THE WORKS OF
ROBERT LOUIS STEVENSON

EDITED BY
CHARLES CURTIS BIGELOW
AND
TEMPLE SCOTT

VOLUME IV

DINING AND RECEPTION-HALL AT VAILIMA

Edition De Luxe

THE WORKS OF
ROBERT LOUIS STEVENSON

VOLUME IV

MASTER OF BALLANTRAE

PRINCE OTTO

The Davos Press
New York

TICONDEROGA EDITION DE LUXE

Limited to One Thousand numbered sets of which this is

No. 116

THE MASTER OF BALLANTRAE

PRINCE OTTO

CONTENTS

THE MASTER OF BALLANTRAE

EDITORIAL NOTE

THE MASTER OF BALLANTRAE was first published serially in *Scribner's Magazine* in 1888-89, and first appeared in book form in August, 1889, issued by Cassell & Co. The preface here included was written in 1889, but was never used until attention was called to it in 1898. It now forms a part of the English edition, but it has never before been prefixed to any American edition of the book.

To

SIR PERCY FLORENCE AND LADY SHELLEY

Here is a tale which extends over many years and travels into many countries. By a peculiar fitness of circumstances the writer began, continued it, and concluded it among distant and diverse scenes. Above all, he was much upon the sea. The character and fortune of the fraternal enemies, the hall and shrubbery of Durrisdeer, the problem of Mackellar's homespun and how to shape it for superior flights; these were his company on deck in many star-reflecting harbours, ran often in his mind at sea to the tune of slatting canvas, and were dismissed (something of the suddenest) on the approach of squalls. It is my hope that these surroundings of its manufacture may to some degree find favour for my story with seafarers and sealovers like yourselves.

And at least here is a dedication from a great way off; written by the loud shores of a subtropical island near upon ten thousand miles from Boscombe Cline and Manor: scenes which rise before me as I write, along with the faces and voices of my friends.

Well, I am for the sea once more; no doubt Sir Percy also. Let us make the signal B. R. D.!

R. L. S.

Waikiki, May 17, 1889.

PREFACE

ALTHOUGH an old, consistent exile, the editor of the following pages revisits now and again the city of which he exults to be a native; and there are few things more strange, more painful, or more salutary, than such revisitations. Outside, in foreign spots, he comes by surprise and awakens more attention than he had expected; in his own city, the relation is reversed, and he stands amazed to be so little recollected. Elsewhere he is refreshed to see attractive faces, to remark possible friends; there he scouts the long streets, with a pang at heart, for the faces and friends that are no more. Elsewhere he is delighted with the presence of what is new, there tormented by the absence of what is old. Elsewhere he is content to be his present self; there he is smitten with an equal regret for what he once was and for what he once hoped to be.

He was feeling all this dimly, as he drove from the station, on his last visit; he was feeling it still as he alighted at the door of his friend, Mr. Johnstone Thomson, W. S., with whom he was to stay. A hearty welcome, a face not altogether changed, a few words that sounded of old days, a laugh provoked and shared, a glimpse in passing of the snowy cloth and bright decanters and the Piranesis on the dining-room wall, brought him to his bedroom with a somewhat lightened cheer, and when he and Mr. Thomson sat down a few minutes later, cheek by jowl, and pledged the past in a preliminary bumper, he was already almost consoled, he had already almost forgiven himself his two unpardonable errors, that he should ever have left his native city, or ever returned to it.

"I have something quite in your way," said Mr. Thomson. "I wished to do honour to your arrival; because, my dear fellow, it is my own youth that comes back along with you;

in a very tattered and withered state, to be sure, but—well!
—all that's left of it."

" A great deal better than nothing," said the editor. " But
what is this which is quite in my way? "

" I was coming to that," said Mr. Thomson: " Fate has
put it in my power to honour your arrival with something
really original by way of dessert. A mystery."

" A mystery? " I repeated.

" Yes," said his friend, " a mystery. It may prove to be
nothing, and it may prove to be a great deal. But in the
meanwhile it is truly mysterious, no eye having looked on it
for near a hundred years; it is highly genteel, for it treats
of a titled family; it ought to be melodramatic, for (according to the superscription) it is concerned with death."

" I think I rarely heard a more obscure or a more promising annunciation," the other remarked. " But what is It? "

" You remember my predecessor's, old Peter M'Brair's,
business? "

" I remember him acutely; he could not look at me without
a pang of reprobation, and he could not feel the pang without betraying it. He was to me a man of a great historical
interest, but the interest was not returned."

" Ah, well, we go beyond him," said Mr. Thomson. " I
dare say old Peter knew as little about this as I do. You see,
I succeeded to a prodigious accumulation of old lawpapers
and old tin boxes, some of them of Peter's hoarding, some of
his father's, John, first of the dynasty, a great man in his
day. Among other collections, were all the papers of the
Durrisdeers."

" The Durrisdeers! " cried I. " My dear fellow, these may
be of the greatest interest. One of them was out in the '45;
one had some strange passages with the devil—you will find
a note of it in Law's *Memorials*, I think; and there was an
unexplained tragedy, I know not what, much later, about a
hundred years ago——"

" More than a hundred years ago," said Mr. Thomson.
" In 1783."

" How do you know that? I mean some death."

PREFACE

" Yes, the lamentable deaths of my lord Durrisdeer and his brother, the Master of Ballantrae (attainted in the troubles)," said Mr. Thomson, with something the tone of a man quoting. " Is that it? "

" To say truth," said I, " I have only seen some dim reference to the things in memoirs; and heard some traditions dimmer still, through my uncle (whom I think you knew). My uncle lived when he was a boy in the neighbourhood of St. Bride's; he has often told me of the avenue closed up and grown over with grass, the great gates never opened, the last lord and his old-maid sister who lived in the back parts of the house, a quiet, plain, poor, humdrum couple it would seem—but pathetic too, as the last of that stirring and brave house—and, to the country folk, faintly terrible from some deformed traditions."

" Yes," said Mr. Thomson. " Henry Graeme Durie, the last lord, died in 1820; his sister, the Honourable Miss Katherine Durie, in '27; so much I know; and by what I have been going over the last few days, they were what you say, decent, quiet people and not rich. To say truth, it was a letter of my lord's that put me on the search for the packet we are going to open this evening. Some papers could not be found; and he wrote to Jack M'Brair suggesting they might be among those sealed up by a Mr. Mackellar. M'Brair answered, that the papers in question were all in Mackellar's own hand, all (as the writer understood) of a purely narrative character; and besides, said he, ' I am bound not to open them before the year 1889.' You may fancy if these words struck me: I instituted a hunt through all the M'Brair repositories; and at last hit upon that packet which (if you have had enough wine) I propose to show you at once."

In the smoking-room, to which my host now led me, was a packet, fastened with many seals and enclosed in a single sheet of strong paper thus endorsed:

" Papers relating to the lives and lamentable deaths of the late Lord Durrisdeer, and his elder brother James, commonly

xvii

called Master of Ballantrae, attainted in the troubles: entrusted into the hands of John M'Brair in the Lawnmarket of Edinburgh, W. S.; this 20th day of September, Anno Domini, 1789; by him to be kept secret until the revolution of one hundred years complete, or until the 20th day of September, 1889; the same compiled and written by me,

> "EPHRAIM MACKELLAR,
> "*For near forty years Land Steward on the estates of His Lordship.*"

As Mr. Thomson is a married man, I will not say what hour had struck when we laid down the last of the following pages; but I will give a few words of what ensued.

"Here," said Mr. Thomson, "is a novel ready to your hand: all you have to do is to work up the scenery, develop the characters, and improve the style."

"My dear fellow," said I, "they are just the three things that I would rather die than set my hand to. It shall be published as it stands."

"But it's so bald," objected Mr. Thomson.

"I believe there is nothing so noble as baldness," replied I, "and I am sure there is nothing so interesting. I would have all literature bald, and all authors (if you like) but one."

"Well, well," said Mr. Thomson, "we shall see."

CONTENTS

THE MASTER OF BALLANTRAE

THE full truth of this odd matter is what the world has long been looking for and public curiosity is sure to welcome. It so befell that I was intimately mingled with the last years and history of the house, and there does not live one man so able as myself to make these matters plain, or so desirous to narrate them faithfully. I knew the Master; on many secret steps of his career I have an authentic memoir in my hand; I sailed with him on his last voyage almost alone; I made one upon that winter's journey of which so many tales have gone abroad, and I was there at the man's death. As for my late Lord Durrisdeer, I served him and loved him near twenty years, and thought more of him the more I knew of him. Altogether, I think it not fit that so much evidence should perish; the truth is a debt I owe my lord's memory, and I think my old years will flow more smoothly and my white hair lie quieter on the pillow when the debt is paid.

The Duries of Durrisdeer and Ballantrae were a strong family in the southwest from the days of David First. A rhyme still current in the country-side—

> Kittle folk are the Durrisdeers,
> They ride wi' ower mony spears—

bears the mark of its antiquity, and the name appears in another, which common report attributes to Thomas of Ercildoune himself—I cannot say how truly, and which some have applied—I dare not say with how much justice—to the events of this narration:

> Twa Duries in Durrisdeer,
>   Ane to tie and ane to ride,
> An ill day for the groom
>   And a waur day for the bride.

1

THE MASTER OF BALLANTRAE

Authentic history besides is filled with their exploits, which (to our modern eyes) seem not very commendable, and the family suffered its full share of those ups and downs to which the great houses of Scotland have been ever liable. But all these I pass over to come to that memorable year 1745 when the foundations of this tragedy were laid.

At that time there dwelt a family of four persons in the house of Durrisdeer, near St. Bride's, on the Solway shore, a chief hold of their race since the Reformation. My old lord, eighth of the name, was not old in years, but he suffered prematurely from the disabilities of age; his place was at the chimney-side; there he sat reading, in a lined gown, with few words for any man and wry words for none, the model of an old retired housekeeper, and yet his mind very well nourished with study, and reputed in the country to be more cunning than he seemed. The Master of Ballantrae, James in baptism, took from his father the love of serious reading; some of his tact perhaps as well, but that which was only policy in the father became black dissimulation in the son. The face of his behavior was merely popular and wild: he sat late at wine, later at the cards; had the name in the country of " an unco man for the lasses," and was ever in the front of broils. But for all he was the first to go in, yet it was observed he was invariably the best to come off, and his partners in mischief were usually alone to pay the piper. This luck or dexterity got him several ill-wishers, but with the rest of the country enhanced his reputation, so that great things were looked for in his future when he should have gained more gravity. One very black mark he had to his name, but the matter was hushed up at the time and so defaced by legends before I came into those parts that I scruple to set it down. If it was true it was a horrid fact in one so young, and if false it was a horrid calumny. I think it notable that he had always vaunted himself quite implacable and was taken at his word, so that he had the addition among his neighbors of " an ill man to cross." Here was altogether a young nobleman (not yet twenty-four in the year '45) who had made a figure in the country beyond his time of life.

2

THE MASTER OF BALLANTRAE

The less marvel if there were little heard of the second son, Mr. Henry (my late Lord Durrisdeer), who was neither very bad nor yet very able, but an honest, solid sort of lad like many of his neighbors. Little heard, I say; but indeed it was a case of little spoken. He was known among the salmon-fishers in the firth, for that was a sport that he assiduously followed; he was an excellent good horse-doctor besides, and took a chief hand almost from a boy in the management of the estates. How hard a part that was in the situation of that family none knows better than myself, nor yet with how little color of justice a man may there acquire the reputation of a tyrant and a miser. The fourth person in the house was Miss Alison Graeme, a near kinswoman, an orphan and the heir to a considerable fortune which her father had acquired in trade. This money was loudly called for by my lord's necessities; indeed the land was deeply mortgaged, and Miss Alison was designed accordingly to be the Master's wife, gladly enough on her side; with how much good will on his is another matter. She was a comely girl, and in those days very spirited and self-willed, for the old lord having no daughter of his own, and my lady being long dead, she had grown up as best she might.

To these four came the news of Prince Charlie's landing, and set them presently by the ears. My lord, like the chimney-keeper that he was, was all for temporizing. Miss Alison held the other side, because it appeared romantical; and the Master (though I have heard they did not agree often) was for this once of her opinion. The adventure tempted him, as I conceive; he was tempted by the opportunity to raise the fortunes of the house, and not less by the hope of paying off his private liabilities, which were heavy beyond all opinion. As for Mr. Henry, it appears he said little enough at first; his part came later on. It took the three a whole day's disputation, before they agreed to steer a middle course, one son going forth to strike a blow for King James, my lord and the other staying at home to keep in favor with King George. Doubtless this was my lord's decision; and as is well known, it was the part played by many considerable families.

But the one dispute settled, another opened. For my lord, Miss Alison and Mr. Henry all held the one view: that it was the cadet's part to go out; and the Master, what with restlessness and vanity, would at no rate consent to stay at home. My lord pleaded, Miss Alison wept, Mr. Henry was very plain spoken; all was of no avail.

"It is the direct heir of Durrisdeer that should ride by his king's bridle," says the master.

"If we were playing a manly part," says Mr. Henry, "there might be sense in such talk. But what are we doing? Cheating at cards!"

"We are saving the house of Durrisdeer, Henry," his father said.

"And see, James," said Mr. Henry, "if I go, and the prince has the upper hand, it will be easy to make your peace with King James. But if you go, and the expedition fails, we divide the right and the title. And what shall I be then?"

"You will be Lord Durrisdeer," said the Master. "I put all I have upon the table."

"I play at no such game," cries Mr. Henry. "I shall be left in such a situation as no man of sense and honor could endure. I shall be neither fish nor flesh!" he cried. And a little after, he had another expression, plainer perhaps than he intended. "It is your duty to be here with my father," said he. "You know well enough you are the favorite."

"Ay?" said the master. "And there spoke Envy! Would you trip up my heels—Jacob?" said he, and dwelled upon the name maliciously.

Mr. Henry went and walked at the low end of the hall without reply; for he had an excellent gift of silence. Presently he came back.

"I am the cadet and I *should* go," said he. "And my lord here is the master, and he says I *shall* go. What say ye to that, my brother?"

"I say this, Harry," returned the Master, "that when very obstinate folk are met, there are only two ways out: Blows—and I think none of us could care to go so far; or

4

the arbitrament of chance—and here is a guinea piece. Will you stand by the toss of the coin?"

"I will stand and fall by it," said Mr. Henry. "Heads, I go; shield, I stay."

The coin was spun and it fell shield. "So there is a lesson for Jacob," says the Master.

"We shall live to repent of this," says Mr. Henry, and flung out of the hall.

As for Miss Alison, she caught up that piece of gold which had just sent her lover to the wars, and flung it clean through the family shield in the great painted window.

"If you loved me as well as I love you, you would have stayed," cried she.

"'I could not love you, dear, so well, loved I not honor more,'" sung the Master.

"Oh!" she cried, "you have no heart—I hope you may be killed!" and she ran from the room, and in tears to her own chamber.

It seems the Master turned to my lord with his most comical manner, and says he, "This looks like a devil of a wife."

"I think you are a devil of a son to me," cried his father, "you that has always been the favorite, to my shame be it spoken. Never a good hour have I gotten of you since you were born; no, never one good hour," and repeated it again the third time. Whether it was the Master's levity, or his insubordination, or Mr. Henry's word about the favorite son, that had so much disturbed my lord, I do not know; but I incline to think it was the last, for I have it by all accounts that Mr. Henry was more made up to from that hour.

Altogether it was in pretty ill blood with his family that the Master rode to the north; which was the more sorrowful for others to remember when it seemed too late. By fear and favor, he had scraped together near upon a dozen men, principally tenants' sons; they were all pretty full when they set forth, and rode up the hill by the old abbey, roaring and singing, the white cockade in every hat. It was a desperate venture for so small a company to cross the most of Scotland unsupported; and (what made folk think so the more) even

as that poor dozen was clattering up the hill, a great ship
of the king's navy, that could have brought them under with
a single boat, lay with her broad ensign streaming in the bay.
The next afternoon, having given the Master a fair start, it
was Mr. Henry's turn; and he rode off, all by himself, to
offer his sword and carry letters from his father to King
George's government. Miss Alison was shut in her room and
did little but weep, till both were gone; only she stitched the
cockade upon the Master's hat and (as John Paul told me) it
was wetted with tears when he carried it down to him.

In all that followed, Mr. Henry and my old lord were true
to their bargain. That ever they accomplished anything is
more than I could learn; and that they were any way strong
on the king's side, more than I believe. But they kept the
letter of loyalty, corresponded with my lord president, sat
still at home, and had little or no commerce with the Master
while that business lasted. Nor was he, on his side, more communicative. Miss Alison, indeed, was always sending him
expresses, but I do not know if she had many answers. Macconochie rode for her once, and found the Highlanders before
Carlisle, and the Master riding by the prince's side in high
favor; he took the letter (so Macconochie tells), opened it,
glanced it through with a mouth like a man whistling, and
stuck it in his belt, whence, on his horse passageing, it fell
unregarded to the ground. It was Macconochie who picked
it up; and he still kept it, and indeed I have seen it in his
hands. News came to Durrisdeer of course, by the common
report, as it goes traveling through a country, a thing always
wonderful to me. By that means the family learned more of
the Master's favor with the prince, and the ground it was said
to stand on; for by a strange condescension in a man so proud
—only that he was a man still more ambitious—he was said
to have crept into notability by truckling to the Irish. Sir
Thomas Sullivan, Colonel Burke, and the rest were his daily
comrades, by which course he withdrew himself from his own
country folk. All the small intrigues he had a hand in
fomenting; thwarted my Lord George upon a thousand
points; was always for the advice that seemed palatable to

6

the prince, no matter if it was good or bad; and seems upon the whole (like the gambler he was all through life) to have had less regard to the chances of the campaign than to the greatness of favor he might aspire to, if (by any luck) it should succeed. For the rest, he did very well in the field; no one questioned that; for he was no coward.

The next was the news of Culloden, which was brought to Durrisdeer by one of the tenants' sons, the only survivor, he declared, of all those that had gone singing up the hill. By an unfortunate chance, John Paul and Macconochie had that very morning found the guinea piece (which was the root of all the evil) sticking in a holly bush; they had been " up the gait," as the servants say at Durrisdeer, to the change-house; and if they had little left of the guinea, they had less of their wits. What must John Paul do but burst into the hall where the family sat at dinner, and cry the news to them that " Tam Macmorland was but new lichtit at the door, and —wirra, wirra—there were nane to come behind him? "

They took the word in silence like folk condemned; only Mr. Henry carrying his palm to his face, and Miss Alison laying her head outright upon her hands. As for my lord, he was like ashes.

" I have still one son," says he. " And, Henry, I will do you this justice, it is the kinder that is left."

It was a strange thing to say in such a moment; but my lord had never forgotten Mr. Henry's speech, and he had years of injustice on his conscience. Still it was a strange thing; and more than Miss Alison could let pass. She broke out and blamed my lord for his unnatural words, and Mr. Henry because he was sitting there in safety when his brother lay dead, and herself because she had given her sweetheart ill words at his departure; calling him the flower of the flock, wringing her hands, protesting her love, and crying on him by his name; so that the servants stood astonished.

Mr. Henry got to his feet and stood holding his chair; it was he that was like ashes now.

" Oh," he burst out suddenly, " I know you loved him ! "

" The world knows that, glory be to God ! " cries she; and

7

then to Mr. Henry: "There is none but me to know one thing—that you were a traitor to him in your heart."

"God knows," groans he, "it was lost love on both sides."

Time went by in the house after that without much change; only they were now three instead of four, which was a perpetual reminder of their loss. Miss Alison's money, you are to bear in mind, was highly needful for the estates; and the one brother being dead, my old lord soon set his heart upon her marrying the other. Day in, day out, he would work upon her, sitting by the chimney-side with his finger in his Latin book, and his eyes set upon her face with a kind of pleasant intentness that became the old gentleman very well. If she wept, he would condole with her, like an ancient man that has seen worse times and begins to think lightly even of sorrow; if she raged, he would fall to reading again in his Latin book, but always with some civil excuse; if she offered (as she often did) to let them have her money in a gift, he would show her how little it consisted with his honor, and remind her, even if he should consent, that Mr. Henry would certainly refuse. *Non vi sed sæpe cadendo* was a favorite word of his; and no doubt this quiet persecution wore away much of her resolve; no doubt, besides, he had a great influence on the girl, having stood in the place of both her parents; and for that matter, she was herself filled with the spirit of the Duries, and would have gone a great way for the glory of Durrisdeer; but not so far, I think, as to marry my poor patron, had it not been (strangely enough) for the circumstance of his extreme unpopularity.

This was the work of Tam Macmorland. There was not much harm in Tam; but he had that grievous weakness, a long tongue; and as the only man in that country who had been out (or rather who had come in again) he was sure of listeners. Those that have the underhand in any fighting, I have observed, are ever anxious to persuade themselves they were betrayed. By Tam's account of it, the rebels had been betrayed at every turn and by every officer they had; they had been betrayed at Derby, and betrayed at Falkirk; the night

march was a step of treachery of my Lord George's; and
Culloden was lost by the treachery of the Macdonalds. This
habit of imputing treason grew upon the fool, till at last he
must have in Mr. Henry also. Mr. Henry (by his account)
had betrayed the lads of Durrisdeer; he had promised to follow with more men, and instead of that he had ridden to King
George. "Ay, and the next day!" Tam would cry. "The
puir, bonnie master and the puir, kind lads that rade wi' him,
were hardly ower the scaur, or he was aff—the Judis! Ay,
weel—he has his way o't: he's to be my lord, nae less, and
there's mony a cauld corp amang the Hieland heather!"
And at this, if Tam had been drinking, he would begin to
weep.

Let any one speak long enough he will get believers. This
view of Mr. Henry's behavior crept about the country by
little and little; it was talked upon by folk that knew the contrary but were short of topics; and it was heard and believed
and given out for gospel by the ignorant and the ill-willing.
Mr. Henry began to be shunned; yet awhile, and the commons
began to murmur as he went by, and the women (who are always the most bold because they are the most safe) to cry
out their reproaches to his face. The Master was cried up
for a saint. It was remembered how he had never had any
hand in pressing the tenants; as, indeed, no more he had, except to spend the money. He was a little wild perhaps, the
folk said; but how much better was a natural, wild lad that
would soon have settled down, than a skinflint and a sneck-
draw, sitting, with his nose in an account book, to persecute
poor tenants. One trollop, who had had a child to the Master
and by all accounts been very badly used, yet made herself
a kind of champion of his memory. She flung a stone one
day at Mr. Henry.

"Whaur's the bonnie lad that trustit ye?" she cried.

Mr. Henry reined in his horse and looked upon her, the
blood flowing from his lip. "Ay, Jess?" says he. "You
too? And yet ye should ken me better." For it was he who
had helped her with money.

The woman had another stone ready, which she made as

9

if she would cast; and he, to ward himself, threw up the hand that held his riding rod.

"What, would you beat a lassie, ye ugly—?" cries she, and ran away screaming as though he had struck her.

Next day, word went about the country like wildfire that Mr. Henry had beaten Jessie Broun within an inch of her life. I give it as one instance of how this snowball grew and one calumny brought another; until my poor patron was so perished in reputation that he began to keep the house like my lord. All this while, you may be sure he uttered no complaints at home; the very ground of the scandal was too sore a matter to be handled; and Mr. Henry was very proud and strangely obstinate in silence. My old lord must have heard of it, by John Paul, if by no one else; and he must at least have remarked the altered habits of his son. Yet even he, it is probable, knew not how high the feeling ran; and as for Miss Alison, she was ever the last person to hear news, and the least interested when she heard them.

In the height of the ill-feeling (for it died away as it came, no man could say why) there was an election forward in the town of St. Bride's, which is the next to Durrisdeer, standing on the Water of Swift; some grievance was fermenting, I forget what, if ever I heard; and it was currently said there would be broken heads ere night, and that the sheriff had sent as far as Dumfries for soldiers. My lord moved that Mr. Henry should be present; assuring him it was necessary to appear, for the credit of the house. "It will soon be reported," said he, "that we do not take the lead in our own country."

"It is a strange lead that I can take," said Mr. Henry; and when they had pushed him further, "I tell you the plain truth," he said, "I dare not show my face."

"You are the first of the house that ever said so," cries Miss Alison.

"We will go all three," said my lord: and sure enough he got into his boots (the first time in four years—a sore business John Paul had to get them on) and Miss Alison into her riding-coat, and all three rode together to St. Bride's.

THE MASTER OF BALLANTRAE

The streets were full of the riff-raff of all the country-side, who had no sooner clapped eyes on Mr. Henry than the hissing began, and the hooting, and the cries of "Judas!" and "Where was the Master?" and "Where were the poor lads that rode with him?" Even a stone was cast; but the more part cried shame at that, for my old lord's sake and Miss Alison's. It took not ten minutes to persuade my lord that Mr. Henry had been right. He said never a word, but turned his horse about, and home again, with his chin upon his bosom. Never a word said Miss Alison; no doubt she thought the more; no doubt her pride was stung, for she was a bonebred Durie; and no doubt her heart was touched to see her cousin so unjustly used. That night she was never in bed; I have often blamed my lady—when I call to mind that night, I readily forgive her all; and the first thing in the morning, she came to the old lord in his usual seat.

"If Henry still wants me," said she, "he can have me now." To himself she had a different speech: "I bring you no love, Henry; but God knows, all the pity in the world."

June the first, 1748, was the day of their marriage. It was December of the same year that first saw me alighting at the doors of the great house; and from there I take up the history of events as they befell under my own observation, like a witness in a court.

I made the last of my journey in the cold end of December, in a mighty dry day of frost; and who should be my guide but Patey Macmorland, brother of Tam! For a tow-headed, bare-legged brat of ten, he had more ill tales upon his tongue than ever I heard the match of; having drunken betimes in his brother's cup. I was still not so old myself; pride had not yet the upper hand of curiosity; and indeed it would have taken any man, that cold morning, to hear all the old clashes of the country and be shown all the places by the way where strange things had fallen out. I had tales of Claverhouse as we came through the bogs, and tales of the devil as we came over the top of the scaur. As we came in by the abbey I heard somewhat of the old monks, and more of the free-traders, who use its ruins for a magazine, landing

11

for that cause within a cannon-shot of Durrisdeer; and along all the road, the Duries and poor Mr. Henry were in the first rank of slander. My mind was thus highly prejudiced against the family I was about to serve: so that I was half surprised when I beheld Durrisdeer itself, lying in a pretty, sheltered bay, under the Abbey Hill; the house most commodiously built in the French fashion or perhaps Italianate, for I have no skill in these arts; and the place the most beautified with gardens, lawns, shrubberies, and trees I had ever seen. The money sunk here unproductively would have quite restored the family; but as it was, it cost a revenue to keep it up.

Mr. Henry came himself to the door to welcome me: a tall, dark young gentleman (the Duries are all black men) of a plain and not cheerful face, very strong in body but not so strong in health: taking me by the hand without any pride, and putting me at home with plain, kind speeches. He led me into the hall, booted as I was, to present me to my lord. It was still daylight; and the first thing I observed was a lozenge of clear glass in the midst of the shield in the painted window, which I remember thinking a blemish on a room otherwise so handsome, with its family portraits, and the pargetted ceiling with pendants, and the carved chimney, in one corner of which my old lord sat reading in his Livy. He was like Mr. Henry, with much the same plain countenance, only more subtle and pleasant, and his talk a thousand times more entertaining. He had many questions to ask me, I remember, of Edinburgh College, where I had just received my mastership of arts, and of the various professors, with whom and their proficiency he seemed well acquainted; and thus, talking of things that I knew, I soon got liberty of speech in my new home.

In the midst of this came Mrs. Henry into the room; she was very far gone, Miss Katharine being due in about six weeks, which made me think less of her beauty at the first sight, and she used me with more condescension than the rest, so that upon all accounts I kept her in the third place of my esteem.

THE MASTER OF BALLANTRAE

It did not take long before all Pate Macmorland's tales were blotted out of my belief, and I was become, what I have ever since remained, a loving servant of the house of Durrisdeer. Mr. Henry had the chief part of my affection. It was with him I worked, and I found him an exacting master, keeping all his kindness for those hours in which we were unemployed, and in the steward's office not only loading me with work but viewing me with a shrewd supervision. At length one day he looked up from his paper with a kind of timidness, and says he: " Mr. Mackellar, I think I ought to tell you that you do very well." That was my first word of commendation, and from that day his jealousy of my performance was relaxed; soon it was " Mr. Mackellar " here and " Mr. Mackellar " there with the whole family, and for much of my service at Durrisdeer I have transacted everything at my own time and to my own fancy, and never a farthing challenged. Even while he was driving me I had begun to find my heart go out to Mr. Henry, no doubt partly in pity—he was a man so palpably unhappy. He would fall into a deep muse over our accounts, staring at the page or out of the window, and at those times the look of his face and the sigh that would break from him awoke in me strong feelings of curiosity and commiseration. One day, I remember, we were late upon some business in the steward's room. This room is in the top of the house, and has a view upon the bay and over a little wooded cape on the long sands; and there, right over against the sun which was then dipping, we saw the freetraders with a great force of men and horses scouring on the beach. Mr. Henry had been staring straight west, so that I marveled he was not blinded by the sun; suddenly he frowns, rubs his hand upon his brow and turns to me with a smile.

" You would not guess what I was thinking," says he. " I was thinking I would be a happier man if I could ride and run the danger of my life with these lawless companions."

I told him I had observed he did not enjoy good spirits, and that it was a common fancy to envy others and think we should be the better of some change, quoting Horace to the point like a young man fresh from college.

13

THE MASTER OF BALLANTRAE

"Why, just so," said he. "And with that we may get back to our accounts."

It was not long before I began to get wind of the causes that so much depressed him. Indeed a blind man must have soon discovered there was a shadow on that house, the shadow of the Master of Ballantrae. Dead or alive (and he was then supposed to be dead) that man was his brother's rival—his rival abroad, where there was never a good word for Mr. Henry and nothing but regret and praise for the Master, and his rival at home, not only with his father and his wife, but with the very servants.

They were two old serving-men that were the leaders. John Paul, a little, bald, solemn, stomachy man, a great professor of piety and (take him for all in all) a pretty faithful servant, was the chief of the Master's faction. None durst go so far as John. He took a pleasure in disregarding Mr. Henry publicly, often with a slighting comparison. My lord and Mrs. Henry took him up, to be sure, but never so resolutely as they should, and he had only to pull his weeping face and begin his lamentations for the Master—"his laddie," as he called him—to have the whole condoned. As for Henry, he let these things pass in silence, sometimes with a sad and sometimes with a black look. There was no rivaling the dead, he knew that, and how to censure an old serving-man for a fault of loyalty was more than he could see. His was not the tongue to do it.

Macconochie was chief upon the other side—an old, ill-spoken, swearing, ranting, drunken dog—and I have often thought it an odd circumstance in human nature that these two serving-men should each have been the champion of his contrary, and blackened their own faults and made light of their own virtues when they beheld them in a master. Macconochie had soon smelled out my secret inclination, took me much into his confidence, and would rant against the Master by the hour, so that even my work suffered. "They're a' daft here," he would cry, "and be damned to them! The Master—the deil's in their thrapples that should call him sae!—it's Mr. Henry should be Master now! They were nane

14

sea fond o' the Master when they had him, I can tell ye that.
Sorrow on his name! Never a guid word did I hear on his
lips, nor naebody else, but just fleering and flyting and pro-
fane cursing—deil ha'e him! There's nane kent his wickedness: him a gentleman! Did ever ye hear tell, Mr. Mackellar,
o' Wully White the wabster? No? Aweel, Wully was an
unco praying kind o' man—a driegh body, nane o' my kind;
I never could abide the sight o' him; onyway he was a great
hand by his way of it, and he up and rebukit the Master for
some of his on-goings. It was a grand thing for the Master
o' Ball'ntrae to tak up a feud wi' a' wabster, was-nae't? "
Macconochie would sneer; indeed he never took the full name
upon his lips but with a sort of a whine of hatred. "But he
did! A fine employ it was—chapping at the man's door and
crying 'boo' in his lum, and puttin' poother in his fire and
pee-oys * in his window, till the man thocht it was auld
Hornie was come seekin' him. Weel, to mak a lang story
short, Wully gaed gyte. At the hinder end they couldnae
get him frae his knees, but he just roared and prayed and
grat straucht on till he got his release. It was fair murder,
a'body said that. Ask John Paul; he was brawly ashamed o'
that game—him that's sic a Christian man! Grand doin's
for the Master o' Ball'ntrae!" I asked him what the Master
had thought of himself. "How would I ken?" says he.
"He never said naething." And on again in his usual manner of banning and swearing, with every now and again a
"Master of Ballantrae" sneered through his nose. It was in
one of these confidences that he showed me the Carlisle letter,
the print of the horseshoe still stamped in the paper. Indeed
that was our last confidence, for he then expressed himself
so ill-naturedly of Mrs. Henry that I had to reprimand him
sharply, and must thenceforth hold him at a distance.

My old lord was uniformly kind to Mr. Henry; he had even
pretty ways of gratitude, and would sometimes clap him on
the shoulder and say, as if to the world at large: "This is a
very good son to me." And grateful he was no doubt, being
a man of sense and justice. But I think that was all, and I

* A kind of firework made with damp powder.

am sure Mr. Henry thought so. The love was all for the dead son. Not that this was often given breath to; indeed with me but once. My lord had asked me one day how I got on with Mr. Henry, and I had told him the truth.

"Ay," said he, looking sideway on the burning fire, "Henry is a good lad, a very good lad," said he. "You have heard, Mr. Mackellar, that I had another son? I am afraid he was not so virtuous a lad as Mr. Henry: but dear me, he's dead, Mr. Mackellar! and while he lived we were all very proud of him, all very proud. If he was not all he should have been in some ways, well, perhaps we loved him better!" This last he said looking musingly in the fire; and then to me, with a great deal of briskness, "But I am rejoiced you do so well with Mr. Henry. You will find him a good master." And with that he opened his book, which was the customary signal of dismission. But it would be little that he read and less that he understood; Culloden field and the Master, these would be the burden of his thought; and the burden of mine was an unnatural jealousy of the dead man for Mr. Henry's sake, that had even then begun to grow on me.

I am keeping Mrs. Henry for the last so that this expression of my sentiment may seem unwarrantably strong: the reader shall judge for himself when I have done. But I must first tell of another matter, which was the means of bringing me more intimate. I had not yet been six months at Durrisdeer when it chanced that John Paul fell sick and must keep his bed; drink was the root of his malady, in my poor thought; but he was tended and indeed carried himself like an afflicted saint; and the very minister who came to visit him professed himself edified when he went away. The third morning of his sickness, Mr. Henry comes to me with something of a hangdog look.

"Mackellar," says he, "I wish I could trouble you upon a little service. There is a pension we pay; it is John's part to carry it; and now that he is sick, I know not to whom I should look unless it was yourself. The matter is very delicate; I could not carry it with my own hand for a sufficient reason; I dare not send Macconochie, who is a talker, and I am—I

16

have—I am desirous this should not come to Mrs. Henry's ears," says he, and flushed to his neck as he said it.

To say truth, when I found I was to carry money to one Jessie Broun, who was no better than she should be, I supposed it was some trip of his own that Mr. Henry was dissembling. I was the more impressed when the truth came out.

It was up a wynd off a side street in St. Bride's that Jessie had her lodging. The place was very ill inhabited, mostly by the free-trading sort; there was a man with a broken head at the entry; halfway up, in a tavern, fellows were roaring and singing, though it was not yet nine in the day. Altogether, I had never seen a worse neighborhood even in the great city of Edinburgh, and I was in two minds to go back. Jessie's room was of a piece with her surroundings and herself no better. She would not give me the receipt (which Mr. Henry had told me to demand, for he was very methodical) until she had sent out for spirits and I had pledged her in a glass; and all the time she carried on in a light-headed, reckless way, now aping the manners of a lady, now breaking into unseemly mirth, now making coquettish advances that oppressed me to the ground. Of the money, she spoke more tragically.

"It's blood money," said she, "I take it for that: blood money for the betrayed. See what I'm brought down to! Ah, if the bonnie lad were back again, it would be changed days. But he's deid—he's lyin' deid amang the Hieland hills —the bonnie lad, the bonnie lad!"

She had a rapt manner of crying on the bonnie lad, clasping her hands and casting up her eyes, that I think she must have learned of strolling players; and I thought her sorrow very much of an affectation, and that she dwelled upon the business because her shame was now all she had to be proud of. I will not say I did not pity her, but it was a loathing pity at the best; and her last change of manner wiped it out. This was when she had had enough of me for an audience and had set her name at last to the receipt. "There!" says she, and taking the most unwomanly oaths upon her tongue, bade me begone and carry it to the Judas who had sent me. It was the first time I had heard the name applied to Mr. Henry; I

17

was staggered besides at her sudden vehemence of word and manner; and got forth from the room, under this shower of curses, like a beaten dog. But even then I was not quit; for the vixen threw up her window and, leaning forth, continued to revile me as I went up the wynd; the free-traders, coming to the tavern door, joined in the mockery; and one had even the inhumanity to set upon me a very savage, small dog, which bit me in the ankle. This was a strong lesson, had I required one, to avoid ill company; and I rode home in much pain from the bite and considerable indignation of mind.

Mr. Henry was in the steward's room, affecting employment, but I could see he was only impatient to hear of my errand.

"Well?" says he, as soon as I came in; and when I had told him something of what passed, and that Jessie seemed an undeserving woman and far from grateful: "She is no friend to me," said he; "but indeed, Mackellar, I have few friends to boast of; and Jessie has some cause to be unjust. I need not dissemble what all the country knows: she was not very well used by one of our family." This was the first time I had heard him refer to the Master even distantly; and I think he found his tongue rebellious, even for that much; but presently he resumed. "This is why I would have nothing said. It would give pain to Mrs. Henry—and to my father," he added with another flush.

"Mr. Henry," said I, "if you will take a freedom at my hands, I would tell you to let that woman be. What service is your money to the like of her? She has no sobriety and no economy; as for gratitude, you will as soon get milk from a whinstone; and if you will pretermit your bounty, it will make no change at all but just to save the ankles of your messengers."

Mr. Henry smiled. "But I am grieved about your ankle," said he, the next moment, with a proper gravity.

"And observe," I continued, "I give you this advice upon consideration; and yet my heart was touched for the woman in the beginning."

"Why, there it is, you see!" said Mr. Henry. "And you

18

are to remember that I knew her once a very decent lass. Besides which, although I speak little of my family, I think much of its repute."

And with that he broke up the talk, which was the first we had together in such confidence. But the same afternoon I had the proof that his father was perfectly acquainted with the business, and that it was only from his wife that Mr. Henry kept it secret.

"I fear you had a painful errand to-day," says my lord to me: "for which, as it enters in no way among your duties, I wish to thank you, and to remind you at the same time (in case Mr. Henry should have neglected) how very desirable it is that no word of it should reach my daughter. Reflections on the dead, Mr. Mackellar, are doubly painful."

Anger glowed in my heart; and I could have told my lord to his face how little he had to do, bolstering up the image of the dead in Mrs. Henry's heart, and how much better he were employed to shatter that false idol. For by this time I saw very well how the land lay between my patron and his wife.

My pen is clear enough to tell a plain tale; but to render the effect of an infinity of small things, not one great enough in itself to be narrated; and to translate the story of looks, and the message of voices when they are saying no great matter; and to put in half a page the essence of near eighteen months: this is what I despair to accomplish. The fault, to be very blunt, lay all in Mrs. Henry. She felt it a merit to have consented to the marriage, and she took it like a martyrdom; in which my old lord, whether he knew it or not, fomented her. She made a merit, besides, of her constancy to the dead; though its name, to a nicer conscience, should have seemed rather disloyalty to the living; and here also my lord gave her his countenance. I suppose he was glad to talk of his loss, and ashamed to dwell on it with Mr. Henry. Certainly, at least, he made a little coterie apart in that family of three, and it was the husband who was shut out. It seems it was an old custom when the family were alone in Durrisdeer, that my lord should take his wine to the chimney-side, and Miss Alison (instead of withdrawing) should bring a stool to his knee and chatter to him privately; and after she had become my patron's wife, the same manner of doing was continued. It should have been pleasant to behold this ancient gentleman so loving with his daughter; but I was too much a partisan of Mr. Henry's to be anything but wroth at his exclusion. Many's the time I have seen him make an obvious resolve, quit the table, and go and join himself to his wife and my Lord Durrisdeer; and on their part, they were never backward to make him welcome, turned to him smilingly as to an intruding child, and took him into their talk with an effort so ill-concealed that he was soon back again beside me at the table; whence (so great is the hall of Durrisdeer) we could but hear the murmur of voices at the chimney. There he would sit and watch, and I along with him; and sometimes by my lord's head sorrowfully shaken, or his hand laid on Mrs. Henry's head, or hers upon his knee as if in consolation, or sometimes by an exchange of tearful looks, we would draw our conclusion that the talk had gone to the old subject and the shadow of the dead was in the hall.

I have hours when I blame Mr. Henry for taking all too patiently; yet we are to remember he was married in pity, and accepted his wife upon that term. And indeed he had small encouragement to make a stand. Once, I remember, he announced he had found a man to replace the pane of the stained window; which, as it was he that managed all the business, was a thing clearly within his attributions. But to the master's fanciers, that pane was like a relic; and on the first word of any change, the blood flew to Mrs. Henry's face.

" I wonder at you!" she cried.

" I wonder at myself," says Mr. Henry, with more of bitterness than I had ever heard him to express.

Thereupon my old lord stepped in with his smooth talk, so that before the meal was at an end all seemed forgotten; only that, after dinner, when the pair had withdrawn as usual to the chimney-side, we could see her weeping with her head upon his knee. Mr. Henry kept up the talk with me upon some topic of the estates—he could speak of little else but business, and was never the best of company; but he kept it up that day with more continuity, his eye straying ever and again to the chimney and his voice changing to another key, but without check of delivery. The pane, however, was not replaced, and I believe he counted it a great defeat.

Whether he was stout enough or no, God knows he was kind enough. Mrs. Henry had a manner of condescension with him, such as (in a wife) would have pricked my vanity into an ulcer; he took it like a favor. She held him at the staff's end; forgot and then remembered and unbent to him, as we do to children; burdened him with cold kindness; reproved him with a change of color and a bitten lip, like one shamed by his disgrace; ordered him with a look of the eye, when she was off her guard; when she was on the watch, pleaded with him for the most natural attentions as though they were unheard-of favors. And to all this, he replied with the most unwearied service; loving, as folk say, the very ground she trod on, and carrying that love in his eyes as bright as a lamp. When Miss Katharine was to be born, nothing would serve but he must stay in the room behind the head of the bed. There he sat, as white (they tell me) as a sheet and the sweat dropping from his brow; and the handkerchief he had in his hand was crushed into a little ball no bigger than a musket bullet. Nor could he bear the sight of Miss Katharine for many a day; indeed I doubt if he was ever what he should have been to my young lady; for the which want of natural feeling he was loudly blamed.

Such was the state of this family down to the 7th of April, 1749, when there befell the first of that series of events which were to break so many hearts and lose so many lives.

On that day I was sitting in my room a little before supper, when John Paul burst open the door with no civility of knocking, and told me there was one below that wished

21

to speak with the steward; sneering at the name of my office.

I asked what manner of man, and what his name was; and this disclosed the cause of John's ill humor; for it appeared the visitor refused to name himself except to me, a sore affront to the majordomo's consequence.

"Well," said I. smiling a little, "I will see what he wants."

I found in the entrance hall a big man very plainly habited and wrapped in a sea-cloak, like one new landed, as indeed he was. Not far off Macconochie was standing, with his tongue out of his mouth and his hand upon his chin, like a dull fellow thinking hard; and the stranger, who had brought his cloak about his face, appeared uneasy. He had no sooner seen me coming than he went to meet me with an effusive manner.

"My dear man," said he, "a thousand apologies for disturbing you, but I'm in the most awkward position. And there's a son of a ramrod there that I should know the looks of, and more betoken I believe that he knows mine. Being in this family, sir, and in a place of some responsibility (which was the cause I took the liberty to send for you), you are doubtless of the honest party?"

"You may be sure at least," says I, "that all of that party are quite safe in Durrisdeer."

"My dear man, it is my very thought," says he. "You see I have just been set on shore here by a very honest man, whose name I cannot remember, and who is to stand off and on for me till morning, at some danger to himself; and, to be clear with you, I am a little concerned lest it should be at some to me. I have saved my life so often, Mr.—I forget your name, which is a very good one—that, faith, I would be very loath to lose it after all. And the son of a ramrod, whom I believe I saw before Carlisle——"

"Oh, sir," said I, "you can trust Macconochie until to-morrow."

"Well, and it's a delight to hear you say so," says the stranger. "The truth is that my name is not a very suitable one in this country of Scotland. With a gentleman like you, my dear man, I would have no concealments of course; and by your leave, I'll just breathe it in your ear. They call me Francis Burke—Colonel Francis Burke; and I am here, at a most damnable risk to myself, to see your masters—if you'll excuse me, my good man, for giving them the name, for I'm sure it's a circumstance I would never have guessed from your appearance. And if you would just be so very obliging as to take my name to them, you might say that I come bearing letters which I am sure they will be very rejoiced to have the reading of."

Colonel Francis Burke was one of the prince's Irishmen, that did his cause such an infinity of hurt and were so much distasted of the Scots at the time of the rebellion; and it came at once into my mind how the Master of Ballantrae had astonished all men by going with that party. In the same moment a strong foreboding of the truth possessed my soul.

"If you will step in here," said I, opening a chamber door, " I will let my lord know."

" And I am sure it's very good of you, Mr. What-is-your-name," says the colonel.

Up to the hall I went, slow footed. There they were all three, my old lord in his place, Mrs. Henry at work by the window, Mr. Henry (as was much his custom) pacing the low end. In the midst was the table laid for supper. I told them briefly what I had to say. My old lord lay back in his seat. Mrs. Henry sprung up standing with a mechanical motion, and she and her husband stared at each other's eyes across the room; it was the strangest, challenging look these two exchanged, and as they looked, the color faded in their faces. Then Mr. Henry turned to me; not to speak, only to sign with his finger; but that was enough, and I went down again for the colonel.

When we returned, these three were in much the same position I had left them in; I believe no word had passed.

" My Lord Durrisdeer, no doubt? " says the colonel, bowing, and my lord bowed in answer. "And this," continues the colonel, "should be the Master of Ballantrae?

"I have never taken that name," said Mr. Henry; "but I am Henry Durie at your service."

Then the colonel turns to Mrs. Henry, bowing with his hat upon his heart and the most killing airs of gallantry. "There can be no mistake about so fine a figure of a lady," says he. "I address the seductive Miss Alison, of whom I have so often heard?"

Once more husband and wife exchanged a look.

"I am Mrs. Henry Durie," said she; "but before my marriage my name was Alison Graeme."

Then my lord spoke up. "I am an old man, Colonel Burke," said he, "and a frail one. It will be mercy on your part to be expeditious. Do you bring me news of—" he hesitated, and then the words broke from him with a singular change of voice—"my son?"

"My dear lord, I will be round with you like a soldier," said the colonel. "I do."

My lord held out a wavering hand; he seemed to wave a signal, but whether it was to give him time or to speak on, was more than we could guess. At length, he got out the one word—"Good?"

"Why, the very best in the creation!" cries the colonel. "For my good friend and admired comrade is at this hour in the fine city of Paris, and as like as not, if I know anything of his habits, he will be drawing in his chair to a piece of dinner. Bedad, I believe the lady's fainting."

Mrs. Henry was indeed the color of death, and drooped against the window frame. But when Mr. Henry made a movement as if to run to her, she straightened with a sort of shiver. "I am well," she said, with her white lips.

Mr. Henry stopped, and his face had a strong twitch of anger. The next moment he had turned to the colonel. "You must not blame yourself," says he, "for this effect on Mrs. Durie. It is only natural; we were all brought up like brother and sister."

Mrs. Henry looked at her husband with something like

relief or even gratitude. In my way of thinking, that speech was the first step he made in her good graces.

" You must try to forgive me, Mrs. Durie, for indeed and I am just an Irish savage," said the colonel, " and I deserve to be shot for not breaking the matter more artistically to a lady. But here are the Master's own letters, one for each of the three of you, and to be sure (if I know anything of my friend's genius) he will tell his own story with a better grace."

He brought the three letters forth as he spoke, arranged them by their superscriptions, presented the first to my lord, who took it greedily, and advanced toward Mrs. Henry holding out the second.

But the lady waved it back. " To my husband," says she, with a choked voice.

The colonel was a quick man, but at this he was somewhat nonplused. " To be sure," says he; " how very dull of me! To be sure." But he still held the letter.

At last Mr. Henry reached forth his hand, and there was nothing to be done but give it up. Mr. Henry took the letters (both hers and his own) and looked upon their outside, with his brows knit hard, as if he were thinking. He had surprised me all through by his excellent behavior, but he was to excel himself now.

" Let me give you a hand to your room," said he to his wife. " This has come something of the suddenest, and at any rate you will wish to read your letter by yourself."

Again she looked upon him with the same thought of wonder, but he gave her no time, coming straight to where she stood. " It will be better so, believe me," said he, " and Colonel Burke is too considerate not to excuse you." And with that he took her hand by the fingers and led her from the hall.

Mrs. Henry returned no more that night, and when Mr. Henry went to visit her next morning, as I heard long afterward, she gave him the letter again, still unopened.

" Oh, read it and be done! " he had cried.

" Spare me that," said she.

And by these two speeches, to my way of thinking, each undid a great part of what they had previously done well. But the letter, sure enough, came into my hands and by me was burned, unopened.

To be very exact as to the adventures of the master after Culloden I wrote not long ago to Colonel Burke, now a Chevalier of the Order of St. Louis, begging him for some notes in writing, since I could scarce depend upon my memory at so great an interval. To confess the truth I have been somewhat embarrassed by his response, for he sent me the complete memoirs of his life, touching only in places on the Master, running to a much greater length than my whole story, and not everywhere (as it seems to me) designed for edification. He begged in his letter, dated from Etten- heim, that I would find a publisher for the whole after I had made what use of it I required, and I think I shall best answer my own purpose and fulfill his wishes by printing certain parts of it in full. In this way my readers will have a detailed and I believe a very genuine account of some essential matters, and if any publisher should take a fancy to the chevalier's manner of narration he knows where to apply for the rest, of which there is plenty at his service. I put in my first extract here, so that it may stand in the place of what the chevalier told us over our wine in the hall of Durrisdeer; but you are to suppose it was not the brutal fact, but a very varnished version that he offered to my lord.

THE MASTER'S WANDERINGS

From the Memoirs of the Chevalier de Burke

. . . I LEFT Ruthven (it's hardly necessary to remark) with much greater satisfaction than I had come to it, but whether I missed my way in the deserts or whether my companions failed me I soon found myself alone. This was a predicament very disagreeable, for I never understood this horrid country or savage people, and the last stroke of the prince's withdrawal had made us of the Irish more unpopular than ever. I was reflecting on my poor chances, when I saw another horseman on the hill, whom I supposed at first to have been a phantom, the news of his death in the very front at Culloden being current in the army generally. This was the Master of Ballantrae, my Lord Durrisdeer's son, a young nobleman of the rarest gallantry and parts, and equally designed by nature to adorn a court and to reap laurels in the field. Our meeting was the more welcome to both, as he was one of the few Scots who had used the Irish with consideration and as he might now be of very high utility in aiding my escape. Yet what founded our particular friendship was a circumstance by itself as romantic as any fable of King Arthur.

This was on the second day of our flight, after we had slept one night in the rain upon the inclination of a mountain. There was an Appin man, Alan Black Stewart (or some such name,* but I have seen him since in France) who chanced to be passing the same way, and had a jealousy of my companion. Very uncivil expressions were exchanged; and Stewart calls upon the master to alight and have it out.

"Why, Mr. Stewart," says the master, "I think at the

* *Note by Mr. Mackellar.*—Should not this be Alan *Breck* Stewart, afterward notorious as the Appin murderer? The chevalier is sometimes very weak on names.

27

present time I would prefer to run a race with you." And with the word claps spurs to his horse.

Stewart ran after us, a childish thing to do, for more than a mile; and I could not help laughing as I looked back at last and saw him on a hill holding his hand to his side and nearly burst with running.

" But all the same," I could not help saying to my companion, " I would let no man run after me for any such proper purpose and not give him his desire. It was a good jest, but it smells a trifle cowardly."

He bent his brows at me. " I do pretty well," says he, " when I saddle myself with the most unpopular man in Scotland, and let that suffice for courage."

" Oh, bedad," says I, " I could show you a more unpopular with the naked eye. And if you like not my company, you can ' saddle ' yourself on some one else."

" Colonel Burke," says he, " do not let us quarrel; and to that effect, let me assure you I am the least patient man in the world."

" I am as little patient as yourself," said I. " I care not who knows that."

" At this rate," said he, reining in, " we shall not go very far. And I propose we do one of two things upon the instant: either quarrel and be done, or make a sure bargain to bear everything at each other's hands."

" Like a pair of brothers? " said I.

" I said no such foolishness," he replied. " I have a brother of my own, and I think no more of him than of a colewort. But if we are to have our noses rubbed together in this course of flight, let us each dare to be ourselves like savages, and each swear that he will neither resent nor deprecate the other. I am a pretty bad fellow at bottom, and I find the pretense of virtues very irksome."

" Oh, I am as bad as yourself," said I. " There is no skim milk in Francis Burke. But which is it to be? Fight or make friends? "

" Why," says he, " I think it will be the best manner to spin a coin for it."

THE MASTER OF BALLANTRAE

This proposition was too highly chivalrous not to take my fancy; and strange as it may seem of two well-born gentlemen of to-day, we spun a half crown (like a pair of ancient paladins) whether we were to cut each other's throats or be sworn friends. A more romantic circumstance can rarely have occurred; and it is one of those points in my memoirs, by which we may may see the old tales of Homer and the poets are equally true to-day, at least of the noble and genteel. The coin fell for peace, and we shook hands upon our bargain. And then it was that my companion explained to me his thought in running away from Mr. Stewart, which was certainly worthy of his political intellect. The report of his death, he said, was a great guard to him; Mr. Stewart, having recognised him, had become a danger; and he had taken the briefest road to that gentleman's silence. "For," says he, "Alan Black is too vain a man to narrate any such story of himself."

Toward afternoon we came down to the shores of that loch for which we were heading; and there was the ship but newly come to anchor. She was the *Sainte-Marie-des-Anges*, out of the port of Havre-de-Grace. The Master, after we had signaled for a boat, asked me if I knew the captain. I told him he was a countryman of mine, of the most unblemished integrity, but, I was afraid, a rather timorous man.

"No matter," says he. "For all that, he should certainly hear the truth."

I asked him if he meant about the battle; for if the captain once knew the standard was down, he would certainly put to sea again at once.

"And even then!" said he; "the arms are now of no sort of utility."

"My dear man," said I, "who thinks of the arms? But to be sure we must remember our friends. They will be close upon our heels, perhaps the prince himself, and if the ship be gone, a great number of valuable lives may be imperiled."

"The captain and the crew have lives also, if you come to that," says Ballantrae.

THE MASTER OF BALLANTRAE

This I declared was but a quibble, and that I would not hear of the captain being told; and then it was that Ballantrae made me a witty answer, for the sake of which (and also because I have been blamed myself in this business of the *Sainte-Marie-des-Anges*) I have related the whole conversation as it passed.

"Frank," says he, "remember our bargain. I must not object to your holding your tongue, which I hereby even encourage you to do; but by the same terms, you are not to resent my telling."

I could not help laughing at this; though I still forewarned him what would come of it.

"The devil may come of it for what I care," says the reckless fellow. "I have always done exactly as I felt inclined."

As is well known, my prediction came true. The captain had no sooner heard the news than he cut his cable and to sea again; and before morning broke we were in the Great Minch.

The ship was very old, and the skipper although the most honest of men (and Irish too) was one of the least capable. The wind blew very boisterous, and the sea raged extremely. All that day we had little heart whether to eat or drink; went early to rest in some concern of mind; and (as if to give us a lesson) in the night the wind chopped suddenly into the northeast, and blew a hurricane. We were awaked by the dreadful thunder of the tempest and the stamping of the mariners on deck; so that I supposed our last hour was certainly come; and the terror of my mind was increased out of all measure by Ballantrae, who mocked at my devotions. It is in hours like these that a man of any piety appears in his true light, and we find (what we are taught as babes) the small trust that can be set in worldly friends; I would be unworthy of my religion if I let this pass without particular remark. For three days we lay in the dark in the cabin, and had but a biscuit to nibble. On the fourth the wind fell, leaving the ship dismasted and heaving on vast billows. The captain had not a guess of whither we were blown; he was stark ignorant of his trade, and could do naught but bless the Holy Virgin; a very good thing too, but scarce the whole of seamanship. It seemed our one hope was to be picked up by another vessel; and if that should prove to be an English ship, it might be no great blessing to the master and myself.

The fifth and sixth days we tossed there helpless. The seventh, some sail was got on her, but she was an unwieldy vessel at the best, and we made little but leeway. All the time, indeed, we had been drifting to the south and west, and during the tempest must have driven in that direction with unheard-of violence. The ninth dawn was cold and black, with a great sea running, and every mark of foul weather. In this situation, we were overjoyed to sight a small ship on the horizon, and to perceive her go about and head for the *Sainte-Marie*. But our gratification did not very long endure; for when she had laid to and lowered a boat, it was immediately filled with disorderly fellows, who sung and shouted as they pulled across to us, and swarmed in on our deck with bare cutlasses, cursing loudly. Their leader was a horrible villain, with his face blacked and his whiskers curled in ringlets: Teach, his name; a most notorious pirate. He stamped about the deck, raving and crying out that his name was Satan and his ship was called " Hell." There was something about him like a wicked child or a half-witted person, that daunted me beyond expression. I whispered in the ear of Ballantrae that I would not be the last to volunteer and only prayed God they might be short of hands; he approved my purpose with a nod.

" Bedad," said I to Master Teach, " if you are Satan, here is a devil for ye."

The word pleased him; and (not to dwell upon these shocking incidents) Ballantrae and I and two others were taken for recruits, while the skipper and all the rest were cast into the sea by the method of walking the plank. It was the first time I had seen this done; my heart died within me at the spectacle; and Master Teach or one of his acolytes (for my head was too much lost to be precise) remarked upon my pale face in a very alarming manner. I had the strength to cut a step or two of a jig and cry out some ribaldry, which saved me for that time; but my legs were like water when I must get down into the skiff among these miscreants; and what with my horror of my company and fear of the monstrous billows, it was all I could do to keep an Irish tongue and break a jest or two as we were pulled aboard. By the blessing of God, there was a fiddle in the pirate ship, which I had no sooner seen than I fell upon; and in my quality of crowder, I had the heavenly good luck to get favor in their eyes. *Crowding Pat* was the name they dubbed me with; and it was little I cared for a name so long as my skin was whole.

What kind of a pandemonium that vessel was, I cannot describe, but she was commanded by a lunatic, and might be called a floating Bedlam. Drinking, roaring, singing, quarreling, dancing, they were never all sober at one time; and there were days together when, if a squall had supervened, it must have sent us to the bottom, or if a king's ship had come along, it would have found us quite helpless for defense. Once or twice we sighted a sail, and if we were sober enough, overhauled it, God forgive us! and if we were all too drunk, she got away, and I would bless the saints under my breath. Teach ruled, if you can call that rule which brought no order, by the terror he created; and I observed the man was very vain of his position. I have known marshals of France, ay, and even Highland chieftains that were less openly puffed up; which throws a singular light on the pursuit of honor and glory. Indeed the longer we live, the more we perceive the sagacity of Aristotle and the other old philosophers; and though I have all my life been eager for legitimate distinctions, I can lay my hand upon my heart, at the end of my career, and declare there is not one—no, nor yet life itself—which is worth acquiring or preserving at the slightest cost of dignity.

It was long before I got private speech of Ballantrae; but at length one night we crept out upon the boltsprit, when the rest were better employed, and commiserated our position.

" None can deliver us but the saints," said I.

" My mind is very different," said Ballantrae; " for I am going to deliver myself. This Teach is the poorest creature possible; we make no profit of him and lie continually open to capture; and," says he, " I am not going to be a tarry pirate for nothing, nor yet to hang in chains if I can help it." And he told me what was in his mind to better the state of the ship in the way of discipline, which would give us safety for the present, and a sooner hope of deliverance when they should have gained enough and should break up their company.

I confessed to him ingenuously that my nerve was quite shook amid these horrible surroundings, and I durst scarce tell him to count upon me.

" I am not very easy frightened," said he, " nor very easy beat."

A few days after there befell an accident which had nearly hanged us all, and offers the most extraordinary picture of the folly that ruled in our concerns. We were all pretty drunk; and some bedlamite spying a sail, Teach put the ship about in chase without a glance, and we began to bustle up the arms and boast of the horrors that should follow. I observed Ballantrae stood quiet in the bows, looking under the shade of his hand; but for my part, true to my policy among these savages, I was at work with the busiest, and passing Irish jests for their diversion.

" Run up the colors," cries Teach. " Show the ——s the Jolly Roger!"

It was the merest drunken braggadocio at such a stage, and might have lost us a valuable prize; but I thought it no part of mine to reason, and I ran up the black flag with my own hand.

Ballantrae steps presently aft with a smile upon his face.

" You may perhaps like to know, you drunken dog," says he, " that you are chasing a king's ship."

Teach roared him the lie; but he ran at the same time

to the bulwarks, and so did they all. I have never seen so many drunken men struck suddenly sober. The cruiser had gone about, upon our impudent display of colors; she was just then filling on the new tack; her ensign blew out quite plain to see; and even as we stared, there came a puff of smoke, and then a report, and a shot plunged in the waves a good way short of us. Some ran to the ropes and got the *Sarah* round with an incredible swiftness. One fellow fell on the rum barrel, which stood broached upon the deck, and rolled it promptly overboard. On my part, I made for the Jolly Roger, struck it, tossed it in the sea, and could have flung myself after, so vexed was I with our mismanagement. As for Teach, he grew as pale as death, and incontinently went down to his cabin. Only twice he came on deck that afternoon; went to the taffrail; took a long look at the king's ship, which was still on the horizon heading after us; and then, without speech, back to his cabin. You may say he deserted us; and if it had not been for one very capable sailor we had on board, and for the lightness of the airs that blew all day, we must certainly have gone to the yardarm.

It is to be supposed Teach was humiliated, and perhaps alarmed for his position with the crew; and the way in which he set about regaining what he had lost was highly characteristic of the man. Early next day we smelled him burning sulphur in his cabin and crying out of " Hell, hell!" which was well understood among the crew, and filled their minds with apprehension. Presently he comes on deck, a perfect figure of fun, his face blacked, his hair and whiskers curled, his belt stuck full of pistols, chewing bits of glass so that the blood ran down his chin, and brandishing a dirk. I do not know if he had taken these manners from the Indians of America, where he was a native; but such was his way, and he would always thus announce that he was wound up to horrid deeds. The first that came near him was the fellow who had sent the rum overboard the day before; him he stabbed to the heart, damning him for a mutineer; and then he capered about the body, raving and swearing and daring us to come on. It was the silliest exhibition; and yet dangerous too, for the cowardly fellow was plainly working himself up to another murder.

All of a sudden Ballantrae stepped forth. "Have done with this play-acting," says he. "Do you think to frighten us with making faces? We saw nothing of you yesterday when you were wanted; and we did well without you, let me tell you that."

There was a murmur and a movement in the crew of pleasure and alarm, I thought, in nearly equal parts. As for Teach, he gave a barbarous howl, and swung his dirk to fling it, an art in which (like many seamen) he was very expert.

"Knock that out of his hand!" says Ballantrae, so sudden and sharp that my arm obeyed him before my mind had understood.

Teach stood like one stupid, never thinking on his pistols.

"Go down to your cabin," cries Ballantrae, "and come on deck again when you are sober. Do you think we are going to hang for you, you black-faced, half-witted, drunken brute and butcher? Go down!" And he stamped his foot at him with such a sudden smartness that Teach fairly ran for it to the companion.

"And now, mates," says Ballantrae, "a word with you. I don't know if you are gentlemen of fortune for the fun of the thing; but I am not. I want to make money, and get ashore again, and spend it like a man. And on one thing my mind is made up: I will not hang if I can help it. Come: give me a hint; I'm only a beginner! Is there no way to get a little discipline and common sense about this business?"

One of the men spoke up: he said by rights they should have a quartermaster; and no sooner was the word out of his mouth, than they were all of that opinion. The thing went by acclamation; Ballantrae was made quartermaster, the rum was put in his charge, laws were passed in imitation of those of a pirate by the name of Roberts; and the last proposal was to make an end of Teach. But Ballantrae was afraid of a more efficient captain, who might be a counterweight to himself, and he opposed this stoutly. Teach, he said, was good enough to board ships and frighten fools with his blacked face and swearing; we could scarce get a better man than Teach for that; and besides, as the man was now disconsidered and as good as deposed, we might reduce his proportion of the plunder. This carried it; Teach's share was cut down to a mere derision, being actually less than mine; and there remained only two points: whether he would consent, and who was to announce to him this resolution.

" Do not let that stick you," says Ballantrae, " I will do that."

And he stepped to the companion and down alone into the cabin to face that drunken savage.

" This is the man for us," cries one of the hands. " Three cheers for the quartermaster!" which were given with a will, my voice among the loudest, and I dare say these plaudits had their effect on Master Teach in the cabin, as we have seen of late days how shouting in the streets may trouble even the minds of legislators.

What passed precisely was never known, though some of the heads of it came to the surface later on; and we were all amazed as well as gratified when Ballantrae came on deck with Teach upon his arm, and announced that all had been consented.

I pass swiftly over those twelve or fifteen months in which we continued to keep the sea in the North Atlantic, getting our food and water from the ships we overhauled and doing on the whole a pretty fortunate business. Sure no one could wish to read anything so ungenteel as the memoirs of a pirate, even an unwilling one like me! Things went extremely better with our designs, and Ballantrae kept his lead to my admiration from that day forth. I would be tempted to suppose that a gentleman must everywhere be first, even aboard a rover; but my birth is every whit as good as any Scottish lord's, and I am not ashamed to confess that I stayed Crowding Pat until the end, and was not much better than the crew's buffoon. Indeed it was no scene to bring out my merits. My health suffered from a variety of reasons; I was more at home to the last on a horse's back than a ship's deck; and to be ingenuous, the fear of the sea was constantly in my mind, battling with the fear of my companions. I need not cry myself up for courage; I have done well on many fields under the eyes of famous generals, and earned my late advancement by an act of the most distinguished valor before many witnesses. But when we must proceed on one of our abordages, the heart of Francis Burke was in his boots; the little egg-shell skiff in which we must set forth, the horrible heaving of the vast billows, the height of the ship that we must scale, the thought of how many might be there in garrison upon their legitimate defense, the scowling heavens which (in that climate) so often looked darkly upon our exploits, and the mere crying of the wind in my ears, were all considerations most unpalatable to my valor. Besides which, as I was always a creature of the nicest sensibility, the scenes that must follow on our success tempted me as little as the chances of defeat. Twice we found women on board; and though I have seen towns sacked, and of late days in France some very horrid public tumults, there was something in the smallness of the numbers engaged and the bleak, dangerous sea-surroundings that made these acts of piracy far the most revolting. I confess ingenuously I could never proceed, unless I was three parts drunk; it was the same even with the crew; Teach himself was fit for no enterprise till he was full of rum; and it was one of the most difficult parts of Ballantrae's performance to serve us with liquor in the proper quantities. Even this he did to admiration; being upon the whole the most capable man I ever met with, and the one of the most natural genius. He did not even scrape favor with the crew, as I did, by continual buffoonery made upon a very anxious heart; but preserved on most occasions a great deal of gravity and distance; so that he was like a parent among a family of young children or a schoolmaster with his boys. What made his part the harder to perform, the men were most inveterate grumblers;

Ballantrae's discipline, little as it was, was yet irksome to their love of license; and what was worse, being kept sober they had time to think. Some of them accordingly would fall to repenting their abominable crimes: one in particular, who was a good Catholic and with whom I would sometimes steal apart for prayer; above all in bad weather, fogs, lashing rain and the like, when we would be the less observed; and I am sure no two criminals in the cart have ever performed their devotions with more anxious sincerity. But the rest, having no such grounds of hope, fell to another pastime, that of computation. All day long they would be telling up their shares or glooming over the result. I have said we were pretty fortunate. But an observation fails to be made: that in this world, in no business that I have tried, do the profits rise to a man's expectations. We found many ships and took many; yet few of them contained much money, their goods were usually nothing to our purpose—what did we want with a cargo of plows or even of tobacco?—and it is quite a painful reflection how many whole crews we have made to walk the plank for no more than a stock of biscuit or an anker or two of spirit.

In the meanwhile, our ship was growing very foul, and it was high time we should make for our *por de carrénage,* which was in the estuary of a river among swamps. It was openly understood that we should then break up and go and squander our proportions of the spoil; and this made every man greedy of a little more, so that our decision was delayed from day to day. What finally decided matters was a trifling accident, such as an ignorant person might suppose incidental to our way of life. But here I must explain: on only one of all the ships we boarded—the first on which we found women—did we meet with any genuine resistance. On that occasion we had two men killed, and several injured, and if it had not been for the gallantry of Ballantrae, we had surely been beat back at last. Everywhere else the defense (where there was any at all) was what the worst troops in Europe would have laughed at; so that the most dangerous part of our employment was to clamber

38

up the side of the ship; and I have even known the poor
souls on board to cast us a line, so eager were they to volunteer instead of walking the plank. This constant im-
munity had made our fellows very soft, so that I understood
how Teach had made so deep a mark upon their minds; for
indeed the company of that lunatic was the chief danger in
our way of life. The accident to which I have referred
was this. We had sighted a little full-rigged ship very close
under our board in a haze; she sailed near as well as we
did—I should be near the truth if I said near as ill; and
we cleared the bow chaser to see if we could bring a spar
or two about their ears. The swell was exceeding great;
the motion of the ship beyond description; it was little
wonder if our gunners should fire thrice and be still quite
broad of what they aimed at. But in the meanwhile the
chase had cleared a stern gun, the thickness of the air con-
cealing them; being better marksmen, their first shot struck
us in the bows, knocked our two gunners into mince-meat,
so that we were all sprinkled with the blood, and plunged
through the deck into the forecastle, where we slept. Ballantrae would have held on; indeed there was nothing in
this *contretemps* to affect the mind of any soldier; but he
had a quick perception of the men's wishes, and it was plain
this lucky shot had given them a sickener of their trade.
In a moment they were all of one mind: the chase was drawing away from us, it was needless to hold on, the *Sarah*
was too foul to overhaul a bottle, it was mere foolery to
keep the sea with her; and on these pretended grounds her
head was incontinently put about and the course laid for
the river. It was strange to see what merriment fell on
that ship's company, and how they stamped about the deck
jesting, and each computing what increase had come to his
share by the death of the two gunners.

We were nine days making our port, so light were the
airs we had to sail on, so foul the ship's bottom; but early
on the tenth, before dawn, and in a light, lifting haze, we
passed the head. A little after, the haze lifted, and fell
again, showing us a cruiser very close. This was a sore

blow, happening so near our refuge. There was a great debate of whether she had seen us, and if so whether it was likely they had recognized the *Sarah*. We were very careful, by destroying every member of those crews we overhauled, to leave no evidence as to our own persons; but the appearance of the *Sarah* herself we could not keep so private; and above all of late, since she had been foul and we had pursued many ships without success, it was plain that her description had been often published. I supposed this alert would have made us separate upon the instant. But here again that original genius of Ballantrae's had a surprise in store for me. He and Teach (and it was the most remarkable step of his success) had gone hand in hand since the first day of his appointment. I often questioned him upon the fact, and never got an answer but once, when he told me he and Teach had an understanding " which would very much surprise the crew if they should hear of it, and would surprise himself a good deal if it was carried out." Well, here again he and Teach were of a mind; and by their joint procurement, the anchor was no sooner down than the whole crew went off on a scene of drunkenness indescribable. By afternoon we were a mere shipful of lunatical persons, throwing of things overboard, howling of different songs at the same time, quarreling and falling together and then forgetting our quarrels to embrace. Ballantrae had bidden me drink nothing and feign drunkenness as I valued my life; and I have never passed a day so wearisomely, lying the best part of the time upon the forecastle and watching the swamps and thickets by which our little basin was entirely surrounded for the eye. A little after dusk Ballantrae stumbled up to my side, feigned to fall, with a drunken laugh, and before he got his feet again whispered to me to " reel down into the cabin and seem to fall asleep upon a locker, for there would be need of me soon." I did as I was told, and coming into the cabin, where it was quite dark, let myself fall on the first locker. There was a man there already: by the way he stirred and threw me off, I could not think he was much in liquor; and yet when I had found another place, he seemed to continue to sleep

on. My heart now beat very hard, for I saw some desperate
matter was in act. Presently down came Ballantrae, lighted
the lamp, looked about the cabin, nodded as if pleased, and on
deck again without a word. I peered out from between my
fingers, and saw there were three of us slumbering, or feigning to slumber, on the lockers: myself, one Dutton and one
Grady, both resolute men. On deck the rest were got to a
pitch of revelry quite beyond the bounds of what is human;
so that no reasonable name can describe the sounds they were
now making. I have heard many a drunken bout in my time,
many on board that very *Sarah*, but never anything the least
like this, which made me early suppose the liquor had been
tampered with. It was a long while before these yells and
howls died out into a sort of miserable moaning, and then to
silence; and it seemed a long while after that before Ballantrae came down again, this time with Teach upon his heels.
The latter cursed at the sight of us three upon the lockers.

"Tut," says Ballantrae, "you might fire a pistol at their
ears. You know what stuff they have been swallowing."

There was a hatch in the cabin floor, and under that the
richest part of the booty was stored against the day of
division. It fastened with a ring and three padlocks, the
keys (for greater security) being divided: one to Teach, one
to Ballantrae, and one to the mate, a man called Hammond.
Yet I was amazed to see they were now all in the one hand;
and yet more amazed (still looking through my fingers) to
observe Ballantrae and Teach bring up several packets, four
of them in all, very carefully made up and with a loop for
carriage.

"And now," says Teach, "let us be going."

'One word," says Ballantrae. "I have discovered there
is another man besides yourself who knows a private path
across the swamp. And it seems it is shorter than yours."

Teach cried out in that case they were undone.

"I do not know that," says Ballantrae. "For there are
several other circumstances with which I must acquaint you.
First of all, there is no bullet in your pistols, which (if you
remember) I was kind enough to load for both of us this

morning. Secondly, as there is some one else who knows a passage, you must think it highly improbable I should saddle myself with a lunatic like you. Thirdly, these gentlemen (who need no longer pretend to be asleep) are those of my party, and will now proceed to gag and bind you to the mast; and when your men awaken (if they ever do awake after the drugs we have mingled in their liquor) I am sure they will be so obliging as to deliver you, and you will have no difficulty, I dare say, to explain the business of the keys."

Not a word said Teach, but looked at us like a frightened baby, as we gagged and bound him.

"Now you see, you moon-calf," says Ballantrae, "why we make four packets. Heretofore you have been called Captain Teach, but I think you are now rather Captain Learn."

That was our last word on board the *Sarah;* we four with our four packets lowered ourselves softly into a skiff, and left that ship behind us as silent as the grave, only for the moaning of some of the drunkards. There was a fog about breast-high on the waters; so that Dutton, who knew the passage, must stand on his feet to direct our rowing; and this, as it forced us to row gently, was the means of our deliverance.

We were yet but a little way from the ship, when it began to come gray, and the birds to fly abroad upon the water. All of a sudden Dutton clapped down upon his hams, and whispered us to be silent for our lives, and hearken. Sure enough, we heard a little faint creak of oars upon one hand, and then again, and further off, a creak of oars upon the other. It was clear we had been sighted yesterday in the morning; here were the cruiser's boats to cut us out; here we were defenseless in their very midst. Sure, never were poor souls more perilously placed; and as we lay there on our oars, praying God the mist might hold, the sweat poured from my brow. Presently we heard one of the boats, where we might have thrown a biscuit in her. "Softly, men," we heard an officer whisper; and I marveled they could not hear the drumming of my heart.

"Never mind the path," says Ballantrae, "we must get

shelter anyhow; let us pull straight ahead for the sides of the basin."

This we did with the most anxious precaution, rowing, as best we could, upon our hands, and steering at a venture in the fog, which was (for all that) our only safety. But Heaven guided us; we touched ground at a thicket; scrambled ashore with our treasure; and having no other way of concealment, and the mist beginning already to lighten, hove down the skiff and let her sink. We were still but new under cover when the sun rose; and at the same time, from the midst of the basin, a great shouting of seamen sprung up, and we knew the *Sarah* was being boarded. I heard afterward the officer that took her got great honor; and it's true the approach was creditably managed, but I think he had an easy capture when he came to board.*

I was still blessing the saints for my escape, when I became aware we were in trouble of another kind. We were here landed at random in a vast and dangerous swamp; and how to come at the path was a concern of doubt, fatigue, and peril. Dutton, indeed, was of opinion we should wait until the ship was gone, and fish up the skiff; for any delay would be more wise than to go blindly ahead in that morass. One went back accordingly to the basin-side and (peering through the thicket) saw the fog already quite drunk up and English colors flying on the *Sarah*, but no movement made to get her under way.

Our situation was now very doubtful. The swamp was an unhealthful place to linger in; we had been so greedy to bring treasures that we had brought but little food; it was highly desirable, besides, that we should get clear of the neighborhood and into the settlements before the news of the capture went abroad; and against all these considerations there was only the peril of the passage on the other side. I think it not wonderful we decided on the active part.

* *Note by Mr. Mackellar.*—This Teach of the *Sarah* must not be confused with the celebrated "Blackbeard." The dates and facts by no means tally. It is possible the second Teach may have at once borrowed the name and imitated the more excessive part of his manners from the first. Even the Master of Ballantrae could make admirers.

THE MASTER OF BALLANTRAE

It was already blistering hot when we set forth to pass the marsh, or rather to strike the path, by compass. Dutton took the compass, and one or other of us three carried his proportion of the treasure; I promise you he kept a sharp eye to his rear, for it was like the man's soul that he must trust us with. The thicket was as close as a bush; the ground very treacherous, so that we often sunk in the most terrifying manner, and must go round about; the heat, besides, was stifling; the air singularly heavy, and the stinging insects abounded in such myriads that each of us walked under his own cloud. It has often been commented on how much better gentlemen of birth endure fatigue than persons of the rabble; so that walking officers, who must tramp in the dirt beside their men, shame them by their constancy. This was well to be observed in the present instance; for here were Ballantrae and I, two gentlemen of the highest breeding, on the one hand; and on the other, Grady, a common mariner, and a man nearly a giant in physical strength. The case of Dutton is not in point, for I confess he did as well as any of us.[*] But as for Grady, he began early to lament his case, tailed in the rear, refused to carry Dutton's packet when it came his turn, clamored continually for rum (of which we had too little) and at last even threatened us from behind with a cocked pistol, unless we should allow him rest. Ballantrae would have fought it out, I believe; but I prevailed with him the other way; and we made a stop and ate a meal. It seemed to benefit Grady little; he was in the rear again at once, growling and bemoaning his lot; and at last, by some carelessness, not having followed properly in our tracks, stumbled into a deep part of the slough where it was mostly water, gave some very dreadful screams, and before we could come to his aid, had sunk along with his booty. His fate and above all these screams of his appalled us to the soul; yet it was on the whole a fortunate circumstance and the means of our deliverance. For it moved Dutton to mount into a tree, whence he

[*]*Note by Mr. Mackellar.*—And is not this the whole explanation? since this Dutton, exactly like the officers, enjoyed the stimulus of some responsibility.

44

was able to perceive and to show me, who had climbed after him, a high piece of the wood which was a landmark for the path. He went forward the more carelessly, I must suppose; for presently we saw him sink a little down, draw up his feet and sink again, and so twice. Then he turned his face to us, pretty white.

"Lend a hand," said he, " I am in a bad place."

"I don't know about that," says Ballantrae, standing still.

Dutton broke out into the most violent oaths, sinking a little lower as he did, so that the mud was nearly to his waist; and plucking a pistol from his belt, " Help me," he cries, " or die and be damned to you!"

"Nay," says Ballantrae, "I did but jest. I am coming." And he set down his own packet and Dutton's, which he was then carrying. "Do not venture near till we see if you are needed," said he to me, and went forward alone to where the man was bogged. He was quiet now, though he still held the pistol; and the marks of terror in his countenance were very moving to behold.

"For the Lord's sake," says he, " look sharp."

Ballantrae was now got close up. "Keep still," says he, and seemed to consider; and then "Reach out both your hands!"

Dutton laid down his pistol, and so watery was the top surface that it went clear out of sight; with an oath he stooped to snatch it; and as he did so Ballantrae leaned forth and stabbed him between the shoulders. Up went his hands over his head, I know not whether with the pain or to ward himself, and the next moment he doubled forward in the mud.

Ballantrae was already over the ankles, but he plucked himself out and came back to me, where I stood with my knees smiting one another. "The devil take you, Francis!" says he. "I believe you are a half-hearted fellow after all. I have only done justice on a pirate. And here we are quite clear of the *Sarah!* Who shall now say that we have dipped our hands in any irregularities?"

I assured him he did me injustice; but my sense of human-

45

ity was so much affected by the horridness of the fact that I could scarce find breath to answer with.

"Come," said he, "you must be more resolved. The need for this fellow ceased when he had shown you where the path ran; and you cannot deny I would have been daft to let slip so fair an opportunity."

I could not deny but he was right in principle; nor yet could I refrain from shedding tears, of which I think no man of valor need have been ashamed; and it was not until I had a share of the rum that I was able to proceed. I repeat I am far from ashamed of my generous emotion; mercy is honorable in the warrior; and yet I cannot altogether censure Ballantrae, whose step was really fortunate, as we struck the path without further misadventure, and the same night, about sundown, came to the edge of the morass.

We were too weary to seek far; on some dry sands, still warm with the day's sun, and close under a wood of pines, we lay down and were instantly plunged in sleep.

We awaked the next morning very early, and began with a sullen spirit a conversation that came near to end in blows. We were now cast on shore in the southern provinces, thousands of miles from any French settlement; a dreadful journey and a thousand perils lay in front of us; and sure, if there was ever need for amity, it was in such an hour. I must suppose that Ballantrae had suffered in his sense of what is truly polite; indeed, and there is nothing strange in the idea, after the sea-wolves we had consorted with so long; and as for myself he fubbed me off unhandsomely, and any gentleman would have resented his behavior.

I told him in what light I saw his conduct: he walked a little off, I following to upbraid him; and at last he stopped me with his hand.

"Frank," says he, "you know what we swore; and yet there is no oath invented would induce me to swallow such expressions, if I did not regard you with sincere affection. It is impossible you should doubt me there: I have given proofs. Dutton I had to take, because he knew the pass, and Grady because Dutton would not move without him; but what call was there to carry you along? You are a perpetual danger to me with your cursed Irish tongue. By rights you should now be in irons in the cruiser. And you quarrel with me like a baby for some trinkets!"

I considered this one of the most unhandsome speeches ever made; and indeed to this day I can scarce reconcile it to my notion of a gentleman that was my friend. I retorted upon him with his Scotch accent, of which he had not so much as some, but enough to be very barbarous and disgusting, as I told him plainly; and the affair would have gone to a great length, but for an alarming intervention.

We had got some way off upon the sand. The place where we had slept, with the packets lying undone and the money scattered openly, was now between us and the pines; and it was out of these the stranger must have come. There he was at least, a great hulking fellow of the country, with a broad-ax on his shoulder, looking open-mouthed, now at the treasure which was just at his feet, and now at our disputation in which we had gone far enough to have weapons in our hands. We had no sooner observed him than he found his legs and made off again among the pines.

This was no scene to put our minds at rest; a couple of armed men in sea-clothes found quarreling over a treasure, not many miles from where a pirate had been captured—here was enough to bring the whole country about our ears. The quarrel was not even made up; it was blotted from our minds; and we got our packets together in the twinkling of an eye and made off, running with the best will in the world. But the trouble was, we did not know in what direction, and must continually return upon our steps. Ballantrae had indeed collected what he could from Dutton; but it's hard to travel upon hearsay; and the estuary, which spreads into a vast irregular harbor, turned us off upon every side with a new stretch of water.

We were near beside ourselves and already quite spent with running, when coming to the top of a dune, we saw we were again cut off by another ramification of the bay. This was a creek, however, very different from those that had arrested us before; being set in rocks, and so precipitously deep that a small vessel was able to lie alongside, made fast with a hawser; and her crew had laid a plank to the shore. Here they had lighted a fire and were sitting at their meal. As for the vessel herself, she was one of those they build in the Bermudas.

The love of gold and the great hatred that everybody has to pirates were motives of the most influential, and would certainly raise the country in our pursuit. Besides, it was now plain we were on some sort of straggling peninsula like the fingers of a hand; and the wrist, or passage to the mainland, which we should have taken at the first, was by this time not improbably secured. These considerations put us on a bolder counsel. For as long as we dared, looking every moment to hear sounds of the chase, we lay among some bushes on the top of the dune; and having by this means secured a little breath and recomposed our appearance, we strolled down at last, with a great affectation of carelessness, to the party by the fire.

It was a trader and his negroes, belonging to Albany in the province of New York, and now on the way home from the Indies with a cargo; his name I cannot recall. We were amazed to learn he had put in here from terror of the *Sarah*; for we had no thought our exploits had been so notorious. As soon as the Albanian heard she had been taken the day before, he jumped to his feet, gave us a cup of spirits for our good news, and sent his negroes to get sail on the Bermudan. On our side, we profited by the dram to become more confidential, and at last offered ourselves as passengers. He looked askance at our tarry clothes and pistols, and replied civilly enough that he had scarce accommodation for himself; nor could either our prayers or our offers of money, in which we advanced pretty far, avail to shake him.

"I see you think ill of us," says Ballantrae, "but I will show you how well we think of you by telling you the truth. We are Jacobite fugitives, and there is a price upon our heads."

At this the Albanian was plainly moved a little. He asked

us many questions as to the Scotch war, which Ballantrae very patiently answered. And then, with a wink, in a vulgar manner, " I guess you and your Prince Charlie got more than you cared about," said he.

" Bedad, and that we did," said I. " And, my dear man, I wish you would set a new example and give us just that much."

This I said in the Irish way, about which there is allowed to be something very engaging. It's a remarkable thing, and a testimony to the love with which our nation is regarded, that this address scarce ever fails in a handsome fellow. I cannot tell how often I have seen a private soldier escape the horse, or a beggar wheedle out a good alms, by a touch of the brogue. And indeed, as soon as the Albanian had laughed at me I was pretty much at rest. Even then, however, he made many conditions and (for one thing) took away our arms, before he suffered us on board, which was the signal to cast off; so that in a moment after we were gliding down the bay with a good breeze and blessing the name of God for our deliverance. Almost in the mouth of the estuary we passed the cruiser, and a little after, the poor *Sarah* with her prize crew; and these were both sights to make us tremble. The Bermudan seemed a very safe place to be in, and our bold stroke to have been fortunately played, when we were thus reminded of the case of our companions. For all that, we had only exchanged traps, jumped out of the frying-pan into the fire, run from the yardarm to the block, and escaped the open hostility of the man-of-war to lie at the mercy of the doubtful faith of our Albanian merchant.

From many circumstances, it chanced we were safer than we could have dared to hope. The town of Albany was at that time much concerned in contraband trade across the desert with the Indians and the French. This, as it was highly illegal, relaxed their loyalty, and as it brought them in relation with the politest people on the earth, divided even their sympathies. In short, they were like all the smugglers in the world, spies and agents ready-made for either party. Our Albanian, besides, was a very honest man indeed, and very greedy; and to crown our luck, he conceived a great delight in our society. Before we had reached the town of New York we had come to a full agreement; that he should carry us as far as Albany upon his ship, and thence put us on a way to pass the boundaries and join the French. For all this we were to pay at a high rate; but beggars cannot be choosers, nor outlaws bargainers.

We sailed, then, up the Hudson River which, I protest, is a very fine stream, and put up at the King's Arms in Albany. The town was full of the militia of the province, breathing slaughter against the French. Governor Clinton was there himself, a very busy man, and, by what I could learn, very near distracted by the factiousness of his Assembly. The Indians on both sides were on the war-path; we saw parties of them bringing in prisoners and (what was much worse) scalps, both male and female, for which they were paid at a fixed rate; and I assure you the sight was not encouraging. Altogether we could scarce have come at a period more unsuitable for our designs; our position in the chief inn was dreadfully conspicuous; our Albanian fubbed us off with a thousand delays and seemed upon the point of a retreat from his engagements; nothing but peril appeared to environ the poor fugitives; and for some time we drowned our concern in a very irregular course of living.

This too proved to be fortunate; and it's one of the remarks that fall to be made upon our escape, how providentially our steps were conducted to the very end. What a humiliation to the dignity of man! My philosophy, the extraordinary genius of Ballantrae, our valor, in which I grant that we were equal—all these might have proved insufficient without the Divine blessing on our efforts. And how true it is, as the church tells us, that the truths of religion are after all quite applicable even to daily affairs! At least it was in the course of our revelry that we made the acquaintance of a spirited youth by the name of Chew. He was one of the most daring of the Indian traders, very well acquainted with the secret paths of the wilderness, needy, dissolute, and by a last good fortune, in some disgrace with his family. Him we persuaded to come to our relief; he privately provided what was needful for our flight; and one day we slipped out of Albany, without a word to our former friend, and embarked a little above, in a canoe.

To the toils and perils of this journey, it would require a pen more elegant than mine to do full justice. The reader must conceive for himself the dreadful wilderness which we had now to thread; its thickets, swamps, precipitous rocks, impetuous rivers, and amazing water-falls. Among these barbarous scenes we must toil all day, now paddling, now carrying our canoe upon our shoulders; and at night we slept about a fire, surrounded by the howling of wolves and other savage animals. It was our design to mount the head-waters of the Hudson, to the neighborhood of Crown Point, where the French had a strong place in the woods, upon Lake Champlain. But to have done this directly were too perilous; and it was accordingly gone upon by such a labyrinth of rivers, lakes, and portages as makes my head giddy to remember. These paths were in ordinary times entirely desert; but the country was now up, the tribes on the war-path, the woods full of Indian scouts. Again and again we came upon these parties, when we least expected them; and one day, in particular, I shall never forget; how, as dawn was coming in, we were suddenly surrounded by five or six of these painted devils, uttering a very dreary sort of cry and brandishing their hatchets. It passed off harmlessly indeed, as did the rest of our encounters; for Chew was well known and highly valued among the different tribes. Indeed, he was a very gallant, respectable young man. But even with the advantage of his companionship, you must not think these meetings were without sensible peril. To prove friendship on our part, it was needful to draw upon our stock of rum—indeed, under whatever disguise, that is the true business of the Indian trader, to keep a traveling public-house in the forest; and when once the braves had got their bottle of *scaura* (as they call this beastly liquor) it behooved us to set forth and paddle for our scalps. Once they were a little drunk, good-by to any sense or decency; they had but the one thought, to get more *scaura;* they might easily take it in their heads to give us chase; and had we been overtaken I had never written these memoirs.

We were come to the most critical portion of our course, where we might equally expect to fall into the hands of French or English, when a terrible calamity befell us. Chew was taken suddenly sick with symptoms like those of poison, and in the course of a few hours expired in the bottom of the canoe. We thus lost at once our guide, our interpreter, our boatman and our passport, for he was all these in one; and found ourselves reduced, at a blow, to the most desperate and irremediable distress. Chew, who took a great pride in his knowledge, had indeed often lectured us on the geography; and Ballantrae, I believe, would listen. But for my part I have always found such information highly tedious; and beyond the fact that we were now in the country of the Adirondack Indians, and not so distant from our destination, could we but have found the way, I was entirely ignorant. The wisdom of my course was soon the more apparent; for with all his pains, Ballantrae was no further advanced than myself. He knew we must continue to go up one stream; then, by way of a portage, down another; and then up a third. But you are to consider, in a mountain country, how many streams come rolling in from every hand. And how is a gentleman, who is a perfect stranger in that part of the world, to tell any one of them from any other? Nor was this our only trouble. We were great novices, besides, in handling a canoe; the portages were almost beyond our strength, so that I have seen us sit down in despair for half an hour at a time without one word; and the appearance of a single Indian, since we had now no means of speaking to them, would have been in all probability the means of our destruction. There is altogether some excuse if Ballantrae showed something of a glooming disposition; his habit of imputing blame to others, quite as capable as himself, was less tolerable, and his language it was not always easy to accept. Indeed, he had contracted on board the pirate ship a manner of address which was in a high degree unusual between gentlemen; and now, when you might say he was in a fever, it increased upon him hugely.

The third day of these wanderings, as we were carrying the canoe upon a rocky portage, she fell and was entirely bilged. The portage was between two lakes, both pretty extensive; the track, such as it was, opened at both ends upon the water, and on both hands was inclosed by the unbroken woods; and the sides of the lakes were quite impassable with bog; so that we beheld ourselves not only condemned to go without our boat and the greater part of our provisions, but to plunge at once into impenetrable thickets and to desert what little guidance we still had—the course of the river. Each stuck his pistols in his belt, shouldered an ax, made a pack of his treasure and as much food as he could stagger under, and deserting the rest of our possessions, even to our swords, which would have much embarrassed us among the woods, we set forth on this deplorable adventure. The labors of Hercules, so finely described by Homer, were a trifle to what we now underwent. Some parts of the forest were perfectly dense down to the ground, so that we must cut our way like mites in a cheese. In some the bottom was full of deep swamp, and the whole wood entirely rotten. I have leaped on a great fallen log and sunk to the knees in touchwood; I have sought to stay myself, in falling, against what looked to be a solid trunk, and the whole thing has whiffed away at my touch like a sheet of paper. Stumbling, falling, bogging to the knees, hewing our way, our eyes almost put out with twigs and branches, our clothes plucked from our bodies, we labored all day, and it is doubtful if we made two miles. What was worse, as we could rarely get a view of the country and were perpetually justled from our path by obstacles, it was impossible even to have a guess in what direction we were moving.

A little before sundown, in an open place with a stream and set about with barbarous mountains, Ballantrae threw down his pack. " I will go no further," said he, and bade me light the fire, damning my blood in terms not proper for a chairman.

I told him to try to forget he had ever been a pirate. and to remember he had been a gentleman.

"Are you mad?" he cried. "Don't cross me here!" And then, shaking his fist at the hills, "To think," cries he, "that I must leave my bones in this miserable wilderness! Would God I had died upon the scaffold like a gentleman!" This he said ranting like an actor; and then sat biting his fingers and staring on the ground, a most unchristian object.

I took a certain horror of the man, for I thought a soldier and a gentleman should confront his end with more philosophy. I made him no reply, therefore, in words; and presently the evening fell so chill that I was glad, for my own sake, to kindle a fire. And yet God knows, in such an open spot, and the country alive with savages, the act was little short of lunacy. Ballantrae seemed never to observe me, but at last, as I was about parching a little corn, he looked up.

"Have you ever a brother?" said he.

"By the blessing of Heaven," said I, "not less than five."

"I have the one," said he, with a strange voice; and then presently, "He shall pay me for all this," he added. And when I asked him what was his brother's part in our distress, "What!" he cried, "he sits in my place, he bears my name, he courts my wife; and I am here alone with a damned Irishman in this tooth-chattering desert! Oh, I have been a common gull!" he cried.

The explosion was in all ways so foreign to my friend's nature that I was daunted out of all my just susceptibility. Sure, an offensive expression, however vivacious, appears a wonderfully small affair in circumstances so extreme! But here there is a strange thing to be noted. He had only once before referred to the lady with whom he was contracted. That was when he came in view of the town of New York, when he had told me, if all had their rights, he was now in sight of his own property, for Miss Graeme enjoyed a large estate in the province. And this was certainly a natural occasion; but now here she was named a second time; and what is surely fit to be observed, in this very month, which was November, '47, and *I believe upon that very day, as we* *sat among those barbarous mountains,* his brother and Miss Graeme were married. I am the least superstitious of men; but the hand of Providence is here displayed too openly not to be remarked.*

The next day, and the next, were passed in similar labors; Ballantrae often deciding on our course by the spinning of a coin; and once, when I expostulated on this childishness, he had an odd remark that I have never forgotten. " I know no better way," said he, " to express my scorn of human reason." I think it was the third day that we found the body of a Christian, scalped and most abominably mangled, and lying in a pudder of his blood, the birds of the desert screaming over him, as thick as flies. I cannot describe how dreadfully this sight affected us; but it robbed me of all strength and all hope for this world. The same day, and only a little after, we were scrambling over a part of the forest that had been burned, when Ballantrae, who was a little ahead, ducked suddenly behind a fallen trunk. I joined him in this shelter, whence we could look abroad without being seen ourselves; and in the bottom of the next vale beheld a large war party of the savages going by across our line. There might be the value of a weak battalion present; all naked to the waist, blacked with grease and suet, and painted with white lead and vermilion, according to their beastly habits. They went one behind another like a string of geese, and at a quickish trot; so that they took but a little while to rattle by and disappear again among the woods. Yet I suppose we endured a greater agony of hesitation and suspense in these few minutes than goes usually to a man's whole life. Whether they were French or English Indians, whether they desired scalps or prisoners, whether we should declare ourselves upon the chance or lie quiet and continue the heart-breaking business of our journey: sure, I think, these were questions to have puzzled the brains of Aristotle himself. Ballantrae turned to me with a face all wrinkled up and his teeth showing in his mouth, like that I have read of people starving; he said no

---

* *Note by Mr. Mackellar.*—A complete blunder: there was at this date no word of the marriage: see above in my own narration.

word, but his whole appearance was a kind of dreadful question.

"They may be of the English side," I whispered; "and think! the best we could then hope, is to begin this over again."

"I know, I know," he said. "Yet it must come to a plunge at last." And he suddenly plucked out his coin, shook it in his closed hands, looked at it, and then lay down with his face in the dust.

Addition by Mr. Mackellar.—I drop the chevalier's narration at this point because the couple quarreled and separated the same day; and the chevalier's account of the quarrel seems to me (I must confess) quite incompatible with the nature of either of the men. Henceforth, they wandered alone, undergoing extraordinary sufferings; until first one and then the other was picked up by a party from Fort St. Frederick. Only two things are to be noted. And first (as most important for my purpose) that the master in the course of his miseries buried his treasure, at a point never since discovered, but of which he took a drawing in his own blood on the lining of his hat. And second, that on his coming thus penniless to the fort, he was welcomed like a brother by the chevalier, who thence paid his way to France. The simplicity of Mr. Burke's character leads him at this point to praise the master exceedingly; to an eye more worldly wise, it would seem it was the chevalier alone that was to be commended. I have the more pleasure in pointing to this really very noble trait of my esteemed correspondent, as I fear I may have wounded him immediately before. I have refrained from comments on any of his extraordinary and (in my eyes) immoral opinions, for I know him to be jealous of respect. But his version of the quarrel is really more than I can reproduce; for I knew the master myself, and a man more insusceptible of fear is not conceivable. I regret this oversight of the chevalier's, and all the more because the tenor of his narrative (set aside a few flourishes) strikes me as highly ingenuous.

YOU can guess on what part of his adventures the colonel principally dwelt. Indeed, if we had heard it all, it is to be thought the current of this business had been wholly altered; but the pirate ship was very gently touched upon. Nor did I hear the colonel to an end even of that which he was willing to disclose; for Mr. Henry, having for some while been plunged in a brown study, rose at last from his seat and (reminding the colonel there were matters that he must attend to) bade me follow him immediately to the office.

Once there, he sought no longer to dissemble his concern, walking to and fro in the room with a contorted face, and passing his hand repeatedly upon his brow.

"We have some business," he began at last; and there broke off, declared we must have wine, and sent for a magnum of the best. This was extremely foreign to his habitudes; and what was still more so, when the wine had come he gulped down one glass upon another like a man careless of appearances. But the drink steadied him.

"You will scarce be surprised, Mackellar," says he, "when I tell you that my brother (whose safety we are all rejoiced to learn) stands in some need of money."

I told him I had misdoubted as much; but the time was not very fortunate as the stock was low.

"Not mine," said he. "There is the money for the mortgage."

I reminded him it was Mrs. Henry's.

"I will be answerable to my wife," he cried violently.

"And then," said I, "there is the mortgage."

"I know," said he, "it is on that I would consult you."

I showed him how unfortunate a time it was to divert this money from its destination; and how by so doing we must lose the profit of our past economies, and plunge back the estate into the mire. I even took the liberty to plead with him; and when he still opposed me with a shake of the head and a bitter, dogged smile, my zeal quite carried me beyond my place. "This is midsummer madness," cried I; "and I for one will be no party to it."

"You speak as though I did it for my pleasure," says he. "But I have a child now; and besides I love order; and to say the honest truth, Mackellar, I had begun to take a pride in the estates." He gloomed for a moment. "But what would you have?" he went on. "Nothing is mine, nothing. This day's news has knocked the bottom out of my life. I have only the name and the shadow of things; only the shadow; there is no substance in my rights."

"They will prove substantial enough before a court," said I.

He looked at me with a burning eye, and seemed to repress the word upon his lips; and I repented what I had said, for I saw that while he spoke of the estate he had still a side-thought to his marriage. And then, of a sudden, he twitched the letter from his pocket, where it lay all crumpled, smoothed it violently on the table, and read these words to me with a trembling tongue. "'My dear Jacob'—this is how he begins!" cries he—"'My dear Jacob, I once called you so, you may remember; and you have now done the business, and flung my heels as high as Criffel.' What do you think of that, Mackellar," says he, "from an only brother? I declare to God I liked him very well; I was always stanch to him; and this is how he writes! But I will not sit down under the imputation"—(walking to and fro)—"I am as good as he, I am a better man than he, I call on God to prove it! I cannot give him all the monstrous sum he asks; he knows the estate to be incompetent; but I will give him what I have, and it is more than he expects. I have borne all this too long. See what he writes further on; read it for yourself: 'I know you are a niggardly dog.' A niggardly dog! I, niggardly? Is that true, Mackellar? You think it is?" I really thought he would have struck me at that. "Oh, you all think so! Well, you shall see, and he shall see, and God shall see. If I ruin the estate and go barefoot, I shall stuff this bloodsucker.

Let him ask all—all, and he shall have it! It is all his by rights. Ah!" he cried, "and I foresaw all this and worse, when he would not let me go." He poured out another glass of wine and was about to carry it to his lips, when I made so bold as lay a finger on his arm. He stopped a moment. "You are right," said he, and flung glass and all in the fireplace. "Come, let us count the money."

I durst no longer oppose him; indeed, I was very much affected by the sight of so much disorder in a man usually so controlled; and we sat down together, counted the money, and made it up in packets for the greater ease of Colonel Burke, who was to be the bearer. This done, Mr. Henry returned to the hall, where he and my old lord sat all night through with their guest.

A little before dawn I was called and set out with the colonel. He would scarce have liked a less responsible convoy, for he was a man who valued himself; nor could we afford him one more dignified, for Mr. Henry must not appear with the free-traders. It was a very bitter morning of wind, and as we went down through the long shrubbery the colonel held himself muffled in his cloak.

"Sir," said I, "this is a great sum of money that your friend requires. I must suppose his necessities to be very great."

"We must suppose so," says he, I thought dryly, but perhaps it was the cloak about his mouth.

"I am only a servant of the family," said I. "You may deal openly with me. I think we are likely to get little good by him?"

"My dear man," said the colonel, "Ballantrae is a gentleman of the most eminent natural abilities, and a man that I admire and that I revere, to the very ground he treads on." And then he seemed to me to pause like one in a difficulty.

"But for all that," said I, "we are likely to get little good by him?"

"Sure, and you can have it your own way, my dear man," says the colonel.

By this time we had come to the side of the creek, where

the boat awaited him. "Well," said he, "I am sure I am very much your debtor for all your civility, Mr. Whatever-your-name-is; and just as a last word, and since you show so much intelligent interest, I will mention a small circumstance that may be of use to the family. For I believe my friend omitted to mention that he has the largest pension on the Scots Fund of any refugee in Paris; and it's the more disgraceful, sir," cries the colonel, warming, "because there's not one dirty penny for myself."

He cocked his hat at me, as if I had been to blame for this partiality; then changed again into his usual swaggering civility, shook me by the hand, and set off down to the boat, with the money under his arms, and whistling as he went the pathetic air of "Shule Aroon." It was the first time I had heard that tune; I was to hear it again, words and all, as you shall learn; but I remember how that little stave of it ran in my head, after the free-traders had bade him "Wheesht, in the deil's name," and the grating of the oars had taken its place, and I stood and watched the dawn creeping on the sea, and the boat drawing away, and the lugger lying with her foresail backed awaiting it.

The gap made in our money was a sore embarrassment; and among other consequences, it had this: that I must ride to Edinburgh, and there raise a new loan on very questionable terms to keep the old afloat; and was thus, for close upon three weeks, absent from the house of Durrisdeer.

What passed in the interval, I had none to tell me; but I found Mrs. Henry, upon my return, much changed in her demeanor; the old talks with my lord for the most part pretermitted; a certain deprecation visible toward her husband, to whom I thought she addressed herself more often; and for one thing, she was now greatly wrapped up in Miss Katharine. You would think the change was agreeable to Mr. Henry! no such matter! To the contrary, every circumstance of alteration was a stab to him; he read in each the avowal of her truant fancies: that constancy to the master of which she was proud while she supposed him dead, she had to blush for now she knew he was alive: and these blushes were the hated spring of her new conduct. I am to conceal no truth; and I will here say plainly, I think this was the period in which Mr. Henry showed the worst. He contained himself, indeed, in public; but there was a deep-seated irritation visible underneath. With me, from whom he had less concealment, he was often grossly unjust; and even for his wife he would sometimes have a sharp retort: perhaps when she had ruffled him with some unwonted kindness; perhaps upon no tangible occasion, the mere habitual tenor of the man's annoyance bursting spontaneously forth. When he would thus forget himself (a thing so strangely out of keeping with the terms of their relation), there went a shock through the whole company; and the pair would look upon each other in a kind of pained amazement.

All the time too, while he was injuring himself by this defect of temper, he was hurting his position by a silence, of which I scarce know whether to say it was the child of generosity or pride. The free-traders came again and again, bringing messengers from the Master, and none departed empty-handed. I never durst reason with Mr. Henry; he gave what was asked of him in a kind of noble rage. Perhaps because he knew he was by nature inclining to the parsimonious, he took a back-foremost pleasure in the recklessness with which he supplied his brother's exigence. Perhaps the falsity of the position would have spurred an humbler man into the same excesses. But the estate (if I may say so) groaned under it; our daily expenses where shown lower and lower; the stables were emptied, all but four roadsters; servants were discharged, which raised a dreadful murmuring in the country and heated up the old disfavor upon Mr. Henry; and at last the yearly visit to Edinburgh must be discontinued.

This was in 1756. You are to suppose that for seven years this bloodsucker had been drawing the life's blood from Durrisdeer; and that all this time my patron had held his peace. It was an effect of devilish malice in the master, that he addressed Mr. Henry alone upon the matter of his demands, and there was never a word to my lord. The family had looked on wondering at our economies. They had lamented, I have no doubt, that my patron had become so great a miser; a fault always despicable, but in the young abhorrent; and Mr. Henry was not yet thirty years of age. Still he had managed the business of Durrisdeer almost from a boy; and they bore with these changes in a silence as proud and bitter as his own, until the coping stone of the Edinburgh visit.

At this time, I believe my patron and his wife were rarely together save at meals. Immediately on the back of Colonel Burke's announcement, Mrs. Henry made palpable advances; you might say she had laid a sort of timid court to her husband, different indeed from her former manner of unconcern and distance. I never had the heart to blame Mr. Henry because he recoiled from these advances; nor yet to censure the wife, when she was cut to the quick by their rejection. But the result was an entire estrangement, so that (as I say) they rarely spoke except at meals. Even the matter of the Edinburgh visit was first broached at table; and it chanced that Mrs. Henry was that day ailing and querulous. She had no sooner understood her husband's meaning than the red flew in her face.

" At last," she cried, " this is too much! Heaven knows what pleasure I have in my life, that I should be denied my only consolation. These shameful proclivities must be trod down! we are already a mark and an eye-sore in the neighborhood; I will not endure this fresh insanity."

" I cannot afford it," says Mr. Henry.

" Afford? " she cried. " For shame! But I have money of my own."

" That is all mine, madam, by marriage," he snarled, and instantly left the room.

My old lord threw up his hands to heaven and he and his daughter, withdrawing to the chimney, gave me a broad hint to be gone. I found Mr. Henry in his usual retreat, the steward's room, perched on the end of the table and plunging his penknife in it, with a very ugly countenance.

" Mr. Henry," said I, " you do yourself too much injustice; and it is time this should cease."

"Oh!" cries he, "nobody minds here. They think it only natural. I have shameful proclivities. I am a niggardly dog," and he drove his knife up to the hilt. "But I will show that fellow," he cried, with an oath, "I will show him which is the more generous."

"This is no generosity," said I, "this is only pride."

"Do you think I want morality?" he asked.

I thought he wanted help, and I should give it him, willingly; and no sooner was Mrs. Henry gone to her room than I presented myself at her door and sought admittance.

She openly showed her wonder. "What do you want with me, Mr. Mackellar?" said she.

"The Lord knows, madam," says I, "I have never troubled you before with any freedoms, but this thing lies too hard upon my conscience, and it will out. Is it possible that two people can be so blind as you and my lord? and have lived all these years with a noble gentleman like Mr. Henry, and understand so little of his nature?"

"What does this mean?" she cried.

"Do you not know where his money goes to? his—and yours—and the money for the very wine he does not drink at table?" I went on. "To Paris—to that man! Eight thousand pounds has he had of us in seven years, and my patron fool enough to keep it secret!"

"Eight thousand pounds!" she repeated. "It is impossible, the estate is not sufficient."

"God knows how we have sweated farthings to produce it," said I. "But eight thousand and sixty is the sum, beside odd shillings. And if you can think my patron miserly after that, this shall be my last interference."

"You need say no more, Mr. Mackellar," said she. "You have done most properly in what you too modestly call your interference. I am much to blame; you must think me indeed a very unobservant wife"—(looking upon me with a strange smile)—"but I shall put this right at once. The Master was always of a very thoughtless nature; but his heart is excellent; he is the soul of generosity. I shall write to him myself.

You cannot think how you have pained me by this communication."

"Indeed, madam, I had hoped to have pleased you," said I, for I raged to see her still thinking of the master.

"And pleased," said she, "and pleased me, of course."

That same day (I will not say but what I watched) I had the satisfaction to see Mr. Henry come from his wife's room in a state most unlike himself; for his face was all bloated with weeping, and yet he seemed to me to walk upon the air. By this, I was sure his wife had made him full amends for once. "Ah," thought I, to myself, "I have done a brave stroke this day."

On the morrow, as _ was seated at my books, Mr. Henry came in softly behind me, took me by the shoulders and shook me in a manner of playfulness. "I find you are a faithless fellow after all," says he; which was his only reference to my part, but the tone he spoke in was more to me than any eloquence of protestation. Nor was this all I had effected; for when the next messenger came (as he did not long afterward) from the Master, he got nothing away with him but a letter. For some while back it had been I myself who had conducted these affairs; Mr. Henry not setting pen to paper, and I only in the dryest and most formal terms. But this letter I did not even see; it would scarce be pleasant reading, for Mr. Henry felt he had his wife behind him for once, and I observed, on the day it was dispatched, he had a very gratified expression.

Things went better now in the family, though it could scarce be pretended they went well. There was now at least no misconception; there was kindness upon all sides; and I believe my patron and his wife might again have drawn together, if he could but have pocketed his pride, and she forgot (what was the ground of all) her brooding on another man. It is wonderful how a private thought leaks out; it is wonderful to me now, how we should all have followed the current of her sentiments; and though she bore herself quietly, and had a very even disposition, yet we should have known whenever her fancy ran to Paris. And would not any one have thought that my disclosure must have rooted up that idol? I think there is the devil in women: all these years passed, never a sight of the man, little enough kindness to remember (by all accounts) even while she had him, the notion of his death intervening, his heartless rapacity laid bare to her: that all should not do, and she must still keep the best place in her heart for this accursed fellow, is a thing to make a plain man rage. I had never much natural sympathy for the passion of love; but this unreason in my patron's wife disgusted me outright with the whole matter. I remember checking a maid, because she sung some bairnly kickshaw while my mind was thus engaged; and my asperity brought about my ears the enmity of all the petticoats about the house; of which I recked very little, but it amused Mr. Henry, who rallied me much upon our joint unpopularity. It is strange enough (for my own mother was certainly one of the salt of the earth and my aunt Dickson, who paid my fees at the university, a very notable woman) but I have never had much toleration for the female sex, possibly not much understanding; and being far from a bold man, I have ever shunned their company. Not only do I see no cause to regret this diffidence in myself, but have invariably remarked the most unhappy consequences follow those who were less wise. So much I thought proper to set down, lest I show myself unjust to Mrs. Henry. And besides the remark arose naturally, on a reperusal of the letter which was the next step in these affairs, and reached me to my sincere astonishment by a private hand, some week or so after the departure of the last messenger.

Letter from COLONEL BURKE (*afterward Chevalier*) *to* MR. MACKELLAR.

" TROYES IN CHAMPAGNE,
" *July* 12, 1756.

" MY DEAR SIR: You will doubtless be surprised to receive a communication from one so little known to you; but on the occasion I had the good fortune to rencontre you at Durrisdeer, I remarked you for a young man of a solid gravity of character: a qualification which I profess I admire and revere next to natural genius or the bold, chivalrous spirit of the soldier. I was besides interested in the noble family which you have the honor to serve or (to speak more by the book) to be the humble and respected friend of; and a conversation I had the pleasure to have with you very early in the morning has remained much upon my mind.

" Being the other day in Paris, on a visit from this famous city where I am in garrison, I took occasion to inquire your name (which I profess I had forgot) at my friend, the Master of B——; and a fair opportunity occurring, I write to inform you of what's new.

" The Master of B—— (when we had last some talk of him together) was in receipt, as I think I then told you, of a highly advantageous pension on the Scots Fund. He next received a company, and was soon after advanced to a regiment of his own. My dear sir, I do not offer to explain this circumstance; any more than why I myself, who have rid at the right hand of princes, should be fubbed off with a pair of colors and sent to rot in a hole at the bottom of the province. Accustomed as I am to courts, I cannot but feel it is no atmosphere for a plain soldier; and I could never hope to advance by similar means, even could I stoop to the endeavor. But our friend has a particular aptitude to succeed by the means of ladies; and if all be true that I have heard, he enjoyed a remarkable protection. It is like this turned against him; for when I had the honor to shake him by the hand, he was but newly released from the Bastille where he had been cast on a sealed letter; and though now released, has both lost his regiment and his pension. My dear sir, the loyalty of a plain Irishman will ultimately succeed in the place of craft; as I am sure a gentleman of your probity will agree.

" Now, sir, the Master is a man whose genius I admire beyond expression, and besides he is my friend; but I thought a little word of this revolution in his fortunes would not come amiss, for in my opinion the man's desperate. He spoke when I saw him of a trip to India (whither I am myself in some hope of accompanying my illustrious countryman, Mr. Lally) ; but for this he would require (as I understood) more money than was readily at his command. You may have heard a military proverb, that it is a good thing to make a bridge of gold to a flying enemy? I trust you will take my meaning; and I subscribe myself, with proper respects to my Lord Durrisdeer, to his son, and to the beauteous Mrs. Durie,

"My dear sir,
"Your obedient humble servant,
"FRANCIS BURKE."

This missive I carried at once to Mr. Henry; and I think there was but the one thought between the two of us : that it had come a week too late. I made haste to send an answer to Colonel Burke, in which I begged him, if he should see the Master, to assure him his next messenger would be attended to. But with all my haste I was not in time to avert what was impending; the arrow had been drawn, it must now fly. I could almost doubt the power of Providence (and certainly His will) to stay the issue of events; and it is a strange thought, how many of us had been storing up the elements of this catastrophe, for how long a time, and with how blind an ignorance of what we did.

From the coming of the colonel's letter, I had a spy-glass in my room, began to drop questions to the tenant folk, and as there was no great secrecy observed and the free-trade (in our part) went by force as much as stealth, I had soon got together a knowledge of the signals in use, and knew pretty well to an hour when any messenger might be expected. I say I questioned the tenants; for with the traders themselves, desperate blades that went habitually armed, I could never bring myself to meddle willingly. Indeed, by what proved in the sequel an unhappy chance, I was an object of scorn to some of these braggadocios; who had not only gratified me with a nickname, but catching me one night upon a by-path and being all (as they would have said) somewhat merry, had caused me to dance for their diversion. The

67

method employed was that of cruelly chipping at my toes
with naked cutlasses, shouting at the same time "Square-
Toes"; and though they did me no bodily mischief, I was
none the less deplorably affected and was indeed for several
days confined to my bed: a scandal on the state of Scotland
on which no comment is required.

It happened on the afternoon of November 7th, in this
same unfortunate year, that I espied during my walk the
smoke of a beacon fire upon the Muckleross. It was drawing
near time for my return; but the uneasiness upon my spirits
was that day so great that I must burst through the thickets
to the edge of what they call the Craig Head. The sun was
already down, but there was still a broad light in the west,
which showed me some of the smugglers treading out their
signal fire upon the Ross, and in the bay the lugger lying
with her sails brailed up. She was plainly but new come to
anchor, and yet the skiff was already lowered and pulling for
the landing-place at the end of the long shrubbery. And this
I knew could signify but one thing: the coming of a messenger for Durrisdeer.

I laid aside the remainder of my terrors, clambered down
the brae—a place I had never ventured through before, and
was hid among the shore-side thickets in time to see the boat
touch. Captain Crail himself was steering, a thing not
usual; by his side there sat a passenger; and the men gave
way with difficulty, being hampered with near upon half a
dozen portmanteaus, great and small. But the business of
landing was briskly carried through; and presently the baggage was all tumbled on shore, the boat on its return voyage
to the lugger, and the passenger standing alone upon the
point of rock, a tall, slender figure of a gentleman, habited
in black, with a sword by his side and a walking-cane upon
his wrist. As he so stood, he waved the cane to Captain Crail
by way of salutation, with something both of grace and
mockery that wrote the gesture deeply on my mind.

No sooner was the boat away with my sworn enemies than
I took a sort of half courage, came forth to the margin of
the thicket, and there halted again, my mind being greatly

pulled about between natural diffidence and a dark forebolding
of the truth. Indeed, I might have stood there swithering
all night, had not the stranger turned, spied me through the
mists, which were beginning to fall, and waved and cried on
me to draw near. I did so with a heart like lead.

"Here, my good man," said he, in the English accent,
"here are some things for Durrisdeer."

I was now near enough to see him, a very handsome figure
and countenance, swarthy, lean, long, with a quick, alert,
black look, as of one who was a fighter and accustomed to
command; upon one cheek he had a mole, not unbecoming; a
large diamond sparkled on his hand; his clothes, although
of the one hue, were of a French and foppish design; his ruf-
fles, which he wore longer than common, of exquisite lace;
and I wondered the more to see him in such a guise, when he
was but newly landed from a dirty smuggling lugger. At
the same time he had a better look at me, toised me a second
time sharply, and then smiled.

"I wager, my friend," says he, "that I know both your
name and your nickname. I divined these very clothes upon
your hand of writing, Mr. Mackellar."

At these words I fell to shaking.

"Oh," says he, "you need not be afraid of me. I bear no
malice for your tedious letters; and it is my purpose to employ you a good deal. You may call me Mr. Bally: it is the
name I have assumed; or rather (since I am addressing so
great a precisian) it is so I have curtailed my own. Come
now, pick up that and that"—indicating two of the portmanteaus. "That will be as much as you are fit to bear, and
the rest can very well wait. Come, lose no more time, if you
please."

His tone was so cutting that I managed to do as he bade
by a sort of instinct, my mind being all the time quite lost.
No sooner had I picked up the portmanteaus than he turned
his back and marched all through the long shrubbery; where
it began already to be dusk, for the wood is thick and ever
green. I followed behind, loaded almost to the dust, though
I profess I was not conscious of the burden; being swallowed

up in the monstrosity of this return and my mind flying like a weaver's shuttle.

On a sudden I set the portmanteaus to the ground and halted. He turned and looked back at me.

" Well? " said he.

" You are the Master of Ballantrae? "

" You will do me the justice to observe," says he, " that I have made no secret with the astute Mackellar."

" And in the name of God," cries I, " what brings you here? Go back, while it is yet time."

" I thank you," said he. " Your master has chosen this way, and not I; but since he has made the choice, he (and you also) must abide by the result. And now pick up these things of mine, which you have set down in a very boggy place, and attend to that which I have made your business."

But I had no thought now of obedience; I came straight up to him. " If nothing will move you to go back," said I; " though sure, under all the circumstances, any Christian or even any gentleman would scruple to go forward——"

" These are gratifying expressions," he threw in.

" If nothing will move you to go back," I continued, " there are still some decencies to be observed. Wait here with your baggage, and I will go forward and prepare your family. Your father is an old man; and "—I stumbled— " there are decencies to be observed."

" Truly," said he, " this Mackellar improves upon acquaintance. But look you here, my man, and understand it once for all—you waste your breath upon me, and I go my own way with inevitable motion."

" Ah! " says I. " Is that so? We shall see then! "

And I turned and took to my heels for Durrisdeer. He clutched at me and cried out angrily, and then I believed I heard him laugh, and then I am certain he pursued me for a step or two, and (I suppose) desisted. One thing at least is sure, that I came but a few minutes later to the door of the great house, nearly strangled for the lack of breath, but quite alone. Straight up the stair I ran, and burst into the hall, and stopped before the family without the power of speech; but I must have carried my story in my looks, for they rose out of their places and stared on me like changelings.

"He has come," I panted at last.

"He?" said Mr. Henry.

"Himself," said I.

"My son?" cried my lord. "Imprudent, imprudent boy! Oh, could he not stay where he was safe?"

Never a word said Mrs. Henry; nor did I look at her, I scarcely knew why.

"Well," said Mr. Henry, with a very deep breath, "and where is he?"

"I left him in the long shrubbery," said I.

"Take me to him," said he.

So we went out together, he and I, without another word from any one; and in the midst of the graveled plot encountered the master strolling up, whistling as he came and beating the air with his cane. There was still light enough overhead to recognize though not to read a countenance.

"Ah, Jacob!" says the Master. "So here is Esau back."

"James," says Mr. Henry, "for God's sake, call me by my name. I will not pretend that I am glad to see you; but I would fain make you as welcome as I can in the house of our fathers."

"Or in *my* house? or *yours?*" says the master. "Which was you about to say? But this is an old sore, and we need not rub it. If you would not share with me in Paris, I hope you will yet scarce deny your elder brother a corner of the fire at Durrisdeer?"

"That is very idle speech," replied Mr. Henry. "And you understand the power of your position excellently well."

"Why, I believe I do," said the other, with a little laugh. And this, though they had never touched hands, was (as we may say) the end of the brothers' meeting; for at this the master turned to me and bade me fetch his baggage.

I, on my side, turned to Mr. Henry for a confirmation; perhaps with some defiance.

THE MASTER OF BALLANTRAE

" As long as the Master is here, Mr. Mackellar, you will
very much oblige me by regarding his wishes as you would
my own," says Mr. Henry. " We are constantly troubling
you ; will you be so good as send one of the servants? " with
an accent on the word.

If this speech were anything at all, it was surely a well-
deserved reproof upon the stranger ; and yet, so devilish was
his impudence, he twisted it the other way.

" And shall we be common enough to say ' Sneck up? ' "
inquires he softly, looking upon me sideways.

Had a kingdom depended on the act, I could not have
trusted myself in words ; even to call a servant was beyond
me ; I had rather serve the man myself than speak ; and
I turned away in silence and went into the long shrubbery, with a heart full of anger and despair. It was dark
under the trees, and I walked before me and forgot what
business I was come upon, till I near broke my shin on the
portmanteaus. Then it was that I remarked a strange particular ; for whereas I had before carried both and scarce
observed it, it was now as much I could do to manage one.
And this, as it forced me to make two journeys, kept me the
longer from the hall.

When I got there the business of welcome was over long
ago ; the company was already at supper ; and by an oversight that cut me to the quick, my place had been forgotten. I had seen one side of the Master's return ; now I
was to see the other. It was he who first remarked my coming
in and standing back (as I did) in some annoyance. He
jumped from his seat.

" And if I have not got the good Mackellar's place ! " cries
he. " John, lay another for Mr. Bally ; I protest he will
disturb no one, and your table is big enough for all."

I could scarce credit my ears, nor yet my senses, when he
took me by the shoulders and thrust me laughing into my
own place ; such an affectionate playfulness was in his voice.
And while John laid the fresh place for him (a thing on
which he still insisted) he went and leaned on his father's
chair and looked down upon him, and the old man turned

about and looked upward on his son, with such a pleasant mutual tenderness that I could have carried my hand to my head in mere amazement.

Yet all was of a piece. Never a harsh word fell from him, never a sneer showed upon his lip. He had laid aside even his cutting English accent, and spoke with the kindly Scots tongue that sets a value on affectionate words; and though his manners had a graceful elegance mighty foreign to our ways in Durrisdeer, it was still a homely courtliness, that did not shame but flattered us. All that he did throughout the meal, indeed, drinking wine with me with a notable respect, turning about for a pleasant word with John, fondling his father's hand, breaking into little merry tales of his adventures, calling up the past with happy reference—all he did was so becoming, and himself so handsome, that I could scarce wonder if my lord and Mrs. Henry sat about the board with radiant faces, or if John waited behind with dropping tears.

As soon as supper was over, Mrs. Henry rose to withdraw.

" This was never your way, Alison," said he.

" It is my way now," she replied; which was notoriously false, " and I will give you a good-night, James, and a welcome—from the dead," said she, and her voice drooped and trembled.

Poor Mr. Henry, who had made rather a heavy figure through the meal, was more concerned than ever; pleased to see his wife withdraw, and yet half displeased, as he thought upon the cause of it; and the next moment altogether dashed by the fervor of her speech.

On my part, I thought I was now one too many; and was stealing after Mrs. Henry, when the Master saw me.

" Now, Mr. Mackellar," says he, " I take this near on an unfriendliness. I cannot have you go; this is to make a stranger of the prodigal son—and let me remind you where —in his own father's house! Come sit ye down, and drink another glass with Mr. Bally."

" Ay, ay, Mr. Mackellar," says my lord, " we must not make a stranger either of him or you. I have been telling

73

my son," he added, his voice brightening as usual on the word, " how much we valued all your friendly service."

So I sat there silent till my usual hour; and might have been almost deceived in the man's nature, but for one passage in which his perfidy appeared too plain. Here was the passage; of which, after what he knows of the brothers' meeting, the reader shall consider for himself. Mr. Henry sitting somewhat dully, in spite of his best endeavors to carry things before my lord, up jumps the Master, passes about the board, and claps his brother on the shoulder.

" Come, come, *Hairry lad*," says he, with a broad accent such as they must have used together when they were boys, " you must not be downcast because your brother has come home. All's yours, that's sure enough, and little I grudge it you. Neither must you grudge me my place beside my father's fire."

" And that is too true, Henry," says my old lord, with a little frown, a thing rare with him. " You have been the elder brother of the parable in the good sense; you must be careful of the other."

" I am easily put in the wrong," said Mr. Henry.

" Who puts you in the wrong? " cried my lord, I thought very tartly for so mild a man. " You have earned my gratitude and your brother's many thousand times; you may count on its endurance, and let that suffice."

" Ay, Harry, that you may," said the Master; and I thought Mr. Henry looked at him with a kind of wildness in his eye.

On all the miserable business that now followed, I have four questions that I asked myself often at the time and ask myself still. Was the man moved by a particular sentiment against Mr. Henry? or by what he thought to be his interest? or by a mere delight in cruelty such as cats display and theologians tell us of the devil? or by what he would have called love? My common opinion halts among the three first; but perhaps there lay at the spring of his behavior an element of all. As thus: Animosity to Mr.

Henry would explain his hateful usage of him when they were alone; the interests he came to serve would explain his very different attitude before my lord; that and some spice of a design of gallantry, his care to stand well with Mrs. Henry; and the pleasure of malice for itself, the pains he was continually at to mingle and oppose these lines of conduct.

Partly because I was a very open friend to my patron, partly because in my letters to Paris I had often given myself some freedom of remonstrance, I was included in his diabolical amusement. When I was alone with him, he pursued me with sneers; before the family, he used me with the extreme of friendly condescension. This was not only painful in itself, not only did it put me continually in the wrong; but there was in it an element of insult indescribable. That he should thus leave me out in his dissimulation, as though even my testimony were too despicable to be considered, galled me to the blood. But what it was to me is not worth notice. I make but memorandum of it here; and chiefly for this reason, that it had one good result, and gave me the quicker sense of Mr. Henry's martyrdom.

It was on him the burden fell. How was he to respond to the public advances of one who never lost a chance of gibing him in private? How was he to smile back on the deceiver and the insulter? He was condemned to seem ungracious. He was condemned to silence. Had he been less proud, had he spoken, who would have credited the truth? The acted calumny had done its work; my lord and Mrs. Henry were the daily witnesses of what went on; they could have sworn in court that the master was a model of long-suffering good-nature and Mr. Henry a pattern of jealousy and thanklessness. And ugly enough as these must have appeared in any one, they seemed tenfold uglier in Mr. Henry; for who could forget that the master lay in peril of his life, and that he had already lost his mistress, his title and his fortune?

" Henry, will you ride with me? " asks the Master one day.

THE MASTER OF BALLANTRAE

And Mr. Henry, who had been goaded by the man all morning, raps out: " I will not."

" I sometimes wish you would be kinder, Henry," says the other wistfully.

I give this for a specimen; but scenes befell continually. Small wonder if Mr. Henry was blamed; small wonder if I fretted myself into something near upon a bilious fever; nay, and at the mere recollection feel a bitterness in my blood.

Sure, never in this world was a more diabolical contrivance; so perfidious, so simple, so impossible to combat. And yet I think again, and I think always, Mrs. Henry might have read between the lines; she might have had more knowledge of her husband's nature; after all these years of marriage, she might have commanded or captured his confidence. And my old lord too, that very watchful gentleman, where was all his observation? But for one thing, the deceit was practiced by a master hand, and might have gulled an angel. For another (in the case of Mrs. Henry), I have observed there are no persons so far away as those who are both married and estranged, so that they seem out of ear-shot or to have no common tongue. For a third (in the case of both of these spectators), they were blinded by old, in-grained predilection. And for a fourth, the risk the Master was supposed to stand in (supposed, I say—you will soon hear why) made it seem the more ungenerous to criticise; and keeping them in a perpetual tender solicitude about his life, blinded them the more effectually to his faults.

It was during this time that I perceived most clearly the effect of manner, and was led to lament most deeply the plainness of my own. Mr. Henry had the essence of a gentleman; when he was moved, when there was any call of circumstance, he could play his part with dignity and spirit; but in the day's commerce (it is idle to deny it) he fell short of the ornamental. The master (on the other hand) had never a movement but it commended him. So it befell that when the one appeared gracious and the other

ungracious, every trick of their bodies seemed to call out
confirmation. Nor that alone; but the more deeply Mr.
Henry floundered in his brother's toils, the more clownish
he grew; and the more the Master enjoyed his spiteful
entertainment, the more engagingly, the more smilingly, he
went! So that the plot, by its own scope and progress,
furthered and confirmed itself.

It was one of the man's arts to use the peril in which,
as I say, he was supposed to stand. He spoke of it to those
who loved him with a gentle pleasantry, which made it the
more touching. To Mr. Henry, he used it as a cruel weapon
of offense. I remember his laying his finger on the clean
lozenge of the painted window, one day when we three were
alone together in the hall. " Here went your lucky guinea,
Jacob," said he. And when Mr. Henry only looked upon
him darkly, " Oh," he added, " you need not look such impotent malice, my good fly. You can be rid of your spider
when you please. How long, oh, Lord? When are you
to be wrought to the point of a denunciation, scrupulous
brother? It is one of my interests in this dreary hole. I
ever loved experiment." Still Mr. Henry only stared upon
him with a glooming brow and a changed color; and at last
the Master broke out in a laugh and clapped him on the
shoulder, calling him a sulky dog. At this my patron leaped
back with a gesture I thought very dangerous; and I must
suppose the Master thought so too; for he looked the least
in the world discountenanced, and I do not remember him
again to have laid hands on Mr. Henry.

But though he had his peril always on his lips in the
one way or the other, I thought his conduct strangely in-
cautious, and began to fancy the government (who had set
a price upon his head) was gone sound asleep. I will not
deny I was tempted with the wish to denounce him; but
two thoughts withheld me: one that if he were thus to end
his life upon an honorable scaffold, the man would be canon-
ized for good in the minds of his father and my patron's
wife; the other, that if I was any way mingled in the matter, Mr. Henry himself would scarce escape some glancings

of suspicion. And in the meanwhile our enemy went in and out more than I could have thought possible, the fact that he was home again was buzzed about all the country-side; and yet he was never stirred. Of all these so many and so different persons who were acquainted with his presence, none had the least greed (as I used to say, in my annoyance) or the least loyalty; and the man rode here and there—fully more welcome, considering the lees of old unpopularity, than Mr. Henry—and considering the free-traders, far safer than myself.

Not but what he had a trouble of his own; and this, as it brought about the gravest consequences, I must now relate. The reader will scarce have forgotten Jessie Broun; her way of life was much among the smuggling party; Captain Crail himself was of her intimates; and she had early word of Mr. Bally's presence at the house. In my opinion she had long ceased to care two straws for the Master's person; but it was become her habit to connect herself continually with the Master's name: that was the ground of all her play-acting; and so, now when he was back, she thought she owed it to herself to grow a haunter of the neighborhood of Durrisdeer. The Master could scarce go abroad but she was there in wait for him; a scandalous figure of a woman, not often sober; hailing him wildly as "her bonny laddie," quoting peddler's poetry, and as I receive the story, even seeking to weep upon his neck. I own I rubbed my hands over this persecution; but the Master, who laid so much upon others, was himself the least patient of men. There were strange scenes enacted in the policies. Some say he took his cane to her, and Jessie fell back upon her former weapon, stones. It is certain at least that he made a motion to Captain Crail to have the woman trepanned, and that the captain refused the proposition with uncommon vehemence. And the end of the matter was victory for Jessie. Money was got together; an interview took place in which my proud gentleman must consent to be kissed and wept upon; and the woman was set up in a public of her own, somewhere on Solway side (but I forget where) and by the only news I ever had of it, extremely ill-frequented.

This is to look forward. After Jessie had been but a little while upon his heels, the Master comes to me one day in the steward's office, and with more civility than usual, "Mackellar," says he, "there is a damned crazy wench comes about here. I cannot well move in the matter myself, which brings me to you. Be so good as see to it; the men must have a strict injunction to drive the wench away."

"Sir," said I, trembling a little, "you can do your own dirty errands for yourself."

He said not a word to that, and left the room.

Presently came Mr. Henry. "Here is news!" cried he. "It seems all is not enough, and you must add to my wretchedness. It seems you have insulted Mr. Bally."

"Under your kind favor, Mr. Henry," said I, "it was he that insulted me, and as I think grossly. But I may have been careless of your position when I spoke; and if you think so when you know all, my dear patron, you have but to say the word. For you I would obey in any point whatever, even to sin, God pardon me!" And thereupon I told him what had passed.

Mr. Henry smiled to himself; a grimmer smile I never witnessed. "You did exactly well," said he. "He shall drink his Jessie Broun to the dregs." And then, spying the Master outside, he opened the window, and crying to him by the name of Mr. Bally, asked him to step up and have a word.

"James," said he, when our persecutor had come in and closed the door behind him, looking at me with a smile as if he thought I was to be humbled, "you brought me a complaint against Mr. Mackellar into which I have inquired. I need not tell you I would always take his word against yours; for we are alone, and I am going to use something of your own freedom. Mr. Mackellar is a gentleman I value; and you must contrive, so long as you are under this roof, to bring yourself into no more collisions with one whom I will support at any possible cost to me or mine. As for the errand upon which you came to him, you must deliver yourself from the consequences of your own cruelty, and none of my servants shall be at all employed in such a case."

"My father's servants, I believe," says the Master.

"Go to him with this tale," said Mr. Henry.

The Master grew very white. He pointed at me with his finger. "I want that man discharged," he said.

"He shall not be," said Mr. Henry.

"You shall pay pretty dear for this," says the Master.

"I have paid so dear already for a wicked brother," said Mr. Henry, "that I am bankrupt even of fears. You have no place left where you can strike me."

"I will show you about that," says the Master, and went softly away.

"What will he do next, Mackellar?" cries Mr. Henry.

"Let me go away," said I. "My dear patron, let me go away; I am but the beginning of fresh sorrows."

"Would you leave me quite alone?" said he.

We were not long in suspense as to the nature of the new assault. Up to that hour the Master had played a very close game with Mrs. Henry; avoiding pointedly to be alone with her, which I took at the time for an effect of decency, but now think to be a most insidious art; meeting her, you may say, at meal-time only; and behaving, when he did so, like an affectionate brother. Up to that hour, you may say he had scarce directly interfered between Mr. Henry and his wife; except in so far as he had maneuvered the one quite forth from the good graces of the other. Now all that was to be changed; but whether really in revenge, or because he was wearying of Durrisdeer and looked about for some diversion, who but the devil shall decide?

From that hour at least began the siege of Mrs. Henry; a thing so deftly carried on that I scarce know if she was aware of it herself, and that her husband must look on in silence. The first parallel was opened (as was made to appear) by accident. The talk fell, as it did often, on the exiles in France; so it glided to the matter of their songs.

"There is one," says the Master, "if you are curious in these matters, that has always seemed to me very moving. The poetry is harsh; and yet, perhaps because of my situation, it has always found the way to my heart. It is supposed to be sung, I should tell you, by an exile's sweetheart; and represents, perhaps, not so much the truth of what she is thinking, as the truth of what he hopes of her, poor soul! in these far lands." And here the master sighed. "I protest it is a pathetic sight when a score of rough Irish, all common sentinels, get to this song; and you may see by their falling tears, how it strikes home to them. It goes thus, father," says he, very adroitly taking my lord for his listener, "and if I cannot get to the end of it, you must think it is a common case with us exiles." And thereupon he struck up the same air as I had heard the colonel whistle; but now to words, rustic indeed, yet most pathetically setting forth a poor girl's aspirations for an exiled lover: of which one verse indeed (or something like it) still sticks by me:

> "O, I will dye my petticoat red,
> With my dear boy I'll beg my bread,
> Though all my friends should wish me dead,
> For Willie among the rushes, O!"

He sung it well even as a song; but he did better yet as a performer. I have heard famous actors, when there was not a dry eye in the Edinburgh theater; a great wonder to behold; but no more wonderful than how the Master played upon that little ballad and on those who heard him like an instrument, and seemed now upon the point of failing, and now to conquer his distress, so that words and music seemed to pour out of his own heart and his own past, and to be aimed direct at Mrs. Henry. And his art went further yet; for all was so delicately touched, it seemed impossible to suspect him of the least design; and so far from making a parade of emotion, you would have sworn he was striving to be calm. When it came to an end we all sat silent for a time; he had chosen the dusk of the afternoon, so that none could see his neighbor's face; but it seemed as if we held our breathing, only my old lord cleared his throat. The first to move was the singer, who got to his feet suddenly and softly, and went and walked softly to and fro in the low end of the hall, Mr. Henry's customary place. We were to suppose that he there struggled down the last of his emotion; for he presently returned and launched into a disquisition on the nature of the Irish (always so much miscalled, and whom he defended) in his natural voice; so that, before the lights were brought we were in the usual course of talk. But even then, methought Mrs. Henry's face was a shade pale; and for another thing, she withdrew almost at once.

The next sign was a friendship this insidious devil struck up with innocent Miss Katharine; so that they were always together, hand in hand, or she climbing on his knee, like a pair of children. Like all his diabolical acts, this cut in several ways. It was the last stroke to Mr. Henry, to see his own babe debauched against him; it made him harsh with the poor innocent, which brought him still a peg lower in his wife's esteem; and (to conclude) it was a bond of union between the lady and the master. Under this influence their old reserve melted by daily stages. Presently there came walks in the long shrubbery, talks in the belvedere, and I know not what tender familiarity. I am sure Mrs. Henry was like many a good woman; she had a whole conscience, but perhaps by the means of a little winking. For even to so dull an observer as myself, it was plain her kindness was of a more moving nature than the sisterly. The tones of her voice appeared more numerous; she had a light and softness in her eye; she was more gentle with all of us, even with Mr. Henry, even with myself; methought she breathed of some quiet, melancholy happiness.

To look on at this, what a torment it was for Mr. Henry! And yet it brought our ultimate deliverance, as I am soon to tell.

THE MASTER OF BALLANTRAE

The purport of the master's stay was no more noble (gild it as they might) than to wring money out. He had some design of a fortune in the French Indies, as the chevalier wrote me; and it was the sum required for this that he came seeking. For the rest of the family it spelled ruin; but my lord, in his incredible partiality, pushed ever for the granting. The family was now so narrowed down (indeed there were no more of them than just the father and the two sons), that it was possible to break the entail, and alienate a piece of land. And to this, at first by hints, and then by open pressure, Mr. Henry was brought to consent. He never would have done so, I am very well assured, but for the weight of the distress under which he labored. But for his passionate eagerness to see his brother gone, he would not thus have broken with his own sentiment and the traditions of his house. And even so, he sold them his consent at a dear rate, speaking for once openly and holding the business up in its own shameful colors.

"You will observe," he said, "this is an injustice to my son, if ever I have one."

"But that you are not likely to have," said my lord.

"God knows!" said Mr. Henry. "And considering the cruel falseness of the position in which I stand to my brother, and that you, my lord, are my father and have the right to command me, I set my hand to this paper. But one thing I will say first: I have been ungenerously pushed, and when next, my lord, you are tempted to compare your sons, I call on you to remember what I have done and what he has done. Acts are the fair test."

My lord was the most uneasy man I ever saw; even in his old face the blood came up. "I think this is not a very wisely chosen moment, Henry, for complaints," said he. "This takes away from the merit of your generosity."

"Do not deceive yourself, my lord," said Mr. Henry. "This injustice is not done from generosity to him, but in obedience to yourself."

"Before strangers—" begins my lord, still more unhappily affected.

THE MASTER OF BALLANTRAE

"There is no one but Mackellar here," said Mr. Henry; "he is my friend. And, my lord, as you make him no stranger to your frequent blame, it were hard if I must keep him one to a thing so rare as my defense."

Almost I believe my lord would have rescinded his decision; but the master was on the watch.

"Ah, Henry, Henry," says he, "you are the best of us still. Rugged and true! Ah, man, I wish I was as good."

And at that instance of his favorite's generosity, my lord desisted from his hesitation, and the deed was signed.

As soon as it could be brought about, the land of Ochterhall was sold for much below its value, and the money paid over to our leech and sent by some private carriage into France. Or so he said; though I have suspected since it did not go so far. And now here was all the man's business brought to a successful head, and his pockets once more bulging with our gold; and yet the point for which we had consented to this sacrifice was still denied us, and the visitor still lingered on at Durrisdeer. Whether in malice, or because the time was not yet come for his adventure to the Indies, or because he had hopes of his design on Mrs. Henry, of from the orders of the government, who shall say? but linger he did and that for weeks.

You will observe I say: from the orders of government; for about this time the man's disreputable secret trickled out.

The first hint I had was from a tenant, who commented on the master's stay and yet more on his security; for this tenant was a Jacobitish sympathizer, and had lost a son at Culloden, which gave him the more critical eye. "There is one thing," said he, "that I cannot but think strange; and that is how he got to Cockermouth."

"To Cockermouth?" said I, with a sudden memory of my first wonder on beholding the man disembark so point-de-vice after so long a voyage.

"Why, yes," says the tenant, "it was there he was picked up by Captain Crail. You thought he had come from France by sea? And so we all did."

THE MASTER OF BALLANTRAE

I turned this news a little in my head, and then carried it to Mr. Henry. "Here is an odd circumstance," said I, and told him.

"What matters how he came, Mackellar, as long as he is here," groans Mr. Henry.

"No, sir," said I, "but think again! Does not this smack a little of some government connivance? You know how much we have wondered already at the man's security."

"Stop," said Mr. Henry. "Let me think of this." And as he thought there came that grim smile upon his face that was a little like the master's. "Give me paper," said he. And he sat without another word and wrote to a gentleman of his acquaintance—I will name no unnecessary names, but he was one in a high place. This letter I dispatched by the only hand I could depend upon in such a case, Macconochie's; and the old man rode hard, for he was back with the reply before even my eagerness had ventured to expect him. Again, as he read it, Mr. Henry had the same grim smile.

"This is the best you have done for me yet, Mackellar," says he. "With this in my hand, I will give him a shog. Watch for us at dinner."

At dinner accordingly, Mr. Henry proposed some very public appearance for the Master; and my lord, as he had hoped, objected to the danger of the course.

"Oh," says Mr. Henry, very easily, "you need no longer keep this up with me. I am as much in the secret as yourself."

"In the secret?" says my lord. "What do you mean, Henry? I give you my word I am in no secret from which you are excluded."

The Master had changed countenance, and I saw he was struck in a joint of his harness.

"How?" says Mr. Henry, turning to him with a huge appearance of surprise. "I see you serve your masters very faithfully; but I had thought you would have been humane enough to set your father's mind at rest."

"What are you talking of? I refuse to have my business

publicly discussed. I order this to cease," cries the Master very foolishly and passionately, and indeed more like a child than a man.

"So much discretion was not looked for at your hands, I can assure you," continued Mr. Henry. "For see what my correspondent writes"—unfolding the paper—"'It is, of course, in the interests both of the government and the gentleman whom we may perhaps best continue to call Mr. Bally, to keep this understanding secret; but it was never meant his own family should continue to endure the suspense you paint so feelingly; and I am pleased mine should be the hand to set these fears at rest. Mr. Bally is as safe in Great Britain as yourself.'"

"Is this possible?" cries my lord, looking at his son, with a great deal of wonder and still more of suspicion in his face.

"My dear father," says the Master, already much recovered, "I am overjoyed that this may be disclosed. My own instructions direct from London bore a very contrary sense, and I was charged to keep the indulgence secret from every one, yourself not excepted, and indeed yourself expressly named—as I can show in black and white, unless I have destroyed the letter. They must have changed their mind very swiftly, for the whole matter is still quite fresh; or rather Henry's correspondent must have misconceived that part, as he seems to have misconceived the rest. To tell you the truth, sir," he continued, getting visibly more easy, "I had supposed this unexplained favor to a rebel was the effect of some application from yourself; and the injunction to secrecy among my family the result of a desire on your part to conceal your kindness. Hence I was the more careful to obey orders. It remains now to guess by what other channel indulgence can have flowed on so notorious an offender as myself; for I do not think your son need defend himself from what seems hinted at in Henry's letter. I have never yet heard of a Durrisdeer who was a turncoat or a spy," says he proudly.

And so it seemed he had swum out of this danger unharmed; but this was to reckon without a blunder he had made, and without the pertinacity of Mr. Henry, who was now to show he had something of his brother's spirit.

" You say the matter is still fresh," says Mr. Henry.

" It is recent," says the Master, with a fair show of stoutness and yet not without a quaver.

" Is it so recent as that? " asks Mr. Henry, like a man a little puzzled, and spreading his letter forth again.

In all the letter there was no word as to the date, but how was the Master to know that?

" It seemed to come late enough for me," says he, with a laugh. And at the sound of that laugh, which rang false like a cracked bell, my lord looked at him again across the table, and I saw his old lips draw together close.

" No," said Mr. Henry, still glancing on his letter, " but I remember your expression. You said it was very fresh."

And here we had a proof of our victory, and the strongest instance yet of my lord's incredible indulgence; for what must he do but interfere to save his favorite from exposure!

" I think, Henry," says he, with a kind of pitiful eagerness, " I think we need dispute no more. We are all rejoiced at last to find your brother safe; we are all at one on that; and as grateful subjects we can do no less than drink to the king's health and bounty."

Thus was the Master extricated; but at least he had been put to his defense, he had come lamely out, and the attraction of his personal danger was now publicly plucked away from him. My lord, in his heart of hearts, now knew his favorite to be a government spy; and Mrs. Henry (however she explained the tale) was notably cold in her behavior to the discredited hero of romance. Thus in the best fabric of duplicity there is some weak point, if you can strike it, which will loosen all; and if, by this fortunate stroke, we had not shaken the idol, who can say how it might have gone with us at the catastrophe?

And yet at the time we seemed to have accomplished nothing. Before a day or two he had wiped off the ill results of his discomfiture, and to all appearance stood as high as ever. As for my Lord Durrisdeer, he was sunk in parental partiality; it was not so much love, which should be an active quality, as an apathy and torpor of his other powers; and forgiveness (so to misapply a noble word) flowed from him in sheer weakness, like the tears of senility. Mrs. Henry's was a different case; and Heaven alone knows what he found to say to her or how he persuaded her from her contempt. It is one of the worst things of sentiment that the voice grows to be more important than the words, and the speaker than that which is spoken. But some excuse the Master must have found, or perhaps he had even struck upon some art to wrest this exposure to his own advantage; for after a time of coldness, it seemed as if things went worse than ever between him and Mrs. Henry. They were then constantly together. I would not be thought to cast one shadow of blame, beyond what is due to a half-willful blindness, on that unfortunate lady; but I do think, in these last days, she was playing very near the fire; and whether I be wrong or not in that, one thing is sure and quite sufficient: Mr. Henry thought so. The poor gentleman sat for days in my room, so great a picture of distress that I could never venture to address him; yet it is to be thought he found some comfort even in my presence and the knowledge of my sympathy. There were times, too, when we talked, and a strange manner of talk it was; there was never a person named, nor an individual circumstance referred to; yet we had the same matter in our mind, and we were each aware of it. It is a strange art that can thus be practiced: to talk for hours of a thing, and never name nor yet so much as hint at it. And I remember I wondered if it was by some such natural skill that the Master made love to Mrs. Henry all day long (as he manifestly did), yet never startled her into reserve.

To show how far affairs had gone with Mr. Henry, I will give some words of his, uttered (as I have cause not to forget) upon the 26th of February, 1757. It was unseasonable weather, a cast back into winter: windless, bitter cold, the world all white with rime, the sky low and gray; the sea black and silent like a quarry hole. Mr. Henry sat close by the fire and debated (as was now common with him) whether " a man " should " do things," whether " interference was wise," and the like general propositions, which each of us particularly applied. I was by the window looking out, when there passed below me the Master, Mrs. Henry and Miss Katharine, that now constant trio. The child was running to and fro delighted with the frost; the Master spoke close in the lady's ear with what seemed (even from so far) a devilish grace of insinuation; and she on her part looked on the ground like a person lost in listening. I broke out of my reserve.

" If I were you, Mr. Henry," said I, " I would deal openly with my lord."

" Mackellar, Mackellar," said he, " you do not see the weakness of my ground. I can carry no such base thoughts to any one: to my father least of all; that would be to fall into the bottom of his scorn. The weakness of my ground," he continued, " lies in myself, that I am not one who engages love. I have their gratitude, they all tell me that: I have a rich estate of it! But I am not present in their minds; they are moved neither to think with me nor to think for me. There is my loss!" He got to his feet and trod down the fire. " But some method must be found, Mackellar," said he, looking at me suddenly over his shoulder; " some way must be found. I am a man of a great deal of patience—far too much—far too much. I begin to despise myself. And yet sure never was a man involved in such a toil!" He fell back to his brooding.

" Cheer up," said I. " It will burst of itself."

" I am far past anger now," says he, which had so little coherency with my own observation that I let both fall.

ON the evening of the interview referred to, the Master
went abroad; he was abroad a great deal of the next
day also, that fatal 27th; but where he went or what he
did, we never concerned ourselves to ask until next day.
If we had done so, and by any chance found out, it might
have changed all. But as all we did was done in ignorance,
and should be so judged, I shall so narrate these passages
as they appeared to us in the moment of their birth, and reserve all that I since discovered for the time of its discovery.
For I have now come to one of the dark parts of my narrative, and must engage the reader's indulgence for my patron.

All the 27th, that rigorous weather endured: a stifling
cold; the folk passing about like smoking chimneys; the
wide hearth in the hall piled high with fuel; some of the
spring birds that had already blundered north into our
neighborhood besieging the windows of the house or trotting
on the frozen turf like things distracted. About noon there
came a blink of sunshine, showing a very pretty, wintery,
frosty landscape of white hills and woods, with Crail's lugger waiting for a wind under the Craig Head, and the
smoke mounting straight into the air from every farm and
cottage. With the coming of night the haze closed in
overhead; it fell dark and still and starless and exceeding
cold: a night the most unseasonable, fit for strange
events.

Mrs. Henry withdrew, as was now her custom, very early.
We had set ourselves of late to pass the evening with a
game of cards; another mark that our visitor was wearying
mightily of the life at Durrisdeer; and we had not been
long at this when my old lord slipped from his place beside
the fire, and was off without a word to seek the warmth of
bed. The three thus left together had neither love nor

90

courtesy to share; not one of us would have sat up one instant to oblige another; yet from the influence of custom and as the cards had just been dealt, we continued the form of playing out the round. I should say we were late sitters; and though my lord had departed earlier than was his custom, twelve was already gone some time upon the clock, and the servants long ago in bed. Another thing I should say, that although I never saw the Master any way affected with liquor, he had been drinking freely and was perhaps (although he showed it not) a trifle heated.

Any way, he now practiced one of his transitions; and so soon as the door closed behind my lord, and without the smallest change of voice, shifted from ordinary civil talk into a stream of insult.

" My dear Henry, it is yours to play," he had been saying, and now continued: " It is a very strange thing how, even in so small a matter as a game of cards, you display your rusticity. You play, Jacob, like a bonnet laird, or a sailor in a tavern. The same dullness, the same petty greed, *cette lenteur d'hébété qui me fait rager;* it is strange I should have such a brother. Even Squaretoes has a certain vivacity when his stake is imperiled; but the dreariness of a game with you, I positively lack language to depict."

Mr. Henry continued to look at his cards, as though very maturely considering some play; but his mind was elsewhere.

" Dear God, will this never be done? " cries the Master. " *Quel lourdeau!* But why do I trouble you with French expressions, which are lost on such an ignoramus? A *lourdeau*, my dear brother, is as we might say a bumpkin, a clown, a clodpole: a fellow without grace, lightness, quickness; any gift of pleasing, any natural brilliancy: such a one as you shall see, when you desire, by looking in the mirror. I tell you these things for your good, I assure you; and besides, Squaretoes " (looking at me and stifling a yawn), " it is one of my diversions in this very dreary spot, to toast you and your master at the fire like chestnuts. I have great pleasure in your case, for I observe the nick-

91

name (rustic as it is), has always the power to make you writhe. But sometimes I have more trouble with this dear fellow here, who seems to have gone to sleep upon his cards. Do you not see the applicability of the epithet I have just explained, dear Henry? Let me show you. For instance, with all those solid qualities which I delight to recognize in you, I never knew a woman who did not prefer me—nor, I think," he continued, with the most silken deliberation, " I think—who did not continue to prefer me."

Mr. Henry laid down his cards. He rose to his feet very softly, and seemed all the while like a person in deep thought. "You coward!" he said gently, as if to himself. And then, with neither hurry nor any particular violence, he struck the Master in the mouth.

The Master sprung to his feet like one transfigured. I had never seen the man so beautiful. " A blow!" he cried. " I would not take a blow from God Almighty."

"Lower your voice," said Mr. Henry. "Do you wish my father to interfere for you again?"

"Gentlemen, gentlemen," I cried, and sought to come between them.

The Master caught me by the shoulder, held me at arm's length, and still addressing his brother: " Do you know what this means?" said he.

" It was the most deliberate act of my life," says Mr. Henry.

" I must have blood, I must have blood for this," says the Master.

" Please God it shall be yours," said Mr. Henry; and he went to the wall and took down a pair of swords that hung there with others, naked. These he presented to the Master by the points. " Mackellar shall see us play fair," said Mr. Henry. " I think it very needful."

" You need insult me no more," said the Master, taking one of the swords at random. " I have hated you all my life."

" My father is but newly gone to bed," said Mr. Henry. " We must go somewhere forth of the house."

"There is an excellent place in the long shrubbery," said the Master.

"Gentlemen," said I, "shame upon you both! Sons of the same mother, would you turn against the life she gave you?"

"Even so, Mackellar," said Mr. Henry, with the same perfect quietude of manner he had shown throughout.

"It is what I will prevent," said I.

And now here is a blot upon my life. At these words of mine the Master turned his blade against my bosom; I saw the light run along the steel; and I threw up my arms and fell to my knees before him on the floor. "No, no," I cried, like a baby.

"We shall have no more trouble with him," said the Master. "It is a good thing to have a coward in the house."

"We must have light," said Mr. Henry, as though there had been no interruption.

"This trembler can bring a pair of candles," said the Master.

To my shame be it said, I was so blinded with the flashing of that bare sword that I volunteered to bring a lantern.

"We do not need a l-l-lantern," said the Master, mocking me. "There is no breath of air. Come, get to your feet, take a pair of lights, and go before. I am close behind with this—" making the blade glitter as he spoke.

I took up the candlesticks and went before them, steps that I would give my hand to recall; but a coward is a slave at the best; and even as I went, my teeth smote each other in my mouth. It was as he had said, there was no breath stirring; a windless stricture of frost had bound the air; and as we went forth in the shine of the candles the blackness was like a roof over our heads. Never a word was said, there was never a sound but the creaking of our steps along the frozen path. The cold of the night fell about me like a bucket of water; I shook as I went with more than terror; but my companions, bareheaded like myself, and fresh from the warm hall, appeared not even conscious of the change.

"Here is the place," said the Master. "Set down the candles."

I did as he bade me, and presently the flames went up as steady as in a chamber in the midst of the frosted trees, and I beheld these two brothers take their places.

"The light is something in my eyes," said the Master.

"I will give you every advantage," replied Mr. Henry, shifting his ground, "for I think you are about to die." He spoke rather sadly than otherwise, yet there was a ring in his voice.

"Henry Durie," said the Master, "two words before I begin. You are a fencer, you can hold a foil; you little know what a change it makes to hold a sword! And by that I know you are to fall. But see how strong is my situation! If you fall, I shift out of this country to where my money is before me. If I fall, where are you? My father, your wife who is in love with me—as you very well know—your child even who prefers me to yourself: how will these avenge me! Had you thought of that, dear Henry?" He looked at his brother with a smile; then made a fencing-room salute.

Never a word said Mr. Henry, but saluted too, and the swords rang together.

I am no judge of the play, but my head besides was gone with cold and fear and horror; but it seems that Mr. Henry took and kept the upper hand from the engagement, crowding in upon his foe with a contained and glowing fury. Nearer and nearer he crept upon the man till, of a sudden, the Master leaped back with a little sobbing oath; and I believe the movement brought the light once more against his eyes. To it they went again, on the fresh ground; but now methought closer, Mr. Henry pressing more outrageously, the Master beyond doubt with shaken confidence. For it is beyond doubt he now recognized himself for lost, and had some taste of the cold agony of fear; or he had never attempted the foul stroke. I cannot say I followed it, my untrained eye was never quick enough to seize details, but it appears he caught his brother's blade with his left hand, a practice not permitted. Certainly Mr. Henry only saved himself by leaping on one side; as certainly the Master, lunging in the air, stumbled on his knee, and before he could move the sword was through his body.

I cried out with a stifled scream, and ran in; but the body was already fallen to the ground, where it writhed a moment like a trodden worm, and then lay motionless.

" Look at his left hand," said Mr. Henry.

" It is all bloody," said I.

" On the inside? " said he.

" It is cut on the inside," said I.

" I thought so," said he, and turned his back.

I opened the man's clothes; the heart was quite still, it gave not a flutter.

" God forgive us, Mr. Henry! " said I. " He is dead."

" Dead? " he repeated, a little stupidly; and then with a rising tone, " Dead? dead? " says he, and suddenly cast his bloody sword upon the ground.

" What must we do? " said I. " Be yourself, sir. It is too late now: you must be yourself."

He turned and stared at me. " Oh, Mackellar! " says he, and put his face in his hands.

I plucked him by the coat. " For God's sake, for all our sakes, be more courageous! " said I. " What must we do? "

He showed me his face with the same stupid stare. " Do? " says he. And with that his eye fell on the body, and " oh! " he cries out, with his hand to his brow, as if he had never remembered; and turning from me, made off toward the house of Durrisdeer at a strange, stumbling run.

I stood a moment, mused; then it seemed to me my duty lay most plain on the side of the living; and I ran after him, leaving the candles on the frosty ground and the body lying in their light under the trees. But run as I pleased, he had the start of me, and was got into the house, and up to the hall, where I found him standing before the fire with his face once more in his hands, and as he so stood, he visibly shuddered.

95

"Mr. Henry, Mr. Henry," I said, "this will be the ruin of us all."

"What is this that I have done?" cries he, and then, looking upon me with a countenance that I shall never forget, "Who is to tell the old man?" he said.

The word knocked at my heart; but it was no time for weakness. I went and poured him out a glass of brandy. "Drink that," said I, "drink it down." I forced him to swallow it like a child; and, being still perished with the cold of the night, I followed his example.

"It has to be told, Mackellar," said he. "It must be told." And he fell suddenly in a seat—my old lord's seat by the chimney-side—and was shaken with dry sobs.

Dismay came upon my soul; it was plain there was no help in Mr. Henry. "Well," said I, "sit there, and leave all to me." And taking a candle in my hand, I set forth out of the room in the dark house. There was no movement; I must suppose that all had gone unobserved; and I was now to consider how to smuggle through the rest with the like secrecy. It was no hour for scruples; and I opened my lady's door without so much as a knock, and passed boldly in.

"There is some calamity happened," she cried, sitting up in bed.

"Madam," said I, "I will go forth again into the passage; and do you get as quickly as you can into your clothes. There is much to be done."

She troubled me with no questions, nor did she keep me waiting. Ere I had time to prepare a word of that which I must say to her, she was on the threshold signing me to enter.

"Madam," said I, "if you cannot be very brave, I must go elsewhere; for if no one helps me to-night, there is an end of the house of Durrisdeer."

"I am very courageous," said she; and she looked at me with a sort of smile, very painful to see, but very brave too.

"It has come to a duel," said I.

"A duel?" she repeated. "A duel! Henry and——"

" And the Master," said I. " Things have been borne so long, things of which you know nothing, which you would not believe if I should tell. But to-night it went too far, and when he insulted you——"

" Stop," said she. " He? Who? "

" Oh, madam! " cried I, my bitterness breaking forth, " do you ask me such a question? Indeed, then, I may go elsewhere for help; there is none here! "

" I do not know in what I have offended you," said she. " Forgive me; put me out of this suspense."

But I dared not tell her yet; I felt not sure of her; and at the doubt and under the sense of impotence it brought with it, I turned on the poor woman with something near to anger.

" Madam," said I, " we are speaking of two men; one of them insulted you, and you ask me which. I will help you to the answer. With one of these men you have spent all your hours; has the other reproached you? To one you have been always kind; to the other, as God sees me and judges between us two, I think not always; has his love ever failed you? To-night one of these two men told the other, in my hearing—the hearing of a hired stranger— that you were in love with him. Before I say one word, you shall answer your own question: Which was it? Nay, madam, you shall answer me another: If it has come to this dreadful end, whose fault is it? "

She stared at me like one dazzled. " Good God! " she said once, in a kind of bursting exclamation; and then a second time, in a whisper to herself, " Great God! In the name of mercy, Mackellar, what is wrong? " she cried. " I am made up; I can hear all."

" You are not fit to hear," said I. " Whatever it was, you shall say first it was your fault."

" Oh! " she cried, with a gesture of wringing her hands, " this man will drive me mad! Can you not put *me* out of your thoughts? "

" I think not once of you," I cried. " I think of none but my dear unhappy master."

" Ah! " she cried, with her hand to her heart, " is Henry dead? "

" Lower your voice," said I. " The other."

I saw her sway like something stricken by the wind, and I know not whether in cowardice or misery, turned aside and looked upon the floor. " These are dreadful tidings," said I at length, when her silence began to put me in some fear; " and you and I behove to be the more bold if the house is to be saved." Still she answered nothing. " There is Miss Katharine besides," I added: " unless we bring this matter through her inheritance is like to be of shame."

I do not know if it was the thought of her child or the naked word shame that gave her deliverance; at least I had no sooner spoken than a sound passed her lips, the like of it I never heard; it was as though she had lain buried under a hill and sought to move that burden. And the next moment she had found a sort of voice.

" It was a fight," she whispered. " It was not—" and she paused upon the word.

" It was a fair fight on my dear master's part," said I. " As for the other, he was slain in the very act of a foul stroke."

" Not now! " she cried.

" Madam," said I, " hatred of that man glows in my bosom like a burning fire; ay, even now he is dead. God knows, I would have stopped the fighting had I dared. It is my shame I did not. But when I saw him fall, if I could have spared one thought from pitying of my master, it had been to exult in that deliverance."

I do not know if she marked; but her next words were:

" My lord? "

" That shall be my part," said I.

" You will not speak to him as you have to me? " she asked.

" Madam," said I, " have you not some one else to think of? Leave my lord to me."

" Some one else? " she repeated.

" Your husband," said I. She looked at me with a countenance illegible. " Are you going to turn your back on
him? " I asked.

Still she looked at me; then her hand went to her heart
again. " No," said she.

" God bless you for that word! " I said. " Go to him
now where he sits in the hall; speak to him—it matters not
what you say; give him you hand; say, ' I know all '; if
God gives you grace enough, say ' Forgive me.' "

" God strengthen you, and make you merciful," said she.
" I will go to my husband."

" Let me light you there," said I, taking up the candle.

" I will find my way in the dark," she said, with a shudder,
and I think the shudder was at me.

So we separated, she downstairs to where a little light
glimmered in the hall door, I along the passage to my lord's
room. It seems hard to say why, but I could not burst in
on the old man as I could on the young woman; with whatever reluctance, I must knock. But his old slumbers were
light, or perhaps he slept not; and at the first summons I
was bidden enter.

He too sat up in bed; very aged and bloodless he looked;
and whereas he had a certain largeness of appearance when
dressed for daylight, he now seemed frail and little, and his
face (the wig being laid aside) not bigger than a child's.
This daunted me; nor less, the haggard surmise of misfortune in his eye. Yet his voice was even peaceful as he inquired my errand. I sat my candle down upon a chair,
leaned on the bed-foot, and looked at him.

" Lord Durrisdeer," said I, " it is very well known to
you that I am a partisan in your family."

" I hope we are none of us partisans," said he. " That
you love my son sincerely, I have always been glad to
recognize."

" Oh, my lord, we are past the hour of these civilities,"
I replied. " If we are to save anything out of the fire, we
must look the fact in its bare countenance. A partisan I
am; partisans we have all been; it is as a partisan that I

am here in the middle of the night to plead before you. Hear me; before I go, I will tell you why."

"I would always hear you, Mr. Mackellar," said he, "and that at any hour, whether of the day or night, for I would be always sure you had a reason. You spoke once before to very proper purpose; I have not forgotten that."

"I am here to plead the cause of my master," I said. "I need not tell you how he acts. You know how he is placed. You know with what generosity he has always met your other—met your wishes," I corrected myself, stumbling at that name of son. "You know—you must know—what he has suffered—what he has suffered about his wife."

"Mr. Mackellar!" cried my lord, rising in bed like a bearded lion.

"You said you would hear me," I continued. "What you do not know, what you should know, one of the things I am here to speak of—is the persecution he must bear in private. Your back is not turned before one whom I dare not name to you falls upon him with the most unfeeling taunts; twits him—pardon me, my lord!—twits him with your partiality, calls him Jacob, calls him clown, pursues him with ungenerous raillery, not to be borne by man. And let but one of you appear, instantly he changes; and my master must smile and courtesy to the man who has been feeding him with insults; I know—for I have shared in some of it, and I tell you the life is insupportable. All these months it has endured; it began with the man's landing; it was by the name of Jacob that my master was greeted the first night."

My lord made a movement as if to throw aside the clothes and rise. "If there be any truth in this—" said he.

"Do I look like a man lying?" I interrupted, checking him with my hand.

"You should have told me at first," he said.

"Ah, my lord, indeed I should, and you may well hate the face of this unfaithful servant!" I cried.

"I will take order," said he, "at once." And again made the movement to rise.

100

Again I checked him. "I have not done," said I. "Would God I had! All this my dear, unfortunate patron has endured without help or countenance. Your own best word, my lord, was only gratitude. Oh, but he was your son, too! He had no other father. He was hated in the country, God knows how unjustly. He had a loveless marriage. He stood on all hands without affection or support, dear, generous, ill-fated, noble heart."

"Your tears do you much honor and me much shame," says my lord, with a palsied trembling. "But you do me some injustice. Henry has been ever dear to me, very dear. James (I do not deny it, Mr. Mackellar), James is perhaps dearer; you have not seen my James in quite a favorable light; he has suffered under his misfortunes; and we can only remember how great and how unmerited these were. And even now his is the more affectionate nature. But I will not speak of him. All that you say of Henry is most true; I do not wonder, I know him to be very magnanimous; you will say I trade upon the knowledge? It is possible; there are dangerous virtues; virtues that tempt the encroacher. Mr. Mackellar, I will make it up to him; I will take order with all this. I have been weak; and what is worse, I have been dull."

"I must not hear you blame yourself, my lord, with that which I have yet to tell upon my conscience," I replied. "You have not been weak; you have been abused by a devilish dissembler. You saw yourself how he had deceived you in the matter of his danger; he has deceived you throughout in every step of his career. I wish to pluck him from your heart; I wish to force your eyes upon your other son; ah, you have a son there!"

"No, no," said he, "two sons—I have two sons."

I made some gesture of despair that struck him; he looked at me with a changed face. "There is much worse behind?" he asked, his voice dying as it rose upon the question.

"Much worse," I answered. "This night he said these words to Mr. Henry: 'I have never known a woman who did not prefer me to you, and I think who did not continue to prefer me.' "

" I will hear nothing against my daughter!" he cried; and from his readiness to stop me in this direction, I conclude his eyes were not so dull as I had fancied, and he had looked on not without anxiety upon the siege of Mrs. Henry.

" I think not of blaming her," cried I. " It is not that. These words were said in my hearing to Mr. Henry; and if you find them not yet plain enough, these others but a little after: ' Your wife who is in love with me.' "

" They have quarreled? " he said.

I nodded.

" I must fly to them," he said, beginning once again to leave his bed.

" No, no! " I cried, holding forth my hands.

" You do not know," said he. " These are dangerous words."

" Will nothing make you understand, my lord? " said I. His eyes besought me for the truth.

I flung myself on my knees by the bedside. " Oh, my lord," cried I, " think on him you have left, think of this poor sinner whom you begot, whom your wife bore to you, whom we have none of us strengthened as we could; think of him, not of yourself; he is the other sufferer—think of him! That is the door for sorrow, Christ's door, God's door; oh, it stands open! Think of him, even as he thought of you. *Who is to tell the old man?* these were his words. It was for that I came; that is why I am here pleading at your feet."

" Let me get up," he cried, thrusting me aside, and was on his feet before myself. His voice shook like a sail in the wind, yet he spoke with a good loudness; his face was like the snow, but his eyes were steady and dry. " Here is too much speech! " said he. " Where was it? "

" In the shrubbery," said I.

" And Mr. Henry? " he asked. And when I had told him he knotted his old face in thought.

" And Mr. James? " says he.

" I have left him lying," said I, " beside the candles."

" Candles? " he cried. And with that he ran to the window, opened it, and looked abroad. " It might be spied from the road."

" Where none goes by at such an hour," I objected.

" It makes no matter," he said. " One might. Hark! " cries he. " What is that? "

It was the sound of men very guardedly rowing in the bay; and I told him so.

" The free-traders," said my lord. " Run at once, Mackellar; put these candles out. I will dress in the meanwhile; and when you return we can debate on what is wisest."

I groped my way downstairs, and out at the door. From quite a far way off a sheen was visible, making points of brightness in the shrubbery; in so black a night it might have been remarked for miles; and I blamed myself bitterly for my incaution: How much more sharply when I reached the place! One of the candlesticks was overthrown, and that taper quenched. The other burned steadily by itself, and made a broad space of light upon the frosted ground. All within that circle seemed, by the force of contrast and the overhanging blackness, brighter than by day. And there was the bloodstain in the midst; and a little further off Mr. Henry's sword, the pommel of which was of silver; but of the body not a trace. My heart thumped upon my ribs, the hair stirred upon my scalp, as I stood there staring; so strange was the sight, so dire the fears it wakened. I looked right and left; the ground was so hard it told no story. I stood and listened till my ears ached, but the night was hollow about me like an empty church; not even a ripple stirred upon the shore; it seemed you might have heard a pin drop in the county.

I put the candle out, and the blackness fell about me groping dark; it was like a crowd surrounding me; and I went back to the house of Durrisdeer, with my chin upon my shoulder, startling, as I went, with craven suppositions. In the door a figure moved to meet me, and I had near screamed with terror ere I recognized Mrs. Henry.

" Have you told him? " says she.

" It was he who sent me," said I. " It is gone. But why are you here? "

" It is gone! " she repeated. " What is gone? "

" The body," said I. " Why are you not with your husband? "

" Gone? " said she. " You cannot have looked. Come back."

" There is no light now," said I. " I dare not."

" I can see in the dark. I have been standing here so long—so long," said she. " Come ; give me your hand."

We returned to the shrubbery hand in hand, and to the fatal place.

" Take care of the blood," said I.

" Blood? " she cried, and started violently back.

" I suppose it will be," said I. " I am like a blind man."

" No," said she, " nothing! Have you not dreamed? "

" Ah, would to God we had! " cried I.

She spied the sword, picked it up, and, seeing the blood, let it fall again with her hands thrown wide. " Ah! " she cried. And then, with an instant courage, handled it the second time and thrust it to the hilt into the frozen ground. " I will take it back and clean it properly," says she, and again looked about her on all sides. " It cannot be that he was dead? " she added.

" There was no flutter of his heart," said I, and then remembering : " Why are you not with your husband? "

" It is no use," said she, " he will not speak to me."

" Not speak to you? " I repeated. " Oh, you have not tried! "

" You have a right to doubt me," she replied, with a gentle dignity.

At this, for the first time, I was seized with sorrow for her. " God knows, madam," I cried, " God knows I am not so hard as I appear ; on this dreadful night, who can veneer his words? But I am a friend to all who are not Henry Durie's enemies!"

"It is hard, then, you should hesitate about his wife," said she.

I saw all at once, like the rending of a veil, how nobly she had borne this unnatural calamity, and how generously my reproaches.

"We must go back and tell this to my lord," said I.

"Him I cannot face," she cried.

"You will find him the least moved of all of us," said I.

"And yet I cannot face him," said she.

"Well," said I, "you can return to Mr. Henry; I will see my lord."

As we walked back, I bearing the candlesticks, she the sword—a strange burden for that woman—she had another thought. "Should we tell Henry?" she asked.

"Let my lord decide," said I.

My lord was nearly dressed when I came to his chamber. He heard me with a frown. "The free-traders," said he. "But whether dead or alive?"

"I thought him—" said I, and paused, ashamed of the word.

"I know; but you may very well have been in error. Why should they remove him if not living?" he asked. "Oh, here is a great door of hope. It must be given out that he departed—as he came—without any note of preparation. We must save all scandal."

I saw he had fallen, like the rest of us, to think mainly of the house. Now that all the living members of the family were plunged in irremediable sorrow, it was strange how we turned to that conjoint abstraction of the family itself, and sought to bolster up the airy nothing of its reputation: not the Duries only, but the hired steward himself.

"Are we to tell Mr. Henry?" I asked him.

"I will see," said he. "I am going first to visit him, then I go forth with you to view the shrubbery and consider."

We went downstairs into the hall. Mr. Henry sat by

the table with his head upon his hand, like a man of stone. His wife stood a little back from him, her hand at her mouth; it was plain she could not move him. My old lord walked very steadily to where his son was sitting; he had a steady countenance too, but methought a little cold; when he was come quite up he held out both his hands and said: "My son!"

With a broken, strangled cry, Mr. Henry leaped up and fell on his father's neck, crying and weeping, the most pitiful sight that ever a man witnessed. "Oh, father," he cried, "you know I loved him; you know I loved him in the beginning; I could have died for him—you know that! I would have given my life for him and you. Oh, say you know that! Oh, say you can forgive me! Oh, father, father, what have I done, what have I done? and we used to be bairns together!" and wept and sobbed, and fondled the old man, and clutched him about the neck, with the passion of a child in terror.

And then he caught sight of his wife, you would have thought for the first time, where she stood weeping to hear him; and in a moment had fallen at her knees. "And oh, my lass," he cried, "you must forgive me, too! Not your husband—I have only been the ruin of your life. But you knew me when I was a lad; there was no harm in Henry Durie then; he meant aye to be a friend to you. It's him —it's the old bairn that played with you—oh, can ye never, never forgive him?"

Throughout all this my lord was like a cold, kind spectator with his wits about him. At the first cry, which was indeed enough to call the house about us, he had said to me over his shoulder, "Close the door." And now he nodded to himself.

"We may leave him to his wife now," says he. "Bring a light, Mr. Mackellar."

Upon my going forth again with my lord, I was aware of a strange phenomenon; for though it was quite dark, and the night not yet old methought I smelled the morning. At the same time there went a tossing through the branches of the evergreens, so that they sounded like a quiet sea; and the air puffed at times against our faces, and the flame of the candle shook. We made the more speed, I believe, being surrounded by this bustle; visited the scene of the duel, where my lord looked upon the blood with stoicism; and passing further on toward the landing-place, came at last upon some evidences of the truth. For first of all, where there was a pool across the path, the ice had been trodden in, plainly by more than one man's weight; next, and but a little further, a young tree was broken; and down by the landing-place, where the traders' boats were usually beached, another stain of blood marked where the body must have been infallibly set down to rest the bearers.

This stain we set ourselves to wash away with the sea-water, carrying it in my lord's hat; and as we were thus engaged there came up a sudden, moaning gust and left us instantly benighted.

"It will come to snow," says my lord; "and the best thing that we could hope. Let us go back now; we can do nothing in the dark."

As we went houseward, the wind being again subsided, we were aware of a strong pattering noise about us in the night; and when we issued from the shelter of the trees, we found it raining smartly.

Throughout the whole of this, my lord's clearness of mind, no less than his activity of body, had not ceased to minister to my amazement. He set the crown upon it in the council we held on our return. The free-traders had certainly secured the Master, though whether dead or alive we were still left to our conjectures; the rain would, long before day, wipe out all marks of the transaction; by this we must profit: the Master had unexpectedly come after the fall of night, it must now be given out he had as suddenly departed before the break of day; and to make all this plausible, it now only remained for me to mount into the man's chamber, and pack and conceal his baggage. True, we still lay at the discretion of the traders; but that was the incurable weakness of our guilt.

107

THE MASTER OF BALLANTRAE

I heard him, as I said, with wonder, and hastened to obey. Mr. and Mrs. Henry were gone from the hall; my lord, for warmth's sake, hurried to his bed; there was still no sign of stir among the servants, and as I went up the tower stair, and entered the dead man's room, a horror of solitude weighed upon my mind. To my extreme surprise, it was all in the disorder of departure. Of his three portmanteaus, two were ready locked, the third lay open and near full. At once there flashed upon me some suspicion of the truth. The man had been going after all; he had but waited upon Crail, as Crail waited upon the wind; early in the night the seamen had perceived the weather changing; the boat had come to give notice of the change and call the passenger aboard, and the boat's crew had stumbled on him lying in his blood. Nay, and there was more behind. This prearranged departure shed some light upon his inconceivable insult of the night before; it was a parting shot; hatred being no longer checked by policy. And for another thing, the nature of that insult, and the conduct of Mrs. Henry, pointed to one conclusion: which I have never verified, and can now never verify until the great assize, the conclusion that he had at last forgotten himself, had gone too far in his advances, and had been rebuffed. It can never be verified, as I say; but as I thought of it that morning among his baggage, the thought was sweet to me like honey.

Into the open portmanteau I dipped a little ere I closed it. The most beautiful lace and linen, many suits of those fine plain clothes in which he loved to appear; a book or two, and those of the best, Cæsar's "Commentaries," a volume of Mr. Hobbes, the "Henriade" of M. de Voltaire, a book upon the Indies, one on the mathematics, far beyond where I have studied: these were what I observed with very mingled feelings. But in the open portmanteau, no papers of any description. This set me musing. It was possible the man was dead; but, since the traders had carried him away, not likely. It was possible he might still die of his wound; but it was also possible he might not. And in this latter case I was determined to have the means of some defense.

One after another I carried his portmanteaus to a loft in the top of the house which we kept locked; went to my own room for my keys, and returning to the loft, had the gratification to find two that fitted pretty well. In one of the portmanteaus there was a shagreen letter-case, which I cut open with my knife; and thenceforth (so far as any credit went) the man was at my mercy. Here was a vast deal of gallant correspondence, chiefly of his Paris days; and what was more to the purpose, here were the copies of his own reports to the English secretary, and the originals of the secretary's answers: a most damning series: such as to publish would be to wreck the Master's honor and to set a price upon his life. I chuckled to myself as I ran through the documents; I rubbed my hands, I sung aloud in my glee. Day found me at the pleasing task, nor did I then remit my diligence, except in so far as I went to the window —looked out for a moment, to see the frost quite gone, the world turned black again, and the rain and the wind driving in the bay—and to assure myself that the lugger was gone from its anchorage, and the master (whether dead or alive) now tumbling on the Irish Sea.

It is proper I should add in this place the very little I have subsequently angled out upon the doings of that night. It took me a long while to gather it; for we dared not openly ask, and the free-traders regarded me with enmity, if not with scorn. It was near six months before we even knew for certain that the man survived; and it was years before I learned from one of Crail's men, turned publican on his ill-gotten gain, some particulars which smack to me of truth. It seems the traders found the Master struggled on one elbow, and now staring round him, and now gazing at the candle or at his hand, which was all bloodied, like a man stupid. Upon their coming he would seem to have found his mind, bade them carry him aboard and hold their tongues; and on the captain asking how he had come in such a pickle, replied with a burst of passionate swearing, and incontinently fainted. They held some debate, but they were momently looking for a wind, they were highly paid to smuggle him to France, and did not care to delay. Besides which, he was well enough liked by these abominable wretches: they supposed him under capital sentence, knew not in what mischief he might have got his wound, and judged it a piece of good nature to remove him out of the way of danger. So he was taken aboard, recovered on the passage over, and was set ashore a convalescent at the Havre de Grace. What is truly notable: he said not a word to any one of the duel, and not a trader knows to this day in what quarrel, or by the hand of what adversary, he fell. With any other man I should have set this down to natural decency; with him, to pride. He could not bear to avow, perhaps even to himself, that he had been vanquished by one whom he had so much insulted and whom he so cruelly despised.

OF the heavy sickness which declared itself next morning, I can think with equanimity as of the last unmingled trouble that befell my master; and even that was perhaps a mercy in disguise; for what pains of the body could equal the miseries of his mind? Mrs. Henry and I had the watching by the bed. My old lord called from time to time to take the news, but would not usually pass the door. Once, I remember, when hope was nigh gone, he stepped to the bedside, looked awhile in his son's face, and turned away with a singular gesture of the head and hand thrown up, that remains upon my mind as something tragic; such grief and such a scorn of sublunary things were there expressed. But the most of the time, Mrs. Henry and I had the room to ourselves, taking turns by night and bearing each other company by day, for it was dreary watching. Mr. Henry, his shaven head bound in a napkin, tossed to and fro without remission, beating the bed with his hands. His tongue never lay; his voice ran continuously like a river, so that my heart was weary with the sound of it. It was notable, and to me inexpressibly mortifying, that he spoke all the while on matters of no import: comings and goings, horses—which he was ever calling to have saddled, thinking perhaps (the poor soul!) that he might ride away from his discomfort—matters of the garden, the salmon nets, and (what I particularly raged to hear) continually of his affairs, ciphering figures and holding disputation with the tenantry. Never a word of his father or his wife, nor of the master, save only for a day or two, when his mind dwelt entirely in the past and he supposed himself a boy again and upon some innocent child's play with his brother. What made this the more affecting: it appeared the Master had then run some peril of his life, for there was a cry—" Oh,

111

Jamie will be drowned—oh, save Jamie!" which he came over and over with a great deal of passion.

This, I say, was affecting, both to Mrs. Henry and myself; but the balance of my master's wanderings did him little justice. It seemed he had set out to justify his brother's calumnies; as though he was bent to prove himself a man of a dry nature, immersed in money-getting. Had I been there alone, I would not have troubled my thumb; but all the while, as I listened, I was estimating the effect on the man's wife, and telling myself that he fell lower every day. I was the one person on the surface of the globe that comprehended him, and I was bound there should be yet another. Whether he was to die there and his virtues perish; or whether he should save his days and come back to that inheritance of sorrows, his right memory, I was bound he should be heartily lamented in the one case and unaffectedly welcomed in the other, by the person he loved the most, his wife.

Finding no occasion of free speech, I bethought me at last of a kind of documentary disclosure; and for some nights, when I was off duty and should have been asleep, I gave my time to the preparation of that which I may call my budget.

But this I found to be the easiest portion of my task, and that which remained, namely, the presentation to my lady, almost more than I had fortitude to overtake. Several days I went about with my papers under my arm, spying for some juncture of talk to serve as introduction. I will not deny but that some offered; only when they did, my tongue clove to the roof of my mouth; and I think I might have been carrying about my packet till this day, had not a fortunate accident delivered me from all my hesitations. This was at night, when I was once more leaving the room, the thing not yet done, and myself in despair at my own cowardice.

"What do you carry about with you, Mr. Mackellar?" she asked. "These last days, I see you always coming in and out with the same armful."

I returned upon my steps without a word, laid the papers before her on the table, and left her to her reading. Of what that was, I am now to give you some idea; and the best will be to reproduce a letter of my own which came first in the budget and of which (according to an excellent habitude) I have preserved the scroll. It will show too the moderation of my part in these affairs, a thing which some have called recklessly in question.

" DURRISDEER.

" 1757.

" HONORED MADAM: I trust I would not step out of my place without occasion; but I see how much evil has flowed in the past to all of your noble house from that unhappy and secretive fault of reticency, and the papers on which I venture to call your attention are family papers and all highly worthy your acquaintance.

" I append a schedule with some necessary observations,

" And am,

" Honored madam,

" Your ladyship's obliged, obedient servant,

" EPHRAIM MACKELLAR.

" Schedule of Papers.

" A. Scroll of ten letters from Ephraim Mackellar to the Honorable James Durie, Esq., by courtesy Master of Ballantrae during the latter's residence in Paris: under dates—" (*follow the dates*)—" *Nota:* to be read in connection with B. and C.

" B. Seven original letters from the said Master of Ballantrae to the said E. Mackellar, under dates—" (*follow the dates*).

" C. Three original letters from the said Master of Ballantrae to the Honorable Henry Durie, Esq., under dates—" (*follow the dates*)—" *Nota:* given me by Mr. Henry to answer: copies of my answers A 4, A 5, and A 9 of these productions. The purport of Mr. Henry's communications, of which I can find no scroll, may be gathered from those of his unnatural brother.

113

THE MASTER OF BALLANTRAE

"D. A correspondence, original and scroll, extending over a period of three years till January of the current year, between the said Master of Ballantrae and —— ——, Under Secretary of State; twenty-seven in all. *Nota:* found among the master's papers."

Weary as I was with watching and distress of mind, it was impossible for me to sleep. All night long I walked in my chamber, revolving what should be the issue and sometimes repenting the temerity of my immixture in affairs so private; and with the first peep of the morning, I was at the sick-room door. Mrs. Henry had thrown open the shutters and even the window, for the temperature was mild. She looked steadfastly before her, where was nothing to see, or only the blue of the morning creeping among woods. Upon the stir of my entrance she did not so much as turn about her face: a circumstance from which I augured very ill.

"Madam," I began; and then again, "Madam"; but could make no more of it. Nor yet did Mrs. Henry come to my assistance with a word. In this pass I began gathering up the papers where they lay scattered on the table; and the first thing that struck me, their bulk appeared to have diminished. Once I ran them through, and twice; but the correspondence with the secretary of state, on which I had reckoned so much against the future, was nowhere to be found. I looked in the chimney; amid the smoldering embers black ashes of paper fluttered in the draught; and at that my timidity vanished.

"Good God, madam," cried I, in a voice not fitting for a sick-room, "good God, madam, what have you done with my papers?"

"I have burned them," said Mrs. Henry, turning about. "It is enough, it is too much, that you and I have seen them."

"This is a fine night's work that you have done!" cried I. "And all to save the reputation of a man that ate bread by the shedding of his comrades' blood, as I do by the shedding of ink."

114

" To save the reputation of that family in which you are a servant, Mr. Mackellar," she returned, " and for which you have already done so much."

" It is a family I will not serve much longer," I cried, " for I am driven desperate. You have stricken the sword out of my hands; you have left us all defenseless. I had always these letters I could shake over his head; and now—what is to do? We are so falsely situate, we dare not show the man the door; the country would fly on fire against us; and I had this one hold upon him—and now it is gone—now he may come back to-morrow, and we must all sit down with him to dinner, go for a stroll with him on the terrace, or take a hand at cards, of all things, to divert his leisure! No, madam; God forgive you, if he can find it in his heart; for I cannot find it in mine."

" I wonder to find you so simple, Mr. Mackellar," said Mrs. Henry. " What does this man value reputation? But he knows how high we prize it; he knows we would rather die than make these letters public; and do you suppose he would not trade upon the knowledge? What you call your sword, Mr. Mackellar, and which had been one indeed against a man of any remnant of propriety, would have been but a sword of paper against him. He would smile in your face at such a threat. He stands upon his degradation, he makes that his strength; it is in vain to struggle with such characters." She cried out this last a little desperately, and then with more quiet: " No, Mr. Mackellar, I have thought upon this matter all night, and there is no way out of it. Papers or no papers, the door of this house stands open for him; he is the rightful heir, forsooth! If we sought to exclude him, all would redound against poor Henry, and I should see him stoned again upon the streets. Ah! if Henry dies, it is a different matter! They have broke the entail for their own good purposes; the estate goes to my daughter; and I shall see who sets a foot upon it. But if Henry lives, my poor Mr. Mackellar, and that man returns, we must suffer; only this time it will be together."

On the whole, I was well pleased with Mrs. Henry's attitude of mind; nor could I even deny there was some cogency in that which she advanced about the papers.

"Let us say no more about it," said I. "I can only be sorry I trusted a lady with the originals, which was an un-business-like proceeding at the best. As for what I said of leaving the service of the family, it was spoken with the tongue only; and you may set your mind at rest. I belong to Durrisdeer, Mrs. Henry, as if I had been born there."

I must do her the justice to say she seemed perfectly relieved; so that we began this morning, as we were to continue for so many years, on a proper ground of mutual indulgence and respect.

The same day, which was certainly predicate to joy, we observed the first signal of recovery in Mr. Henry; and about three of the following afternoon he found his mind again, recognizing me by name with the strongest evidences of affection. Mrs. Henry was also in the room, at the bed-foot; but it did not appear that he observed her. And indeed (the fever being gone) he was so weak that he made but the one effort and sunk again into a lethargy. The course of his restoration was now slow but equal; every day his appetite improved; every week we were able to remark an increase both of strength and flesh; and before the end of the month he was out of bed and had even begun to be carried in his chair upon the terrace.

It was perhaps at this time that Mrs. Henry and I were the most uneasy in mind. Apprehension for his days was at an end; and a worse fear succeeded. Every day we drew consciously nearer to a day of reckoning; and the days passed on, and still there was nothing. Mr. Henry bettered in strength, he held long talks with us on a great diversity of subjects, his father came and sat with him and went again; and still there was no reference to the late tragedy or to the former troubles which had brought it on. Did he remember, and conceal his dreadful knowledge? or was the whole blotted from his mind? this was the problem that kept us watching and trembling all day when we were in his company, and

116

held us awake at night when we were in our lonely beds. We knew not even which alternative to hope for, both appearing so unnatural and pointing so directly to an unsound brain. Once this fear offered, I observed his conduct with sedulous particularity. Something of the child he exhibited: a cheerfulness quite foreign to his previous character, an interest readily aroused, and then very tenacious, in small matters which he had heretofore despised. When he was stricken down, I was his only confidant, and I may say his only friend, and he was on terms of division with his wife; upon his recovery all was changed, the past forgotten, the wife first and even single in his thoughts. He turned to her with all his emotions like a child to its mother, and seemed secure of sympathy; called her in all his needs with something of that querulous familiarity that marks a certainty of indulgence; and I must say, in justice to the woman, he was never disappointed. To her, indeed, this changed behavior was inexpressibly affecting; and I think she felt it secretly as a reproach; so that I have seen her, in early days, escape out of the room that she might indulge herself in weeping. But to me the change appeared not natural; and viewing it along with all the rest, I began to wonder, with many head-shakings, whether his reason were perfectly erect.

As this doubt stretched over many years, endured indeed until my master's death, and clouded all our subsequent relations, I may well consider of it more at large. When he was able to resume some charge of his affairs I had many opportunities to try him with precision. There was no lack of understanding, nor yet of authority; but the old continuous interest had quite departed; he grew readily fatigued and fell to yawning; and he carried into money relations, where it is certainly out of place, a facility that bordered upon slackness. True, since we had no longer the exactions of the master to contend against there was the less occasion to raise strictness into principle or do battle for a farthing. True again, there was nothing excessive in these relaxations, or I would have been no party to them. But the whole thing marked a change, very slight yet very perceptible; and though no man could say my master had gone at all out of his mind, no man could deny that he had drifted from his character. It was the same to the end, with his manner and appearance. Some of the heat of the fever lingered in his veins: his movements a little hurried, his speech notably more voluble, yet neither truly amiss. His whole mind stood open to happy impressions, welcoming these and making much of them; but the smallest suggestion of trouble or sorrow he received with visible impatience and dismissed again with immediate relief. It was to this temper that he owed the felicity of his later days; and yet here it was, if anywhere, that you could call the man insane. A great part of this life consists in contemplating what we cannot cure; but Mr. Henry, if he could not dismiss solicitude by an effort of the mind, must instantly and at whatever cost annihilate the cause of it; so that he played alternately the ostrich and the bull. It is to this strenuous cowardice of pain that I have to set down all the unfortunate and excessive steps of his subsequent career. Certainly this was the reason of his beating McManus, the groom, a thing so much out of all his former practice and which awakened so much comment at the time. It is to this again that I must lay the total loss of near upon two hundred pounds, more than the half of which I could have saved, if his impatience would have suffered me. But he preferred loss or any desperate extreme to a continuance of mental suffering.

All this has led me far from our immediate trouble— whether he remembered or had forgotten his late dreadful act, and if he remembered, in what light he viewed it. The truth burst upon us suddenly, and was indeed one of the chief surprises of my life. He had been several times abroad, and was now beginning to walk a little with an arm, when it chanced I should be left alone with him upon the terrace. He turned to me with a singular furtive smile, such as schoolboys use when in fault, and says he, in a private whisper and without the least preface:

"Where have you buried him?"

I could not make one sound in answer.

"Where have you buried him?" he repeated. "I want to see his grave."

I conceived I had best take the bull by the horns. "Mr. Henry," said I, "I have news to give that will rejoice you exceedingly. In all human likelihood your hands are clear of blood. I reason from certain indices, and by these it should appear your brother was not dead, but was carried in a swound on board the lugger. By now he may be perfectly recovered."

What there was in his countenance I could not read. "James?" he asked.

"Your brother James," I answered. "I would not raise a hope that may be found deceptive, but in my heart I think it very probable he is alive."

"Ah!" says Mr. Henry, and suddenly rising from his seat with more alacrity than he had yet discovered, set one finger on my breast and cried at me in a kind of screaming whisper, "Mackellar"—these were his words—"nothing can kill that man. He is not mortal. He is bound upon my back to all eternity—to all God's eternity!" says he, and sitting down again, fell upon a stubborn silence.

A day or two after, with the same secret smile, and first looking about as if to be sure we were alone, "Mackellar," said he, "when you have any intelligence be sure and let me know. We must keep an eye upon him or he will take us when we least expect."

"He will not show face here again," said I.

"Oh, yes, he will," said Mr. Henry. "Wherever I am there will he be." And again he looked all about him.

"You must not dwell upon this thought, Mr. Henry," said I.

"No," said he, "that is very good advice. We will never think of it except when you have news. And we do not know yet," he added; "he may be dead."

The manner of his saying this convinced me thoroughly of what I had scarce ventured to suspect—that so far from suffering any penitence for the attempt he did but lament his failure. This was a discovery I kept to myself, fearing it might do him a prejudice with his wife. But I might have saved myself the trouble; she had divined it for herself, and found the sentiment quite natural. Indeed, I could not but say that there were three of us all of the same mind, nor could any news have reached Durrisdeer more generally welcome than tidings of the Master's death.

This brings me to speak of the exception, my old lord. As soon as my anxiety for my old master began to be relaxed I was aware of a change in the old gentleman, his father, that seemed to threaten mortal consequences.

His face was pale and swollen; as he sat in the chimney-side with his Latin he would drop off sleeping and the book roll in the ashes; some days he would drag his foot, others stumble in speaking. The amenity of his behavior appeared more extreme; full of excuses for the least trouble, very thoughtful for all; to myself of a most flattering civility. One day that he had sent for his lawyer and remained a long while private he met me as he was crossing the hall with painful footsteps and took me kindly by the hand. " Mr. Mackellar," said he, " I have had many occasions to set a proper value on your services, and to-day when I recast my will I have taken the freedom to name you for one of my executors. I believe you bear love enough to our house to render me this service." At that very time he passed the greater portion of his days in slumber, from which it was often difficult to rouse him; seemed to have lost all count of years, and had several times (particularly on waking) called for his wife and for an old servant whose very gravestone was now green with moss. If I had been put to my oath I must have declared he was incapable of testing, and yet there was never a will drawn more sensible in every trait, or showing a more excellent judgment both of persons and affairs.

His dissolution, though it took not very long, proceeded by infinitesimal gradations. His faculties decayed together steadily; the power of his limbs was almost gone, he was extremely deaf, his speech had sunk into mere mumblings; and yet to the end he managed to discover something of his former courtesy and kindness, pressing the hand of any that helped him, presenting me with one of his Latin books in which he had laboriously traced my name, and in a thousand ways reminding us of the greatness of that loss, which it might almost be said we had already suffered. To the end, the power of articulation returned to him in flashes; it seemed he had only forgotten the art of speech as a child forgets his lesson, and at times he would call some part of it to mind. On the last night of his life, he suddenly broke silence with these words from Virgil: " *Gnatique pratisque, alma, precor, miserere,*" perfectly uttered and with a fitting accent. At the sudden clear sound of it, we started from our several occupations; but it was in vain we turned to him; he sat there silent and to all appearances fatuous. A little later, he was had to bed with more difficulty than ever before; and some time in the night, without any mortal violence, his spirit fled.

At a far later period I chanced to speak of these particulars with a doctor of medicine, a man of so high a reputation that I scruple to adduce his name. By his view of it, father and son both suffered from the same affection; the father from the strain of his unnatural sorrows, the son perhaps in the excitation of the fever, each had ruptured a vessel on the brain; and there was probably (my doctor added) some predisposition in the family to accidents of that description. The father sunk, the son recovered all the externals of a healthy man; but it is like there was some destruction in those delicate tissues where the soul resides and does her earthly business; her heavenly, I would fain hope, cannot be thus obstructed by material accidents. And yet upon a more mature opinion, it matters not one jot; for He who shall pass judgment on the records of our life is the same that formed us in frailty.

The death of my old lord was the occasion of a fresh surprise to us who watched the behavior of his successor. To any considering mind the two sons had between them slain their father; and he who took the sword might be even said to have slain him with his hand. But no such thought appeared to trouble my new lord. He was becomingly grave; I could scarce say sorrowful, or only with a pleasant sorrow; talking of the dead with a regretful cheerfulness, relating old examples of his character, smiling at them with a good conscience; and when the day of the funeral came round doing the honors with exact propriety. I could perceive, besides, that he found a solid gratification in his accession to the title; the which he was punctilious in exacting.

And now there came upon the scene a new character, and one that played his part too in the story; I mean the present lord, Alexander, whose birth (17th July, 1757) filled the cup of my poor master's happiness. There was nothing then left him to wish for; nor yet leisure to wish for it. Indeed, there never was a parent so fond and doting as he showed himself. He was continually uneasy in his son's absence. Was the child abroad? the father would be watching the clouds in case it rained. Was it night? he would rise out of his bed to observe its slumbers. His conversation grew even wearyful to strangers, since he talked of little but his son. In matters relating to the estate all was designed with a particular eye to Alexander; and it would be: "Let us put it in hand at once, that the wood may be grown against Alexander's majority;" or "this will fall in again handsomely for Alexander's marriage." Every day this absorption of the man's nature became more observable, with many touching and some very blameworthy particulars. Soon the child could walk abroad with him, at first on the terrace hand in hand, and afterward at large about the policies; and this grew to be my lord's chief occupation. The sound of their two voices (audible a great way off, for they spoke loud) became familiar in the neighborhood; and for my part I found it more agreeable than the sound of birds. It was pretty to see the pair returning, full of briers, and the father as flushed and sometimes as bemuddied as the child; for they were equal sharers in all sorts of boyish entertainment, digging in the beach, damming of streams, and what not; and I have seen them gaze through a fence at cattle with the same childish contemplation.

The mention of these rambles brings me to a strange scene

of which I was a witness. There was one walk I never followed myself without emotion, so often had I gone there upon miserable errands, so much had there befallen against the house of Durrisdeer. But the path lay handy from all points beyond the Muckle Ross; and I was driven, although much against my will, to take my use of it perhaps once in the two months. It befell when Mr. Alexander was of the age of seven or eight, I had some business on the far side in the morning, and entered the shrubbery on my homeward way, about nine of a bright forenoon. It was that time of year when the woods are all in their spring colors, the thorns all in flower, and the birds in the high season of their singing. In contrast to this merriment, the shrubbery was only the more sad and I the more oppressed by its associations. In this situation of spirit, it struck me disagreeably to hear voices a little way in front, and to recognize the tones of my lord and Mr. Alexander. I pushed ahead, and came presently into their view. They stood together in the open space where the duel was, my lord with his hand on his son's shoulder and speaking with some gravity. At least, as he raised his head upon my coming, I thought I could perceive his countenance to lighten.

"Ah," says he, "here comes the good Mackellar. I have just been telling Sandie the story of this place, and how there was a man whom the devil tried to kill, and how near he came to kill the devil instead."

I had thought it strange enough he should bring the child into that scene; that he should actually be discoursing of his act, passed measure. But the worst was yet to come; for he added, turning to his son: "You can ask Mackellar; he was here and saw it."

"Is it true, Mr. Mackellar?" asked the child. "And did you really see the devil?"

"I have not heard the tale," I replied; "and I am in a press of business." So far I said a little sourly, fencing with the embarrassment of the position; and suddenly the bitterness of the past and the terror of that scene by candle-light rushed in upon my mind; I bethought me that, for a difference of a second's quickness in parade, the child before me might have never seen the day; and the emotion that always fluttered round my heart in that dark shrubbery burst forth in words. " But so much is true," I cried, " that I have met the devil in these woods and seen him foiled here; blessed be God that we escaped with life—blessed be God that one stone yet stands upon another in the walls of Durrisdeer; and oh, Mr. Alexander, if ever you come by this spot, though it was a hundred years hence and you came with the gayest and the highest in the land, I would step aside and remember a bit prayer."

My lord bowed his head gravely. " Ah," says he, " Mackellar is always in the right. Come, Alexander, take your bonnet off." And with that he uncovered and held out his hand. " Oh, Lord," said he, " I thank thee, and my son thanks thee, for thy manifold great mercies. Let us have peace for a little; defend us from the evil man. Smite him, oh, Lord, upon the lying mouth!" The last broke out of him like a cry; and at that, whether remembered anger choked his utterance, or whether he perceived this was a singular sort of prayer, at least he came suddenly to a full stop; and after a moment set back his hat upon his head.

" I think you have forgot a word, my lord," said I. " ' Forgive us our trespasses as we forgive them that trespass against us. For thine is the kingdom, and the power, and the glory, for ever and ever. Amen.' "

" Ah, that is easy saying," said my lord. " That is very easy saying, Mackellar. But for me to forgive? I think I would cut a very silly figure, if I had the affectation to pretend it."

" The bairn, my lord," said I, with some severity, for I thought his expressions little fitted for the ears of children.

" Why, very true," said he. " This is dull work for a bairn. Let's go nesting."

I forget if it was the same day, but it was soon after, my lord, finding me alone, opened himself a little more on the same head.

" Mackellar," he said, " I am now a very happy man."

"I think so indeed, my lord," said I, "and the sight of it gives me a light heart."

"There is an obligation in happiness, do you not think so?" says he musingly.

"I think so indeed," says I, "and one in sorrow too. If we are not here to try to do the best, in my humble opinion, the sooner we are away the better for all parties."

"Ay, but if you were in my shoes, would you forgive him?" asks my lord.

The suddenness of the attack a little graveled me. "It is a duty laid upon us strictly," said I.

"Hut!" said he. "These are expressions! Do you forgive the man yourself?"

"Well—no!" said I. "God forgive me, I do not."

"Shake hands upon that!" cries my lord, with a kind of joviality.

"It is an ill sentiment to shake hands upon," said I, "for Christian people. I think I will give you mine on some more evangelical occasion."

This I said, smiling a little; but as for my lord, he went from the room laughing aloud.

For my lord's slavery to the child, I can find no expression adequate. He lost himself in that continual thought; business, friends, and wife being all alike forgotten or only remembered with a painful effort, like that of one struggling with a posset. It was most notable in the matter of his wife. Since I had known Durrisdeer she had been the burden of his thought and the loadstone of his eyes; and now, she was quite cast out. I have seen him come to the door of a room, look round, and pass my lady over as though she were a dog before the fire; it would be Alexander he was seeking, and my lady knew it well. I have heard him speak to her so ruggedly that I nearly found it in my heart to intervene; the cause would still be the same, that she had in some way thwarted Alexander. Without doubt this was in the nature of a judgment on my lady. Without doubt she had the tables turned upon her as only Providence can do it; she who had been cold so many years to every mark of tenderness, it was her part now to be neglected; the more praise to her that she played it well.

An odd situation resulted: that we had once more two parties in the house, and that now I was of my lady's. Not that ever I lost the love I bore my master. But for one thing, he had the less use for my society. For another, I could not but compare the case of Mr. Alexander with that of Miss Katharine; for whom my lord had never found the least attention. And for a third, I was wounded by the change he discovered to his wife, which struck me in the nature of an infidelity. I could not but admire besides the constancy and kindness she displayed. Perhaps her sentiment to my lord, as it had been founded from the first in pity, was that rather of a mother than a wife; perhaps it pleased her (if I may so say) to behold her two children so happy in each other; the more as one had suffered so unjustly in the past. But for all that, and though I could never trace in her one spark of jealousy, she must fall back for society on poor, neglected Miss Katharine; and I, on my part, came to pass my spare hours more and more with the mother and daughter. It would be easy to make too much of this division, for it was a pleasant family as families go; still the thing existed; whether my lord knew it or not, I am in doubt. I do not think he did, he was bound up so entirely in his son; but the rest of us knew it and (in a manner) suffered from the knowledge.

What troubled us most, however, was the great and growing danger to the child. My lord was his father over again; it was to be feared the son would prove a second Master. Time has proved these fears to have been quite exaggerate. Certainly there is no more worthy gentleman to-day in Scotland than the seventh Lord Durrisdeer. Of my own exodus from his employment, it does not become me to speak, above all in a memorandum written only to justify his father.* . . .

*[EDITOR'S NOTE.—Five pages of Mr. Mackellar's MS. are here omitted. I have gathered from their perusal an impression that Mr. Mackellar, in his old age, was rather an exacting servant. Against the seventh Lord Durrisdeer (with whom, at any rate, we have no concern) nothing material is alleged.—R. L. S.]

THE MASTER OF BALLANTRAE

But our fear at the time was lest he should turn out, in the person of his son, a second edition of his brother. My lady had tried to interject some wholesome discipline; she had been glad to give that up, and now looked on with secret dismay; sometimes she even spoke of it by hints; and sometimes when there was brought to her knowledge some monstrous instance of my lord's indulgence she would betray herself in a gesture or perhaps an exclamation. As for myself, I was haunted by the thought both day and night; not so much for the child's sake as for the father's. The man had gone to sleep, he was dreaming a dream, and any rough wakening must infallibly prove mortal. That he should survive its death was inconceivable; and the fear of its dishonor made me cover my face.

It was this continual preoccupation that screwed me up at last to a remonstrance; a matter worthy to be narrated in detail. My lord and I sat one day at the same table upon some tedious business of detail; I have said that he had lost his former interest in such occupations; he was plainly itching to be gone, and he looked fretful, weary, and, methought, older than I had ever previously observed. I suppose it was the haggard face that put me suddenly upon my enterprise.

" My lord," said I, with my head down, and feigning to continue my occupation—" or rather let me call you again by the name of Mr. Henry, for I fear your anger and want you to think upon old times———"

" My good Mackellar! " said he; and that in tones so kindly that I had near forsook my purpose. But I called to mind that I was speaking for his good, and stuck to my colors.

" Has it never come in upon your mind what you are doing? " I asked.

" What I am doing? " he repeated. " I was never good at guessing riddles."

" What you are doing with your son," said I.

" Well," said he, with some defiance in his tone, " and what am I doing with my son? "

" You father was a very good man," says I, straying from the direct path. " But do you think he was a wise father? "

There was a pause before he spoke, and then: " I say nothing against him," he replied. " I had the most cause perhaps; but I say nothing."

" Why, there it is," said I. " You had the cause at least. And yet your father was a good man; I never knew a better, save on the one point, nor yet a wiser. Where he stumbled, it is highly possible another man should fall. He had the two sons——"

My lord rapped suddenly and violently on the table.

" What is this? " cried he. " Speak out! "

" I will, then," said I, my voice almost strangled with the thumping of my heart. " If you continue to indulge Mr. Alexander, you are following in your father's footsteps: Beware, my lord, lest (when he grows up) your son should follow in the Master's."

I had never meant to put the thing so crudely; but in the extreme of fear, there comes a brutal kind of courage, the most brutal indeed of all; and I burned my ships with that plain word. I never had the answer. When I lifted my head, my lord had risen to his feet, and the next moment he fell heavily on the floor. The fit or seizure endured not very long; he came to himself vacantly, put his hand to his head which I was then supporting, and says he, in a broken voice: " I have been ill," and a little after: " Help me! " I got him to his feet, and he stood pretty well, though he kept hold of the table. " I have been ill, Mackellar," he said again. " Something broke, Mackellar—or was going to break, and then all swam away. I think I was very angry. Never you mind, Mackellar, never you mind, my man. I wouldnae hurt a hair upon your head. Too much has come and gone. It's a certain thing between us two. But I think, Mackellar, I will go to Mrs. Henry—I think I will go to Mrs. Henry," said he, and got pretty steadily from the room, leaving me overcome with penitence.

Presently the door flew open, and my lady swept in with flashing eyes. " What is all this? " she cried. " What have you done to my husband? Will nothing teach you your position in this house? Will you never cease from making and meddling?"

"My lady," said I, "since I have been in this house, I have had plenty of hard words. For awhile they were my daily diet, and I swallowed them all. As for to-day, you may call me what you please; you will never find the name hard enough for such a blunder. And yet I meant it for the best."

I told her all with ingenuity, even as it is written here; and when she had heard me out, she pondered, and I could see her animosity fall. "Yes," she said, "you meant well indeed. I have had the same thought myself, or the same temptation rather, which makes me pardon you. But, dear God, can you not understand that he can bear no more? He can bear no more!" she cried. "The cord is stretched to snapping. What matters the future, if he have one or two good days?"

"Amen," said I. "I will meddle no more. I am pleased enough that you should recognize the kindness of my meaning."

"Yes," said my lady, "but when it came to the point, I have to suppose your courage failed you; for what you said was said cruelly." She paused, looking at me; then suddenly smiled a little, and said a singular thing: "Do you know what you are, Mr. Mackellar? You are an old maid."

No more incident of any note occurred in the family until the return of that ill-starred man, the Master. But I have to place here a second extract from the memoirs of Chevalier Burke, interesting in itself and highly necessary for my purpose. It is our only sight of the master on his Indian travels; and the first word in these pages of Secundra Dass. One fact, it is to observe, appears here very clearly, which if we had known some twenty years ago, how many calamities and sorrows had been spared!—that Secundra Dass spoke English.

(Extracted from his Memoirs)

HERE was I, therefore, on the streets of that city, the name of which I cannot call to mind, while even then I was so ill acquainted with its situation that I knew not whether to go south or north. The alert being sudden, I had run forth without shoes or stockings; my hat had been struck from my head in the mellay; my kit was in the hands of the English; I had no companion but the cipaye, no weapon but my sword, and the devil a coin in my pocket. In short I was for all the world like one of those calendars with whom Mr. Galland has made us acquainted in his elegant tales. These gentlemen, you will remember, were forever falling in with extraordinary incidents; and I was myself upon the brink of one so astonishing that I protest I cannot explain it to this day.

The cipaye was a very honest man, he had served many years with the French colors, and would have let himself be cut to pieces for any of the brave countrymen of Mr. Lally. It is the same fellow (his name has quite escaped me) of whom I have narrated already a surprising instance of generosity of mind: when he found Mr. de Fessac and myself upon the ramparts, entirely overcome with liquor, and covered us with straw while the commandant was passing by. I consulted him therefore with perfect freedom. It was a fine question what to do; but we decided at last to escalade a garden wall, where we could certainly sleep in the shadow of the trees, and might perhaps find an occasion to get hold of a pair of slippers and a turban. In that part of the city we had only the difficulty of the choice, for it was a quarter consisting entirely of walled gardens, and the lanes which divided them were at that hour of the night deserted. I gave the cipaye a back, and we had soon dropped into a large enclosure full of trees. The place was soaking with the dew which, in that country, is exceedingly unwholesome, above all to whites; yet my fatigue was so extreme that I was already half asleep, when the cipaye recalled me to my senses. In the far end of the inclosure a bright light had suddenly shone out, and continued to burn steadily among the leaves. It was a circumstance highly unusual in such a place and hour; and in our situation it behooved us to proceed with some timidity. The cipaye was sent to reconnoiter, and pretty soon returned with the intelligence that we had fallen extremely amiss, for the house belonged to a white man, who was in all likelihood English.

" Faith," says I, " if there's a white man to be seen, I will have a look at him; for the Lord be praised! there are more sorts than the one!"

The cipaye led me forward accordingly to a place from which I had a clear view upon the house. It was surrounded with a wide veranda; a lamp, very well trimmed, stood upon the floor of it, and on either side of the lamp there sat a man, cross-legged after the Oriental manner. Both, besides, were bundled up in muslin like two natives; and yet one of them was not only a white man, but a man very well known to me and the reader: being indeed that very master of Ballantrae of whose gallantry and genius I have had to speak so often. Word had reached me that he was come to the Indies; though we had never met at least, and I heard little of his occupations. But sure, I had no sooner recognized him, and found myself in the arms of so old a comrade, than I supposed my tribulations were quite done. I stepped plainly forth into the light of the moon, which shone exceeding strong, and hailing Ballantrae by name, made him in a few words master of my grievous situation. He turned, started the least thing in the world, looked me fair in the face while I was speaking, and when I had done, addressed himself to his companion in the barbarous native dialect. The second person, who was of an extraordinary delicate appearance, with legs like walking-canes and fingers like the stalk of a tobacco pipe * now rose to his feet.

* *Note by Mr. Mackellar.*—Plainly Secundra Dass.—E. McK.

" The sahib," says he, " understands no English language.
I understand it myself, and I see you make some small mistake—oh, which may happen very often! But the sahib
would be glad to know how you come in a garden."

" Ballantrae!" I cried. " Have you the damned impudence to deny me to my face? "

Ballantrae never moved a muscle, staring at me like an
image in a pagoda.

" The sahib understands no English language," says the
native, as glib as before. " He be glad to know how you come
in a garden."

" Oh, the divil fetch him!" says I. " He would be glad
to know how I come in a garden, would he? Well now, my
dear man, just have the civility to tell the sahib, with my kind
love, that we are two soldiers here whom he never met and
never heard of, but the cipaye is a broth of a boy, and I am
a broth of a boy myself; and if we don't get a full meal of
meat, and a turban, and slippers, and the value of a gold
mohur in small change as a matter of convenience, my friend,
I could lay my finger on a garden where there is going to be
trouble."

They carried their comedy so far as to converse awhile
in Hindoostanee; and then says the Hindoo, with the same
smile, but sighing as if he were tired of the repetition: " The
sahib would be glad to know how you come in a garden."

" Is that the way of it? " says I, and laying my hand on
my sword-hilt, I bade the cipaye draw.

Ballantrae's Hindoo, still smiling, pulled out a pistol from
his bosom, and though Ballantrae himself never moved a
muscle, I knew him well enough to be sure he was prepared.

" The sahib thinks you better go away," says the Hindoo.

Well, to be plain, it was what I was thinking myself; for
the report of a pistol would have been, under Providence, the
means of hanging the pair of us.

" Tell the sahib, I consider him no gentleman," says I, and
turned away with a gesture of contempt.

I was not gone three steps when the voice of the Hindoo
called me back. " The sahib would be glad to know if you

are a damn low Irishman," says he; and at the words Ballantrae smiled and bowed very low.

"What is that?" says I.

"The sahib say you ask your friend Mackellar," says the Hindoo. "The sahib he cry quits."

"Tell the sahib I will give him a cure for the Scots fiddle when next we meet," cried I.

The pair were still smiling as I left.

There is little doubt some flaws may be picked in my own behavior; and when a man, however gallant, appeals to posterity with an account of his exploits, he must almost certainly expect to share the fate of Cæsar and Alexander, and to meet with some detractors. But there is one thing that can never be laid at the door of Francis Burke: he never turned his back on a friend. . . .

(Here follows a passage which the Chevalier Burke has been at the pains to delete before sending me his manuscript. Doubtless it was some very natural complaint of what he supposed to be an indiscretion on my part; though, indeed, I can call none to mind. Perhaps Mr. Henry was less guarded; or it is just possible the Master found the means to examine my correspondence, and himself read the letter from Troyes: in revenge for which this cruel jest was perpetrated on Mr. Burke in his extreme necessity. The master, for all his wickedness, was not without some natural affection; I believe he was sincerely attached to Mr. Burke in the beginning; but the thought of treachery dried up the springs of his very shallow friendship, and his detestable nature appeared naked. —E. McK.)

IT is a strange thing that I should be at a stick for a date—the date, besides, of an incident that changed the very nature of my life, and sent us all into foreign lands. But the truth is I was stricken out of all my habitudes, and find my journals very ill redd-up,* the day not indicated sometimes for a week or two together, and the whole fashion of the thing like that of a man near desperate. It was late in March at least, or early in April, 1764. I had slept heavily and wakened with a premonition of some evil to befall. So strong was this upon my spirit that I hurried downstairs in my shirt and breeches, and my hand (I remember) shook upon the rail. It was a cold, sunny morning with a thick white frost; the blackbirds sung exceeding sweet and loud about the house of Durrisdeer, and there was a noise of the sea in all the chambers. As I came by the door of the hall another sound arrested me, of voices talking. I drew nearer and stood like a man dreaming. Here was certainly a human voice, and that in my own master's house, and yet I knew it not; certainly human speech, and that in my native land; and yet listen as I pleased, I could not catch one syllable. An old tale started up in my mind of a fairy wife (or perhaps only a wandering stranger), that came to the place of my fathers some generations back, and stayed the matter of a week, talking often in a tongue that signified nothing to the hearers; and went again as she had come, under cloud of night, leaving not so much as a name behind her. A little fear I had, but more curiosity; and I opened the hall door and entered.

The supper things still lay upon the table; the shutters were still closed, although day peeped in the divisions; and the great room was lighted only with a single taper and some lurching reverberation of the fire. Close in the chimney sat two men. The one that was wrapped in a cloak and wore

* Ordered.

134

boots, I knew at once: it was the bird of ill omen back again. Of the other, who was set close to the red embers, and made up into a bundle like a mummy, I could but see that he was an alien, of a darker hue than any man of Europe, very frailly built, with a singular tall forehead and a secret eye. Several bundles and a small valise were on the floor; and to judge by the smallness of this luggage, and by the condition of the master's boots, grossly patched by some unscrupulous country cobbler, evil had not prospered.

He rose upon my entrance; our eyes crossed; and I know not why it should have been, but my courage rose like a lark on a May morning.

"Ha!" said I, "is this you?"—and I was pleased with the unconcern of my own voice.

"It is even myself, worthy Mackellar," says the Master.

"This time you have brought the black dog visibly upon your back," I continued.

"Referring to Secundra Dass?" asked the Master. "Let me present you. He is a native gentleman of India."

"Hum!" said I. "I am no great lover either of you or your friends, Mr. Bally. But I will let a little daylight in and have a look at you." And so saying, I undid the shutters of the eastern window.

By the light of the morning I could perceive the man was changed. Later, when we were all together, I was more struck to see how lightly time had dealt with him, but the first glance was otherwise.

"You are getting an old man," said I.

A shade came upon his face. "If you could see yourself," said he, "you would perhaps not dwell upon the topic."

"Hut!" I returned; "old age is nothing to me. I think I have been always old, and I am now, I thank God, better known and more respected. It is not every one that can say that, Mr. Bally! The lines in *your* brow are calamities; your life begins to close in upon you like a prison; death will soon be rapping at the door, and I see not from what source you are to draw your consolations."

Here the Master addressed himself to Secundra Dass in

Hindoostanee, from which I gathered (I freely confess, with a high degree of pleasure) that my remarks annoyed him. All this while, you may be sure, my mind had been busy upon other matters even while I rallied my enemy, and chiefly as to how I should communicate secretly and quickly with my lord. To this, in the breathing-space now given me, I turned all the forces of my mind, when, suddenly shifting my eyes, I was aware of the man himself standing in the doorway, and to all appearance quite composed. He had no sooner met my looks than he stepped across the threshold. The Master heard him coming, and advanced upon the other side; about four feet apart these brothers came to a full pause and stood exchanging steady looks, and then my lord smiled, bowed a little forward and turned briskly away.

"Mackellar," says he, "we must see to breakfast for these travelers."

It was plain the Master was a trifle disconcerted, but he assumed the more impudence of speech and manner. "I am as hungry as a hawk," says he. "Let it be something good, Henry."

My lord turned to him with the same hard smile. "Lord Durrisdeer," says he.

"Oh, never in the family!" returned the Master.

"Every one in this house renders me my proper title," says my lord. "If it please you to make an exception I will leave you to consider what appearance it will bear to strangers, and whether it may not be translated as an effect of impotent jealousy."

I could have clapped my hands together with delight: the more so as my lord left no time for any answer, but bidding me with a sign to follow him, went straight out of the hall.

"Come quick," says he; "we have to sweep vermin from the house." And he sped through the passage with so swift a step that I could scarce keep up with him straight to the door of John Paul, the which he opened without summons and walked in. John was to all appearance sound asleep, but my lord made no pretense of waking him.

"John Paul," said he, speaking as quietly as ever I heard

him, "you served my father long or I would pack you from
the house like a dog. If in half an hour's time I find you gone
you shall continue to receive your wages in Edinburgh. If
you linger here or in St. Bride's—the old man, old servant
and altogether—I shall find some very astonishing way to
make you smart for your disloyalty. Up and begone. The
door you let them in by will serve for your departure. I do
not choose my son shall see your face again."

"I am rejoiced to find you bear the thing so quietly," said
I when we were forth again by ourselves.

"Quietly!" cries he, and put my hand suddenly against
his heart, which struck upon his bosom like a sledge.

At this revelation I was filled with wonder and fear. There
was no constitution could bear so violent a strain—his least
of all that was unhinged already—and I decided in my mind
that we must bring this monstrous situation to an end.

"It would be well, I think, if I took word to my lady,"
said I. Indeed, he should have gone himself, but I counted
(not in vain) on his indifference.

"Ay," says he, "do. I will hurry breakfast; we must all
appear at the table, even Alexander; it must appear we are
untroubled."

I ran to my lady's room, and with no preparatory cruelty
disclosed my news.

"My mind was long ago made up," said she. "We must
make our packets secretly to-day and leave secretly to-night.
Thank Heaven, we have another house! The first ship that
sails shall bear us to New York."

"And what of him?" I asked.

"We leave him Durrisdeer," she cried. "Let him work his
pleasure upon that."

"Not so, by your leave," said I. "There shall be a dog
at his heels that can hold fast. Bed he shall have, and board,
and a horse to ride upon, if he behave himself; but the keys
(if you think well of it, my lady) shall be left in the hands
of one Mackellar. There will be good care taken; trust him
for that."

"Mr. Mackellar," she cried, "I thank you for that

137

thought! All shall be left in your hands. If we must go into a savage country, I bequeath it to you to take our vengeance. Send Macconochie to St. Bride's, to arrange privately for horses and to call the lawyer. My lord must leave procuration."

At that moment my lord came to the door, and we opened our plan to him.

"I will never hear of it," he cried; "he would think I feared him. I will stay in my own house, please God, until I die. There lives not the man can beard me out of it. Once and for all, here I am and here I stay, in spite of all the devils in hell." I can give no idea of the vehemency of his words and utterance; but we both stood aghast, and I in particular, who had been a witness of his former self-restraint.

My lady looked at me with an appeal that went to my heart and recalled me to my wits. I made her a private sign to go, and, when my lord and I were alone, went up to him where he was racing to and fro in one end of the room like a half lunatic, and set my hand firmly on his shoulder.

"My lord," says I, "I am going to be the plaindealer once more; if for the last time, so much the better, for I am grown weary of the part."

"Nothing will change me," he answered. "God forbid I should refuse to hear you; but nothing will change me." This he said firmly, with no signal of the former violence, which already raised my hopes.

"Very well," said I. "I can afford to waste my breath." I pointed to a chair, and he sat down and looked at me. "I can remember a time when my lady very much neglected you," said I.

"I never spoke of it while it lasted," returned my lord, with a high flush of color; "and it is all changed now."

"Do you know how much?" I said. "Do you know how much it is all changed? The tables are turned, my lord! It is my lady that now courts you for a word, a look, ay, and courts you in vain. Do you know with whom she passes her days while you are out gallivanting in the policies? My lord, she is glad to pass them with a certain dry old grieve * of

* Land steward.

the name of Ephraim Mackellar; and I think you may be able to remember what that means, for I am the more in a mistake or you were once driven to the same company yourself."

" Mackellar!" cries my lord, getting to his feet. " Oh, my God, Meckellar!"

" It is neither the name of Mackellar nor the name of God that can change the truth," said I; " and I am telling you the fact. Now, for you, that suffered so much, to deal out the same suffering to another, is that the part of any Christian? But you are so swallowed up in your new friend that the old are all forgotten. They are all clean vanished from your memory. And yet they stood by you at the darkest; my lady not the least. And does my lady ever cross your mind? Does it ever cross your mind what she went through that night?—or what manner of a wife she has been to you thence-forward?—or in what kind of a position she finds herself to-day? Never. It is your pride to stay and face him out, and she must stay along with him. Oh, my lord's pride—that's the great affair! And yet she is the woman, and you are a great, hulking man! She is the woman that you swore to protect; and, more betoken, the own mother of that son of yours!"

" You are speaking very bitterly, Mackellar," said he; " but, the Lord knows, I fear you are speaking very true. I have not proved worthy of my happiness. Bring my lady back."

My lady was waiting near at hand to learn the issue. When I brought her in, my lord took a hand of each of us and laid them both upon his bosom. " I have had two friends in my life," said he. " All the comfort ever I had, it came from one or other. When you two are in a mind, I think I would be an ungrateful dog—" He shut his mouth very hard, and looked on us with swimming eyes. " Do what ye like with me," says he, " only don't think—" He stopped again. " Do what ye please with me. God knows I love and honor you." And dropping our two hands, he turned his back and went and gazed out of the window. But my lady ran after, calling his name, and threw herself upon his neck in a passion of weeping.

I went out and shut the door behind me, and stood and thanked God from the bottom of my heart.

At the breakfast board, according to my lord's design, we were all met. The master had by that time plucked off his patched boots and made a toilet suitable to the hour; Secundra Dass was no longer bundled up in wrappers, but wore a decent plain black suit, which misbecame him strangely; and the pair were at the great window looking forth, when the family entered. They turned; and the black man (as they had already named him in the house) bowed almost to his knees, but the Master was for running forward like one of the family. My lady stopped him, courtesying low from the far end of the hall, and keeping her children at her back. My lord was a little in front: so there were the three cousins of Durrisdeer face to face. The hand of time was very legible on all. I seemed to read in their changed faces a *memento mori;* and what affected me still more, it was the wicked man that bore his years the handsomest. My lady was quite transfigured into the matron, a becoming woman for the head of a great tableful of children and dependents. My lord was grown slack in his limbs; he stooped; he walked with a running motion, as though he had learned again from Mr. Alexander; his face was drawn; it seemed a trifle longer than of old; and it wore at times a smile very singularly mingled, and which (in my eyes) appeared both bitter and pathetic. But the Master still bore himself erect, although perhaps with effort; his brow barred about the center with imperious lines, his mouth set as for command. He had all the gravity and something of the splendor of Satan in the " Paradise Lost." I could not help but see the man with admiration, and was only surprised that I saw him with so little fear.

But indeed (as long as we were at the table) it seemed as if his authority were quite vanished and his teeth all drawn. We had known him a magician that controlled the elements; and here he was, transformed into an ordinary gentleman, chatting like his neighbors at the breakfast board. For now the father was dead, and my lord and lady reconciled, in what ear was he to pour his calumnies? It came upon me in a kind of vision how hugely I had overrated the man's subtlety. He had his malice still, he was false as ever; and, the occasion being gone that made his strength, he sat there impotent; he was still the viper, but now spent his venom on a file. Two more thoughts occurred to me while yet we sat at breakfast: the first, that he was abashed—I had almost said distressed—to find his wickedness quite unavailing; the second, that perhaps my lord was in the right, and we did amiss to fly from our dismasted enemy. But my poor master's leaping heart came in my mind, and I remembered it was for his life we played the coward.

When the meal was over, the Master followed me to my room, and taking a chair (which I had never offered him), asked me what was to be done with him.

"Why, Mr. Bally," said I, "the house will still be open to you for a time."

"For a time?" says he. "I do not know if I quite take your meaning."

"It is plain enough," said I. "We keep you for our reputation; as soon as you shall have publicly disgraced yourself by some of your misconduct, we shall pack you forth again.

"You are become an impudent rogue," said the Master, bending his brows at me dangerously.

"I learned in a good school," I returned. "And you must have perceived yourself that with my old lord's death your power is quite departed. I do not fear you now, Mr. Bally; I think even—God forgive me—that I take a certain pleasure in your company."

He broke out in a burst of laughter, which I clearly saw to be assumed.

"I have come with empty pockets," says he after a pause.

"I do not think there will be any money going," I replied. "I would advise you not to build on that."

141

" I shall have something to say on that point," he returned.

" Indeed? " said I. " I have not a guess what it will be, then."

" Oh, you affect confidence," said the master. " I have still one strong position—that you people fear a scandal, and I enjoy it."

" Pardon me, Mr. Bally," says I. " We do not in the least fear a scandal against you."

He laughed again. " You have been studying repartee," he said. " But speech is very easy, and sometimes very deceptive. I warn you fairly: you will find me vitriol in the house. You would do wiser to pay money down, and see my back." And with that he waved his hand to me and left the room.

A little after my lord came with the lawyer, Mr. Carlyle; a bottle of old wine was brought, and we all had a glass before we fell to business. The necessary deeds were then prepared and executed, and the Scotch estates made over in trust to Mr. Carlyle and myself.

" There is one point, Mr. Carlyle," said my lord, when these affairs had been adjusted, " on which I wish that you would do us justice. This sudden departure coinciding with my brother's return will be certainly commented on. I wish you would discourage any conjunction of the two."

" I will make a point of it, my lord," said Mr. Carlyle. " The Mas—Mr. Bally does not then accompany you? "

" It is a point I must approach," said my lord. " Mr. Bally remains at Durrisdeer under the care of Mr. Mackellar; and I do not mean that he shall even know our destination."

" Common report, however—" began the lawyer.

" Ah, but Mr. Carlyle, this is to be a secret quite among ourselves," interrupted my lord. " None but you and Mackellar are to be made acquainted with my movements."

" And Mr. Bally stays here? Quite so," said Mr. Carlyle. " The powers you leave—" then he broke off again. " Mr. Mackellar, we have a rather heavy weight upon us."

"No doubt, sir," said I.

"No doubt," said he. "Mr. Bally will have no voice?"

"He will have no voice," said my lord, "and I hope no influence. Mr. Bally is not a good adviser."

"I see," said the lawyer. "By the way, has Mr. Bally means?"

"I understand him to have nothing," replied my lord. "I give him table, fire, and candle in this house."

"And in the matter of an allowance? If I am to share the responsibility, you will see how highly desirable it is that I should understand your views," said the lawyer. "On the question of an allowance?"

"There will be no allowance," said my lord. "I wish Mr. Bally to live very private. We have not always been gratified with his behavior."

"And in the matter of money," I added, "he has shown himself an infamous bad husband. Glance your eye upon that document, Mr. Carlyle, where I have brought together the different sums the man has drawn from the estate in the last fifteen or twenty years. The total is pretty."

Mr. Carlyle made the motion of whistling. "I had no guess of this," said he. "Excuse me once more, my lord, if I appear to push you; but it is really desirable I should penetrate your intentions: Mr. Mackellar might die, when I should find myself alone upon this trust. Would it not be rather your lordship's preference that Mr. Bally should —ahem—should leave the country?"

My lord looked at Mr. Carlyle. "Why do you ask that?" said he.

"I gather, my lord, that Mr. Bally is not a comfort to his family," says the lawyer with a smile.

My lord's face became suddenly knotted. "I wish he was in hell," cried he, and filled himself a glass of wine, but with a hand so tottering that he spilled the half into his bosom. This was the second time that, in the midst of the most regular and wise behavior, his animosity had spurted out. It startled Mr. Carlyle, who observed my lord thenceforth with covert curiosity, and to me it restored the certainty that we were acting for the best in view of my lord's health and reason.

Except for this explosion, the interview was very successfully conducted. No doubt Mr. Carlyle would talk; as lawyers do, little by little. We could thus feel we had laid the foundations of a better feeling in the country; and the man's own misconduct would certainly complete what we had begun. Indeed, before his departure, the lawyer showed us there had already gone abroad some glimmerings of the truth.

" I should perhaps explain to you, my lord," said he, pausing, with his hat in his hand, " that I have not been altogether surprised with your lordship's dispositions in the case of Mr. Bally. Something of this nature oozed out when he was last in Durrisdeer. There was some talk of a woman at St. Bride's to whom you had behaved extremely handsome, and Mr. Bally with no small degree of cruelty. There was the entail again, which was much controverted. In short, there was no want of talk, back and forward; and some of our wiseacres took up a strong opinion. I remained in suspense, as became one of my cloth; but Mr. Mackellar's docket here has finally opened my eyes. I do not think, Mr. Mackellar, that you and I will give him that much rope."

The rest of that important day passed prosperously through. It was our policy to keep the enemy in view, and I took my turn to be his watchman with the rest. I think his spirits rose as he perceived us to be so attentive: and I know that mine insensibly declined. What chiefly daunted me was the man's singular dexterity to worm himself into our troubles. You may have felt (after a horse accident) the hand of a bone-setter artfully divide and interrogate the muscles, and settle strongly on the injured place? It was so with the Master's tongue that was so cunning to question, and his eyes that were so quick to observe. I seemed to have said nothing, and yet to have let all out. Before I knew where I was, the man was condoling with

me on my lord's neglect of my lady and myself, and his
hurtful indulgence to his son. On this last point I perceived him (with panic fear) to return repeatedly. The boy
had displayed a certain shrinking from his uncle; it was
strong in my mind his father had been fool enough to in-
doctrinate the same, which was no wise beginning: and when
I looked upon the man before me, still so handsome, so
apt a speaker, with so great a variety of fortunes to relate, I saw he was the very personage to captivate a boyish
fancy.

John Paul had left only that morning; it was not to
be supposed he had been altogether dumb upon his favorite subject: so that here would be Mr. Alexander in
the part of Dido, with a curiosity inflamed to hear; and
there would be the Master like a diabolical Æneas, full of
matter the most pleasing in the world to any youthful
ear, such as battles, sea disasters, flights, the forests of the
west, and (since his later voyage) the ancient cities of the
Indies. How cunningly these baits might be employed, and
what an empire might be so founded, little by little, in the
mind of any boy, stood obviously clear to me. There was
no inhibition, so long as the man was in the house, that
would be strong enough to hold these two apart; for if
it be hard to charm serpents, it is no very difficult thing
to cast a glamour on a little chip of manhood not very long
in breeches. I recalled an ancient sailor-man who dwelt in
a lone house beyond the Figgate Whins (I believe he called
it after Portobello), and how the boys would troop out of
Leith on a Saturday, and sit and listen to his swearing tales,
as thick as crows about a carrion: a thing I often remarked
as I went by, a young student, on my own more meditative
holiday diversion. Many of these boys went, no doubt, in
the face of an express command; many feared and even
hated the old brute of whom they made their hero; and I
have seen them flee from him when he was tipsy, and stone
him when he was drunk. And yet there they came each
Saturday! How much more easily would a boy like Mr.
Alexander fall under the influence of a high-looking, high-

spoken gentleman adventurer who should conceive the fancy to entrap him; and the influence gained, how easy to employ it for the child's perversion!

I doubt if our enemy had named Mr. Alexander three times, before I perceived which way his mind was aiming— all this train of thought and memory passed in one pulsation through my own—and you may say I started back as though an open hole had gaped across a pathway. Mr. Alexander: there was the weak point, there was the Eve in our perishable paradise; and the serpent was already hissing on the trail.

I promise you I went the more heartily about the preparations; my last scruple gone, the danger of delay written before me in huge characters. From that moment forth, I seem not to have sat down or breathed. Now I would be at my post with the Master and his Indian; now in the garret buckling a valise; now sending forth Macconochie by the side postern and the wood-path to bear it to the trysting-place; and again, snatching some words of counsel with my lady. This was the *verso* of our life in Durrisdeer that day; but on the *recto* all appeared quite settled, as of a family at home in its paternal seat; and what perturbation may have been observable the Master would set down to the blow of his unlooked-for coming and the fear he was accustomed to inspire.

Supper went creditably off, cold salutations passed, and the company trooped to their respective chambers. I attended the Master to the last. We had put him next door to his Indian, in the north wing; because that was the most distant and could be severed from the body of the house with doors. I saw he was a kind friend or a good master (whichever it was) to his Secundra Dass: seeing to his comfort; mending the fire with his own hand, for the Indian complained of cold; inquiring as to the rice on which the stranger made his diet; talking with him pleasantly in the Hindoo-stanee, while I stood by, my candle in my hand, and affected to be overcome with slumber. At length the master observed my signals of distress. "I perceive," says he, "that you have all your ancient habits: early to bed and early to rise. Yawn yourself away!"

Once in my own room, I made the customary motions of undressing, so that I might time myself; and when the cycle was complete, set my tinder-box ready and blew out my taper. The matter of an hour afterward I made a light again, put on my shoes of list that I had worn by, my lord's sick-bed, and set forth into the house to call the voyagers. All were dressed and waiting—my lord, my lady, Miss Katharine, Mr. Alexander, my lady's woman Christie; and I observed the effect of secrecy even upon quite innocent persons, that one after another showed in the chink of the door a face as white as paper. We slipped out of the side postern into a night of darkness, scarce broken by a star or two; so that at first we groped and stumbled and fell among the bushes. A few hundred yards up the wood-path Macconochie was waiting us with a great lantern; so the rest of the way we went easy enough, but still in a kind of guilty silence. A little beyond the abbey the path debouched on the main road; and some quarter of a mile further, at the place called Eagles, where the moors begin, we saw the lights of the two carriages stand shining by the wayside. Scarce a word or two was uttered at our parting, and these regarded business; a silent grasping of hands, a turning of faces aside, and the thing was over; the horses broke into a trot, the lamplight sped like will-o'-the-wisp upon the broken moorland, it dipped beyond Stony Brae; and there were Macconochie and I alone with our lantern on the road. There was one thing more to wait for; and that was the reappearance of the coach upon Cartmore. It seems they must have pulled up upon the summit, looked back for a last time, and seen our lantern not yet moved away from the place of separation. For a lamp was taken from a carriage, and waved three times up and down by way of a farewell. And then they were gone indeed, having looked their last on the kind roof of Durrisdeer, their faces toward a barbarous country. I never knew before the greatness of that vault of night in which we two poor serv-

147

ing-men, the one old and the one elderly, stood for the first time deserted; I had never felt before my own dependency upon the countenance of others. The sense of isolation burned in my bowels like a fire. It seemed that we who remained at home were the true exiles; and that Durrisdeer, and Solwayside, and all that made my country native, its air good to me, and its language welcome, had gone forth and was for over the sea with my old masters.

The remainder of that night I paced to and fro on the smooth highway, reflecting on the future and the past. My thoughts, which at first dwelled tenderly on those who were just gone, took a more manly temper as I considered what remained for me to do. Day came upon the inland mountain-tops, and the fowls began to cry and the smoke of homesteads to arise in the brown bosom of the moors, before I turned my face homeward and went down the path to where the roof of Durrisdeer shone in the morning by the sea.

At the customary hour I had the Master called, and awaited his coming in the hall with a quiet mind. He looked about him at the empty room and the three covers set.

"We are a small party," said he. "How comes that?"

"This is the party to which we must grow accustomed," I replied.

He looked at me with sudden sharpness. "What is all this?" said he.

"You and I and your friend Mr. Dass are now all the company," I replied. "My lord, my lady, and the children are gone upon a voyage."

"Upon my word!" said he. "Can this be possible? I have indeed fluttered your Volscians in Corioli! But this is no reason why our breakfast should go cold. Sit down, Mr. Mackellar, if you please"—taking, as he spoke, the head of the table, which I had designed to occupy myself—"and as we eat, you can give me the details of this evasion."

I could see he was more affected than his language carried, and I determined to equal him in coolness. "I was about to ask you to take the head of the table," said I;

148

"for though I am now thrust into the position of your host, I could never forget that you were, after all, a member of the family."

For awhile he played the part of entertainer, giving directions to Macconochie, who received them with an evil grace, and attending specially upon Secundra. "And where has my good family withdrawn to?" he asked carelessly.

"Ah, Mr. Bally, that is another point!" said I. "I have no orders to communicate their destination."

"To me," he corrected.

"To any one," said I.

"It is the less pointed," said the Master; "*c'est de bon ton:* my brother improves as he continues. And I, dear Mr. Mackellar?"

"You will have bed and board, Mr. Bally," said I. "I am permitted to give you the run of the cellar, which is pretty reasonably stocked. You have only to keep well with me, which is no very difficult matter, and you shall want neither for wine nor a saddle-horse."

He made an excuse to send Macconochie from the room.

"And for money?" he inquired. "Have I to keep well with my good friend Mackellar for my pocket-money also? This is a pleasing return to the principles of boyhood."

"There was no allowance made," said I; "but I will take it on myself to see you are supplied in moderation."

"In moderation?" he repeated. "And you will take it on yourself?" He drew himself up and looked about the hall at the dark row of portraits. "In the name of my ancestors, I thank you," says he; and then, with a return to irony: "But there must certainly be an allowance for Secundra Dass?" he said. "It is not possible they have omitted that."

"I will make a note of it and ask instructions when I write," said I.

And he, with a sudden change of manner, and leaning forward with an elbow on the table: "Do you think this entirely wise?"

"I execute my orders, Mr. Bally," said I.

THE MASTER OF BALLANTRAE

"Profoundly modest," said the Master; "perhaps not equally ingenuous. You told me yesterday my power was fallen with my father's death. How comes it, then, that a peer of the realm flees under cloud of night out of a house in which his fathers have stood several sieges? that he conceals his address, which must be a matter of concern to his gracious majesty and to the whole republic? and that he should leave me in possession, and under the paternal charge of his invaluable Mackellar? This smacks to me of a very considerable and genuine apprehension."

I sought to interrupt him with some not very truthful denegation; but he waved me down and pursued his speech.

"I say it smacks of it," he said, "but I will go beyond that, for I think the apprehension grounded. I came to this house with some reluctancy. In view of the manner of my last departure, nothing but necessity could have induced me to return. Money, however, is that which I must have. You will not give with a good grace; well, I have the power to force it from you. Inside of a week, without leaving Durrisdeer, I will find out where these fools are fled to. I will follow; and when I have run my quarry down I will drive a wedge into that family that shall once more burst it into shivers. I shall see then whether my Lord Durrisdeer" (said with indescribable scorn and rage) "will choose to buy my absence; and you will all see whether, by that time, I decide for profit or revenge."

I was amazed to hear the man so open. The truth is, he was consumed with anger at my lord's successful flight, felt himself to figure as a dupe, and was in no humor to weigh language.

"Do you consider this entirely wise?" said I, copying his words.

"These twenty years I have lived by my poor wisdom," he answered, with a smile that seemed almost foolish in its vanity.

"And come out a beggar in the end," said I, "if beggar be a strong enough word for it."

"I would have you observe, Mr. Mackellar," cried he, with a sudden, imperious heat in which I could not but admire him, "that I am scrupulously civil; copy me in that, and we shall be the better friends."

Throughout this dialogue I had been incommoded by the observation of Secundra Dass. Not one of us, since the first word, had made a feint of eating; our eyes were in each other's faces—you might say, in each other's bosoms; and those of the Indian troubled me with a certain changing brightness, as of comprehension. But I brushed the fancy aside; telling myself once more he understood no English; only, from the gravity of both voices and the occasional scorn and anger in the master's, smelled out there was something of import in the wind.

For the matter of three weeks we continued to live together in the house of Durrisdeer, the beginning of that most singular chapter of my life—what I must call my intimacy with the Master. At first he was somewhat changeable in his behavior; now civil, now returning to his old manner of flouting me to my face; and in both I met him halfway. Thanks be to Providence, I had now no measure to keep with the man; and I was never afraid of black brows, only of naked swords. So that I found a certain entertainment in these bouts of incivility, and was not always ill-inspired in my rejoinders. At last (it was at supper) I had a droll expression that entirely vanquished him. He laughed again and again; and "Who would have guessed," he cried, "that this old wife had any wit under his petticoats?"

"It is no wit, Mr. Bally," said I; "a dry Scot's humor, and something of the driest." And indeed I never had the least pretension to be thought a wit.

From that hour he was never rude with me, but all passed between us in a manner of pleasantry. One of our chief times of daffing * was when he required a horse, another bottle, or some money; he would approach me then after the manner of a schoolboy, and I would carry it on by way of

* Fooling.

being his father; on both sides, with an infinity of mirth. I could not but perceive that he thought more of me, which tickled that poor part of mankind, the vanity. He dropped besides (I must suppose unconsciously) into a manner that was not only familiar, but even friendly; and this, on the part of one who had so long detested me, I found the more insidious. He went little abroad; sometimes even refusing invitations. "No," he would say, "what do I care for these thick-headed bonnet-lairds? I will stay at home, Mackellar; and we shall share a bottle quietly and have one of our good talks." And indeed meal-time at Durrisdeer must have been a delight to any one, by reason of the brilliancy of the discourse. He would often express wonder at his former indifference to my society. "But, you see," he would add, "we were upon opposite sides. And so we are to-day; but let us never speak of that. I would think much less of you if you were not stanch to your employer." You are to consider, he seemed to me quite impotent for any evil; and how it is a most engaging form of flattery when (after many years) tardy justice is done to a man's character and parts. But I have no thought to excuse myself. I was to blame; I let him cajole me; and, in short, I think the watch-dog was going sound asleep, when he was suddenly aroused.

I should say the Indian was continually traveling to and fro in the house. He never spoke, save in his own dialect and with the master; walked without sound; and was always turning up where you would least expect him fallen into a deep abstraction, from which he would start (upon your coming) to mock you with one of his groveling obeisances. He seemed so quiet, so frail, and so wrapped in his own fancies, that I came to pass him over without much regard, or even to pity him for a harmless exile from his country. And yet without doubt the creature was still eavesdropping; and without doubt it was through his stealth and my security that our secret reached the master.

It was one very wild night, after supper, and when we had been making more than usually merry, that the blow fell on me.

" This is all very fine," says the Master, " but we should do better to be buckling our valise."

" Why so? " I cried. " Are you leaving? "

" We are all leaving to-morrow in the morning," said he. " For the port of Glasgow first; thence for the province of New York."

I suppose I must have groaned aloud.

" Yes," he continued, " I boasted; I said a week, and it has taken me near twenty days. But never mind; I shall make it up; I will go the faster."

" Have you the money for this voyage? " I asked.

" Dear and ingenuous personage, I have," said he. " Blame me, if you choose, for my duplicity; but while I have been wringing shillings from my daddy, I had a stock of my own put by against a rainy day. You will pay for your own passage, if you choose to accompany us on our flank march; I have enough for Secundra and myself, but not more; enough to be dangerous, not enough to be generous. There is, however, an outside seat upon the chaise which I will let you have upon a moderate commutation; so that the whole menagerie can go together, the house-dog, the monkey, and the tiger."

" I go with you," said I.

" I count upon it," said the master. " You have seen me foiled, I mean you shall see me victorious. To gain that, I will risk wetting you like a sop in this wild weather."

" And at least," I added, " you know very well you could not throw me off."

" Not easily," said he. " You put your finger on the point with your usual excellent good sense. I never fight with the inevitable."

" I suppose it is useless to appeal to you," said I.

" Believe me, perfectly," said he.

" And yet if you would give me time, I could write—" I began.

" And what would be my Lord Durrisdeer's answer? " asks he.

" Ay," said I, " that is the rub."

153

" And at any rate, how much more expeditious that I should go myself!" says he. " But all this is quite a waste of breath. At seven to-morrow the chaise will be at the door. For I start from the door, Mackellar; I do not skulk through woods and take my chaise upon the wayside—shall we say, at Eagles?"

My mind was now thoroughly made up. " Can you spare me a quarter of an hour at St. Bride's?" said I. " I have a little necessary business with Carlyle."

" An hour, if you prefer," said he. " I do not seek to deny that the money for your seat is an object to me; and you could always get the first to Glasgow with saddle-horses."

" Well," said I, " I never thought to leave old Scotland."

" It will brisken you up," says he.

" This will be an ill journey for some one," I said. " I think, sir, for you. Something speaks in my bosom; and so much it says plain, That this is an ill-omened journey."

" If you take to prophecy," says he, " listen to that."

There came up a violent squall off the open Solway, and the rain was dashed on the great windows.

" Do ye ken what that bodes, warlock?" said he, in a broad accent: " that there'll be a man Mackellar unco sick at sea."

When I got to my chamber I sat there under a painful excitation, hearkening to the turmoil of the gale which struck full upon that gable of the house. What with the pressure on my spirits, the eldritch cries of the wind among the turret tops, and the perpetual trepidation of the masoned house, sleep fled my eyelids utterly. I sat by my taper, looking on the black panes of the window where the storm appeared continually on the point of bursting in its entrance; and upon that empty field I beheld a perspective of consequences that made the hair to rise upon my scalp. The child corrupted, the home broken up, my master dead or worse than dead, my mistress plunged in desolation—all these I saw before me painted brightly on the darkness; and the outcry of the wind appeared to mock at my inaction.

THE chaise came to the door in a strong drenching mist. We took our leave in silence: the house of Durrisdeer standing with drooping gutters and windows closed, like a place dedicate to melancholy. I observed the Master kept his head out, looking back on the splashed walls and glimmering roofs, till they were suddenly swallowed in the mist; and I must suppose some natural sadness fell upon the man at this departure; or was it some prevision of the end? At least, upon our mounting the long brae from Durrisdeer, as we walked side by side in the wet, he began first to whistle and then to sing the saddest of our country tunes, which sets folk weeping in a tavern, "Wandering Willie." The set of words he used with it I have not heard elsewhere, and could never come by any copy; but some of them which were the most appropriate to our departure linger in my memory. One verse began:

> Home was home then, my dear, full of kindly faces;
> Home was home then, my dear, happy for the child.

And ended somewhat thus:

> Now, when day dawns on the brow of the moorland,
> Lone stands the house and the chimney-stone is cold.
> Lone let it stand, now the folks are all departed,
> The kind hearts, the true hearts, that loved the place of old.

I could never be a judge of the merit of these verses; they were so hallowed by the melancholy of the air, and were sung (or rather " soothed ") to me by a master singer at a time so fitting. He looked in my face when he had done, and saw that my eyes watered.

"Ah, Mackellar," said he, "do you think I have never a regret?"

155

"I do not think you could be so bad a man," said I, "if you had not all the machinery to be a good one."

"No, not all," says he: "not all. You are there in error. The malady of not wanting, my evangelist." But methought he sighed as he mounted again into the chaise.

All day long we journeyed in the same miserable weather: the mist besetting us closely, the heavens incessantly weeping on my head. The road lay over moorish hills, where was no sound but the crying of the moor-fowl in the wet heather and the pouring of the swollen burns. Sometimes I would doze off in slumber, when I would find myself plunged at once in some foul and ominous nightmare, from the which I would awaken strangling. Sometimes, if the way was steep and the wheels turning slowly, I would overhear the voices from within, talking in that tropical tongue which was to me as inarticulate as the piping of the fowls. Sometimes, at a longer ascent, the Master would set foot to ground and walk by my side, mostly without speech. And all the time, sleeping or waking, I beheld the same black perspective of approaching ruin; and the same pictures rose in my view, only they were now painted upon hill-side mist. One, I remember, stood before me with the colors of a true illusion. It showed me my lord seated at a table in a small room; his head, which was at first buried in his hands, he slowly raised, and turned upon me a countenance from which hope had fled. I saw it first on the black window panes, my last night in Durrisdeer; it haunted and returned upon me half the voyage through; and yet it was no effect of lunacy, for I have come to a ripe old age with no decay of my intelligence; nor yet (as I was then tempted to suppose) a heaven-sent warning of the future, for all manner of calamities befell, not that calamity—and I saw many pitiful sights, but never that one.

It was decided we should travel on all night; and it was singular, once the dusk had fallen, my spirits somewhat rose. The bright lamps, shining forth into the mist and on the smoking horses and the hodding post-boy, gave me perhaps an outlook intrinsically more cheerful than what day had shown; or perhaps my mind had become wearied of its melancholy. At least, I spent some waking hours, not without satisfaction in my thoughts, although wet and weary in my body; and fell at last into a natural slumber without dreams. Yet I must have been at work even in the deepest of my sleep; and at work with at least a measure of intelligence. For I started broad awake, in the very act of crying out to myself.

Home was home then, my dear, happy for the child,

stricken to find in it an appropriateness, which I had not yesterday observed, to the Master's detestable purpose in the present journey.

We were then close upon the city of Glasgow, where we were soon breakfasting together at an inn, and where (as the devil would have it) we found a ship in the very article of sailing. We took places in the cabin; and, two days after, carried our effects on board. Her name was the *Nonesuch*, a very ancient ship and very happily named. By all accounts this should be her last voyage; people shook their heads upon the quays, and I had several warnings offered me by strangers in the street, to the effect that she was rotten as a cheese, too deeply loaden, and must infallibly founder if we met a gale. From this it fell out we were the only passengers; the captain, McMurtrie, was a silent, absorbed man with the Glasgow or Gaelic accent; the mates ignorant, rough seafarers, come in through the hawsehole; and the master and I were cast upon each other's company.

The *Nonesuch* carried a fair wind out of the Clyde, and for near upon a week we enjoyed bright weather and a sense of progress. I found myself (to my wonder) a born seaman, in so far at least as I was never sick; yet I was far from tasting the usual serenity of my health. Whether it was the motion of the ship on the billows, the confinement, the salted food, or all of these together, I suffered from a blackness of spirit and a painful strain upon my temper.

157

THE MASTER OF BALLANTRAE

The nature of my errand on that ship perhaps contributed; I think it did no more: the malady (whatever it was) sprung from my environment; and if the ship were not to blame, then it was the Master. Hatred and fear are ill bedfellows; but (to my shame be it spoken) I have tasted those in other places, lain down and got up with them, and eaten and drunk with them, and yet never before, nor after, have I been so poisoned through and through, in soul and body, as I was on board the *Nonesuch*. I freely confess my enemy set me a fair example of forbearance; in our worst days displayed the most patient geniality, holding me in conversation as long as I would suffer, and when I had rebuffed his civility, stretching himself on deck to read. The book he had on board with him was Mr. Richardson's famous "Clarissa"; and among other small attentions he would read me passages aloud; nor could any elocutionist have given with greater potency the pathetic portions of that work. I would retort upon him with passages out of the Bible, which was all my library—and very fresh to me, my religious duties (I grieve to say it) being always and even to this day extremely neglected. He tasted the merits of the work like the connoisseur he was; and would sometimes take it from my hand, turn the leaves over like a man that knew his way, and give me, with his fine declamation, a Roland for my Oliver. But it was singular how little he applied his reading to himself; it passed high above his head like summer thunder: Lovelace and Clarissa, the tales of David's generosity, the psalms of his penitence, the solemn questions of the book of Job, the touching poetry of Isaiah—they were to him a source of entertainment only, like the scraping of a fiddle in a change-house. This outer sensibility and inner toughness set me against him; it seemed of a piece with that impudent grossness which I knew to underlie the veneer of his fine manners; and sometimes my gorge rose against him as though he were deformed—and sometimes I would draw away as though from something partly spectral. I had moments when I thought of him as of a man of pasteboard—as though, if one should strike smartly through the buckram of his countenance, there would be found a mere vacuity within. This horror (not merely fanciful, I think) vastly increased my detestation of his neighborhood; I began to feel something shiver within me on his drawing near; I had at times a longing to cry out; there were days when I thought I could have struck him. This frame of mind was doubtless helped by shame, because I had dropped during our last days at Durrisdeer into a certain toleration of the man; and if any one had then told me I should drop into it again, I must have laughed in his face. It is possible he remained unconscious of this extreme fever of my resentment; yet I think he was too quick; and rather that he had fallen, in a long life of idleness, into a positive need of company which obliged him to confront and tolerate my unconcealed aversion. Certain at least, that he loved the note of his own tongue, as indeed he entirely loved all the parts and properties of himself: a sort of imbecility which almost necessarily attends on wickedness. I have seen him driven, when I proved recalcitrant, to long discourses with the skipper: and this, although the man plainly testified his weariness, fiddling miserably with both hand and foot, and replying only with a grunt.

After the first week out we fell in with foul winds and heavy weather. The sea was high. The *Nonesuch*, being an old-fashioned ship and badly loaden, rolled beyond belief; so that the skipper trembled for his masts and I for my life. We made no progress on our course. An unbearable ill-humor settled on the ship; men, mates and master, girding at one another all day long. A saucy word on the one hand, and a blow on the other, made a daily incident. There were times when the whole crew refused their duty; and we of the after-guard were twice got under arms (being the first time that ever I bore weapons) in the fear of mutiny.

In the midst of our evil season sprung up a hurricane of wind; so that all supposed she must go down. I was shut in the cabin from noon of one day till sundown of the next; the Master was somewhere lashed on deck. Secundra had eaten of some drug and lay insensible; so you may say I passed these hours in an unbroken solitude. At first I was terrified beyond motion and almost beyond thought, my mind appearing to be frozen. Presently there stole in on me a ray of comfort. If the *Nonesuch* foundered, she would carry down with her into the deeps of that unsounded sea the creature whom we all so feared and hated; there would be no more Master of Ballantrae, the fish would sport among his ribs; his schemes all brought to nothing, his harmless enemies at peace. At first, I have said, it was but a ray of comfort; but it had soon grown to be broad sunshine. The thought of the man's death, of his deletion from this world which he imbittered for so many, took possession of my mind. I hugged it, I found it sweet in my belly. I conceived the ship's last plunge, the sea bursting upon all sides into the cabin, the brief mortal conflict there, all by myself, in that closed place; I numbered the horrors, I had almost said with satisfaction; I felt I could bear all and more, if the *Nonesuch* carried down with her, overtook by the same ruin, the enemy of my poor master's house. Toward noon of the second day the screaming of the wind abated; the ship lay not so perilously over; and it began to be clear to me that we were past the height of the tempest. As I hope for mercy, I was singly disappointed. In the selfishness of that vile, absorbing passion of hatred, I forgot the case of our innocent shipmates and thought but of myself and my enemy. For myself, I was already old, I had never been young, I was not formed for the world's pleasures, I had few affections; it mattered not the toss of a silver tester whether I was drowned there and then in the Atlantic, or dribbled out a few more years, to die, perhaps no less terribly, in a deserted sick-bed. Down I went upon my knees—holding on by the locker, or else I had been instantly dashed across the tossing cabin—and, lifting up my voice in the midst of that clamor of the abating hurricane, impiously prayed for my own death. " Oh, God," I cried, " I would be liker a man if I rose and struck this creature down; but thou madest me a coward from my mother's womb. Oh, Lord, thou madest me so, thou knowest my weakness, thou knowest that any face of death will set me shaking in my shoes. But lo! here is thy servant ready, his mortal weakness laid aside. Let me give my life for this creature's; take the two of them, Lord! take the two, and have mercy on the innocent!" In some such words as these, only yet more irreverent and with more sacred adjurations, I continued to pour forth my spirit; God heard me not, I must suppose in mercy; and I was still absorbed in my agony of supplication, when some one, removing the tarpaulin cover, let the light of the sunset pour into the cabin. I stumbled to my feet ashamed, and was seized with surprise to find myself totter and ache like one that had been stretched upon the rack. Secundra Dass, who had slept off the effects of his drug, stood in a corner not far off, gazing at me with wild eyes; and from the open skylight the captain thanked me for my supplications.

"It's you that saved the ship, Mr. Mackellar," says he. "There is no craft of seamanship that could have kept her floating: well may we say: 'Except the Lord the city keep, the watchman watch in vain!'"

I was abashed by the captain's error; abashed, also, by the surprise and fear with which the Indian regarded me at first, and the obsequious civilities with which he soon began to cumber me. I know now that he must have overheard and comprehended the peculiar nature of my prayers. It is certain, of course, that he at once disclosed the matter to his patron; and looking back with greater knowledge, I can now understand, what so much puzzled me at the moment, those singular and (so to speak) approving smiles with which the Master honored me. Similarly, I can understand a word that I remember to have fallen from him in conversation that same night; when, holding up his hand and smiling, "Ah, Mackellar," said he, "not every man is so great a coward as he thinks he is—nor yet so good a Christian." He did not guess how true he spoke! For the fact is, the thoughts which had come to me in the violence of the storm retained their hold upon my spirit; and the words that rose to my lips unbidden in the instancy of prayer continued to sound in my ears: With what shameful consequences, it is fitting I should honestly relate; for I could not support a part of such disloyalty as to describe the sins of others and conceal my own.

The wind fell, but the sea hove ever the higher. All night the *Nonesuch* rolled outrageously; the next day dawned, and the next, and brought no change. To cross the cabin was scarce possible; old, experienced seamen were cast down upon the deck, and one cruelly mauled in the concussion; every board and block in the old ship cried out aloud; and the great bell by the anchor-bitts continually and dolefully rang. One of these days the master and I sate alone together at the break of the poop. I should say the *Nonesuch* carried a high, raised poop. About the top of it ran considerable bulwarks, which made the ship unweatherly; and these, as they approached the front on each side, ran down in a fine, old-fashioned, carven scroll to join the bulwarks of the waist. From this disposition, which seems designed rather for ornament than use, it followed there was a discontinuance of protection: and that, besides, at the very margin of the elevated part where (in certain movements of the ship) it might be the most needful. It was here we were sitting: our feet hanging down, the master betwixt me and the side, and I holding on with both hands to the grating of the cabin skylight; for it struck me it was a dangerous position, the more so as I had continually before my eyes a measure of our evolutions in the person of the Master, which stood out in the break of the bulwarks against the sun. Now his head would be in the zenith and his shadow fall quite beyond the *Nonesuch* on the further side; and now he would swing down till he was underneath my feet, and the line of the sea leaped high above him like the ceiling of a room. I looked on upon this with a growing fascination, as birds are said to look on snakes. My mind besides was troubled with an astonishing diversity of noises; for now that we had all sails spread in the vain hope to bring her to the sea, the ship sounded like a factory with their reverberations. We spoke first of the mutiny with which we had been threatened;

this led us on to the topic of assassination; and that offered a temptation to the Master more strong than he was able to resist. He must tell me a tale, and show me at the same time how clever he was and how wicked. It was a thing he did always with affectation and display; generally with a good effect. But this tale, told in a high key in the midst of so great a tumult, and by a narrator who was one moment looking down at me from the skies and the next peering up from under the soles of my feet—this particular tale, I say, took hold upon me in a degree quite singular.

"My friend the count," it was thus that he began his story, "had for an enemy a certain German baron, a stranger in Rome. It matters not what was the ground of the count's enmity; but as he had a firm design to be revenged, and that with safety to himself, he kept it secret even from the baron. Indeed that is the first principle of vengeance; and hatred betrayed is hatred impotent. The count was a man of a curious, searching mind; he had something of the artist; if anything fall for him to do, it must always be done with an exact perfection, not only as to the result but in the very means and instruments, or he thought the thing miscarried. It chanced he was one day riding in the outer suburbs, when he came to a disused byroad branching off into the moor which lies about Rome. On the one hand was an ancient Roman tomb; on the other a deserted house in a garden of evergreen trees. This road brought him presently into a field of ruins, in the midst of which, in the side of a hill, he saw an open door and (not far off) a single stunted pine no greater than a currant bush. The place was desert and very secret: a voice spoke in the count's bosom that there was something here to his advantage. He tied his horse to the pine tree, took his flint and steel in his hand to make a light, and entered into the hill. The doorway opened on a passage of old Roman masonry, which shortly after branched in two. The count took the turning to the right, and followed it, groping forward in the dark, till he was brought up by a kind of fence about elbow-high, which extended quite across the passage. Sounding for-

163

ward with his foot, he found an edge of polished stone, and then vacancy. All his curiosity was now awakened, and, getting some rotten sticks that lay about the floor, he made a fire. In front of him was a profound well: doubtless some neighboring peasant had once used it for his water, and it was he that had set up the fence. A long while the count stood leaning on the rail and looking down into the pit. It was of Roman foundation, and, like all that nation set their hands to, built as for eternity: the sides were still straight and the joints smooth; to a man who should fall in, no escape was possible. 'Now,' the count was think-ing, 'a strong impulsion brought me to this place: what for? what have I gained? why should I be sent to gaze into this well?'—when the rail of the fence gave suddenly, under his weight, and he came within an ace of falling headlong in. Leaping back to save himself, he trod out the last flicker of his fire, which gave him thenceforward no more light, only an incommoding smoke. 'Was I sent here to my death?' says he, and shook from head to foot. And then a thought flashed in his mind. He crept forth on hands and knees to the brink of the pit and felt above him in the air. The rail had been fast to a pair of uprights; it had only broken from the one, and still depended from the other. The count set it back again as he had found it, so that the place meant death to the first comer, and groped out of the catacomb like a sick man. The next day, riding in the Corso with the baron, he purposely betrayed a strong preoccupation. The other (as he had designed) inquired into the cause; and he (after some fencing) admitted that his spirits had been dashed by an unusual dream. This was calculated to draw on the baron—a superstitious man who affected the scorn of superstition. Some rallying followed; and then the count (as if suddenly carried away) called on his friend to beware, for it was of him that he had dreamed. You know enough of human nature, my excellent Mackellar, to be certain of one thing: I mean, that the baron did not rest till he had heard the dream. The count (sure that he would never desist) kept him in play till his curiosity was highly inflamed, and then suffered himself with seeming reluctance to be overborne. ' I warn you,' says he, ' evil will come of it; something tells me so. But since there is to be no peace either for you or me except on this condition, the blame be on your own head! This was the dream. I beheld you riding, I know not where, yet I think it must have been near Rome, for on your one hand was an ancient tomb and on the other a garden of evergreen trees. Methought I cried and cried upon you to come back in a very agony of terror; whether you heard me, I know not, but you went doggedly on. The road brought you to a desert place among ruins: where was a door in a hillside, and hard by the door a misbegotten pine. Here you dismounted (I still crying on you to beware), tied your horse to the pine tree, and entered resolutely in by the door. Within it was dark; but in my dream I could still see you, and still besought you to hold back. You felt your way along the right-hand wall, took a branching passage to the right, and came to a little chamber, where was a well with a railing. At this (I know not why) my alarm for you increased a thousand-fold, so that I seemed to scream myself hoarse with warnings, crying it was still time and bidding you begone at once from that vestibule. Such was the word I used in my dream, and it seemed then to have a clear significancy; but to-day and awake, I profess I know not what it means. To all my outcry you rendered not the least attention, leaning the while upon the rail and looking down intently in the water. And then there was made to you a communication, I do not think I even gathered what it was, but the fear of it plucked me clean out of my slumber, and I awoke shaking and sobbing. And now,' continues the count, ' I thank you from my heart for your insistency. This dream lay on me like a load; and now I have told it in plain words and in the broad daylight, it seems no great matter.' ' I do not know,' says the baron. ' It is in some points strange. A communication, did you say? Oh, it is an odd dream. It will make a story to amuse our friends.' ' I am not so sure,' says the count. ' I am sensible of some reluctancy. Let us rather

THE MASTER OF BALLANTRAE

forget it.' 'By all means,' says the baron. And (in fact) the dream was not again referred to. Some days after the count proposed a ride in the fields, which the baron (since they were daily growing faster friends) very readily accepted. On the way back to Rome the count led them insensibly by a particular route. Presently he reined in his horse, clapped his hand before his eyes, and cried out aloud. Then he showed his face again (which was now quite white, for he was a consummate actor) and stared upon the baron. 'What ails you?' cries the baron. 'What is wrong with you?' 'Nothing,' cries the count. 'It is nothing. A seizure, I know not what. Let us hurry back to Rome.' But in the meanwhile the baron had looked about him; and there, on the left-hand side of the way as they went back to Rome, he saw a dusty by-road with a tomb upon the one hand and a garden of evergreen trees upon the other. 'Yes,' says he, with a changed voice. 'Let us by all means hurry back to Rome. I fear you are not well in health.' 'Oh, for God's sake!' cries the count, shuddering. 'Back to Rome and let me get to bed.' They made their return with scarce a word; and the count, who should by rights have gone into society, took to his bed and gave out he had a touch of country fever. The next day the baron's horse was found tied to the pine, but himself was never heard of from that hour. And now, was that a murder?" says the Master, breaking sharply off.

"Are you sure he was a count?" I asked.

"I am not certain of the title," said he, "but he was a gentleman of family, and the Lord deliver you, Mackellar, from an enemy so subtle!"

These last words he spoke down at me smiling, from high above; the next he was under my feet. I continued to follow his evolutions with a childish fixity; they made me giddy and vacant, and I spoke as in a dream.

"He hated the baron with a great hatred?" I asked.

"His belly moved when the man came near him," said the Master.

"I have felt that same," said I.

" Verily! " cried the Master. " Here is news indeed! I wonder—do I flatter myself? or am I the cause of these ventral perturbations? "

He was quite capable of choosing out a graceful posture, even with no one to behold him but myself, and all the more if there were any element of peril. He sat now with one knee flung across the other, his arms on his bosom, fitting the swing of the ship with an exquisite balance, such as a feather-weight might overthrow. All at once I had the vision of my lord at the table with his head upon his hands; only now, when he showed me his countenance, it was heavy with reproach. The words of my own prayer—*I were liker a man if I struck this creature down*—shot at the same time into my memory, I called my energies together, and (the ship then heeling downward toward my enemy) thrust at him swiftly with my foot. It was written I should have the guilt of this attempt without the profit. Whether from my own uncertainty or his incredible quickness, he escaped the thrust, leaping to his feet and catching hold at the same moment of a stay.

I do not know how long a time passed by: I lying where I was upon the deck, overcome with terror and remorse and shame: he standing with the stay in his hand, backed against the bulwarks, and regarding me with an expression singularly mingled. At last he spoke.

" Mackellar," said he, " I make no reproaches, but I offer you a bargain. On your side, I do not suppose you desire to have this exploit made public; on mine, I own to you freely, I do not care to draw my breath in a perpetual terror of assassination by the man I sit at meat with. Promise me—but no," says he, breaking off, " you are not yet in the quiet possession of your mind; you might think I had extorted the promise from your weakness; and I would leave no door open for casuistry to come in—that dishonesty of the conscientious. Take time to meditate."

With that he made off up the sliding deck like a squirrel and plunged into the cabin. About half an hour later he returned: I still lying as he had left me.

167

" Now," says he, " will you give me your troth as a Christian and a faithful servant of my brother's that I shall have no more to fear from your attempts? "

" I give it you," said I.

" I shall require your hand upon it," says he.

" You have the right to make conditions," I replied, and we shook hands.

He sat down at once in the same place and the old perilous attitude.

" Hold on! " cried I, covering my eyes. " I cannot bear to see you in that posture. The least irregularity of the sea might plunge you overboard."

" You are highly inconsistent," he replied, smiling, but doing as I asked. " For all that, Mackellar, I would have you to know you have risen forty feet in my esteem. You think I cannot set a price upon fidelity? But why do you suppose I carry that Secundra Dass about the world with me? Because he would die or do murder for me to-morrow; and I love him for it. Well, you may think it odd, but I like you the better for this afternoon's performance. I thought you were magnetized with the Ten Commandments; but no—God damn my soul! " he cries, " the old wife has blood in his body after all! which does not change the fact," he continued, smiling again, " that you have done well to give your promise; for I doubt if you would ever shine in your new trade."

" I suppose," said I, " I should ask your pardon and God's for my attempt. At any rate I have passed my word, which I will keep faithfully. But when I think of those you persecute—" I paused.

" Life is a singular thing," said he, " and mankind a very singular people. You suppose yourself to love my brother. I assure you it is merely custom. Interrogate your memory; and when first you came to Durrisdeer, you will find you considered him a dull, ordinary youth. He is as dull and ordinary now, though not so young. Had you instead fallen in with me, you would to-day be as strong upon my side."

" I would never say you were ordinary, Mr. Bally," I

returned; "but here you prove yourself dull. You have just shown your reliance on my word. In other terms, that is my conscience—the same which starts instinctively back from you, like the eye from a strong light."

"Ah!" says he, "but I mean otherwise. I mean, had I met you in my youth. You are to consider I was not always as I am to-day; nor (had I met in with a friend of your description) should I have ever been so."

"Hut, Mr. Bally," says I, "you would have made a mock of me; you would never have spent ten civil words on such a squaretoes."

But he was now fairly started on his new course of justification, with which he wearied me throughout the remainder of the passage. No doubt in the past he had taken pleasure to paint himself unnecessarily black, and made a vaunt of his wickedness, bearing it for a coat of arms. Nor was he so illogical as to abate one item of his old confessions. " But now that I know you are a human being," he would say, " I can take the trouble to explain myself. For I assure you I am human too, and have my virtues like my neighbors." I say he wearied me, for I had only the one word to say in answer: twenty times I must have said it: " Give up your present purpose and return with me to Durrisdeer; then I will believe you."

Thereupon he would shake his head at me. " Ah, Mackellar, you might live a thousand years and never understand my nature," he would say. " This battle is now committed, the hour of reflection quite past, the hour for mercy not yet come. It began between us when we span a coin in the hall of Durrisdeer now twenty years ago; we have had our ups and downs, but never either of us dreamed of giving in, and as for me, when my glove is cast life and honor go with it."

" A fig for your honor!" I would say. " And by your leave, these warlike similitudes are something too high-sounding for the matter in hand. You want some dirty money, there is the bottom of your contention, and as for your means, what are they?—to stir up sorrow in a family that

never harmed you, to debauch (if you can) your own born
nephew and to wring the heart of your born brother! A
foot-pad that kills an old granny in a woolen mutch with a
dirty bludgeon, and that for a shilling-piece and a paper
of snuff—there is all the warrior that you are."

When I would attack him thus (or somewhat thus) he
would smile and sigh like a man misunderstood. Once I remember, he defended himself more at large and had some
curious sophistries, worth repeating for a light upon his
character.

"You are very like a civilian to think war consists in
drums and banners," said he. "War (as the ancients said
very wisely) is *ultima ratio*. When we take our advantage
unrelentingly, then we make war. Ah, Mackellar, you are a
devil of a soldier in the steward's room at Durrisdeer, or the
tenants do you sad injustice!"

"I think little of what war is or is not," I replied. "But
you weary me with claiming my respect. Your brother is
a good man, and you are a bad one—neither more nor less."

"Had I been Alexander——" he began.

"It is so we all dupe ourselves," I cried. "Had I been
St. Paul, it would have been all one; I would have made the
same hash of that career that you now see me making of
my own."

"I tell you," he cried, bearing down my interruption,
"had I been the least petty chieftain in the highlands, had
I been the least king of naked negroes in the African desert,
my people would have adored me. A bad man, am I? Ah,
but I was born for a good tyrant! Ask Secundra Dass;
he will tell you I treat him like a son. Cast in your lot
with me to-morrow, become my slave, my chattel, a thing
I can command as I command the powers of my own limbs
and spirit—you will see no more that dark side that I turn
upon the world in anger. I must have all or none. But
where all is given, I give it back with usury. I have a
kingly nature: there is my loss!"

"It has been hitherto rather the loss of others," I remarked; "which seems a little on the hither side of royalty."

" Tilly vally! " cried he. " Even now, I tell you I would spare that family in which you take so great an interest: yes, even now—to-morrow I would leave them to their petty welfare, and disappear in that forest of cutthroats and thimbleriggers that we call the world. I would do it to-morrow!" says he. " Only—only——"

" Only what? " I asked.

" Only they must beg it on their bended knees. I think in public too," he added, smiling. " Indeed, Mackellar, I doubt if there be a hall big enough to serve my purpose for that act of reparation."

" Vanity, vanity! " I moralized. " To think that this great force for evil should be swayed by the same sentiment that sets a lassie mincing to her glass! "

" Oh, there are double words for everything; the word that swells, the word that belittles; you cannot fight me with a word! " said he. " You said the other day that I relied on your conscience: were I in your humor of detraction, I might say I build upon your vanity. It is your pretension to be *un homme de parole;* 'tis mine not to accept defeat. Call it vanity, call it virtue, call it greatness of soul—what signifies the expression? But recognize in each of us a common strain; that we both live for an idea."

It will be gathered from so much familiar talk, and so much patience on both sides, that we now lived together upon excellent terms. Such was again the fact, and this time more seriously than before. Apart from disputations such as that which I have tried to reproduce, not only consideration reigned, but I am tempted to say even kindness. When I fell sick (as I did shortly after our great storm) he sat by my berth to entertain me with his conversation, and treated me with excellent remedies, which I accepted with security. Himself commented on the circumstance. " You see," says he, " you begin to know me better. A very little while ago, upon this lonely ship, where no one but myself has any smattering of science, you would have made sure I had designs upon your life. And observe, it is since I found you had designs upon my own that I have shown you most respect. You will tell me if this speaks of a small mind." I found little to reply. In so far as regarded myself, I believed him to mean well; I am perhaps the more a dupe of his dissimulation, but I believed (and I still believe) that he regarded me with genuine kindness. Singular and sad fact! so soon as this change began, my animosity abated, and these haunting visions of my master passed utterly away. So that, perhaps, there was truth in the man's last vaunting word to me, uttered on the second day of July, when our long voyage was at last brought almost to an end, and we lay becalmed at the sea end of the vast harbor of New York in a gasping heat which was presently exchanged for a surprising water-fall of rain. I stood on the poop regarding the green shores near at hand, and now and then the light smoke of the little town, our destination. And as I was even then devising how to steal a march on my familiar enemy, I was conscious of a shade of embarrassment when he approached me with his hand extended.

"I am now to bid you farewell," said he, "and that forever. For now you go among my enemies, where all your former prejudices will revive. I never yet failed to charm a person when I wanted; even you, my good friend—to call you so for once—even you have now a very different portrait of me in your memory, and one that you will never quite forget. The voyage has not lasted long enough, or I should have wrote the impression deeper. But now all is at an end, and we are again at war. Judge by this little interlude how dangerous I am; and tell those fools "—pointing with his finger to the town—" to think twice and thrice before they set me at defiance."

I HAVE mentioned I was resolved to steal a march upon the Master; and this, with the complicity of Captain Mc-Murtrie, was mighty easily effected; a boat being partly loaded on the one side of our ship and the master placed on board of it, the while a skiff put off from the other carrying me alone. I had no more trouble in finding a direction to my lord's house, whither I went at top speed, and which I found to be on the outskirts of the place, a very suitable mansion, in a fine garden, with an extraordinary large barn, byre, and stable all in one. It was here my lord was walking when I arrived; indeed it had become his chief place of frequentation, and his mind was now filled with farming. I burst in upon him breathless, and gave him my news; which was indeed no news at all, several ships having outsailed the *Nonesuch* in the interval.

" We have been expecting you long," said my lord; " and indeed, of late days, ceased to expect you any more. I am glad to take your hand again, Mackellar. I thought you had been at the bottom of the sea."

" Ah, my lord, would God I had!" cried I. " Things would have been better for yourself."

" Not in the least," says he grimly. " I could not ask better. There is a long score to pay, and now—at last—I can begin to pay it."

I cried out against his security.

" Oh," says he, " this is not Durrisdeer, and I have taken my precautions. His reputation awaits him, I have prepared a welcome for my brother. Indeed, fortune has served me; for I found here a merchant of Albany who knew him after the '45 and had mighty convenient suspicions of a murder; some one of the name of Chew it was, another Albanian. No one here will be surprised if I deny him my door; he will not be suffered to address my children, nor even to salute my wife;

173

as for myself, I make so much exception for a brother that he may speak to me. I should lose my pleasure else," says my lord, rubbing his palms.

Presently he bethought himself, and set men off running with billets, to summon the magnates of the province. I cannot recall what pretext he employed; at least it was successful; and when our ancient enemy appeared upon the scene he found my lord pacing in front of his house under some trees of shade, with the governor upon one hand and various notables upon the other. My lady, who was seated in the veranda, rose with a very pinched expression and carried her children into the house.

The Master, well dressed and with an elegant walking-sword, bowed to the company in a handsome manner and nodded to my lord with familiarity. My lord did not accept the salutation, but looked upon his brother with bended brows.

"Well, sir," says he, at last, "what ill wind brings you hither of all places, where (to our common disgrace) your reputation has preceded you?"

"Your lordship is pleased to be civil," cries the Master with a fine start.

"I am pleased to be very plain," returned my lord; "because it is needful you should clearly understand your situation. At home, where you were so little known, it was still possible to keep appearances; that would be quite vain in this province; and I have to tell you that I am quite resolved to wash my hands of you. You have already ruined me almost to the door, as you ruined my father before me; whose heart you also broke. Your crimes escape the law; but my friend the governor has promised protection to my family. Have a care, sir!" cries my lord, shaking his cane at him: "if you are observed to utter two words to any of my innocent household, the law shall be stretched to make you smart for it."

"Ah!" says the Master, very slowly. "And so this is the advantage of a foreign land! These gentlemen are unacquainted with our story, I perceive. They do not know that I am the Lord Durrisdeer; they do not know you are my younger brother, sitting in my place under a sworn family compact; they do not know (or they would not be seen with you in familiar correspondence) that every acre is mine before God Almighty—and every doit of the money you withhold from me, you do it as a thief, a perjurer, and a disloyal brother!"

"General Clinton," I cried, "do not listen to his lies. I am the steward of the estate, and there is not one word of truth in it. The man is a forfeited rebel turned into a hired spy; there is his story in two words."

It was thus that (in the heat of the moment) I let slip his infamy.

"Fellow," said the governor, turning his face sternly on the Master, "I know more of you than you think for. We have some broken ends of your adventures in the provinces, which you will do very well not to drive me to investigate. There is the disappearance of Mr. Jacob Chew with all his merchandise; there is the matter of where you came ashore from with so much money and jewels, when you were picked up by a Bermudan out of Albany. Believe me, if I let these matters lie it is in commiseration for your family and out of respect for my valued friend, Lord Durrisdeer."

There was a murmur of applause from the provincials.

"I should have remembered how a title would shine out in such a hole as this," says the Master, white as a sheet; "no matter how unjustly come by. It remains for me then to die at my lord's door, where my dead body will form a very cheerful ornament."

"Away with your affectations!" cried my lord. "You know very well I have no such meaning; only to protect myself from calumny and my home from your intrusion. I offer you a choice. Either I shall pay your passage home on the first ship, when you may perhaps be able to resume your occupations under government, although God knows I would rather see you on the highway! Or, if that likes you not, stay here and welcome! I have inquired the least sum on which body and soul can be decently kept together in New York; so much you shall have, paid weekly; and if you cannot labor with your hands to better it, high time you should

betake yourself to learn! The condition is, that you speak
with no member of my family except myself," he added.

I do not think I have ever seen any man so pale as was
the Master; but he was erect and his mouth firm.

"I have been met here with some very unmerited insults,"
said he, "from which I have certainly no idea to take refuge
by flight. Give me your pittance; I take it without shame,
for it is mine already—like the shirt upon your back; and
I choose to stay until these gentlemen shall understand me
better. Already they must spy the cloven hoof; since with
all your pretended eagerness for the family honor, you
take a pleasure to degrade it in my person."

"This is all very fine," says my lord; "but to us who
know you of old, you must be sure it signifies nothing.
You take that alternative out of which you think that you
can make the most. Take it, if you can, in silence; it will
serve you better in the long run, you may believe me, than
this ostentation of ingratitude."

"Oh, gratitude, my lord!" cries the Master, with a
mounting intonation and his forefinger very conspicuously
lifted up. "Be at rest; it will not fail you. It now remains
that I should salute these gentlemen whom we have wearied
with our family affairs."

And he bowed to each in succession, settled his walking-
sword, and took himself off, leaving every one amazed at
his behavior, and me not less so at my lord's.

We were now to enter on a changed phase of this family
division. The Master was by no manner of means so helpless as my lord supposed, having at his hand and entirely
devoted to his service an excellent artist in all sorts of goldsmith work. With my lord's allowance, which was not so
scanty as he had described it, the pair could support life;
and all the earnings of Secundra Dass might be laid upon one
side for any future purpose. That this was done, I have no
doubt. It was in all likelihood the Master's design to gather
a sufficiency, and then proceed in quest of that treasure
which he had buried long before among the mountains; to

which, if he had confined himself, he would have been more happily inspired. But unfortunately for himself and all of us, he took counsel of his anger. The public disgrace of his arrival (which I sometimes wonder he could manage to survive) rankled in his bones; he was in that humor when a man (in the words of the old adage) will cut off his nose to spite his face; and he must make himself a public spectacle, in the hopes that some of the disgrace might spatter on my lord.

He chose, in a poor quarter of the town, a lonely small house of boards, overhung with some acacias. It was furnished in front with a sort of hutch opening, like that of a dog's kennel, but about as high as a table from the ground, in which the poor man that built it had formerly displayed some wares; and it was this which took the master's fancy and possibly suggested his proceedings. It appears, on board the pirate ship, he had acquired some quickness with the needle; enough at least to play the part of tailor in the public eye; which was all that was required by the nature of his vengeance. A placard was hung above the hutch, bearing these words in something of the following disposition:

JAMES DURIE

FORMERLY MASTER OF BALLANTRAE

CLOTHES NEATLY CLOUTED.

———

SECUNDRA DASS

DECAYED GENTLEMAN OF INDIA

FINE GOLDSMITH WORK.

Underneath this, when he had a job, my gentleman sat withinside tailor-wise and busily stitching. I say, when he had a job; but such customers as came were rather for Secundra, and the master's sewing would be more in the manner of Penelope's. He could never have designed to gain even butter to his bread by such a means of livelihood; enough for him that there was the name of Durie dragged in the dirt on the placard, and the sometime heir of that proud family set up cross-legged in public for a reproach upon his brother's meanness. And in so far his device succeeded, that there was murmuring in the town and a party formed highly inimical to my lord. My lord's favor with the governor laid him more open on the other side; my lady (who was never so well received in the colony) met with painful innuendoes; in a party of women where it would be the topic most natural to introduce, she was almost debarred from the naming of needlework; and I have seen her return with a flushed countenance and vow that she would go abroad no more.

In the meanwhile, my lord dwelt in his decent mansion, immersed in farming; a popular man with his intimates, and careless or unconscious of the rest. He laid on flesh; had a bright, busy face; even the heat seemed to prosper with him; and my lady (in despite of her own annoyances) daily blessed Heaven her father should have left her such a paradise. She had looked on from a window upon the Master's humiliation; and from that hour appeared to feel at ease. I was not so sure myself; as time went on there seemed to me a something not quite wholesome in my lord's condition; happy he was, beyond a doubt, but the grounds of this felicity were secret; even in the bosom of his family he brooded with manifest delight upon some private thought; and I conceived at last the suspicion (quite unworthy of us both) that he kept a mistress somewhere in the town. Yet he went little abroad, and his day was very fully occupied; indeed there was but a single period, and that pretty early in the morning while Mr. Alexander was at his lesson-book, of which I was not certain of the disposition. It should be borne in mind, in the defense of that which I now did, that I was always in some fear my lord was not quite justly in his reason; and with our enemy sitting so still in the same town with us, I did well to be upon my guard. Accordingly

THE MASTER OF BALLANTRAE

I made a pretext, had the hour changed at which I taught Mr. Alexander the foundation of ciphering and the mathematic, and set myself instead to dog my master's footsteps.

Every morning, fair or foul, he took his gold-headed cane, set his hat on the back of his head—a recent habitude, which I thought to indicate a burning brow—and betook himself to make a certain circuit. At the first his way was among pleasant trees and beside a graveyard, where he would sit awhile, if the day were fine, in meditation. Presently the path turned down to the water-side and came back along the harbor front and past the master's booth. As he approached this second part of his circuit my Lord Durrisdeer began to pace more leisurely, like a man delighted with the air and scene; and before the booth, halfway between that and the water's edge, would pause a little, leaning on his staff. It was the hour when the Master sate within upon his board and plied his needle. So these two brothers would gaze upon each other with hard faces; and then my lord move on again, smiling to himself.

It was but twice that I must stoop to that ungrateful necessity of playing spy. I was then certain of my lord's purpose in his rambles and of the secret source of his delight. Here was his mistress; it was hatred and not love that gave him healthful colors. Some moralists might have been relieved by the discovery, I confess that I was dismayed. I found this situation of two brethren not only odious in itself, but big with possibilities of further evil; and I made it my practice, in so far as many occupations would allow, to go by a shorter path and be secretly present at their meeting. Coming down one day a little late, after I had been near a week prevented, I was struck with surprise to find a new development. I should say there was a bench against the Master's house, where customers might sit to parley with the shopman; and here I found my lord seated, nursing his cane and looking pleasantly forth upon the day. Not three feet from him sat the master stitching. Neither spoke; nor (in this new situation) did my lord so much as

179

cast a glance upon his enemy. He tasted his neighborhood, I must suppose, less indirectly in the bare proximity of person; and, without doubt, drank deep of hateful pleasures.

He had no sooner come away than I openly joined him.

" My lord, my lord," said I, " this is no manner of behavior."

" I grow fat upon it," he replied; and not merely the words, which were strange enough, but the whole character of his expression shocked me.

" I warn you, my lord, against this indulgency of evil feeling," said I. " I know not to which it is more perilous, the soul or the reason: but you go the way to murder both."

" You cannot understand," said he. " You had never such mountains of bitterness upon your heart."

" And if it were no more," I added, " you will surely goad the man to some extremity."

" To the contrary: I am breaking his spirit," says my lord.

Every morning for hard upon a week my lord took his same place upon the bench. It was a pleasant place, under the green acacias, with a sight upon the bay and shipping, and a sound (from some way off) of mariners singing at their employ. Here the two sate without speech or any external movement beyond that of the needle or the Master biting off a thread, for he still clung to his pretense of industry; and here I made a point to join them, wondering at myself and my companions. If any of my lord's friends went by, he would hail them cheerfully, and cry out he was there to give some good advice to his brother, who was now (to his delight) grown quite industrious. And even this the Master accepted with a steady countenance; what was in his mind, God knows, or perhaps Satan only.

All of a sudden, on a still day of what they call the Indian summer, when the woods were changed into gold and pink and scarlet, the Master laid down his needle and burst into a fit of merriment. I think he must have been preparing it a long while in silence, for the note in itself was pretty naturally pitched; but breaking suddenly from so extreme a silence and in circumstances so averse from mirth, it sounded ominously to my ear.

"Henry," said he, "I have for once made a false step, and for once you have had the wit to profit by it. The farce of the cobbler ends to-day; and I confess to you (with my compliments) that you have had the best of it. Blood will out; and you have certainly a choice idea of how to make yourself unpleasant."

Never a word said my lord; it was just as though the Master had not broken silence.

"Come," resumed the Master, "do not be sulky, it will spoil your attitude. You can now afford (believe me) to be a little gracious; for I have not merely a defeat to accept. I had meant to continue this performance till I had gathered enough money for a certain purpose; I confess ingenuously I have not the courage. You naturally desire my absence from this town; I have come round by another way to the same idea. And I have a proposition to make; or if your lordship prefers, a favor to ask."

"Ask it," says my lord.

"You may have heard that I had once in this country a considerable treasure," returned the master: "it matters not whether or no—such is the fact; and I was obliged to bury it in a spot of which I have sufficient indications. To the recovery of this, has my ambition now come down; and as it is my own you will not grudge it me."

"Go and get it," says my lord. "I make no opposition."

"Yes," said the Master, "but to do so I must find men and carriage. The way is long and rough, and the country infested with wild Indians. Advance me only so much as shall be needful: either as a lump sum, in lieu of my allowance, or if you prefer it as a loan, which I shall repay on my return. And then, if you so decide, you may have seen the last of me."

My lord stared him steadily in the eyes; there was a hard smile upon his face, but he uttered nothing.

"Henry," said the Master, with a formidable quietness, and drawing at the same time somewhat back—"Henry, I had the honor to address you."

"Let us be stepping homeward," says my lord to me, who was plucking at his sleeve; and with that he rose, stretched himself, settled his hat, and still without a syllable of response, began to walk steadily along the shore.

I hesitated awhile between the two brothers, so serious a climax did we seem to have reached. But the Master had resumed his occupation, his eyes lowered, his hand seemingly as deft as ever; and I decided to pursue my lord.

"Are you mad?" I cried, so soon as I had overtook him. "Would you cast away so fair an opportunity?"

"Is it possible you should still believe in him?" inquired my lord, almost with a sneer.

"I wish him forth of this town," I cried. "I wish him anywhere and anyhow but as he is."

"I have said my say," returned my lord, "and you have said yours. There let it rest."

But I was bent on dislodging the Master. That sight of him patiently returning to his needlework was more than my imagination could digest. There was never a man made, and the master the least of any, that could accept so long a series of insults. The air smelled blood to me. And I vowed there should be no neglect of mine if, through any chink of possibility, crime could be yet turned aside. That same day, therefore, I came to my lord in his business room, where he sat upon some trivial occupation.

"My lord," said I, "I have found a suitable investment for my small economies. But these are unhappily in Scotland; it will take some time to lift them, and the affair presses. Could your lordship see his way to advance me the amount against my note?"

He read me awhile with keen eyes. "I have never inquired into the state of your affairs, Mackellar," says he. "Beyond the amount of your caution, you may not be worth a farthing, for what I know."

"I have been a long while in your service, and never told

a lie, nor yet asked a favor for myself," said I, "until to-day."

"A favor for the Master," he returned quietly. "Do you take me for a fool, Mackellar? Understand it once and for all; I treat this beast in my own way; fear nor favor shall not move me; and before I am hoodwinked, it will require a trickster less transparent than yourself. I ask service, loyal service; not that you should make and mar behind my back, and steal my own money to defeat me."

"My lord," said I, "these are very unpardonable expressions."

"Think once more, Mackellar," he replied; "and you will see they fit the fact. It is your own subterfuge that is unpardonable. Deny (if you can) that you designed this money to evade my orders with, and I will ask your pardon freely. If you cannot, you must have the resolution to hear your conduct go by its own name."

"If you think I had any design but to save you—" I began.

"Oh, my old friend," said he, "you know very well what I think! Here is my hand to you with all my heart; but of money, not one rap."

Defeated upon this side, I went straight to my room, wrote a letter, ran with it to the harbor, for I knew a ship was on the point of sailing; and came to the Master's door a little before dusk. Entering without the form of any knock, I found him sitting with his Indian at a simple meal of maize porridge with some milk. The house within was clean and poor; only a few books upon a shelf distinguished it, and (in one corner) Secundra's little bench.

"Mr. Bally," said I, "I have near five hundred pounds laid by in Scotland, the economies of a hard life. A letter goes by yon ship to have it lifted; have so much patience till the return ship comes in, and it is all yours, upon the same condition you offered to my lord this morning."

He rose from the table, came forward, took me by the shoulders, and looked me in the face, smiling.

"And yet you are very fond of money!" said he. "And

yet you love money beyond all things else, except my brother!"

"I fear old age and poverty," said I, "which is another matter."

"I will never quarrel for a name. Call it so!" he replied. "Ah, Mackellar, Mackellar, if this were done from any love to me, how gladly would I close upon your offer!"

"And yet," I eagerly answered, "I say it to my shame, but I cannot see you in this poor place without compunction. It is not my single thought, nor my first; and yet it's there! I would gladly see you delivered. I do not offer it in love, and far from that; but as God judges me—and I wonder at it too!—quite without enmity."

"Ah," says he, still holding my shoulders and now gently shaking me, "you think of me more than you suppose. 'And I wonder at it too,'" he added, repeating my expression and I suppose something of my voice. "You are an honest man, and for that cause I spare you."

"Spare me?" I cried.

"Spare you," he repeated, letting me go and turning away. And then fronting me once more: "You little know what I would do with it, Mackellar! Did you think I had swallowed my defeat indeed? Listen: my life has been a series of unmerited cast-backs. That fool, Prince Charlie, mismanaged a most promising affair: there fell my first fortune. In Paris I had my foot once more high upon the ladder: that time it was an accident, a letter came to the wrong hand, and I was bare again. A third time I found my opportunity; I built up a place for myself in India with an infinite patience; and then Clive came, my rajah was swallowed up, and I escaped out of the convulsion, like another Æneas, with Secundra Dass upon my back. Three times I have had my hand upon the highest station; and I am not yet three-and-forty. I know the world as few men know it when they come to die, court and camp, the east and the west; I know where to go. I see a thousand openings. I am now at the height of my resources, sound of health, of inordinate ambition. Well, all this I resign; I care not if I die and the world never hear of me; I care only for one thing, and that I will have. Mind yourself: lest, when the roof falls, you too should be crushed under the ruins."

As I came out of his house, all hope of intervention quite destroyed, I was aware of a stir on the harbor side, and, raising my eyes, there was a great ship newly come to anchor. It seems strange I could have looked upon her with so much indifference, for she brought death to the brothers of Durrisdeer. After all the desperate episodes of this contention, the insults, the opposing interests, the fraternal duel in the shrubbery, it was reserved for some poor devil in Grub Street, scribbling for his dinner and not caring what he scribbled, to cast a spell across four thousand miles of the salt sea, and send forth both these brothers into savage and wintery deserts, there to die. But such a thought was distant from my mind; and while all the provincials were fluttered about me by the unusual animation of their port, I passed throughout their midst on my return homeward, quite absorbed in the recollection of my visit and the master's speech.

The same night there was brought to us from the ship a little packet of pamphlets. The next day my lord was under engagement to go with the governor upon some party of pleasure; the time was nearly due, and I left him for a moment alone in his room and skimming through the pamphlets. When I returned his head had fallen upon the table, his arms lying abroad among the crumpled papers.

" My lord, my lord! " I cried as I ran forward, for I supposed he was in some fit.

He sprung up like a figure upon wires, his countenance deformed with fury, so that in a strange place I should scarce have known him. His hand at the same time flew above his head as though to strike me down. " Leave me alone! " he screeched; and I fled, as fast as my shaking legs would bear me, for my lady. She too lost no time; but when we returned he had the door locked within, and only cried to us from the other side to leave him be. We looked in each other's faces, very white: each supposing the blow had come at last.

"I will write to the governor to excuse him," says she. "We must keep our strong friends." But when she took up the pen it flew out of her fingers. "I cannot write," said she. "Can you?"

"I will make a shift, my lady," said I.

She looked over me as I wrote. "That will do," she said, when I had done. "Thank God, Mackellar, I have you to lean upon! But what can it be now? what, what can it be?"

In my own mind, I believed there was no explanation possible and none required: it was my fear that the man's madness had now simply burst forth its way, like the long-smothered flames of a volcano; but to this (in mere mercy to my lady) I durst not give expression.

"It is more to the purpose to consider our own behavior," said I. "Must we leave him there alone?"

"I do not dare disturb him," she replied. "Nature may know best; it may be nature that cries to be alone; and we grope in the dark. Oh, yes, I would leave him as he is."

"I will then dispatch this letter, my lady, and return here, if you please, to sit with you," said I.

"Pray do," cries my lady.

All afternoon we sat together, mostly in silence, watching my lord's door. My own mind was busy with the scene that had just passed, and its singular resemblance to my vision. I must say a word upon this, for the story has gone abroad with great exaggeration, and I have even seen it printed and my own name referred to for particulars. So much was the same: here was my lord in a room, with his head upon the table, and when he raised his face it wore such an expression as distressed me to the soul. But the room was different, my lord's attitude at the table not at all the same, and his face, when he disclosed it, expressed a painful degree of fury instead of that haunting despair which had always (except once, already referred to) characterized it in the vision. There is the whole truth at last before the public; and if the differences be great, the coincidence was

yet enough to fill me with uneasiness. All afternoon, as I
say, I sat and pondered upon this quite to myself; for my
lady had trouble of her own, and it was my last thought to
vex her with fancies. About the midst of our time of waiting she conceived an ingenious scheme, had Mr. Alexander
fetched and bade him knock at his father's door. My lord
sent the boy about his business, but without the least violence
whether of manner or expression; so that I began to entertain a hope the fit was over.

At last, as the night fell and I was lighting a lamp
that stood there trimmed, the door opened and my lord
stood within upon the threshold. The light was not so
strong that we could read his countenance; when he spoke
methought his voice a little altered but yet perfectly steady.

"Mackellar," said he, "carry this note to its destination
with your own hand. It is highly private. Find the person
alone when you deliver it."

"Henry," says my lady, "you are not ill?"

"No, no," says he querulously, "I am occupied. Not at
all; I am only occupied. It is a singular thing a man must
be supposed to be ill when he has any business! Send me
supper to this room, and a basket of wine: I expect the visit
of a friend. Otherwise I am not to be disturbed."

And with that he once more shut himself in.

The note was addressed to one Captain Harris, at a tavern
on the port-side. I knew Harris (by reputation) for a
dangerous adventurer, highly suspected of piracy in the
past, and now following the rude business of an Indian
trader. What my lord should have to say to him, or he to
my lord, it passed my imagination to conceive: or yet how
my lord had heard of him, unless by a disgraceful trial from
which the man was recently escaped. Altogether I went upon
the errand with reluctance, and from the little I saw of the
captain, returned from it with sorrow. I found him in a
foul-smelling chamber, sitting by a guttering candle and an
empty bottle; he had the remains of a military carriage,
or rather perhaps it was an affectation, for his manners
were low.

" Tell my lord, with my service, that I will wait upon his lordship in the inside of half an hour," says he, when he had read the note; and then had the servility, pointing to his empty bottle, to propose that I should buy him liquor.

Although I returned with my best speed, the captain followed close upon my heels, and he stayed late into the night. The cock was crowing a second time when I saw (from my chamber window) my lord lighting him to the gate, both men very much affected with their potations and sometimes leaning one upon the other to confabulate. Yet the next morning my lord was abroad again early with a hundred pounds of money in his pocket. I never supposed that he returned with it; and yet I was quite sure it did not find its way to the Master, for I lingered all morning within view of the booth.

That was the last time my Lord Durrisdeer passed his own inclosure till we left New York; he walked in his barn or sat and talked with his family, all much as usual; but the town saw nothing of him, and his daily visits to the master seemed forgotten. Nor yet did Harris reappear; or not until the end.

I was now much oppressed with a sense of the mysteries in which we had begun to move. It was plain, if only from his change of habitude, my lord had something on his mind of a grave nature; but what it was, whence it sprung, or why he should now keep the house and garden, I could make no guess at. It was clear, even to probation, the pamphlets had some share in this revolution; I read all I could find, and they were all extremely insignificant and of the usual kind of party scurrility; even to a high politician, I could spy out no particular matter of offense, and my lord was a man rather indifferent on public questions. The truth is, the pamphlet which was the spring of this affair, lay all the time on my lord's bosom. There it was that I found it at last, after he was dead, in the midst of the north wilderness; in such a place, in such dismal circumstances, I was to read for the first time these idle, lying words of a whig pamphleteer declaiming against indulgency to Jacobites: " Another notorious rebel, the *M——r* of *B——e*, is to have his title restored," the passage ran. "This business has been long in hand, since he rendered some very disgraceful services in Scotland and France. His brother, *L——d D——r*, is known to be no better than himself in inclination; and the supposed heir, who is now to be set aside, was bred up in the most detestable principles. In the old phrase, it is *six of the one and half a dozen of the other*, but the favor of such a reposition is too extreme to be passed over." A man in his right wits could not have cared two straws for a tale so manifestly false; that government should ever entertain the notion, was inconceivable to any reasoning creature, unless possibly the fool that penned it; and my lord, though never brilliant, was ever remarkable for sense. That he should credit such a rodomontade, and carry the pamphlet on his bosom and the words in his heart, is the clear proof of the man's lunacy. Doubtless the mere mention of Mr. Alexander, and the threat directly held out against the child's succession, precipitated that which had so long impended. Or else my master had been truly mad for a long time, and we were too dull or too much used to him, and did not perceive the extent of his infirmity.

About a week after the day of the pamphlets I was late upon the harbor-side, and took a turn toward the master's, as I often did. The door opened, a flood of light came forth upon the road, and I beheld a man taking his departure with friendly salutations. I cannot say how singularly I was shaken to recognize the adventurer Harris. I could not but conclude it was the hand of my lord that had brought him there; and prolonged my walk in very serious and apprehensive thought. It was late when I came home, and there was my lord making up his portmanteau for a voyage.

"Why do you come so late?" he cried. "We leave to-morrow for Albany, you and I together; and it is high time you were about your preparations."

"For Albany, my lord?" I cried. "And for what earthly purpose?"

"Change of scene," said he.

And my lady, who appeared to have been weeping, gave me the signal to obey without more parley. She told me a little later (when we found occasion to exchange some words) that he had suddenly announced his intention after a visit from Captain Harris, and her best endeavors, whether to dissuade him from the journey or to elicit some explanation of its purpose, had alike proved unavailing.

WE made a prosperous voyage up that fine river of
the Hudson, the weather grateful, the hills singularly
beautified with the colors of the autumn. At Albany we
had our residence at an inn, where I was not so blind and
my lord not so cunning but what I could see he had some
design to hold me prisoner. The work he found for me to
do was not so pressing that we should transact it apart
from necessary papers in the chamber of an inn; nor was
it of such importance that I should be set upon as many
as four or five scrolls of the same document. I submitted
in appearance; but I took private measures on my own
side, and had the news of the town communicated to me
daily by the politeness of our host. In this way I received
at last a piece of intelligence for which, I may say, I had
been waiting. Captain Harris (I was told) with "Mr.
Mountain, the trader," had gone by up the river in a boat.
I would have feared the landlord's eye, so strong the sense
of some complicity upon my master's part oppressed me.
But I made out to say I had some knowledge of the captain, although none of Mr. Mountain, and to inquire who
else was of the party. My informant knew not; Mr. Mountain had come ashore upon some needful purchases; had
gone round the town buying, drinking and prating; and it
seemed the party went upon some likely venture, for he had
spoken much of great things he would do when he returned.
No more was known, for none of the rest had come ashore,
and it seemed they were pressed for time to reach a certain
spot before the snow should fall.

And sure enough the next day there fell a sprinkle even
in Albany; but it passed as it came, and was but a reminder
of what lay before us. I thought of it lightly then, knowing
so little as I did of that inclement province; the retrospect

191

is different; and I wonder at times if some of the horror of
these events which I must now rehearse flowed not from the
foul skies and savage winds to which we were exposed, and
the agony of cold that we must suffer.

The boat having passed by, I thought at first we should
have left the town. But no such matter. My lord continued his stay in Albany where he had no ostensible affairs,
and kept me by him, far from my due employment, and
making a pretense of occupation. It is upon this passage I
expect, and perhaps deserve censure. I was not so dull
but what I had my own thoughts. I could not see the master intrust himself into the hands of Harris, and not suspect
some underhand contrivance. Harris bore a villainous reputation, and he had been tampered with in private by my
lord; Mountain, the trader, proved, upon inquiry, to be
another of the same kidney; the errand they were all gone
upon being the recovery of ill-gotten treasures, offered in
itself a very strong incentive to foul play; and the character of the country where they journeyed promised im-
punity to deeds of blood. Well, it is true I had all these
thoughts and fears, and guesses of the Master's fate. But
you are to consider I was the same man that sought to dash
him from the bulwarks of a ship in the mid-sea; the same
that, a little before, very impiously but sincerely offered
God a bargain, seeking to hire God to be my bravo. It is
true again that I had a good deal melted toward our enemy.
But this I always thought of as a weakness of the flesh and
even culpable; my mind remaining steady and quite bent
against him. True yet again that it was one thing to assume on my own shoulders the guilt and danger of a criminal
attempt, and another to stand by and see my lord imperil
and besmirch himself. But this was the very ground of my
inaction. For (should I any way stir in the business) I
might fail indeed to save the Master, but I could not miss
to make a by-word of my lord.

Thus it was that I did nothing; and upon the same reasons, I am still strong to justify my course. We lived meanwhile in Albany; but though alone together in a strange

place, had little traffic beyond formal salutations. My lord had carried with him several introductions to chief people of the town and neighborhood; others he had before encountered in New York; with this consequence, that he went much abroad, and I am sorry to say was altogether too convivial in his habits. I was often in bed, but never asleep, when he returned; and there was scarce a night when he did not betray the influence of liquor. By day he would still lay upon me endless tasks, which he showed considerable ingenuity to fish up and to renew, in the manner of Penelope's web. I never refused, as I say, for I was hired to do his bidding; but I took no pains to keep my penetration under a bushel, and would sometimes smile in his face.

"I think I must be the devil, and you Michael Scott," I said to him one day. "I have bridged Tweed and split the Eildons; and now you set me to the rope of sand."

He looked at me with shining eyes and looked away again, his jaw chewing; but without words.

"Well, well, my lord," said I, "your will is my pleasure. I will do this thing for the fourth time; but I would beg of you to invent another task against to-morrow, for by my troth, I am weary of this one."

"You do not know what you are saying," returned my lord, putting on his hat and turning his back to me. "It is a strange thing you should take a pleasure to annoy me. A friend—but that is a different affair. It is a strange thing. I am a man that has had ill-fortune all my life through. I am still surrounded by contrivances. I am always treading in plots," he burst out. "The whole world is banded against me."

"I would not talk wicked nonsense if I were you," said I; "but I will tell you what I *would* do—I would put my head in cold water, for you had more last night than you could carry."

"Do you think that?" said he, with a manner of interest highly awakened. "Would that be good for me? It's a thing I never tried."

"I mind the days when you had no call to try, and I wish,

my lord, that they were back again," said I. " But the plain truth is, if you continue to exceed, you will do yourself a mischief.

" I don't appear to carry drink the way I used to," said my lord. " I get overtaken, Mackellar. But I will be more upon my guard."

" That is what I would ask of you," I replied. " You are to bear in mind that you are Mr. Alexander's father; give the bairn a chance to carry his name with some responsibility."

" Ay, ay," said he. " Ye're a very sensible man, Mackellar, and have been long in my employ. But I think if you have nothing more to say to me, I will be stepping. If you have nothing more to say? " he added, with that burning, childish eagerness that was now so common with the man.

" No, my lord, I have nothing more," said I, dryly enough.

" Then I think I will be stepping," says my lord, and stood and looked at me fidgeting with his hat, which he had taken off again. " I suppose you will have no errands? No. I am to meet Sir William Johnson, but I will be more upon my guard." He was silent for a time, and then, smiling: " Do you call to mind a place, Mackellar—it's a little below Engles—where the burn runs very deep under a wood of rowans? I mind being there when I was a lad—dear, it comes over me like an old song! I was after the fishing, and I made a bonny cast. Eh, but I was happy. I wonder, Mackellar, why I am never happy now? "

" My lord," said I, " if you would drink with more moderation you would have the better chance. It is an old by-word that the bottle is a false consoler."

" No doubt," said he, " no doubt. Well, I think I will be going."

" Good-morning, my lord," said I.

" Good-morning, good-morning," said he, and so got himself at last from the apartment.

I give that for a fair specimen of my lord in the morning; and I must have described my patron very ill if the reader does not perceive a notable falling off. To behold the man thus fallen; to know him accepted among his companions for a poor, muddled toper, welcome (if he were welcome at all) for the bare consideration of his title; and to recall the virtues he had once displayed against such odds of fortune; was not this a thing at once to rage and to be humbled at?

In his cups, he was more excessive. I will give but the one scene, close upon the end, which is strongly marked upon my memory to this day, and at the time affected me almost with horror.

I was in bed, lying there awake, when I heard him stumbling on the stair and singing. My lord had no gift of music, his brother had all the graces of the family, so that when I say singing, you are to understand a manner of high, caroling utterance, which was truly neither speech nor song. Something not unlike is to be heard upon the lips of children, ere they learn shame; from those of a man grown elderly it had a strange effect. He opened the door with noisy precaution; peered in, shading his candle; conceived me to slumber; entered, set his light upon the table, and took off his hat. I saw him very plain; a high, feverish exultation appeared to broil in his veins, and he stood and smiled and smirked upon the candle. Presently he lifted up his arm, snapped his fingers, and fell to undress. As he did so, having once more forgot my presence, he took back to his singing; and now I could hear the words, which were those from the old song of the " Twa Corbies " endlessly repeated:

> " And over his banes when they are bare
> The wind sall blaw for evermair! "

I have said there was no music in the man. His strains had no logical succession except in so far as they inclined a little to the minor mode; but they exercised a rude potency upon the feelings, and followed the words, and signified the feelings of the singer with barbaric fitness. He took it first in the time and manner of a rant; presently this ill-favored gleefulness abated, he began to dwell upon the notes more feelingly, and sunk at last into a degree of maudlin pathos that was to me scarce bearable. By equal steps, the original briskness of his acts declined; and when he was stripped to his breeches he sat on the bedside and fell to whimpering. I know nothing less respectable than the tears of drunkenness, and turned my back impatiently on this poor sight.

But he had started himself (I am to suppose) on that slippery descent of self-pity; on the which, to a man unstrung by old sorrows and recent potations, there is no arrest except exhaustion. His tears continued to flow, and the man to sit there, three parts naked, in the cold air of the chamber. I twitted myself alternately with inhumanity and sentimental weakness, now half rising in my bed to interfere, now reading myself lessons of indifference and courting slumber, until, upon a sudden, the *quantum mutatus ab illo* shot into my mind; and recalling to remembrance his old wisdom, constancy, and patience, I was overborne with a pity almost approaching the passionate, not for my master alone but for the sons of man.

At this I leaped from my place, went over to his side and laid a hand on his bare shoulder, which was cold as stone. He uncovered his face and showed it me all swollen and begrutten * like a child's; and at the sight my impatience partially revived.

"Think shame to yourself," said I. "This is bairnly conduct. I might have been sniveling myself, if I had cared to swill my belly with wine. But I went to my bed sober like a man. Come; get into yours, and have done with this pitiable exhibition."

"Oh, Mackellar," said he, "my heart is wae!"

"Wae?" cried I. "For a good cause, I think. What words were these you sung as you came in? Show pity to others, we then can talk of pity to yourself. You can be the one thing or the other, but I will be no party to halfway houses. If you're a striker, strike, and if you're a bleater, bleat!"

"Cry!" cries he, with a burst, "that's it—strike! that's talking! Man, I've stood it all too long. But when they

* Tear-marked.

laid a hand upon the child, when the child's threatened "
—his momentary vigor whimpering off—" my child, my
Alexander! "—and he was at his tears again.

I took him by the shoulders and shook him. " Alexander! " said I. " Do you even think of him? Not you! Look
yourself in the face like a brave man, and you'll find you're
but a self-deceiver. The wife, the friend, the child, they're
all equally forgot, and you sunk in a mere bog of selfishness."

" Mackellar," said he, with a wonderful return to his old
manner and appearance, " you may say what you will of
me, but one thing I never was—I was never selfish."

" I will open your eyes in your despite," said I. " How
long have we been here? and how often have you written to
your family? I think this is the first time you were ever
separate; have you written at all? Do they know if you are
dead or living? "

I had caught him here too openly; it braced his better
nature; there was no more weeping, he thanked me very
penitently, got to bed and was soon fast asleep; and the
first thing he did the next morning was to sit down and begin
a letter to my lady; a very tender letter it was too, though
it was never finished. Indeed all communication with New
York was transacted by myself; and it will be judged I
had a thankless task of it. What to tell my lady and in
what words, and how far to be false and how far cruel, was
a thing that kept me often from my slumber.

All this while, no doubt, my lord waited with growing
impatiency for news of his accomplices. Harris, it is to be
thought, had promised a high degree of expedition; the
time was already overpast when word was to be looked for;
and suspense was a very evil counselor to a man of an im-
paired intelligence. My lord's mind throughout this interval
dwelled almost wholly in the wilderness, following that party
with whose deeds he had so much concern. He continually
conjured up their camps and progresses, the fashion of the
country, the perpetration in a thousand different manners
of the same horrid fact, and that consequent spectacle of
the master's bones lying scattered in the wind. These pri-

vate, guilty considerations I would continually observe to peep forth in the man's talk, like rabbits from a hill. And it is the less wonder if the scene of his meditations began to draw him bodily.

It is well known what pretext he took. Sir William Johnson had a diplomatic errand in these parts; and my lord and I (from curiosity, as was given out) went in his company. Sir William was well attended and liberally supplied. Hunters brought us venison, fish was taken for us daily in the streams, and brandy ran like water. We proceeded by day and encamped by night in the military style, sentinels were set and changed; every man had his named duty; and Sir William was the spring of all. There was much in this that might at times have entertained me; but for our misfortune, the weather was extremely harsh, the days were in the beginning open, but the nights frosty from the first. A painful keen wind blew most of the time, so that we sat in the boat with blue fingers, and at night, as we scorched our faces at the fire, the clothes upon our back appeared to be of paper. A dreadful solitude surrounded our steps; the land was quite dispeopled, there was no smoke of fires, and save for a single boat of merchants on the second day, we met no travelers. The season was indeed late, but this desertion of the waterways impressed Sir William himself; and I have heard him more than once express a sense of intimidation. "I have come too late I fear; they must have dug up the hatchet," he said; and the future proved how justly he had reasoned.

I could never depict the blackness of my soul upon this journey. I have none of those minds that are in love with the unusual: to see the winter coming and to lie in the field so far from any house, oppressed me like a nightmare; it seemed, indeed, a kind of awful braving of God's power; and this thought, which I dare say only writes me down a coward, was greatly exaggerated by my private knowledge of the errand we were come upon. I was besides encumbered by my duties to Sir William, whom it fell upon me to entertain; for my lord was quite sunk into a state bordering on *pervigilium*, watching the woods with a rapt eye, sleeping scarce at all, and speaking sometimes not twenty words in a whole day. That which he said was still coherent; but it turned almost invariably upon the party for whom he kept his crazy lookout. He would tell Sir William often, and always as if it were a new communication, that he had " a brother somewhere in the woods," and beg that the sentinels should be directed " to inquire for him." " I am anxious for news of my brother," he would say. And sometimes, when we were under way, he would fancy he spied a canoe far off upon the water or a camp on the shore, and exhibit painful agitation. It was impossible but Sir William should be struck with these singularities; and at last he led me aside, and hinted his uneasiness. I touched my head and shook it; quite rejoiced to prepare a little testimony against possible disclosures.

" But in that case," cries Sir William, " is it wise to let him go at large? "

" Those that know him best," said I, " are persuaded that he should be humored."

" Well, well," replied Sir William, " it is none of my affairs. But if I had understood, you would never have been here."

Our advance into this savage country had thus uneventfully proceeded for about a week when we encamped for a night at a place where the river ran among considerable mountains clothed in wood. The fires were lighted on a level space at the water's edge; and we supped and lay down to sleep in the customary fashion. It chanced the night fell murderously cold; the stringency of the frost seized and bit me through my coverings, so that pain kept me wakeful; and I was afoot again before the peep of day, crouching by the fires or trotting to and fro at the stream's edge, to combat the aching of my limbs. At last dawn began to break upon hoar woods and mountains, the sleepers rolled in their robes, and the boisterous river dashing among spears of ice. I stood looking about me, swaddled in my stiff coat of a bull's fur, and the breath smoking from my scorched nostrils, when, upon a sudden, a singular, eager cry rang from the borders of the wood. The sentries answered it, the sleepers sprung to their feet; one pointed, the rest followed his direction with their eyes, and there, upon the edge of the forest and betwixt two trees, we beheld the figure of a man reaching forth his hands like one in ecstasy. The next moment he ran forward, fell on his knees at the side of the camp, and burst in tears.

This was John Mountain, the trader, escaped from the most horrid perils; and his first word, when he got speech, was to ask if we had seen Secundra Dass.

"Seen what?" cries Sir William.

"No," said I, "we have seen nothing of him. Why?"

"Nothing?" says Mountain. "Then I was right after all." With that he struck his palm upon his brow. "But what takes him back?" he cried. "What takes the man back among dead bodies? There is some damned mystery here."

This was a word which highly aroused our curiosity, but I shall be more perspicacious if I narrate these incidents in their true order. Here follows a narrative which I have compiled out of three sources, not very consistent in all points:

First, a written statement by Mountain, in which everything criminal is cleverly smuggled out of view.

Second, two conversations with Secundra Dass; and

Third, many conversations with Mountain himself, in which he was pleased to be entirely plain; for the truth is he regarded me as an accomplice.

NARRATIVE OF THE TRADER, MOUNTAIN

The crew that went up the river under the joint command of Captain Harris and the Master numbered in all nine persons, of whom (if I except Secundra Dass) there was not one that had not merited the gallows. From Harris downward the voyagers were notorious in that colony for desperate, bloody-minded miscreants; some were reputed pirates, the most hawkers of rum; all ranters and drinkers;

all fit associates, embarking together without remorse, upon
this treacherous and murderous design. I could not hear
there was much discipline or any set captain in the gang;
but Harris and four others, Mountain himself, two Scotch-
men—Pinkerton and Hastie—and a man of the name of
Hicks, a drunken shoemaker, put their heads together and
agreed upon the course. In a material sense, they were well
enough provided; and the Master in particular brought with
him a tent where he might enjoy some privacy and shelter.

Even this small indulgence told against him in the minds
of his companions. But indeed he was in a position so entirely false (and even ridiculous) that all his habit of command and arts of pleasing were here thrown away. In the
eyes of all, except Secundra Dass, he figured as a common
gull and designated victim; going unconsciously to death;
yet he could not but suppose himself the contriver and the
leader of the expedition; he could scarce help but so conduct himself; and at the least hint of authority or condescension, his deceivers would be laughing in their sleeves.
I was so used to see and to conceive him in a high, authoritative attitude that when I had conceived his position on this
journey I was pained and could have blushed. How soon he
may have entertained a first surmise we cannot know; but
it was long, and the party had advanced into the wilderness
beyond the reach of any help ere he was fully awakened to
the truth.

It fell thus. Harris and some others had drawn apart
into the woods for consultation, when they were startled by
a rustling in the brush. They were all accustomed to the
arts of Indian warfare, and Mountain had not only lived
and hunted, but fought and earned some reputation with
the savages. He could move in the woods without noise,
and follow a trail like a hound; and upon the emergence
of this alert, he was deputed by the rest to plunge into the
thicket for intelligence. He was soon convinced there
was a man in his close neighborhood, moving with precaution but without art among the leaves and branches; and
coming shortly to a place of advantage, he was able to

observe Secundra Dass crawling briskly off with many backward glances. At this he knew not whether to laugh or cry; and his accomplices, when he had returned and reported, were in much the same dubiety. There was now no danger of an Indian onslaught; but on the other hand, since Secundra Dass was at the pains to spy upon them, it was highly probable he knew English, and if he knew English it was certain the whole of their design was in the Master's knowledge. There was one singularity in the position. If Secundra Dass knew and concealed his knowledge of English, Harris was a proficient in several of the tongues of India, and as his career in that part of the world had been a great deal worse than profligate, he had not thought proper to remark upon the circumstance. Each side had thus a spy-hole on the counsels of the other. The plotters, so soon as this advantage was explained, returned to camp; Harris, hearing the Hindoostanee was once more closeted with his master, crept to the side of the tent; and the rest, sitting about the fire with their tobacco, awaited his report with impatience. When he came at last his face was very black. He had overheard enough to confirm the worst of his suspicions. Secundra Dass was a good English scholar; he had been some days creeping and listening, the Master was now fully informed of the conspiracy, and the pair proposed on the morrow to fall out of line at a carrying place and plunge at a venture in the woods: preferring the full risk of famine, savage beasts, and savage men to their position in the midst of traitors.

What, then, was to be done? Some were for killing the Master on the spot; but Harris assured them that would be a crime without profit, since the secret of the treasure must die along with him that buried it. Others were for desisting at once from the whole enterprise and making for New York; but the appetizing name of treasure, and the thought of the long way they had already traveled, dissuaded the majority. I imagine they were dull fellows for the most part. Harris, indeed, had some acquirements, Mountain was no fool, Hastie was an educated man; but even these had manifestly failed in life, and the rest were the dregs of colonial rascality. The conclusion they reached, at least, was more the offspring of greed and hope than reason. It was to temporize, to be wary and watch the Master, to be silent and supply no further aliment to his suspicions, and to depend entirely (as well as I make out) on the chance that their victim was as greedy, hopeful, and irrational as themselves, and might, after all, betray his life and treasure.

Twice, in the course of the next day, Secundra and the Master must have appeared to themselves to have escaped; and twice they were circumvented. The Master, save that the second time he grew a little pale, displayed no sign of disappointment, apologized for the stupidity with which he had fallen aside, thanked his recapturers as for a service, and rejoined the caravan with all his usual gallantry and cheerfulness of mien and bearing. But it is certain he had smelled a rat; for from thenceforth he and Secundra spoke only in each other's ear, and Harris listened and shivered by the tent in vain. The same night it was announced they were to leave the boats and proceed by foot: a circumstance which (as it put an end to the confusion of the portages) greatly lessened the chances of escape.

And now there began between the two sides a silent contest, for life on the one hand, for riches on the other. They were now near that quarter of the desert in which the Master himself must begin to play the part of guide; and using this for a pretext of prosecution, Harris and his men sat with him every night about the fire, and labored to entrap him into some admission. If he let slip his secret, he knew well it was the warrant for his death; on the other hand, he durst not refuse their questions, and must appear to help them to the best of his capacity, or he practically published his mistrust. And yet Mountain assures me the man's brow was never ruffled. He sat in the midst of these jackals, his life depending by a thread, like some easy, witty householder at home by his own fire; an answer he had for everything —as often as not, a jesting answer; avoided threats, evaded insults; talked, laughed, and listened with an open countenance; and, in short, conducted himself in such a manner as must have disarmed suspicion, and went near to stagger knowledge. Indeed Mountain confessed to me they would soon have disbelieved the captain's story, and supposed their designated victim still quite innocent of their designs, but for the fact that he continued (however ingeniously) to give the slip to questions, and the yet stronger confirmation of his repeated efforts to escape. The last of these, which brought things to a head, I am now to relate. And first I should say that by this time the temper of Harris's companions was utterly worn out; civility was scarce pretended; and for one very significant circumstance, the Master and Secundra had been (on some pretext) deprived of weapons. On their side, however, the threatened pair kept up the parade of friendship handsomely; Secundra was all bows, the master all smiles; and on the last night of the truce he had even gone so far as to sing for the diversion of the company. It was observed that he had also eaten with unusual heartiness, and drank deep: doubtless from design.

At least, about three in the morning, he came out of the tent into the open air, audibly mourning and complaining, with all the manner of a sufferer from surfeit. For some while Secundra publicly attended on his patron, who at last became more easy, and fell asleep on the frosty ground behind the tent: the Indian returning within. Some time after the sentry was changed; had the Master pointed out to him, where he lay in what is called a robe of buffalo; and thenceforth kept an eye upon him (he declared) without remission. With the first of the dawn, a draught of wind came suddenly and blew open one side the corner of the robe; and with the same puff, the Master's hat whirled in the air and fell some yards away.

The sentry, thinking it remarkable the sleeper should not awaken, thereupon drew near: and the next moment, with a great shout, informed the camp their prisoner was escaped. He had left behind his Indian, who (in the first vivacity of the surprise) came near to pay the forfeit of his life, and was, in fact, inhumanly mishandled; but Secundra, in the midst of threats and cruelties, stuck to it with extraordinary loyalty that he was quite ignorant of his Master's plans, which might indeed be true, and of the manner of his escape, which was demonstrably false. Nothing was therefore left to the conspirators but to rely entirely on the skill of Mountain. The night had been frosty, the ground quite hard; and the sun was no sooner up than a strong thaw set in. It was Mountain's boast that few men could have followed that trail, and still fewer (even of the native Indians) found it. The Master had thus a long start before his pursuers had the scent, and he must have traveled with surprising energy for a pedestrian so unused, since it was near noon before Mountain had a view of him. At this conjuncture the trader was alone, all his companions following, at his own request, several hundred yards in the rear; he knew the Master was unarmed; his heart was besides heated with the exercise and lust of hunting; and seeing the quarry so close, so defenseless, and seemingly so fatigued, he vaingloriously determined to effect the capture with his single hand. A step or two further brought him to one margin of a little clearing; on the other, with his arms folded and his back to a huge stone, the Master sat. It is possible Mountain may have made a rustle, it is certain, at least, the Master raised his head and gazed directly at that quarter of the thicket where his hunter lay. "I could not be sure he saw me," Mountain said; "he just looked my way like a man with his mind made up, and all the courage ran out of me like rum out of a bottle." And presently, when the Master looked away again, and appeared to resume those meditations in which he had sat immersed before the trader's coming, Mountain slunk stealthily back and returned to seek the help of his companions.

And now began the chapter of surprises, for the scout had scarce informed the others of his discovery, and they were yet preparing their weapons for a rush upon the fugitive, when the man himself appeared in their midst, walking openly and quietly, with his hands behind his back.

" Ah, men!" says he, on his beholding them. " Here is a fortunate encounter. Let us get back to camp."

Mountain had not mentioned his own weakness or the Master's disconcerting gaze upon the thicket, so that (with all the rest) his return appeared spontaneous. For all that, a hubbub arose; oaths flew, fists were shaken, and guns pointed.

" Let us get back to camp," said the Master. " I have an explanation to make, but it must be laid before you all. And in the meanwhile I would put up these weapons, one of which might very easily go off and blow away your hopes of treasure. I would not kill," says he, smiling, " the goose with the golden eggs."

The charm of his superiority once more triumphed; and the party, in no particular order, set off on their return. By the way he found occasion to get a word or two apart with Mountain.

" You are a clever fellow and a bold," says he, " but I am not so sure that you are doing yourself justice. I would have you to consider whether you would not do better, ay, and safer, to serve me instead of serving so commonplace a rascal as Mr. Harris. Consider of it," he concluded, dealing the man a gentle tap upon the shoulder, " and don't be in haste. Dead or alive, you will find me an ill man to quarrel with."

When they were come back to the camp, where Harris and Pinkerton stood guard over Secundra, these two ran upon the Master like viragoes, and were amazed out of measure when they were bidden by their comrades to " stand back and hear what the gentleman had to say." The Master had not flinched before their onslaught; nor, at this proof of the ground he had gained, did he betray the least sufficiency.

" Do not let us be in haste," says he. " Meat first and public speaking after."

With that they made a hasty meal; and as soon as it was done, the Master, leaning on one elbow, began his speech. He spoke long, addressing himself to each except Harris, finding for each (with the same exception) some particular flattery. He called them "bold, honest blades," declared he had never seen a more jovial company, work better done, or pains more merrily supported. "Well, then," says he, "some one asks me 'Why the devil I ran away?' But that is scarce worth answer, for I think you all know pretty well. But you know only pretty well: that is a point I shall arrive at presently, and be you ready to remark it when it comes. There is a traitor here: a double traitor: I will give you his name before I am done; and let that suffice for now. But here comes some other gentleman and asks me 'Why in the devil I came back?' Well, before I answer that question, I have one to put to you. It was this cur here, this Harris, that speaks Hindoostanee?" cries he, rising on one knee and pointing fair at the man's face, with a gesture indescribably menacing; and when he had been answered in the affirmative, "Ah!" says he, "then are all my suspicions verified, and I did rightly to come back. Now, men, hear the truth for the first time." Thereupon he launched forth in a long story, told with extraordinary skill how he had all along suspected Harris, how he had found the confirmation of his fears, and how Harris must have misrepresented what passed between Secundra and himself. At this point he made a bold stroke with excellent effect. "I suppose," says he, "you think you are going shares with Harris, I suppose you think you will see to that yourselves; you would naturally not think so flat a rogue could cozen you. But have a care! These half idiots have a sort of cunning, as the skunk has its stench; and it may be news to you that Harris has taken care of himself already. Yes, for him the treasure is all money in the bargain. You must find it or go starve. But he has been paid beforehand; my brother paid him to destroy me; look at him, if you doubt —look at him, grinning and gulping, a detected thief!" Thence, having made this happy impression, he explained how he had escaped, and thought better of it, and at last concluded to come back, lay the truth before the company, and take his chance with them once more: persuaded, as he was, they would instantly depose Harris and elect some other leader. "There is the whole truth," said he: "and with one exception, I put myself entirely in your hands. What is the exception? There he sits," he cried, pointing once more to Harris; "a man that has to die! Weapons and conditions are all one to me; put me face to face with him, and if you give me nothing but a stick, in five minutes I will show you a sop of broken carrion fit for dogs to roll in."

It was dark night when he made an end; they had listened in almost perfect silence; but the firelight scarce permitted any one to judge, from the look of his neighbors, with what result of persuasion or conviction. Indeed, the Master had set himself in the brightest place, and kept his face there, to be the center of men's eyes: doubtless on a profound calculation. Silence followed for awhile, and presently the whole party became involved in disputation: the Master lying on his back with his hands knit under his head and one knee flung across the other, like a person unconcerned in the result. And here, I dare say, his bravado carried him too far and prejudiced his case. At least, after a cast or two backward and forward, opinion settled finally against him. It's possible he hoped to repeat the business of the pirate ship, and be himself, perhaps, on hard enough conditions, elected leader; and things went so far that way that Mountain actually threw out the proposition. But the rock he split upon was Hastie. This fellow was not well liked, being sour and slow, with an ugly, glowering disposition, but he had studied some time for the Church at Edinburgh College, before ill conduct had destroyed his prospects, and he now remembered and applied what he had learned. Indeed, he had not proceeded very far, when the Master rolled carelessly upon one side, which was done (in Mountain's opinion) to conceal the beginnings of despair upon his countenance. Hastie dismissed the most of what they had heard as nothing to the matter: what they wanted was the treasure. All that was said of Harris might be true, and they would have to see to that in time. But what had that to do with the treasure?

THE MASTER OF BALLANTRAE

They had heard a vast of words; but the truth was just
this, that Mr. Durie was damnably frightened and had several times run off. Here he was—whether caught or come
back was all one to Hastie: the point was to make an end
of the business. As for the talk of deposing and electing
captains, he hoped they were all free men and could attend
their own affairs. That was dust flung in their eyes, and so
was the proposal to fight Harris. "He shall fight no one
in this camp, I can tell him that," said Hastie. "We had
trouble enough to get his arms away from him, and we
should look pretty fools to give them back again. But if
it's excitement the gentleman is after, I can supply him with
more than perhaps he cares about. For I have no intention
to spend the remainder of my life in these mountains; already
I have been too long; and I propose that he shall immediately tell us where that treasure is, or else immediately be
shot. And there," says he, producing his weapon, "there
is the pistol that I mean to use."

"Come, I call you a man," cries the Master, sitting up and
looking at the speaker with an air of admiration.

"I didn't ask you to call me anything," returned Hastie;
"what is it to be?"

"That's an idle question," said the Master. "Needs
must when the devil drives. The truth is we are within easy
walk of the place, and I will show it you to-morrow."

With that, as if all were quite settled, and settled exactly
to his mind, he walked off to his tent, whither Secundra
had preceded him.

I cannot think of these last turns and wriggles of my old
enemy except with admiration; scarce even pity is mingled
with the sentiment, so strongly the man supported, so boldly
resisted his misfortunes. Even at that hour, when he perceived himself quite lost, when he saw he had but effected
an exchange of enemies, and overthrown Harris to set Hastie
up, no sign of weakness appeared in his behavior, and he
withdrew to his tent, already determined (I must suppose)
upon affronting the incredible hazard of his last expedient
with the same easy, assured, genteel expression and de-

meanor as he might have left a theater withal to join a supper of the wits. But doubtless within, if we could see there, his soul trembled.

Early in the night, word went about the camp that he was sick; and the first thing the next morning he called Hastie to his side, and inquired most anxiously if he had any skill in medicine. As a matter of fact, this was a vanity of that fallen divinity student's to which he had cunningly addressed himself. Hastie examined him; and being flattered, ignorant, and highly suspicious, knew not in the least whether the man was sick or malingering. In this state, he went forth again to his companions; and (as the thing which would give himself most consequence either way) announced that the patient was in a fair way to die.

"For all that," he added, with an oath, "and if he bursts by the wayside, he must bring us this morning to the treasure."

But there were several in the camp (Mountain among the number) whom this brutality revolted. They would have seen the Master pistoled, or pistoled him themselves, without the smallest sentiment of pity; but they seem to have been touched by his gallant fight and unequivocal defeat the night before; perhaps, too, they were even already beginning to oppose themselves to their new leader; at least, they now declared that (if the man was sick) he should have a day's rest in spite of Hastie's teeth.

The next morning he was manifestly worse, and Hastie himself began to display something of humane concern, so easily does even the pretense of doctoring awaken sympathy. The third, the Master called Mountain and Hastie to the tent, announced himself to be dying, gave them full particulars as to the position of the cache, and begged them to set out incontinently on the quest, so that they might see if he deceived them, and (if they were at first unsuccessful), he should be able to correct their error.

But here arose a difficulty on which he doubtless counted. None of these men would trust another, none would consent to stay behind. On the other hand, although the Master seemed extremely low, spoke scarce above a whisper, and lay much of the time insensible, it was still possible it was a fraudulent sickness; and if all went treasure-hunting it might prove they had gone upon a wild-goose chase, and return to find their prisoner flown. They concluded, therefore, to hang idling round the camp, alleging sympathy to their reason; and certainly, so mingled are our dispositions, several were sincerely (if not very deeply) affected by the natural peril of the man whom they callously designed to murder. In the afternoon Hastie was called to the bedside to pray: the which (incredible as it must appear) he did with unction; about eight at night the wailing of Secundra announced that all was over, and before ten the Indian, with a link stuck in the ground, was toiling at the grave. Sunrise of next day beheld the Master's burial, all hands attending with great decency of demeanor; and the body was laid in the earth wrapped in a fur robe, with only the face uncovered; which last was of a waxy whiteness, and had the nostrils plugged according to some Oriental habit of Secundra's. No sooner was the grave filled than the lamentations of the Indian once more struck concern to every heart; and it appears this gang of murderers, so far from resenting his outcries, although both distressful and (in such a country) perilous to their own safety, roughly but kindly endeavored to console him.

But if human nature is even in the worst of men occasionally kind, it is still, and before all things, greedy; and they soon turned from the mourner to their own concerns. The cache of the treasure being hard by, although yet unidentified, it was concluded not to break camp; and the day passed, on the part of the voyagers, in unavailing exploration of the woods, Secundra the while lying on his master's grave. That night they placed no sentinel, but lay all together about the fire, in the customary woodman fashion, the heads outward, like the spokes of a wheel. Morning found them in the same disposition; only Pinkerton, who lay on Mountain's right, between him and Hastie, had (in the hours of darkness) been secretly butchered, and there lay, still wrapped as to his body in his mantle, but offering above that ungodly and horrific spectacle of the scalped head. The gang were that morning as pale as a company of phantoms, for the pertinacity of Indian war (or, to speak more correctly, Indian murder), was well known to all. But they laid the chief blame on their unsentineled posture; and fired with the neighborhood of the treasure, determined to continue where they were. Pinkerton was buried hard by the Master; the survivors again passed the day in exploration, and returned in a mingled humor of anxiety and hope, being partly certain they were now close on the discovery of what they sought, and on the other hand (with the return of darkness) were infected with the fear of Indians. Mountain was the first sentry; he declares he neither slept nor yet sat down, but kept his watch with a perpetual and straining vigilance, and it was even with unconcern that (when he saw by the stars his time was up) he drew near the fire to waken his successor. This man (it was Hicks the shoemaker) slept on the lee-side of the circle, somewhat further off in consequence than those to windward, and in a place darkened by the blowing smoke. Mountain stooped and took him by the shoulder; his hand was at once smeared by some adhesive wetness; and (the wind at the moment veering) the firelight shone upon the sleeper and showed him, like Pinkerton, dead and scalped.

It was clear they had fallen in the hands of one of those matchless Indian bravos, that will sometimes follow a party for days, and in spite of indefatigable travel and unsleeping watch, continue to keep up with their advance and steal a scalp at every resting place. Upon this discovery the treasure seekers, already reduced to a poor half dozen, fell into mere dismay, seized a few necessaries, and deserting the remainder of their goods, fled outright into the forest. Their fire, they left still burning, and their dead comrade unburied. All day they ceased not to flee, eating by the way, from hand to mouth; and since they feared to sleep, continued to advance at random even in the hours of darkness. But the limit of man's endurance is soon reached; when they rested at last, it was to sleep profoundly; and when they woke, it was to find that the enemy was still upon their heels, and death and mutilation had once more lessened and deformed their company.

By this, they had become light-headed, they had quite missed their path in the wilderness, their stores were already running low. With the further horrors, it is superfluous that I should swell this narrative, already too prolonged. Suffice it to say, that when at length a night passed by innocuous, and they might breathe again in the hope that the murderer had at last desisted from pursuit, Mountain and Secundra were alone. The trader is firmly persuaded their unseen enemy was some warrior of his own acquaintance, and that he himself was spared by favor. The mercy extended to Secundra he explains on the ground that the East Indian was thought to be insane; partly from the fact that, through all the horrors of the flight and while others were casting away their very food and weapons, Secundra continued to stagger forward with a mattock on his shoulder; and partly because in the last days and with a great degree of heat and fluency, he perpetually spoke with himself in his own language. But he was sane enough when it came to English.

"You think he will be gone quite away?" he asked, upon their blessed awakening in safety.

"I pray God so, I believe so, I dare to believe so," Mountain had replied almost with incoherence as he described the scene to me.

And indeed he was so much distempered that until he met us the next morning he could scarce be certain whether he had dreamed, or whether it was a fact, that Secundra had thereupon turned directly about and returned without a word upon their footprints, setting his face for these wintery and hungry solitudes, along a path whose every stage was milestoned with a mutilated corpse.

MOUNTAIN'S story, as it was laid before Sir William Johnson and my lord, was shorn, of course, of all the earlier particulars, and the expedition described to have proceeded uneventfully, until the master sickened. But the latter part was very forcibly related, the speaker visibly thrilling to his recollections; and our then situation, on the fringe of the same desert, and the private interests of each, gave him an audience prepared to share in his emotions. For Mountain's intelligence not only changed the world for my Lord Durrisdeer, but materially affected the designs of Sir William Johnson.

These I find I must lay more at length before the reader. Word had reached Albany of dubious import; it had been rumored some hostility was to be put in act; and the Indian diplomatist had, thereupon, sped into the wilderness, even at the approach of winter, to nip that mischief in the bud. Here, on the borders, he learned that he was come too late; and a difficult choice was thus presented to a man (upon the whole) not any more bold than prudent. His standing with the painted braves may be compared to that of my Lord President Culloden among the chiefs of our own Highlanders at the '45; that is as much as to say, he was, to these men, reason's only speaking trumpet, and counsels of peace and moderation, if they were to prevail at all, must prevail singly through his influence. If, then, he should return, the province must lie open to all the abominable tragedies of Indian war—the houses blaze, the wayfarer be cut off, and the men of the woods collect their usual disgusting spoil of human scalps. On the other side, to go further forth, to risk so small a party deeper in the desert to carry words of peace among warlike savages already rejoicing to return to war: here was an extremity from which it was easy to perceive his mind revolted.

"I have come too late," he said more than once, and would fall into a deep consideration, his head bowed in his hands, his foot patting the ground.

At length he raised his face and looked upon us, that is to say, upon my lord, Mountain, and myself, sitting close round a small fire, which had been made for privacy in one corner of the camp.

"My lord, to be quite frank with you, I find myself in two minds," said he. "I think it very needful I should go on, but not at all proper I should any longer enjoy the pleasure of your company. We are here still upon the water-side; and I think the risk to southward no great matter. Will not yourself and Mr. Mackellar take a single boat's crew and return to Albany?"

My lord, I should say, had listened to Mountain's narrative, regarding him throughout with a painful intensity of gaze; and since the tale concluded, had sat as in a dream. There was something very daunting in his look; something to my eyes not rightly human; the face, lean, and dark, and aged, the mouth painful, the teeth disclosed in a perpetual rictus; the eyeball swimming clear of the lids upon a field of bloodshot white. I could not behold him myself without a jarring irritation, such as (I believe) is too frequently the uppermost feeling on the sickness of those dear to us. Others, I could not but remark, were scarce able to support his neighborhood—Sir William eviting to be near him, Mountain dodging his eye, and, when he met it, blanching and halting in his story. At this appeal, however, my lord appeared to recover his command upon himself.

"To Albany?" said he, with a good voice.

"Not short of it, at least," replied Sir William. "There is no safety nearer at hand."

"I would be very sweir * to return," says my lord. "I am not afraid—of Indians," he added, with a jerk.

"I wish that I could say so much," returned Sir William, smiling; "although, if any man durst say it, it should be myself. But you are to keep in view my responsibility, and that as the voyage has now become highly dangerous, and

* Unwilling.

your business—if you ever had any," says he, "brought quite to a conclusion by the distressing family intelligence you have received, I should be hardly justified if I even suffered you to proceed, and run the risk of some obloquy if anything regrettable should follow."

My lord turned to Mountain. "What did he pretend he died of?" he asked.

"I don't think I understand your honor," said the trader, pausing like a man very much affected, in the dressing of some cruel frost-bites.

For a moment my lord seemed at a full stop; and then, with some irritation, "I ask you what he died of. Surely that's a plain question," said he.

"Oh, I don't know," said Mountain. "Hastie even never knew. He seemed to sicken natural, and just passed away."

"There it is, you see!" concluded my lord, turning to Sir William.

"Your lordship is too deep for me," replied Sir William.

"Why," says my lord, "this is a matter of succession; my son's title may be called in doubt; and the man being supposed to be dead of nobody can tell what, a great deal of suspicion would be naturally roused."

"But, God damn me, the man's buried!" cried Sir William.

"I will never believe that," returned my lord, painfully trembling. "I'll never believe it!" he cried again, and jumped to his feet. "Did he *look* dead?" he asked of Mountain.

"Look dead?" repeated the trader. "He looked white. Why, what would he be at? I tell you, I put the sods upon him."

My lord caught Sir William by the coat with a hooked hand. "This man has the name of my brother," says he, "but it's well understood that he was never canny."

"Canny?" says Sir William. "What is that?"

"He's not of this world," whispered my lord, "neither him nor the black deil that serves him. I have struck my sword throughout his vitals," he cried, "I have felt the hilt dirl * on his breast-bone, and the hot blood spurt in my very face, time and again, time and again!" he repeated, with a gesture indescribable. "But he was never dead for that," said he, and I sighed aloud. "Why should I think he was dead now? No, not till I see him rotting," says he.

Sir William looked across at me, with a long face. Mountain forgot his wounds, staring and gaping.

"My lord," said I, "I wish you would collect your spirits." But my throat was so dry, and my own wits so scattered, I could add no more.

"No," says my lord, "it's not to be supposed that he would understand me. Mackellar does, for he kens all, and has seen him buried before now. This is a very good servant to me, Sir William, this man Mackellar; he buried him with his own hands—he and my father—by the light of two siller candlesticks. The other man is a familiar spirit; he brought him from Coromandel. I would have told ye this long syne, Sir William, only it was in the family." These last remarks he made with a kind of melancholy composure, and his time of aberration seemed to pass away. "You can ask yourself what it all means," he proceeded. "My brother falls sick, and dies, and is buried, as so they say; and all seems very plain. But why did the familiar go back? I think ye must see for yourself it's a point that wants some clearing."

"I will be at your service, my lord, in half a minute," said Sir William, rising. "Mr. Mackellar, two words with you," and he led me without the camp, the frost crunching in our steps, the trees standing at our elbow hoar with frost, even as on that night in the long shrubbery. "Of course, this is midsummer madness?" said Sir William, so soon as we were gotten out of hearing.

"Why, certainly," said I. "The man is mad. I think that manifest."

"Shall I seize and bind him?" asked Sir William. "I will upon your authority. If these are all ravings, that should certainly be done."

I looked down upon the ground, back at the camp with its bright fires and the folk watching us, and about me on the

* Ring.

woods and mountains; there was just the one way that I could not look, and that was in Sir William's face.

" Sir William," said I, at last, " I think my lord not sane, and have long thought him so. But there are degrees in madness; and whether he should be brought under restraint— Sir William, I am no fit judge," I concluded.

" I will be the judge," said he. " I ask for facts. Was there, in all that jargon, any word of truth or sanity? Do you hesitate? " he asked. " Am I to understand you have buried this gentleman before? "

" Not buried," said I; and then, taking up courage at last, " Sir William," said I, " unless I were to tell you a long story, which much concerns a noble family (and myself not in the least), it would be impossible to make this matter clear to you. Say the word, and I will do it, right or wrong. And, at any rate, I will say so much, that my lord is not so crazy as he seems. This is a strange matter, into the tail of which you are unhappily drifted."

" I desire none of your secrets," replied Sir William; " but I will be plain, at the risk of incivility, and confess that I take little pleasure in my present company."

" I would be the last to blame you," said I, " for that."

" I have not asked either for your censure or your praise, sir," returned Sir William. " I desire simply to be quit of you; and to that effect, I put a boat and complement of men at your disposal."

" This is fairly offered," said I, after reflection. " But you must suffer me to say a word upon the other side. We have a natural curiosity to learn the truth of this affair; I have some of it myself; my lord (it is very plain) has but too much. The matter of the Indian's return is enigmatical."

" I think so myself," Sir William interrupted, " and I propose (since I go in that direction) to probe it to the bottom. Whether or not the man has gone like a dog to die upon his master's grave, his life, at least, is in great danger, and I propose, if I can, to save it. There is nothing against his character? "

" Nothing, Sir William," I replied.

" And the other? " he said. " I have heard my lord, of course; but, from the circumstances of his servant's loyalty, I must suppose he had some noble qualities."

" You must not ask me that! " I cried. " Hell may have noble flames. I have known him a score of years, and always hated, and always admired, and always slavishly feared him."

" I appear to intrude again upon your secrets," said Sir William, " believe me, inadvertently. Enough that I will see the grave, and (if possible) rescue the Indian. Upon these terms, can you persuade your master to return to Albany? "

" Sir William," said I, " I will tell you how it is. You do not see my lord to advantage; it will seem even strange to you that I should love him; but I do, and I am not alone. If he goes back to Albany it must be by force, and it will be the death-warrant of his reason, and perhaps his life. That is my sincere belief; but I am in your hands, and ready to obey, if you will assume so much responsibility as to command."

" I will have no shred of responsibility; it is my single endeavor to avoid the same," cried Sir William. " You insist upon following this journey up; and be it so! I wash my hands of the whole matter."

With which word he turned upon his heel and gave the order to break camp; and my lord, who had been hovering near by, came instantly to my side.

" Which is it to be? " said he.

" You are to have your way," I answered. " You shall see the grave."

The situation of the Master's grave was, between guides, easily described; it lay, indeed, beside a chief landmark of the wilderness, a certain range of peaks, conspicuous by their design and altitude, and the source of many brawling tributaries to that inland sea, Lake Champlain. It was therefore possible to strike for it direct, instead of following back the blood-stained trail of the fugitives, and to cover, in some sixteen hours of march, a distance which their perturbed wanderings had extended over more than sixty. Our boats we left under a guard upon the river; it was, indeed, probable we should return to find them frozen fast; and the small equipment with which we set forth upon the expedition included not only an infinity of furs to protect us from the cold, but an arsenal of snowshoes to render travel possible, when the inevitable snow should fall. Considerable alarm was manifested at our departure; the march was conducted with soldierly precaution, the camp at night sedulously chosen and patroled; and it was a consideration of this sort that arrested us, the second day, within not many hundred yards of our destination—the night being already imminent, the spot in which we stood well qualified to be a strong camp for a party of our numbers; and Sir William, therefore, on a sudden thought, arresting our advance.

Before us was the high range of mountains toward which we had been all day deviously drawing near. From the first light of the dawn, their silver peaks had been the goal of our advance across a tumbled lowland forest, thrid with rough streams, and strewn with monstrous bowlders; the peaks (as I say) silver, for already at the higher altitudes the snow fell nightly; but the woods and the low ground only breathed upon with frost. All day heaven had been charged with ugly vapors, in the which the sun swam and glimmered like a shilling piece; all day the wind blew on our left cheek, barbarous cold, but very pure to breathe. With the end of the afternoon, however, the wind fell; the clouds, being no longer re-enforced, were scattered or drunk up; the sun set behind us with some wintery splendor, and the white brow of the mountains shared its dying glow.

It was dark ere we had supper; we ate in silence, and the meal was scarce dispatched before my lord slunk from the fireside to the margin of the camp, whither I made haste to follow him. The camp was on high ground overlooking a frozen lake, perhaps a mile in its longest measurement; all about us the forest lay in heights and hollows; above rose the white mountains; and higher yet, the moon rode in a fair sky. There was no breath of air; nowhere a twig creaked; and the sounds of our own camp were hushed and swallowed up in the surrounding stillness. Now that the sun and the wind were both gone down, it appeared almost warm, like a night of July; a singular illusion of the sense, when earth, air, and water were strained to bursting with the extremity of frost.

My lord (or what I still continued to call by his loved name) stood with his elbow in one hand, and his chin sunk in the other, gazing before him on the surface of the wood. My eyes followed his, and rested almost pleasantly upon the frosted contexture of the pines, rising in moonlit hillocks, or sinking in the shadow of small glens. Hard by, I told myself, was the grave of our enemy, now gone where the wicked cease from troubling, the earth heaped forever on his once so active limbs. I could not but think of him as somehow fortunate, to be thus done with man's anxiety and weariness, the daily expense of spirit, and that daily river of circumstance to be swum through, at any hazard, under the penalty of shame or death. I could not but think how good was the end of that long travel; and with that, my mind swung at a tangent to my lord. For was not my lord dead also? a maimed soldier, looking vainly for discharge, lingering derided in the line of battle? A kind man, I remembered him; wise, with a decent pride, a son perhaps too dutiful, a husband only too loving, one that could suffer and be silent, one whose hand I loved to press. Of a sudden, pity caught in my wind-pipe with a sob; I could have wept aloud to remember and behold him; and standing thus by his elbow, under the broad moon, I prayed fervently either that he should be released or I strengthened to persist in my affection.

" Oh God," said I, " this was the best man to me and to himself, and now I shrink from him. He did no wrong, or not till he was broke with sorrows; these are but his honorable wounds that we begin to shrink from. Oh, cover them up, oh, take him away, before we hate him! "

I was still so engaged in my own bosom, when a sound broke suddenly upon the night. It was neither very loud nor very near; yet, bursting as it did from so profound and so prolonged a silence, it startled the camp like an alarm of trumpets. Ere I had taken breath Sir William was beside me, the main part of the voyagers clustered at his back, intently giving ear. Methought, as I glanced at them across my shoulder, there was a whiteness, other than moonlight, on their cheeks; and the rays of the moon reflected with a sparkle on the eyes of some, and the shadows lying black under the brows of others (according as they raised or bowed the head to listen) gave to the group a strange air of animation and anxiety. My lord was to the front, crouching a little forth, his hand raised as for silence; a man turned to stone. And still the sounds continued, breathlessly renewed, with a precipitate rhythm.

Suddenly Mountain spoke in a loud, broken whisper, as of a man relieved. "I have it now," he said; and, as we all turned to hear him, "the Indian must have known the cache," he added. "That is he—he is digging out the treasure."

"Why, to be sure!" exclaimed Sir William. "We were geese not to have supposed so much."

"The only thing is," Mountain resumed, "the sound is very close to our old camp. And again, I do not see how he is there before us, unless the man had wings!"

"Greed and fear are wings," remarked Sir William. "But this rogue has given us an alert, and I have a notion to return the compliment. What say you, gentlemen, shall we have a moonlight hunt?"

It was so agreed; dispositions were made to surround Secundra at his task: some of Sir William's Indians hastened in advance; and a strong guard being left at our headquarters, we set forth along the uneven bottom of the forest; frost crackling, ice sometimes loudly splitting underfoot; and overhead the blackness of pine woods, and the broken brightness of the moon. Our way led down into a hollow of the land; and as we descended the sounds diminished and had almost died away. Upon the other slope it was more open, only dotted with a few pines, and several vast and scattered rocks that made inky shadows in the moonlight. Here the sounds began to reach us more distinctly; we could now perceive the ring of iron, and more exactly estimate the furious degree of haste with which the digger plied his instrument. As we neared the top of the ascent a bird or two winged aloft and hovered darkly in the moonlight; and the next moment we were gazing through a fringe of trees upon a singular picture.

A narrow plateau, overlooked by the white mountains, and encompassed nearer hand by woods, lay bare to the strong radiance of the moon. Rough goods, such as make the wealth of foresters, were sprinkled here and there upon the ground in meaningless disarray. About the midst a tent stood, silvered with frost; the door open, gaping on the black interior. At the one end of this small stage lay what seemed the tattered remnants of a man. Without doubt we had arrived upon the scene of Harris' encampment; there were the goods scattered in the panic of flight; it was in yon tent the Master breathed his last; and the frozen carrion that lay before us was the body of the drunken shoemaker. It was always moving to come upon the theater of any tragic incident; to come upon it after so many days, and to find it (in the seclusion of a desert) still unchanged, must have impressed the mind of the most careless. And yet it was not that which struck us into pillars of stone; but the sight (which yet we had been half expecting) of Secundra, ankle deep in the grave of his late master. He had cast the main part of his raiment by, yet his frail arms and shoulders glistened in the moonlight with a copious sweat; his face was contracted with anxiety and expectation; his blows resounded on the grave, as thick sobs; and behind him, strangely deformed and ink-black upon the frosty ground, the creature's shadow repeated and parodied his swift gesticulations. Some night-birds arose from the boughs upon our coming, and then settled back; but Secundra, absorbed in his toil, heard or heeded not at all.

I heard Mountain whisper to Sir William: " Good God, it's the grave! He's digging him up! " It was what we had all guessed, and yet to hear it put in language thrilled me. Sir William violently started.

" You damned sacrilegious hound! " he cried. " What's this? "

Secundra leaped in the air, a little breathless cry escaped

223

him, the tool flew from his grasp, and he stood one instant staring at the speaker. The next, swift as an arrow, he sped for the woods upon the further side; and the next again, throwing up his hands with a violent gesture of resolution, he had begun already to retrace his steps.

"Well, then you come, you help——" he was saying. But by now my lord had stepped beside Sir William; the moon shone fair upon his face, and the words were still upon Secundra's lips when he beheld and recognized his Master's enemy. "Him!" he screamed, clasping his hands and shrinking on himself.

"Come, come," said Sir William, "there is none here to do you harm, if you be innocent; and if you be guilty, your escape is quite cut off. Speak, what do you here among the graves of the dead and the remains of the unburied?"

"You no murderer?" inquired Secundra. "You true man? You see me safe?"

"I will see you safe, if you be innocent," returned Sir William. "I have said the thing, and I see not wherefore you should doubt it."

"There all murderers," cried Secundra, "that is why! He kill—murderer," pointing to Mountain; "there two hire-murderers"—pointing to my lord and myself—"all gallows-murderers! Ah, I see you all swing in a rope. Now I go save the sahib; he see you swing in a rope. The sahib," he continued, pointing to the grave, "he not dead. He bury, he not dead."

My lord uttered a little noise, moved nearer to the grave, and stood and stared in it.

"Buried and not dead?" exclaimed Sir William. "What kind of rant is this?"

"See, sahib!" said Secundra. "The sahib and I alone with murderers; try all way to escape, no way good. Then try this way: good way in warm climate, good way in India; here in this damn cold place, who can tell? I tell you pretty good hurry: you help, you light a fire, help rub."

"What is the creature talking of?" cried Sir William. "My head goes round."

THE MASTER OF BALLANTRAE

" I tell you I bury him alive," said Secundra. " I teach him swallow his tongue. Now dig him up pretty good hurry, and he not much worse. You light a fire."

Sir William turned to the nearest of his men. " Light a fire," said he. " My lot seems to be cast with the insane."

" You good man," returned Secundra. " Now I go dig the sahib up."

He returned as he spoke to the grave, and resumed his former toil. My lord stood rooted, and I at my lord's side: fearing I knew not what.

The frost was not yet very deep, and presently the Indian threw aside his tool and began to scoop the dirt by handfuls. Then he disengaged a corner of a buffalo robe: and then I saw hair catch among his fingers; yet a moment more, and the moon shone on something white. Awhile Secundra crouched upon his knees, scraping with delicate fingers, breathing with puffed lips; and when he moved aside I beheld the face of the Master wholly disengaged. It was deadly white, the eyes closed, the ears and nostrils plugged, the cheeks fallen, the nose sharp as if in death; but for all he had lain so many days under the sod, corruption had not approached him and (what strangely affected all of us) his lips and chin were mantled with a swarthy beard.

" My God! " cried Mountain, " he was as smooth as a baby when we laid him there! "

" They say hair grows upon the dead," observed Sir William, but his voice was thick and weak.

Secundra paid no heed to our remarks, digging swift as a terrier, in the loose earth; every moment the form of the master, swathed in his buffalo robe, grew more distinct in the bottom of that shallow trough; the moon shining strong, and the shadows of the standers-by, as they drew forward and back, falling and flitting over his emergent countenance. The sight held us with a horror not before experienced. I dared not look my lord in the face, but for as long as it lasted I never observed him to draw breath; and a little in the background one of the men (I know not whom) burst into a kind of sobbing.

225

THE MASTER OF BALLANTRAE

" Now," said Secundra, " you help me lift him out."

Of the flight of time I have no idea; it may have been three hours, and it may have been five, that the Indian labored to reanimate his master's body. One thing only I know, that it was still night, and the moon was not yet set, although it had sunk low, and now barred the plateau with long shadows, when Secundra uttered a small cry of satisfaction; and, leaning swiftly forth, I thought I could myself perceive a change upon that icy countenance of the unburied. The next moment I beheld his eyelids flutter; the next they rose entirely, and the week-old corpse looked me for a moment in the face.

So much display of life I can myself swear to. I have heard from others that he visibly strove to speak, that his teeth showed in his beard, and that his brow was contorted as with an agony of pain and effort. And this may have been; I do not know, I was otherwise engaged. For, at that first disclosure of the dead man's eyes, my Lord Durrisdeer fell to the ground, and when I raised him up he was a corpse.

Day came, and still Secundra could not be persuaded to desist from his unavailing efforts. Sir William, leaving a small party under my command, proceeded on his embassy with the first light; and still the Indian rubbed the limbs and breathed in the mouth of the dead body. You would think such labors might have vitalized a stone; but, except for that one moment (which was my lord's death), the black spirit of the Master held aloof from its discarded clay; and by about the hour of noon even the faithful servant was at length convinced. He took it with unshaken quietude.

" Too cold," said he, " good way in India, no good here." And, asking for some food, which he ravenously devoured as soon as it was set before him, he drew near to the fire and took his place at my elbow. In the same spot, as soon as he had eaten, he stretched himself out, and fell into a childlike slumber, from which I must arouse him, some hours afterward, to take his part as one of the mourners at the double funeral. It was the same throughout; he seemed to have outlived at once and with the same effort, his grief for his master and his terror of myself and Mountain.

One of the men left with me was skilled in stonecutting; and before Sir William returned to pick us up I had chiseled on a bowlder this inscription, with a copy of which I may fitly bring my narrative to a close:

J. D.,

HEIR TO A SCOTTISH TITLE,

A MASTER OF THE ARTS AND GRACES,

ADMIRED IN EUROPE, ASIA, AMERICA,

IN WAR AND PEACE,

IN THE TENTS OF SAVAGE HUNTERS AND THE

CITADELS OF KINGS, AFTER SO MUCH

ACQUIRED, ACCOMPLISHED, AND

ENDURED, LIES HERE FOR-

GOTTEN.

H. D.,

HIS BROTHER,

AFTER A LIFE OF UNMERITED DISTRESS,

BRAVELY SUPPORTED,

DIED ALMOST IN THE SAME HOUR,

AND SLEEPS IN THE SAME GRAVE

WITH HIS FRATERNAL ENEMY.

———

THE PIETY OF HIS WIFE AND ONE OLD SERV-

ANT RAISED THIS STONE

TO BOTH.

PRINCE OTTO

EDITORIAL NOTE

PRINCE OTTO: A Romance, was originally published in *Longman's Magazine* April-October, 1885. The story grew out of an incomplete, discarded tragedy called Semiramis and was begun in San Francisco in 1879 or 1880. Stevenson originally planned to call it THE FOREST STATE, or the Greenwood State but before completing the story he changed the title to PRINCE OTTO. Much work was done upon it at Hyères, the end being reached in 1884; but it was not published in book form until November, 1885, when it appeared with the imprint of Chatto & Windus upon the title-page.

TO NELLY VAN DE GRIFT

(Mrs. Adulfo Sanchez, of Monterey)

At last, after so many years, I have the pleasure of reintroducing you to Prince Otto, *whom you will remember a very little fellow, no bigger in fact than a few sheets of memoranda written for me by your kind hand. The sight of his name will carry you back to an old wooden house embowered in creepers; a house that was far gone in the respectable stages of antiquity and seemed indissoluble from the green garden in which it stood, and that yet was a sea-traveller in its younger days, and had come round the Horn piecemeal in the belly of a ship, and might have heard the seamen stamping and shouting and the note of the boatswain's whistle. It will recall to you the nondescript inhabitants now so widely scattered:—the two horses, the dog, and the four cats, some of them still looking in your face as you read these lines;—the poor lady, so unfortunately married to an author;—the China boy, by this time, perhaps, baiting his line by the banks of a river in the Flowery Land;—and in particular the Scot who was then sick apparently unto death, and whom you did so much to cheer and keep in good behaviour.*

You may remember that he was full of ambitions and designs: so soon as he had his health again completely, you may remember the fortune he was to earn, the journeys he was to go upon, the delights he was to enjoy and confer, and (among other matters) the masterpiece he was to make of Prince Otto!

Well, we will not give in that we are finally beaten. We read together in those days the story of Braddock, and how, as he was carried dying from the scene of his defeat, he promised himself to do better another time: a story that will always touch a brave heart, and a dying speech worthy of a more fortunate commander. I try to be of Braddock's mind. I still mean to get my health again; I still purpose, by hook or crook, this book or the next, to launch a masterpiece; and

DEDICATION

I still intend—some how, some time or other—to see your face and to hold your hand.

Meanwhile, this little paper traveller goes forth instead, crosses the great seas and the long plains and the dark mountains, and comes at last to your door in Monterey, charged with tender greetings. Pray you, take him in. He comes from a house where (even as in your own) there are gathered together some of the waifs of our company at Oakland; a house—for all its outlandish Gaelic name and distant station —where you are well-beloved.

R. L. S.

SKERRYVORE,
 BOURNEMOUTH.

CONTENTS

BOOK I

Prince Errant

BOOK II

Of Love and Politics

235

CONTENTS

BOOK I

PRINCE ERRANT

PRINCE ERRANT

CHAPTER I

IN WHICH THE PRINCE DEPARTS ON AN ADVENTURE

YOU shall seek in vain upon the map of Europe for the bygone state of Grünewald. An independent principality, an infinitesimal member of the German Empire, she played, for several centuries, her part in the discord of Europe; and, at last, in the ripeness of time and at the spiriting of several bald diplomatists, vanished like a morning ghost. Less fortunate than Poland, she left not a regret behind her; and the very memory of her boundaries has faded.

It was a patch of hilly country covered with thick wood. Many streams took their beginning in the glens of Grünewald, turning mills for the inhabitants. There was one town, Mittwalden, and many brown, wooden hamlets, climbing roof above roof, along the steep bottom of dells, and communicating by covered bridges over the larger of the torrents. The hum of watermills, the splash of running water, the clean odour of pine sawdust, the sound and smell of the pleasant wind among the innumerable army of the mountain pines, the dropping fire of huntsmen, the dull stroke of the wood-axe, intolerable roads, fresh trout for supper in the clean bare chamber of an inn, and the song of birds and the music of the village-bells—these were the recollections of the Grünewald tourist.

North and east the foothills of Grünewald sank with varying profile into a vast plain. On these sides many small states bordered with the principality, Gerolstein, an extinct grand duchy, among the number. On the south it marched with the comparatively powerful kingdom of Seaboard Bohemia, celebrated for its flowers and mountain bears, and inhabited by a people of singular simplicity and tenderness of heart. Several intermarriages had, in the course of centuries, united the crowned families of Grünewald and maritime Bohemia; and the last Prince of Grünewald, whose history I purpose to relate, drew his descent through Perdita, the only daughter of King Florizel the First of Bohemia. That these intermarriages had in some degree mitigated the rough, manly stock of the first Grünewalds, was an opinion widely held within the borders of the principality. The charcoal burner, the mountain sawyer, the wielder of the broad axe among the congregated pines of Grünewald, proud of their hard hands, proud of their shrewd ignorance and almost savage lore, looked with an unfeigned contempt on the soft character and manners of the sovereign race.

The precise year of grace in which this tale begins shall be left to the conjecture of the reader. But for the season of the year (which, in such a story, is the more important of the two) it was already so far forward in the spring, that when mountain people heard horns echoing all day about the north-west corner of the principality, they told themselves that Prince Otto and his hunt were up and out for the last time till the return of autumn.

At this point the borders of Grünewald descend somewhat steeply, here and there breaking into crags; and this shaggy and trackless country stands in a bold contrast to the cultivated plain below. It was traversed at that period by two roads alone; one, the imperial highway, bound to Brandenau in Gerolstein, descended the slope obliquely and by the easiest gradients. The other ran like a fillet across the very forehead of the hills, dipping into savage gorges, and wetted by the spray of tiny waterfalls. Once it passed beside a certain tower or castle, built sheer upon the margin of a formidable cliff, and commanding a vast prospect of the skirts of Grünewald and the busy plains of Gerolstein. The Felsenburg (so this tower was called) served now as a prison, now as a hunting-seat; and for all it stood so lonesome to the naked eye, with the aid of a good glass the burghers of Brandenau could

PRINCE ERRANT

count its windows from the lime-tree terrace where they walked at night.

In the wedge of forest hillside enclosed between the roads, the horns continued all day long to scatter tumult; and at length, as the sun began to draw near to the horizon of the plain, a rousing triumph announced the slaughter of the quarry. The first and second huntsman had drawn somewhat aside, and from the summit of a knoll gazed down before them on the drooping shoulders of the hill and across the expanse of plain. They covered their eyes, for the sun was in their faces. The glory of its going down was somewhat pale. Through the confused tracery of many thousands of naked poplars, the smoke of so many houses, and the evening steam ascending from the fields, the sails of a windmill on a gentle eminence moved very conspicuously, like a donkey's ears. And hard by, like an open gash, the imperial highroad ran straight sunward, an artery of travel.

There is one of nature's spiritual ditties, that has not yet been set to words or human music: "The Invitation to the Road;" an air continually sounding in the ears of gipsies, and to whose inspiration our nomadic fathers journeyed all their days. The hour, the season, and the scene, all were in delicate accordance. The air was full of birds of passage, steering westward and northward over Grünewald, an army of specks to the up-looking eye. And below, the great practicable road was bound for the same quarter.

But to the two horsemen on the knoll this spiritual ditty was unheard. They were, indeed, in some concern of mind, scanning every fold of the subjacent forest, and betraying both anger and dismay in their impatient gestures.

"I do not see him, Kuno," said the first huntsman, "nowhere—not a trace, not a hair of the mare's tail! No, sir, he's off; broke cover and got away. Why, for twopence I would hunt him with the dogs!"

"Mayhap, he's gone home," said Kuno, but without conviction.

"Home!" sneered the other. "I give him twelve days to get home. No, it's begun again; it's as it was three years

241

ago, before he married; a disgrace! Hereditary prince, hereditary fool! There goes the government over the borders on a grey mare. What's that? No, nothing—no, I tell you, on my word, I set more store by a good gelding or an English dog. That for your Otto!"

"He's not my Otto," growled Kuno.

"Then I don't know whose he is," was the retort.

"You would put your hand in the fire for him to-morrow," said Kuno, facing round.

"Me!" cried the huntsman. "I would see him hanged! I'm a Grünewald patriot—enrolled, and have my medal, too; and I would help a prince! I'm for liberty and Gondremark."

"Well, it's all one," said Kuno. "If anybody said what you said, you would have his blood, and you know it."

"You have him on the brain," retorted his companion. "There he goes!" he cried, the next moment.

And sure enough, about a mile down the mountain, a rider on a white horse was seen to flit rapidly across a heathy open and vanish among the trees on the farther side.

"In ten minutes he'll be over the border into Gerolstein," said Kuno. "It's past cure."

"Well, if he founders that mare, I'll never forgive him," added the other, gathering his reins.

And as they turned down from the knoll to rejoin their comrades, the sun dipped and disappeared, and the woods fell instantly into the gravity and greyness of the early night.

CHAPTER II

THE night fell upon the Prince while he was threading green tracks in the lower valleys of the wood; and though the stars came out overhead and displayed the interminable order of the pine-tree pyramids, regular and dark like cypresses, their light was of small service to a traveller in such lonely paths, and from thenceforth he rode at random. The austere face of nature, the uncertain issue of his course, the open sky and the free air delighted him like wine; and the hoarse chafing of a river on his left sounded in his ears agreeably.

It was past eight at night before his toil was rewarded and he issued at last out of the forest on the firm white highroad. It lay downhill before him, with a sweeping eastward trend, faintly bright between the thickets; and Otto paused and gazed upon it. So it ran, league after league, still joining others, to the farthest ends of Europe, there skirting the sea-surge, here gleaming in the lights of cities; and the innumerable army of tramps and travellers moved upon it in all lands as by a common impulse, and were now in all places drawing near to the inn door and the night's rest. The pictures swarmed and vanished in his brain; a surge of temptation, a beat of all his blood, went over him, to set spur to the mare and to go on into the unknown for ever. And then it passed away; hunger and fatigue, and that habit of middling actions which we call common sense, resumed their empire; and in that changed mood, his eye lighted upon two bright windows on his left hand, between the road and river.

He turned off by a by-road, and in a few minutes he was knocking with his whip on the door of a large farmhouse, and a chorus of dogs from the farmyard were making angry answer. A very tall, old, white-headed man came, shading a candle, at the summons. He had been of great strength in his time, and of a handsome countenance; but now he was fallen away, his teeth were quite gone, and his voice when he spoke was broken and falsetto.

" You will pardon me," said Otto. " I am a traveller and have entirely lost my way."

" Sir," said the old man, in a very stately, shaky manner, " you are at the River Farm, and I am Killian Gottesheim, at your disposal. We are here, sir, at about an equal distance from Mittwalden in Grünewald and Brandenau in Gerolstein: six leagues to either, and the road excellent; but there is not a wine bush, not a carter's alehouse, anywhere between. You will have to accept my hospitality for the night; rough hospitality, to which I make you freely welcome; for, sir," he added with a bow, " it is God who sends the guest."

" Amen. And I most heartily thank you," replied Otto, bowing in his turn.

" Fritz," said the old man, turning towards the interior, " lead round this gentleman's horse; and you, sir, condescend to enter."

Otto entered a chamber occupying the greater part of the ground-floor of the building. It had probably once been divided; for the farther end was raised by a long step above the nearer, and the blazing fire and the white supper-table seemed to stand upon a daïs. All around were dark, brass-mounted cabinets and cupboards; dark shelves carrying ancient country crockery; guns and antlers and broadside ballads on the wall; a tall old clock with roses on the dial; and down in one corner the comfortable promise of a wine barrel. It was homely, elegant, and quaint.

A powerful youth hurried out to attend on the grey mare; and when Mr. Killian Gottesheim had presented him to his daughter Ottilia, Otto followed to the stable as became, not perhaps the Prince, but the good horseman. When he returned, a smoking omelette and some slices of home-cured ham were waiting him; these were followed by a ragout and a cheese; and it was not until his guest had entirely satisfied his hunger, and the whole party drew about the fire over the wine jug, that Killian Gottesheim's elaborate courtesy permitted him to address a question to the Prince.

" You have perhaps ridden far, sir? " he inquired.

" I have, as you say, ridden far," replied Otto; " and, as you have seen, I was prepared to do justice to your daughter's cookery."

" Possibly, sir, from the direction of Brandenau? " continued Killian.

" Precisely: and I should have slept to-night, had I not wandered, in Mittwalden," answered the Prince, weaving in a patch of truth, according to the habit of all liars.

" Business leads you to Mittwalden? " was the next question.

" Mere curiosity," said Otto. " I have never yet visited the principality of Grünewald."

" A pleasant state, sir," piped the old man, nodding, " a very pleasant state, and a fine race, both pines and people. We reckon ourselves part Grünewalders here, lying so near the borders; and the river there is all good Grünewald water, every drop of it. Yes, sir, a fine state. A man of Grünewald now will swing me an axe over his head that many a man of Gerolstein could hardly lift; and the pines, why, deary me, there must be more pines in that little state, sir, than people in this whole big world. 'Tis twenty years now since I crossed the marshes, for we grow home-keepers in old age; but I mind it as if it was yesterday. Up and down, the road keeps right on from here to Mittwalden; and nothing all the way but the good green pine-trees, big and little, and water power! water power at every step, sir. We once sold a bit of forest, up there beside the highroad; and the sight of minted money that we got for it, has set me ciphering ever since what all the pines in Grünewald would amount to."

" I suppose you see nothing of the Prince? " inquired Otto.

" No," said the young man, speaking for the first time, " nor want to."

" Why so? is he so much disliked? " asked Otto.

" Not what you might call disliked," replied the old gentleman, " but despised, sir."

" Indeed," said the Prince, somewhat faintly.

" Yes, sir, despised," nodded Killian, filling a long pipe, " and, to my way of thinking, justly despised. Here is a man with great opportunities, and what does he do with them? He hunts, and he dresses very prettily—which is a thing to be ashamed of in a man—and he acts plays; and if he does aught else, the news of it has not come here."

" Yet these are all innocent," said Otto. " What would you have him do—make war? "

" No, sir," replied the old man. " But here it is; I have been fifty years upon this River Farm, and wrought in it, day in, day out; I have ploughed and sowed and reaped, and risen early, and waked late; and this is the upshot: that all these years it has supported me and my family; and been the best friend that ever I had, set aside my wife; and now, when my time comes, I leave it a better farm than when I found it. So it is, if a man works hearty in the order of nature, he gets bread and he receives comfort, and whatever he touches breeds. And it humbly appears to me, if that Prince was to labour on his throne, as I have laboured and wrought in my farm, he would find both an increase and a blessing."

" I believe with you, sir," Otto said; " and yet the parallel is inexact. For the farmer's life is natural and simple; but the prince's is both artificial and complicated. It is easy to do right in the one, and exceedingly difficult not to do wrong in the other. If your crop is blighted, you can take off your bonnet and say, ' God's will be done '; but if the prince meets with a reverse, he may have to blame himself for the attempt. And perhaps, if all the kings in Europe were to confine them-selves to innocent amusement, the subjects would be the better off."

" Ay," said the young man Fritz, " you are in the right of it there. That was a true word spoken. And I see you are like me, a good patriot and an enemy to princes."

Otto was somewhat abashed at this deduction, and he made haste to change his ground. " But," said he, " you surprise me by what you say of this Prince Otto. I have heard him, I must own, more favourably painted. I was told he was, in his heart, a good fellow, and the enemy of no one but himself."

"And so he is, sir," said the girl, "a very handsome, pleasant prince; and we know some who would shed their blood for him."

"O! Kuno!" said Fritz. "An ignoramus!"

"Ay, Kuno, to be sure," quavered the old farmer. "Well, since this gentleman is a stranger to these parts, and curious about the Prince, I do believe that story might divert him. This Kuno, you must know, sir, is one of the hunt servants, and a most ignorant, intemperate man: a right Grünewalder, as we say in Gerolstein. We know him well, in this house; for he has come as far as here after his stray dogs; and I make all welcome, sir, without account of state or nation. And, indeed, between Gerolstein and Grünewald the peace has held so long that the roads stand open like my door; and a man will make no more of the frontier than the very birds themselves."

"Ay," said Otto, "it has been a long peace—a peace of centuries."

"Centuries, as you say," returned Killian: "the more the pity that it should not be for ever. Well, sir, this Kuno was one day in fault, and Otto, who has a quick temper, up with his whip and thrashed him, they do say, soundly. Kuno took it as best he could, but at last he broke out, and dared the Prince to throw his whip away and wrestle like a man; for we are all great at wrestling in these parts, and it's so that we generally settle our disputes. Well, sir, the Prince did so; and being a weakly creature, found the tables turned; for the man whom he had just been thrashing like a negro slave, lifted him with a back grip and threw him heels overhead."

"He broke his bridle-arm," cried Fritz—"and some say his nose. Serve him right, say I! Man to man, which is the better at that?"

"And then?" asked Otto.

"O, then, Kuno carried him home; and they were the best of friends from that day forth. I don't say it's a discredit-

247

able story, you observe," continued Mr. Gottesheim; "but it's droll, and that's the fact. A man should think before he strikes; for, as my nephew says, man to man was the old valuation."

"Now, if you were to ask me," said Otto, "I should perhaps surprise you. I think it was the Prince that conquered."

"And, sir, you would be right," replied Killian, seriously. "In the eyes of God, I do not question but you would be right; but men, sir, look at these things differently, and they laugh."

"They made a song of it," observed Fritz. "How does it go? Ta-tum-ta-ra. . . ."

"Well," interrupted Otto, who had no great anxiety to hear the song, "the Prince is young; he may yet mend."

"Not so young, by your leave," cried Fritz. "A man of forty."

"Thirty-six," corrected Mr. Gottesheim.

"O," cried Ottilia, in obvious disillusion, "a man of middle age! And they said he was so handsome when he was young!"

"And bald, too," added Fritz.

Otto passed his hand among his locks. At that moment he was far from happy, and even the tedious evenings at Mittwalden Palace began to smile upon him by comparison.

"O, six-and-thirty!" he protested. "A man is not yet old at six-and-thirty. I am that age myself."

"I should have taken you for more, sir," piped the old farmer. "But if that be so, you are of an age with Master Ottekin, as people call him; and, I would wager a crown, have done more service in your time. Though it seems young by comparison with men of a great age like me, yet it's some way through life for all that; and the mere fools and fiddlers are beginning to grow weary and to look old. Yes, sir, by six-and-thirty, if a man be a follower of God's laws, he should have made himself a home and a good name to live by; he should have got a wife and a blessing on his marriage; and his works, as the Word says, should begin to follow him."

PRINCE ERRANT

"Ah, well, the Prince is married," cried Fritz, with a coarse burst of laughter.

"That seems to entertain you, sir," said Otto.

"Ay," said the young boor. "Did you not know that? I thought all Europe knew it!" And he added a pantomime of a nature to explain his accusation to the dullest.

"Ah, sir," said Mr. Gottesheim, "it is very plain that you are not from hereabouts! But the truth is, that the whole princely family and Court are rips and rascals, not one to mend another. They live, sir, in idleness and—what most commonly follows it—corruption. The Princess has a lover; a Baron, as he calls himself, from East Prussia; and the Prince is so little of a man, sir, that he holds the candle. Nor is that the worst of it, for this foreigner and his paramour are suffered to transact the State affairs, while the Prince takes the salary and leaves all things to go to wrack. There will follow upon this some manifest judgment which, though I am old, I may survive to see."

"Good man, you are in the wrong about Gondremark," said Fritz, showing a greatly increased animation; "but for all the rest, you speak the God's truth like a good patriot. As for the Prince, if he would take and strangle his wife, I would forgive him yet."

"Nay, Fritz," said the old man, "that would be to add iniquity to evil. For you perceive, sir," he continued, once more addressing himself to the unfortunate Prince, "this Otto has himself to thank for these disorders. He has his young wife and his principality, and he has sworn to cherish both."

"Sworn at the altar!" echoed Fritz. "But put your faith in princes!"

"Well, sir, he leaves them both to an adventurer from East Prussia," pursued the farmer; "leaves the girl to be seduced and to go on from bad to worse, till her name's become a taproom by-word, and she not yet twenty; leaves the country to be overtaxed, and bullied with armaments, and jockied into war——"

"War!" cried Otto.

249

"So they say, sir; those that watch their ongoings, say to war," asseverated Killian. "Well, sir, that is very sad; it is a sad thing for this poor, wicked girl to go down to hell with people's curses; it's a sad thing for a tight little happy country to be misconducted; but whoever may complain, I humbly conceive, sir, that this Otto cannot. What he has worked for, that he has got; and may God have pity on his soul, for a great and a silly sinner's!"

"He has broke his oath; then he is a perjurer. He takes the money and leaves the work; why, then plainly he's a thief. A cuckold he was before, and a fool by birth. Better me that!" cried Fritz, and snapped his fingers.

"And now, sir, you will see a little," continued the farmer, "why we think so poorly of this Prince Otto. There's such a thing as a man being pious and honest in the private way; and there is such a thing, sir, as a public virtue; but when a man has neither, the Lord lighten him! Even this Gondremark, that Fritz here thinks so much of——"

"Ay," interrupted Fritz, "Gondremark's the man for me. I would we had his like in Gerolstein."

"He is a bad man," said the old farmer, shaking his head; "and there was never good begun by the breach of God's commandments. But so far I will go with you: he is a man that works for what he has."

"I tell you he's the hope of Grünewald," cried Fritz. "He doesn't suit some of your high-and-dry, old, ancient ideas; but he's a downright modern man—a man of the new lights and the progress of the age. He does some things wrong; so they all do; but he has the people's interests next his heart; and you mark me—you, sir, who are a Liberal, and the enemy of all their governments, you please to mark my words—the day will come in Grünewald, when they take out that yellow-headed skulk of a Prince and that dough-faced Messalina of a Princess, march 'em back foremost over the borders, and proclaim the Baron Gondremark first President. I've heard them say it in a speech. I was at a meeting once at Brandenau, and the Mittwalden delegates spoke up for fifteen thousand. Fifteen thousand, all brigaded, and each man with a medal round his neck to rally by. That's all Gondremark."

"Ay, sir, you see what it leads to: wild talk to-day, and wilder doings to-morrow," said the old man. "For there is one thing certain: that this Gondremark has one foot in the Court backstairs, and the other in the Masons' lodges. He gives himself out, sir, for what nowadays they call a patriot: a man from East Prussia!"

"Give himself out!" cried Fritz. "He is! He is to lay by his title as soon as the Republic is declared; I heard it in a speech."

"Lay by Baron to take up President?" returned Killian. "King Log, King Stork. But you'll live longer than I, and you will see the fruits of it."

"Father," whispered Ottilia, pulling at the speaker's coat, "surely the gentleman is ill."

"I beg your pardon," cried the farmer, rewaking to hospitable thoughts; "can I offer you anything?"

"I thank you. I am very weary," answered Otto. "I have presumed upon my strength. If you would show me to a bed, I should be grateful."

"Ottilia, a candle!" said the old man. "Indeed, sir, you look pale. A little cordial water? No? Then follow me, I beseech you, and I will bring you to the stranger's bed. You are not the first by many who has slept well below my roof," continued the old gentleman, mounting the stairs before his guest; "for good food, honest wine, a grateful conscience, and a little pleasant chat before a man retires, are worth all the possets and apothecary's drugs. See, sir," and here he opened a door and ushered Otto into a little whitewashed sleeping-room, "here you are in port. It is small, but it is airy, and the sheets are clean and kept in lavender. The window, too, looks out above the river, and there's no music like a little river's. It plays the same tune (and that's the favourite) over and over again, and yet does not weary of it like men fiddlers. It takes the mind out of doors; and though we should be grateful for good houses, there is, after all, no house like God's out-of-doors. And lastly, sir, it quiets a man down like saying his prayers. So here, sir, I take my kind leave of you until to-morrow; and it is my prayerful wish that you may slumber like a prince."

And the old man, with the twentieth courteous inclination, left his guest alone.

CHAPTER III

IN WHICH THE PRINCE COMFORTS AGE AND BEAUTY AND
DELIVERS A LECTURE ON DISCRETION IN LOVE

THE Prince was early abroad: in the time of the first
chorus of birds, of the pure and quiet air, of the slant-
ing sunlight and the mile-long shadows. To one who had
passed a miserable night, the freshness of that hour was
tonic and reviving; to steal a march upon his slumbering
fellows, to be the Adam of the coming day, composed and
fortified his spirit; and the Prince, breathing deep and
pausing as he went, walked in wet fields beside his shadow,
and was glad.

A trellised path led down into the valley of the brook,
and he turned to follow it. The stream was a break-neck,
boiling highland river. Hard by the farm, it leaped a
little precipice in a thick grey-mare's tail of twisted filaments,
and then lay and worked and bubbled in a lynn. Into the
middle of this quaking pool a rock protruded, shelving
to a cape; and thither Otto scrambled and sat down
to ponder.

Soon the sun struck through the screen of branches and
thin early leaves that made a hanging bower above the
fall; and the golden lights and flitting shadows fell upon
and marbled the surface of that seething pot; and rays
plunged deep among the turning waters; and a spark, as
bright as a diamond, lit upon the swaying eddy. It began
to grow warm where Otto lingered, warm and heady; the
lights swam, weaving their maze across the shaken pool; on
the impending rock, reflections danced like butterflies;
and the air was fanned by the waterfall as by a swinging
curtain.

Otto, who was weary with tossing and beset with horrid

phantoms of remorse and jealousy, instantly fell dead in love with that sun-chequered, echoing corner. Holding his feet, he stared out of a drowsy trance, wondering, admiring, musing, losing his way among uncertain thoughts. There is nothing that so apes the external bearing of free will, as that unconscious bustle, obscurely following liquid laws, with which a river contends among obstructions. It seems the very play of man and destiny, and as Otto pored on these recurrent changes, he grew, by equal steps, the sleepier and the more profound. Eddy and Prince were alike jostled in their purpose, alike anchored by intangible influences in one corner of the world. Eddy and Prince were alike useless, starkly useless, in the cosmology of men. Eddy and Prince —Prince and Eddy.

It is probable he had been some while asleep when a voice recalled him from oblivion. " Sir," it was saying; and looking round, he saw Mr. Killian's daughter, terrified by her boldness and making bashful signals from the shore. She was a plain, honest lass, healthy and happy and good, and with that sort of beauty that comes of happiness and health. But her confusion lent her for the moment an additional charm.

" Good morning," said Otto, rising and moving towards her. " I arose early and was in a dream."

" O, sir! " she cried, " I wish to beg of you to spare my father; for I assure your Highness, if he had known who you was, he would have bitten his tongue out sooner. And Fritz, too—how he went on! But I had a notion; and this morning I went straight down into the stable, and there was your Highness's crown upon the stirrup-irons! But, oh, sir, I made certain you would spare them; for they were as innocent as lambs."

" My dear," said Otto, both amused and gratified, " you do not understand. It is I who am in the wrong; for I had no business to conceal my name and lead on these gentlemen to speak of me. And it is I who have to beg of you, that you will keep my secret and not betray the discourtesy of which I was guilty. As for any fear of me, your friends are safe in Gerolstein; and even in my own territory, you must be well aware I have no power."

"O, sir," she said, curtsying, "I would not say that: the huntsmen would all die for you."

"Happy Prince!" said Otto. "But although you are too courteous to avow the knowledge, you have had many opportunities of learning that I am a vain show. Only last night we heard it very clearly stated. You see the shadow flitting on this hard rock. Prince Otto, I am afraid, is but the moving shadow, and the name of the rock is Gondremark. Ah! if your friends had fallen foul of Gondremark! But happily the younger of the two admires him. And as for the old gentleman your father, he is a wise man and an excellent talker, and I would take a long wager he is honest."

"O, for honest, your Highness, that he is!" exclaimed the girl. "And Fritz is as honest as he. And as for all they said, it was just talk and nonsense. When country-folk get gossiping, they go on, I do assure you, for the fun; they don't as much as think of what they say. If you went to the next farm, it's my belief you would hear as much against my father."

"Nay, nay," said Otto, "there you go too fast. For all that was said against Prince Otto——"

"O, it was shameful!" cried the girl.

"Not shameful—true," returned Otto. "Oh, yes—true. I am all they said of me—all that and worse."

"I never!" cried Ottilia. "Is that how you do? Well, you would never be a soldier. Now if any one accuses me, I get up and give it them. O, I defend myself. I wouldn't take a fault at another person's hands, no, not if I had it on my forehead. And that's what you must do, if you mean to live it out. But, indeed, I never heard such nonsense. I should think you was ashamed of yourself! You're bald then, I suppose?"

"O no," said Otto, fairly laughing. "There I acquit myself: not bald!"

"Well, and good?" pursued the girl. "Come now, you

255

know you are good, and I'll make you say so. . . . Your Highness, I beg your humble pardon. But there's no disrespect intended. And anyhow, you know you are."

"Why, now, what am I to say?" replied Otto. "You are a cook, and excellently well you do it; I embrace the chance of thanking you for the ragout. Well now, have you not seen good food so bedevilled by unskilful cookery that no one could be brought to eat the pudding? That is me, my dear. I am full of good ingredients, but the dish is worthless. I am—I give it you in one word—sugar in the salad."

"Well, I don't care, you're good," reiterated Ottilia, a little flushed by having failed to understand.

"I will tell you one thing," replied Otto: "You are!"

"Ah, well, that's what they all said of you," moralised the girl; "such a tongue to come round—such a flattering tongue!"

"O, you forget, I am a man of middle age," the Prince chuckled.

"Well, to speak to you, I should think you was a boy; and Prince or no Prince, if you came worrying where I was cooking, I would pin a napkin to your tails. . . . And, O Lord, I declare I hope your Highness will forgive me," the girl added. "I can't keep it in my mind."

"No more can I," cried Otto. "That is just what they complain of!"

They made a loverly-looking couple; only the heavy pouring of that horse-tail of water made them raise their voices above lovers' pitch. But to a jealous onlooker from above, their mirth and close proximity might easily give umbrage; and a rough voice out of the tuft of brambles began calling on Ottilia by name. She changed colour at that. "It is Fritz," she said. "I must go."

"Go, my dear, and I need not bid you go in peace, for I think you have discovered that I am not formidable at close quarters," said the Prince, and made her a fine gesture of dismissal.

So Ottilia skipped up the bank, and disappeared into the

thicket, stopping once for a single blushing bob—blushing, because she had in the interval once more forgotten and remembered the stranger's quality.

Otto returned to his rock promontory; but his humour had in the meantime changed. The sun now shone more fairly on the pool; and over its brown welling surface, the blue of heaven and the golden green of the spring foliage danced in fleeting arabesque. The eddies laughed and brightened with essential colour. And the beauty of the dell began to rankle in the Prince's mind; it was so near to his own borders, yet without. He had never had much of the joy of possessorship in any of the thousand and one beautiful and curious things that were his; and now he was conscious of envy for what was another's. It was, indeed, a smiling, dilettante sort of envy; but yet there it was: the passion of Ahab for the vineyard, done in little; and he was relieved when Mr. Killian appeared upon the scene.

"I hope, sir, that you have slept well under my plain roof," said the old farmer.

"I am admiring this sweet spot that you are privileged to dwell in," replied Otto, evading the inquiry.

"It is rustic," returned Mr. Gottesheim, looking around him with complacency, "a very rustic corner; and some of the land to the west is most excellent fat land, excellent deep soil. You should see my wheat in the ten-acre field. There is not a farm in Grünewald, no, nor many in Gerolstein, to match the River Farm. Some sixty—I keep thinking when I sow—some sixty, and some seventy, and some an hundredfold; and my own place, six score! But that, sir, is partly the farming."

"And the stream has fish?" asked Otto.

"A fish-pond," said the farmer. "Ay, it is a pleasant bit. It is pleasant even here, if one had time, with the brook drumming in that black pool, and the green things hanging all about the rocks, and, dear heart, to see the very pebbles! all turned to gold and precious stones! But you have come to that time of life, sir, when, if you will excuse me, you must look to have the rheumatism set in. Thirty to forty is, as one may say, their seedtime. And this is a damp cold corner for the early morning and an empty stomach. If I might humbly advise you, sir, I would be moving."

"With all my heart," said Otto, gravely. "And so you have lived your life here?" he added, as they turned to go.

"Here I was born," replied the farmer, "and here I wish I could say I was to die. But fortune, sir, fortune turns the wheel. They say she is blind, but we will hope she only sees a little farther on. My grandfather and my father and I, we have all tilled these acres, my furrow following theirs. All the three names are on the garden bench, two Killians and one Johann. Yes, sir, good men have prepared themselves for the great change in my old garden. Well do I mind my father, in a woollen night-cap, the good soul, going round and round to see the last of it. "Killian," said he, "do you see the smoke of my tobacco? Why," said he, "that is man's life." It was his last pipe, and I believe he knew it; and it was a strange thing, without doubt, to leave the trees that he had planted, and the son that he had begotten, ay, sir, and even the old pipe with the Turk's head that he had smoked since he was a lad and went a-courting. But here we have no continuing city; and as for the eternal, it's a comfortable thought that we have other merits than our own. And yet you would hardly think how sore it goes against the grain with me, to die in a strange bed."

"And must you do so? For what reason?" Otto asked.

"The reason? The place is to be sold; three thousand crowns," replied Mr. Gottesheim. "Had it been a third of that, I may say without boasting that, what with my credit and my savings, I could have met the sum. But at three thousand, unless I have singular good fortune and the new proprietor continues me in office, there is nothing left me but to budge."

Otto's fancy for the place redoubled at the news, and

became joined with other feelings. If all he heard were true, Grünewald was growing very hot for a sovereign Prince; it might be well to have a refuge; and if so, what more delightful hermitage could man imagine? Mr. Gottesheim, besides, had touched his sympathies. Every man loves in his soul to play the part of the stage deity. And to step down to the aid of the old farmer, who had so roughly handled him in talk, was the ideal of a Fair Revenge. Otto's thoughts brightened at the prospect, and he began to regard himself with a renewed respect.

"I can find you, I believe, a purchaser," he said, "and one who would continue to avail himself of your skill."

"Can you, sir, indeed?" said the old man. "Well, I shall be heartily obliged; for I begin to find a man may practise resignation all his days, as he takes physic, and not come to like it in the end."

"If you will have the papers drawn, you may even burthen the purchase with your interest," said Otto. "Let it be assured to you through life."

"Your friend, sir," insinuated Killian, "would not, perhaps, care to make the interest reversible? Fritz is a good lad."

"Fritz is young," said the Prince, drily; "he must earn consideration, not inherit."

"He has long worked upon the place, sir," insisted Mr. Gottesheim; "and at my great age, for I am seventy-eight come harvest, it would be a troublesome thought to the proprietor how to fill my shoes. It would be a care spared to assure yourself of Fritz. And I believe he might be tempted by a permanency."

"The young man has unsettled views," returned Otto.

"Possibly the purchaser——" began Killian.

A little spot of anger burned in Otto's cheek. "I am the purchaser," he said.

"It was what I might have guessed," replied the farmer, bowing with an aged, obsequious dignity. "You have made an old man very happy; and I may say, indeed, that I have entertained an angel unawares. Sir, the great people of this

world—and by that I mean those who are great in station
—if they had only hearts like yours, how they would make
the fires burn and the poor sing!"

"I would not judge them hardly, sir," said Otto. "We
all have our frailties."

"Truly, sir," said Mr. Gottesheim, with unction. "And
by what name, sir, am I to address my generous landlord?"

The double recollection of an English traveller, whom he
had received the week before at court, and of an old English
rogue called Transome, whom he had known in youth, came
pertinently to the Prince's help. "Transome," he answered,
"is my name. I am an English traveller. It is, to-day,
Tuesday. On Thursday, before noon, the money shall be
ready. Let us meet, if you please, in Mittwalden, at the
'Morning Star.'"

"I am, in all things lawful, your servant to command,"
replied the farmer. "An Englishman! You are a great race
of travellers. And has your lordship some experience of
land?"

"I have had some interest of the kind before," returned
the Prince; "not in Gerolstein, indeed. But fortune, as
you say, turns the wheel, and I desire to be beforehand with
her revolutions."

"Very right, sir, I am sure," said Mr. Killian.

They had been strolling with deliberation; but they were
now drawing near to the farmhouse, mounting by the trellised pathway to the level of the meadow. A little before
them, the sound of voices had been some while audible, and
now grew louder and more distinct with every step of their
advance. Presently, when they emerged upon the top of the
bank, they beheld Fritz and Ottilia some way off; he, very
black and bloodshot, emphasising his hoarse speech with
the smacking of his fist against his palm; she, standing a
little way off in blowsy, voluble distress.

"Dear me!" said Mr. Gottesheim, and made as if he
would turn aside.

But Otto went straight towards the lovers, in whose dis-
sension he believed himself to have a share. And, indeed,

as soon as he had seen the Prince, Fritz had stood tragic, as if awaiting and defying his approach.

"O, here you are!" he cried, as soon as they were near enough for easy speech. "You are a man at least, and must reply. What were you after? Why were you two skulking in the bush? God!" he broke out, turning again upon Ottilia, "to think that I should waste my heart on you!"

"I beg your pardon," Otto cut in. "You were addressing me. In virtue of what circumstance am I to render you an account of this young lady's conduct? Are you her father? her brother? her husband?"

"O, sir, you know as well as I," returned the peasant. "We keep company, she and I. I love her, and she is by way of loving me; but all shall be above-board, I would have her to know. I have a good pride of my own."

"Why, I perceive I must explain to you what love is," said Otto. "Its measure is kindness. It is very possible that you are proud; but she, too, may have some self-esteem; I do not speak for myself. And perhaps, if your own doings were so curiously examined, you might find it inconvenient to reply."

"These are all set-offs," said the young man. "You know very well that a man is a man, and a woman only a woman. That holds good all over, up and down. I ask you a question, I ask it again, and here I stand." He drew a mark and toed it.

"When you have studied liberal doctrines somewhat deeper," said the Prince, "you will perhaps change your note. You are a man of false weights and measures, my young friend. You have one scale for women, another for men; one for princes, and one for farmer-folk. On the prince who neglects his wife you can be most severe. But what of the lover who insults his mistress? You use the name of love. I should think this lady might very fairly ask to be delivered from love of such a nature. For if I, a stranger, had been one-tenth part so gross and so discourteous, you would most righteously have broke my head.

It would have been in your part, as lover, to protect her from such insolence. Protect her first, then, from yourself."

" Ay," quoth Mr. Gottesheim, who had been looking on with his hands behind his tall old back, " ay, that's scripture truth."

Fritz was staggered, not only by the Prince's imperturbable superiority of manner, but by a glimmering consciousness that he himself was in the wrong. The appeal to liberal doctrines had, besides, unmanned him.

" Well," said he, " if I was rude, I'll own to it. I meant no ill, and did nothing out of my just rights; but I am above all these old vulgar notions too; and if I spoke sharp, I'll ask her pardon."

" Freely granted, Fritz," said Ottilia.

" But all this doesn't answer me," cried Fritz. " I ask what you two spoke about. She says she promised not to tell; well, then, I mean to know. Civility is civility; but I'll be no man's gull. I have a right to common justice, if I *do* keep company!"

" If you will ask Mr. Gottesheim," replied Otto, " you will find I have not spent my hours in idleness. I have, since I arose this morning, agreed to buy the farm. So far I will go to satisfy a curiosity which I condemn."

" O, well, if there was business, that's another matter," returned Fritz. " Though it beats me why you could not tell. But, of course, if the gentleman is to buy the farm, I suppose there would naturally be an end."

" To be sure," said Mr. Gottesheim, with a strong accent of conviction.

But Ottilia was much braver. " There now!" she cried in triumph. " What did I tell you? I told you I was fighting your battles. Now you see! Think shame of your suspicious temper! You should go down upon your bended knees both to that gentleman and me."

CHAPTER IV

A LITTLE before noon Otto, by a triumph of manœuvring, effected his escape. He was quit in this way of the ponderous gratitude of Mr. Killian, and of the confidential gratitude of poor Ottilia; but of Fritz he was not quit so readily. That young politician, brimming with mysterious glances, offered to lend his convoy as far as to the highroad; and Otto, in fear of some residuary jealousy and for the girl's sake, had not the courage to gainsay him; but he regarded his companion with uneasy glances, and devoutly wished the business at an end. For some time Fritz walked by the mare in silence; and they had already traversed more than half the proposed distance when, with something of a blush, he looked up and opened fire.

"Are you not," he asked, "what they call a socialist?"

"Why, no," returned Otto, "not precisely what they call so. Why do you ask?"

"I will tell you why," said the young man. "I saw from the first that you were a red progressional, and nothing but the fear of old Killian kept you back. And there, sir, you were right: old men are always cowards. But nowadays, you see, there are so many groups: you can never tell how far the likeliest kind of man may be prepared to go; and I was never sure you were one of the strong thinkers, till you hinted about women and free love."

"Indeed," cried Otto, "I never said a word of such a thing."

"Not you!" cried Fritz. "Never a word to compromise! You was sowing seed: ground-bait, our president calls it. But it's hard to deceive me, for I know all the agitators and their ways, and all the doctrines; and between

263

you and me," lowering his voice, " I am myself affiliated.
O, yes, I am a secret society man, and here is my medal."
And drawing out a green ribbon that he wore about his neck,
he held up, for Otto's inspection, a pewter medal bearing
the imprint of a Phœnix and the legend, *Libertas*. " And
so now you see you may trust me," added Fritz. " I am
none of your ale-house talkers; I am a convinced revolutionary." And he looked meltingly upon Otto.

" I see," replied the Prince; " that is very gratifying.
Well, sir, the great thing for the good of one's country
is, first of all, to be a good man. All springs from there.
For my part, although you are right in thinking that I
have to do with politics, I am unfit by intellect and temper
for a leading *rôle*. I was intended, I fear, for a subaltern.
Yet we have all something to command, Mr. Fritz, if it be
only our own temper; and a man about to marry must
look closely to himself. The husband's, like the prince's,
is a very artificial standing; and it is hard to be kind in
either. Do you follow that? "

" O, yes, I follow that," replied the young man, sadly
chop-fallen over the nature of the information he had elic-
ited; and then brightening up: " Is it," he ventured, " is
it for an arsenal that you have bought the farm? "

" We'll see about that," the Prince answered, laughing.
" You must not be too zealous. And in the meantime, if I
were you, I would say nothing on the subject."

" O, trust me, sir, for that," cried Fritz, as he pocketed
a crown. " And you've let nothing out; for I suspected
—I might say I knew it—from the first. And mind you,
when a guide is required," he added, " I know all the forest
paths."

Otto rode away, chuckling. This talk with Fritz had
vastly entertained him; nor was he altogether discontented
with his bearing at the farm; men, he was able to tell himself, had behaved worse under smaller provocation. And,
to harmonise all, the road and the April air were both delightful to his soul.

Up and down, and to and fro, ever mounting through

the wooded foothills, the broad, white highroad wound onward into Grünewald. On either hand the pines stood coolly rooted—green moss prospering, springs welling forth between their knuckled spurs; and though some were broad and stalwart, and others spiry and slender, yet all stood firm in the same attitude and with the same expression, like a silent army presenting arms.

The road lay all the way apart from towns and villages, which it left on either hand. Here and there, indeed, in the bottom of green glens, the Prince could spy a few congregated roofs, or perhaps above him, on a shoulder, the solitary cabin of a woodman. But the highway was an international undertaking, and with its face set for distant cities, scorned the little life of Grünewald. Hence it was exceeding solitary. Near the frontier Otto met a detachment of his own troops marching in the hot dust; and he was recognised and somewhat feebly cheered as he rode by. But from that time forth and for a long while he was alone with the great woods.

Gradually the spell of pleasure relaxed; his own thoughts returned, like stinging insects, in a cloud; and the talk of the night before, like a shower of buffets, fell upon his memory. He looked east and west for any comforter; and presently he was aware of a cross-road coming steeply down hill, and a horseman cautiously descending. A human voice or presence, like a spring in the desert, was now welcome in itself, and Otto drew bridle to await the coming of this stranger. He proved to be a very red-faced, thick-lipped countryman, with a pair of fat saddle-bags and a stone bottle at his waist; who, as soon as the Prince hailed him, jovially, if somewhat thickly, answered. At the same time he gave a beery yaw in the saddle. It was clear his bottle was no longer full.

"Do you ride towards Mittwalden?" asked the Prince.

"As far as the cross-road to Tannenbrunn," the man replied. "Will you bear company?"

"With pleasure. I have even waited for you on the chance," answered Otto.

265

PRINCE OTTO

By this time they were close alongside; and the man, with the countryfolk instinct, turned his cloudy vision first of all on his companion's mount. "The devil!" he cried. "You ride a bonny mare, friend!" And then, his curiosity being satisfied about the essential, he turned his attention to that merely secondary matter, his companion's face. He started. "The Prince!" he cried, saluting, with another yaw that came near dismounting him. "I beg your pardon, your Highness, not to have reco'nised you at once."

The Prince was vexed out of his self-possession. "Since you know me," he said, "it is unnecessary we should ride together. I will precede you, if you please." And he was about to set spur to the grey mare, when the half-drunken fellow, reaching over, laid his hand upon the rein.

"Hark you," he said, "prince or no prince, that is not how one man should conduct himself with another. What! You'll ride with me incog. and set me talking! But if I know you, you'll preshede me, if you please! Spy!" And the fellow, crimson with drink and injured vanity, almost spat the word into the Prince's face.

A horrid confusion came over Otto. He perceived that he had acted rudely, grossly presuming on his station. And perhaps a little shiver of physical alarm mingled with his remorse, for the fellow was very powerful and not more than half in the possession of his senses. "Take your hand from my rein," he said, with a sufficient assumption of command; and when the man, rather to his wonder, had obeyed: "You should understand, sir," he added, "that while I might be glad to ride with you as one person of sagacity with another, and so receive your true opinions, it would amuse me very little to hear the empty compliments you would address to me as Prince."

"You think I would lie, do you?" cried the man with the bottle, purpling deeper.

"I know you would," returned Otto, entering entirely into his self-possession. "You would not even show me the medal you wear about your neck." For he had caught a glimpse of a green ribbon at the fellow's throat.

PRINCE ERRANT

The change was instantaneous: the red face became mottled with yellow; a thick-fingered, tottering hand made a clutch at the tell-tale ribbon. "Medal!" the man cried, wonderfully sobered. "I have no medal."

"Pardon me," said the Prince. "I will even tell you what that medal bears: a Phœnix burning, with the word *Libertas*." The medalist remaining speechless, "You are a pretty fellow," continued Otto, smiling, "to complain of incivility from the man whom you conspire to murder."

"Murder!" protested the man. "Nay, never that; nothing criminal for me!"

"You are strangely misinformed," said Otto. "Conspiracy itself is criminal, and insures the pain of death. Nay, sir, death it is; I will guarantee my accuracy. Not that you need be so deplorably affected, for I am no officer. But those who mingle with politics should look at both sides of the medal."

"Your Highness . . ." began the knight of the bottle.

"Nonsense! you are a Republican," cried Otto; "what have you to do with highnesses? But let us continue to ride forward. Since you so much desire it, I cannot find it in my heart to deprive you of my company. And for that matter, I have a question to address to you. Why, being so great a body of men—for you are a great body—fifteen thousand, I have heard, but that will be understated: am I right?"

The man gurgled in his throat.

"Why, then, being so considerable a party," resumed Otto, "do you not come before me boldly with your wants? —what do I say? with your commands? Have I the name of being passionately devoted to my throne? I can scarce suppose it. Come, then; show me your majority, and I will instantly resign. Tell this to your friends; assure them from me of my docility; assure them that, however they conceive of my deficiencies, they cannot suppose me more unfit to be a ruler than I do myself. I am one of the worst princes in Europe; will they improve on that?"

"Far be it from me . . ." the man began.

PRINCE OTTO

" See, now, if you will not defend my government!" cried Otto. " If I were you, I would leave conspiracies. You are as little fit to be a conspirator as I to be a king."

" One thing I will say out," said the man. " It is not so much you that we complain of; it's your lady."

" Not a word, sir," said the Prince; and then after a moment's pause, and in tones of some anger and contempt: " I once more advise you to have done with politics," he added; " and when next I see you, let me see you sober. A morning drunkard is the last man to sit in judgment even upon the worst of princes."

" I have had a drop, but I had not been drinking," the man replied, triumphing in a sound distinction. " And if I had, what then? Nobody hangs by me. But my mill is standing idle, and I blame it on your wife. Am I alone in that? Go round and ask. Where are the mills? Where are the young men that should be working? Where is the currency? All paralysed. No, sir, it is not equal; for I suffer for your faults—I pay for them, by George, out of a poor man's pocket. And what have you to do with mine? Drunk or sober, I can see my country going to hell, and I can see whose fault it is. And so now, I've said my say, and you may drag me to a stinking dungeon; what care I? I've spoke the truth, and so I'll hold hard, and not intrude upon your Highness's society."

And the miller reined up and, clumsily enough, saluted.

" You will observe, I have not asked your name," said Otto. " I wish you a good ride," and he rode on hard. But let him ride as he pleased, this interview with the miller was a chokepear, which he could not swallow. He had begun by receiving a reproof in manners, and ended by sustaining a defeat in logic, both from a man whom he despised. All his old thoughts returned with fresher venom. And by three in the afternoon, coming to the cross-roads for Beckstein, Otto decided to turn aside and dine there leisurely. Nothing at least could be worse than to go on as he was going.

In the inn at Beckstein he remarked, immediately upon his entrance, an intelligent young gentleman dining, with

a book in front of him. He had his own place laid close
to the reader, and with a proper apology, broke ground
by asking what he read.

"I am perusing," answered the young gentleman, "the
last work of the Herr Doctor Hohenstockwitz, cousin and
librarian of your Prince here in Grünewald—a man of great
erudition and some lambencies of wit."

"I am acquainted," said Otto, "with the Herr Doctor,
though not yet with his work."

"Two privileges that I must envy you," replied the
young man, politely: "an honour in hand, a pleasure in
the bush."

"The Herr Doctor is a man much respected, I believe, for
his attainments?" asked the Prince.

"He is, sir, a remarkable instance of the force of intellect," replied the reader. "Who of our young men know
anything of his cousin, all reigning Prince although he be?
Who but has heard of Doctor Gotthold? But intellectual
merit, alone of all distinctions, has its base in nature."

"I have the gratification of addressing a student—perhaps an author?" Otto suggested.

The young man somewhat flushed. "I have some claim
to both distinctions, sir, as you suppose," said he; "there
is my card. I am the licentiate Roederer, author of several
works on the theory and practice of politics."

"You immensely interest me," said the Prince; "the
more so as I gather that here in Grünewald we are on the
brink of revolution. Pray, since these have been your special
studies, would you augur hopefully of such a movement?"

"I perceive," said the young author, with a certain vine-
gary twitch, "that you are unacquainted with my opuscula.
I am a convinced authoritarian. I share none of those illu-
sory, Utopian fancies with which empirics blind themselves
and exasperate the ignorant. The day of these ideas is,
believe me, past, or at least passing."

"When I look about me——" began Otto.

"When you look about you," interrupted the licentiate,
"you behold the ignorant. But in the laboratory of opinion,

beside the studious lamp, we begin already to discard these figments. We begin to return to nature's order, to what I might call, if I were to borrow from the language of therapeutics, the expectant treatment of abuses. You will not misunderstand me," he continued: " a country in the condition in which we find Grünewald, a prince such as your Prince Otto, we must explicitly condemn; they are behind the age. But I would look for a remedy not to brute convulsions, but to the natural supervenience of a more able sovereign. I should amuse you, perhaps," added the licentiate, with a smile, " I think I should amuse you if I were to explain my notion of a prince. We who have studied in the closet, no longer, in this age, propose ourselves for active service. The paths, we have perceived, are incompatible. I would not have a student on the throne, though I would have one near by for an adviser. I would set forward as prince a man of a good, medium understanding, lively rather than deep; a man of courtly manner, possessed of the double art to ingratiate and command, receptive, accommodating, seductive. I have been observing you since your first entrance. Well, sir, were I a subject of Grünewald I should pray heaven to set upon the seat of government just such another as yourself."

" The devil, you would! " exclaimed the Prince.

The licentiate, Roederer, laughed most heartily. " I thought I should astonish you," he said. " These are not the ideas of the masses."

" They are not, I can assure you," Otto said.

" Or rather," distinguished the licentiate, " not to-day. The time will come, however, when these ideas shall prevail."

" You will permit me, sir, to doubt it," said Otto.

" Modesty is always admirable," chuckled the theorist. " But yet I assure you, a man like you, with such a man as, say, Doctor Gotthold at your elbow, would be, for all practical issues, my ideal ruler."

At this rate the hours sped pleasantly for Otto. But the licentiate unfortunately slept that night at Beckstein, where he was, being dainty in the saddle and given to half stages. And to find a convoy to Mittwalden, and thus mitigate the company of his own thoughts, the Prince had to make favour with a certain party of wood merchants from various states of the empire, who had been drinking together somewhat noisily at the far end of the apartment.

The night had already fallen when they took the saddle. The merchants were very loud and mirthful; each had a face like a nor'west moon; and they played pranks with each others' horses, and mingled songs and choruses, and alternately remembered and forgot the companion of their ride. Otto thus combined society and solitude, hearkening now to their chattering and empty talk, now to the voices of the encircling forest. The starlit dark, the faint wood airs, the clank of the horseshoes making broken music, accorded together and attuned his mind. And he was still in a most equal temper when the party reached the top of that long hill that overlooks Mittwalden.

Down in the bottom of a bowl of forest, the lights of the little formal town glittered in a pattern, street crossing street; away by itself on the right, the palace was glowing like a factory.

Although he knew not Otto, one of the wood merchants was a native of the state. "There," said he, pointing to the palace with his whip, " there is Jezebel's inn."

"What, do you call it that? " cried another, laughing.

" Ay, that's what they call it," returned the Grünewalder; and he broke into a song, which the rest, as people well acquainted with the words and air, instantly took up in chorus. Her Serene Highness Amalia Seraphina, Princess of Grünewald, was the heroine, Gondremark the hero of this ballad. Shame hissed in Otto's ears. He reined up short and sat stunned in the saddle; and the singers continued to descend the hill without him.

The song went to a rough, swashing, popular air; and long after the words became inaudible the swing of the music, rising and falling, echoed insult in the Prince's brain. He fled the sounds. Hard by him on his right a road struck towards the palace, and he followed it through the thick shadows and branching alleys of the park. It was a busy place on a fine summer's afternoon, when the court and burghers met and saluted; but at that hour of the night in the early spring it was deserted to the roosting birds. Hares rustled among the covert; here and there a statue stood glimmering, with its eternal gesture; here and there the echo of an imitation temple clattered ghostly to the trampling of the mare. Ten minutes brought him to the upper end of his own home garden, where the small stables opened, over a bridge, upon the park. The yard clock was striking the hour of ten; so was the big bell in the palace bell-tower; and, farther off, the belfries of the town. About the stable all else was silent but the stamping of stalled horses and the rattle of halters. Otto dismounted; and as he did so a memory came back to him: a whisper of dishonest grooms and stolen corn, once heard, long forgotten, and now recurring in the nick of opportunity. He crossed the bridge, and, going up to a window, knocked six or seven heavy blows in a particular cadence, and, as he did so, smiled. Presently a wicket was opened in the gate, and a man's head appeared in the dim starlight.

"Nothing to-night," said a voice.

"Bring a lantern," said the Prince.

"Dear heart a' mercy!" cried the groom. "Who's that?"

"It is I, the Prince," replied Otto. "Bring a lantern, take in the mare, and let me through into the garden."

The man remained silent for a while, his head still projecting through the wicket.

"His Highness!" he said at last. "And why did your Highness knock so strange?"

"It is a superstition in Mittwalden," answered Otto, "that it cheapens corn."

With a sound like a sob the groom fled. He was very white when he returned, even by the light of the lantern; and his hand trembled as he undid the fastenings and took the mare.

"Your Highness," he began at last, "for God's sake . . ." And there he paused, oppressed with guilt.

PRINCE ERRANT

" For God's sake, what? " asked Otto, cheerfully. " For God's sake, let us have cheaper corn, say I. Good-night! " And he strode off into the garden, leaving the groom petrified once more.

The garden descended by a succession of stone terraces to the level of the fish-pond. On the far side the ground rose again, and was crowned by the confused roofs and gables of the palace. The modern pillared front, the ball-room, the great library, the princely apartments, the busy and illuminated quarters of that great house, all faced the town. The garden side was much older; and here it was almost dark; only a few windows quietly lighted at various elevations. The great square tower rose, thinning by stages like a telescope; and on the top of all the flag hung motionless.

The garden, as it now lay in the dusk and glimmer of the starshine, breathed of April violets. Under night's cavern arch the shrubs obscurely bustled. Through the plotted terraces and down the marble stairs the Prince rapidly descended, fleeing before uncomfortable thoughts. But, alas! from these there is no city of refuge. And now, when he was about mid-way of the descent, distant strains of music began to fall upon his ear from the ball-room, where the court was dancing. They reached him faint and broken, but they touched the keys of memory; and through and above them, Otto heard the ranting melody of the wood merchants' song. Mere blackness seized upon his mind. Here he was coming home; the wife was dancing, the husband had been playing a trick upon a lackey; and meanwhile, all about them, they were a by-word to their subjects. Such a prince, such a husband, such a man, as this Otto had become! And he sped the faster onward.

Some way below he came unexpectedly upon a sentry; yet a little further, and he was challenged by a second; and as he crossed the bridge over the fish-pond, an officer making the rounds stopped him once more. The parade of watch was more than usual; but curiosity was dead in Otto's mind, and he only chafed at the interruption. The porter of the

273

back postern admitted him, and started to behold him so
disordered. Thence, hasting by private stairs and passages,
he came at length unseen to his own chamber, tore off his
clothes, and threw himself upon his bed in the dark. The
music of the ball-room still continued to a very lively measure; and still, behind that, he heard in spirit the chorus of
the merchants clanking down the hill.

BOOK II

OF LOVE AND POLITICS

OF LOVE AND POLITICS

CHAPTER I

WHAT HAPPENED IN THE LIBRARY

AT a quarter before six on the following morning Doctor Gotthold was already at his desk in the library; and with a small cup of black coffee at his elbow, and an eye occasionally wandering to the busts and the long array of many-coloured books, was quietly reviewing the labours of the day before. He was a man of about forty, flaxen-haired, with refined features a little worn, and bright eyes somewhat faded. Early to bed and early to rise, his life was devoted to two things: erudition and Rhine wine. An ancient friendship existed latent between him and Otto; they rarely met, but when they did it was to take up at once the thread of their suspended intimacy. Gotthold, the virgin priest of knowledge, had envied his cousin, for half a day, when he was married; he had never envied him his throne.

Reading was not a popular diversion at the court of Grünewald; and that great, pleasant, sunshiny gallery of books and statues was, in practice, Gotthold's private cabinet. On this particular Wednesday morning, however, he had not been long about his manuscript when a door opened and the Prince stepped into the apartment. The Doctor watched him as he drew near, receiving, from each of the embayed windows in succession, a flush of morning sun; and Otto looked so gay, and walked so airily, he was so well dressed and brushed and frizzled, so point-de-vice, and of such a sovereign elegance, that the heart of his cousin the recluse was rather moved against him.

"Good morning, Gotthold," said Otto, dropping in a chair.

" Good morning, Otto," returned the librarian. " You are an early bird. Is this an accident, or do you begin reforming? "

" It is about time, I fancy," answered the Prince.

" I cannot imagine," said the Doctor. " I am too sceptical to be an ethical adviser; and as for good resolutions, I believed in them when I was young. They are the colours of hope's rainbow."

" If you come to think of it," said Otto, " I am not a popular sovereign." And with a look he changed his statement to a question.

" Popular? Well, there I would distinguish," answered Gotthold, leaning back and joining the tips of his fingers. " There are various kinds of popularity; the bookish, which is perfectly impersonal, as unreal as the nightmare; the politician's, a mixed variety; and yours, which is the most personal of all. Women take to you; footmen adore you; it is as natural to like you as to pat a dog; and were you a saw-miller you would be the most popular citizen in Grünewald. As a prince—well, you are in the wrong trade. It is perhaps philosophical to recognise it as you do."

" Perhaps philosophical? " repeated Otto.

" Yes, perhaps. I would not be dogmatic," answered Gotthold.

" Perhaps philosophical, and certainly not virtuous," Otto resumed.

" Not of a Roman virtue," chuckled the recluse.

Otto drew his chair nearer to the table, leaned upon it with his elbow, and looked his cousin squarely in the face. " In short," he asked, " not manly? "

" Well," Gotthold hesitated, " not manly, if you will." And then with a laugh, " I did not know that you gave yourself out to be manly," he added. " It was one of the points that I inclined to like about you; inclined, I believe, to admire. The names of virtues exercise a charm on most of us; we must lay claim to all of them, however incompatible; we must all be both daring and prudent; we must

all vaunt our pride and go to the stake for our humility.
Not so you. Without compromise you were yourself: a
pretty sight. I have always said it: none so void of all
pretence as Otto."

" Pretence and effort both!" cried Otto. " A dead dog
in a canal is more alive. And the question, Gotthold, the
question that I have to face is this: Can I not, with effort
and self-denial, can I not become a tolerable sovereign?"

" Never," replied Gotthold. " Dismiss the notion. And
besides, dear child, you would not try."

" Nay, Gotthold, I am not to be put by," said Otto. " If
I am constitutionally unfit to be a sovereign, what am I
doing with this money, with this palace, with these guards?
And I—a thief—am to execute the law on others?"

" I admit the difficulty," said Gotthold.

" Well, can I not try?" continued Otto. " Am I not
bound to try? And with the advice and help of such a man
as you——"

" Me!" cried the librarian. " Now, God forbid!"

Otto, though he was in no very smiling humour, could
not forbear to smile. " Yet I was told last night," he
laughed, " that with a man like me to impersonate, and a
man like you to touch the springs, a very possible government could be composed."

" Now I wonder in what diseased imagination," Gotthold said, " that preposterous monster saw the light of
day?"

" It was one of your own trade—a writer, one Roederer,"
said Otto.

" Roederer! an ignorant puppy!" cried the librarian.

" You are ungrateful," said Otto. " He is one of your
professed admirers."

" Is he?" cried Gotthold, obviously impressed. " Come,
that is a good account of the young man. I must read
his stuff again. It is the rather to his credit, as our views
are opposite. The east and west are not more opposite.
Can I have converted him? But no; the incident belongs
to Fairyland."

"You are not then," asked the Prince, "an authoritarian?"

"I? God bless me, no!" said Gotthold. "I am a red, dear child."

"That brings me then to my next point, and by a natural transition. If I am so clearly unfitted for my post," the Prince asked; "if my friends admit it, if my subjects clamour for my downfall, if revolution is preparing at this hour, must I not go forth to meet the inevitable? should I not save these horrors and be done with these absurdities? in a word, should I not abdicate? O, believe me, I feel the ridicule, the vast abuse of language," he added, wincing, "but even a principulus like me cannot resign; he must make a great gesture, and come buskined forth, and abdicate."

"Ay," said Gotthold, "or else stay where he is. What gnat has bitten you to-day? Do you not know that you are touching, with lay hands, the very holiest inwards of philosophy, where madness dwells? Ay, Otto, madness; for in the serene temples of the wise, the inmost shrine, which we carefully keep locked, is full of spiders' webs. All men, all, are fundamentally useless; nature tolerates, she does not need, she does not use them: sterile flowers! All—down to the fellow swinking in a byre, whom fools point out for the exception—all are useless; all weave ropes of sand; or like a child that has breathed on a window, write and obliterate, write and obliterate, idle words! Talk of it no more. That way, I tell you, madness lies." The speaker rose from his chair and then sat down again. He laughed a little laugh, and then, changing his tone, resumed: "Yes, dear child, we are not here to do battle with giants; we are here to be happy like the flowers, if we can be. It is because you could, that I have always secretly admired you. Cling to that trade; believe me, it is the right one. Be happy, be idle, be airy. To the devil with all casuistry! and leave the state to Gondremark, as heretofore. He does it well enough, they say; and his vanity enjoys the situation."

"Gotthold," cried Otto, "what is this to me? Useless

is not the question; I cannot rest at uselessness; I must be useful or I must be noxious—one or other. I grant you the whole thing, prince and principality alike, is pure absurdity, a stroke of satire; and that a banker or the man who keeps an inn has graver duties. But now, when I have washed my hands of it three years, and left all—labour, responsibility, and honour and enjoyment too, if there be any—to Gondremark and to—Seraphina——" He hesitated at the name, and Gotthold glanced aside. " Well," the Prince continued, " what has come of it? Taxes, army, cannon—why, it's like a box of lead soldiers! And the people sick at the folly of it, and fired with the injustice! And war, too—I hear of war—war in this teapot! What a complication of absurdity and disgrace! And when the inevitable end arrives—the revolution—who will be to blame in the sight of God, who will be gibbeted in public opinion? I! Prince Puppet! "

" I thought you had despised public opinion," said Gotthold.

" I did," said Otto, sombrely, " but now I do not. I am growing old. And then, Gotthold, there is Seraphina. She is loathed in this country that I brought her to and suffered her to spoil. Yes, I gave it her as a plaything, and she has broken it: a fine Prince, an admirable Princess! Even her life—I ask you, Gotthold, is her life safe? "

" It is safe enough to-day," replied the librarian; " but since you ask me seriously, I would not answer for to-morrow. She is ill-advised."

" And by whom? By this Gondremark, to whom you counsel me to leave my country," cried the Prince. " Rare advice! The course that I have been following all these years, to come at last to this. O, ill-advised! if that were all! See now, there is no sense in beating about the bush between two men: you know what scandal says of her? "

Gotthold, with pursed lips, silently nodded.

" Well, come, you are not very cheering as to my conduct as the Prince; have I even done my duty as a husband? " Otto asked.

PRINCE OTTO

" Nay, nay," said Gotthold, earnestly and eagerly, " this is another chapter. I am an old celibate, an old monk. I cannot advise you in your marriage."

" Nor do I require advice," said Otto, rising. " All of this must cease." And he began to walk to and fro with his hands behind his back.

" Well, Otto, may God guide you!" said Gotthold, after a considerable silence. " I cannot."

" From what does all this spring?" said the Prince, stopping in his walk. " What am I to call it? Diffidence? The fear of ridicule? Inverted vanity? What matter names, if it has brought me to this? I could never bear to be bustling about nothing; I was ashamed of this toy kingdom from the first; I could not tolerate that people should fancy I believed in a thing so patently absurd! I would do nothing that cannot be done smiling. I have a sense of humour forsooth! I must know better than my maker. And it was the same thing in my marriage," he added more hoarsely. " I did not believe this girl could care for me; I must not intrude; I must preserve the foppery of my indifference. What an impotent picture!"

" Ay, we have the same blood," moralised Gotthold. " You are drawing, with fine strokes, the character of the born sceptic."

" Sceptic?—coward!" cried Otto. " Coward is the word. A springless, putty-hearted, cowering coward!"

And as the Prince rapped out the words in tones of unusual vigour, a little, stout, old gentleman, opening a door behind Gotthold, received them fairly in the face. With his parrot's beak for a nose, his pursed mouth, his little goggling eyes, he was the picture of formality; and in ordinary circumstances, strutting behind the drum of his corporation, he impressed the beholder with a certain air of frozen dignity and wisdom. But at the smallest contrariety, his trembling hands and disconnected gestures betrayed the weakness at the root. And now, when he was thus surprisingly received in that library of Mittwalden Palace, which was the customary haunt of silence, his hands went up into the air as if he had been shot, and he cried aloud with the scream of an old woman.

"O!" he gasped, recovering, "Your Highness! I beg ten thousand pardons. But your Highness at such an hour in the library!—a circumstance so unusual as your Highness's presence was a thing I could not be expected to foresee."

"There is no harm done, Herr Cancellarius," said Otto.

"I came upon the errand of a moment: some papers I left over night with the Herr Doctor," said the Chancellor of Grünewald. "Herr Doctor, if you will kindly give me them, I will intrude no longer."

Gotthold unlocked a drawer and handed a bundle of manuscript to the old gentleman, who prepared, with fitting salutations, to take his departure.

"Herr Greisengesang, since we have met," said Otto, "let us talk."

"I am honoured by his Highness's commands," replied the Chancellor.

"All has been quiet since I left?" asked the Prince, resuming his seat.

"The usual business, your Highness," answered Greisengesang; "punctual trifles: huge, indeed, if neglected, but trifles when discharged. Your Highness is most zealously obeyed."

"Obeyed, Herr Cancellarius?" returned the Prince. "And when have I obliged you with an order? Replaced, let us rather say. But to touch upon these trifles; instance me a few."

"The routine of government, from which your Highness has so wisely dissociated his leisure . . ." began Greisengesang.

"We will leave my leisure, sir," said Otto. "Approach the facts."

"The routine of business was proceeded with," replied the official, now visibly twittering.

"It is very strange, Herr Cancellarius, that you should so persistently avoid my questions," said the Prince. "You tempt me to suppose a purpose in your dulness. I have asked you whether all was quiet: do me the pleasure to reply."

"Perfectly—O, perfectly quiet," jerked the ancient puppet, with every signal of untruth.

"I make a note of these words," said the Prince, gravely. "You assure me, your sovereign, that since the date of my departure nothing has occurred of which you owe me an account."

"I take your Highness, I take the Herr Doctor to witness," cried Greisengesang, "that I have had no such expression."

"Halt!" said the Prince; and then, after a pause: "Herr Greisengesang, you are an old man, and you served my father before you served me," he added. "It consists neither with your dignity nor mine, that you should babble excuses and stumble possibly upon untruths. Collect your thoughts; and then categorically inform me of all you have been charged to hide."

Gotthold, stooping very low over his desk, appeared to have resumed his labours; but his shoulders heaved with subterranean merriment. The Prince waited, drawing his handkerchief quietly through his fingers.

"Your Highness, in this informal manner," said the old gentleman at last, "and being unavoidably deprived of documents, it would be difficult, it would be impossible, to do justice to the somewhat grave occurrences which have transpired."

"I will not criticise your attitude," replied the Prince. "I desire that, between you and me, all should be done gently; for I have not forgotten, my old friend, that you were kind to me from the first, and for a period of years a faithful servant. I will thus dismiss the matters on which you waive immediate inquiry. But you have certain papers actually in your hand. Come, Herr Greisengesang, there is at least one point for which you have authority. Enlighten me on that."

"On that?" cried the old gentleman. "O, that is a trifle; a matter, your Highness, of police; a detail of a purely administrative order. These are simply a selection of the papers seized upon the English traveller."

"Seized?" echoed Otto. "In what sense? Explain yourself."

"Sir John Crabtree," interposed Gotthold, looking up, "was arrested yesterday evening."

"Is this so, Herr Cancellarius?" demanded Otto, sternly.

"It was judged right, your Highness," protested Greisengesang. "The decree was in due form, invested with your Highness's authority by procuration. I am but an agent; I had no status to prevent the measure."

"This man, my guest, has been arrested," said the Prince. "On what grounds, sir? With what colour of pretence?"

The Chancellor stammered.

"Your Highness will perhaps find the reason in these documents," said Gotthold, pointing with the tail of his pen.

Otto thanked his cousin with a look. "Give them to me," he said, addressing the Chancellor.

But that gentleman visibly hesitated to obey. "Baron von Gondremark," he said, "has made the affair his own. I am in this case a mere messenger; and as such, I am not clothed with any capacity to communicate the documents I carry. Herr Doctor, I am convinced you will not fail to bear me out."

"I have heard a great deal of nonsense," said Gotthold, "and most of it from you; but this beats all."

"Come, sir," said Otto, rising, "the papers I command."

Herr Greisengesang instantly gave way.

"With your Highness's permission," he said, "and laying at his feet my most submiss apologies, I will now hasten to attend his further orders in the Chancery."

"Herr Cancellarius, do you see this chair?" said Otto. "There is where you shall attend my further orders. O, now, no more!" he cried, with a gesture, as the old man opened his lips. "You have sufficiently marked your zeal to your employer; and I begin to weary of a moderation you abuse."

The Chancellor moved to the appointed chair and took his seat in silence.

" And now," said Otto, opening the roll, " what is all this? it looks like the manuscript of a book."

" It is," said Gotthold, " the manuscript of a book of travels."

" You have read it, Doctor Hohenstockwitz? " asked the Prince.

" Nay, I but saw the title page," replied Gotthold. " But the roll was given to me open, and I heard no word of any secrecy."

Otto dealt the Chancellor an angry glance.

" I see," he went on. " The papers of an author seized at this date of the world's history, in a state so petty and so ignorant as Grünewald, here is indeed an ignominious folly. Sir," to the Chancellor, " I marvel to find you in so scurvy an employment. On your conduct to your Prince I will not dwell; but to descend to be a spy! For what else can it be called? To seize the papers of this gentleman, the private papers of a stranger, the toil of a life, perhaps—to open, and to read them. And what have we to do with books? The Herr Doctor might perhaps be asked for his advice; but we have no *index expurgatorius* in Grünewald. Had we but that, we should be the most absolute parody and farce upon this tawdry earth."

Yet, even while Otto spoke, he had continued to unfold the roll; and now, when it lay fully open, his eye rested on the title page elaborately written in red ink. It ran thus:

" Memoirs
of a Visit to the Various
Courts of Europe
by
Sir John Crabtree, Baronet."

Below was a list of chapters, each bearing the name of one of the European Courts; and among these the nineteenth and the last upon the list was dedicated to Grünewald.

" Ah! The Court of Grünewald! " said Otto, " that should be droll reading." And his curiosity itched for it.

" A methodical dog, this English Baronet," said Gotthold.

OF LOVE AND POLITICS

" Each chapter written and finished on the spot. I shall look for his work when it appears."

" It would be odd, now, just to glance at it," said Otto, wavering.

Gotthold's brow darkened, and he looked out of window.

But though the Prince understood the reproof, his weakness prevailed. " I will," he said, with an uneasy laugh, " I will, I think, just glance at it."

So saying, he resumed his seat and spread the traveller's manuscript upon the table.

CHAPTER II

IT may well be asked (*it was thus the English traveller began his nineteenth chapter*) why I should have chosen
Grünewald out of so many other states equally petty, formal,
dull, and corrupt. Accident, indeed, decided, and not I; but
I have seen no reason to regret my visit. The spectacle of
this small society macerating in its own abuses was not perhaps instructive, but I have found it exceedingly diverting.

The reigning Prince, Otto Johann Friedrich, a young man
of imperfect education, questionable valour, and no scintilla
of capacity, has fallen into entire public contempt. It was
with difficulty that I obtained an interview, for he is frequently absent from a court where his presence is unheeded,
and where his only *rôle* is to be a cloak for the amours of his
wife. At last, however, on the third occasion when I visited
the palace, I found this sovereign in the exercise of his in-
glorious function, with the wife on one hand and the lover on
the other. He is not ill-looking; he has hair of a ruddy gold,
which naturally curls, and his eyes are dark, a combination
which I always regard as the mark of some congenital de-
ficiency, physical or moral; his features are irregular but
pleasing; the nose perhaps a little short, and the mouth a
little womanish; his address is excellent, and he can express
himself with point. But to pierce below these externals is to
come on a vacuity of any sterling quality, a deliquescence of
the moral nature, a frivolity and inconsequence of purpose
that mark the nearly perfect fruit of a decadent age. He
has a worthless smattering of many subjects, but a grasp of
none. " I soon weary of a pursuit," he said to me, laughing;
it would almost appear as if he took a pride in his incapacity

and lack of moral courage. The results of his dilettantism are to be seen in every field; he is a bad fencer, a second-rate horseman, dancer, shot; he sings—I have heard him—and he sings like a child; he writes intolerable verses in more than doubtful French; he acts like a common amateur; and in short there is no end to the number of the things that he does, and does badly. His one manly taste is for the chase. In sum, he is but a plexus of weaknesses; the singing chambermaid of the stage, tricked out in man's apparel and mounted on a circus horse. I have seen this poor phantom of a prince riding out alone or with a few huntsmen, disregarded by all, and I have been even grieved for the bearer of so futile and melancholy an existence. The last Merovingians may have looked not otherwise.

The Princess Amalia Seraphina, a daughter of the Grand Ducal house of Toggenburg-Tannhäuser, would be equally inconsiderable if she were not a cutting instrument in the hands of an ambitious man. She is much younger than the Prince, a girl of two-and-twenty, sick with vanity, superficially clever, and fundamentally a fool. She has a redbrown rolling eye, too large for her face, and with sparks of both levity and ferocity; her forehead is high and narrow, her figure thin and a little stooping. Her manners, her conversation, which she interlards with French, her very tastes and ambitions, are alike assumed; and the assumption is ungracefully apparent: Hoyden playing Cleopatra. I should judge her to be incapable of truth. In private life a girl of this description embroils the peace of families, walks attended by a troop of scowling swains, and passes, once at least, through the divorce court; it is a common and, except to the cynic, an uninteresting type. On the throne, however, and in the hands of a man like Gondremark, she may become the authoress of serious public evils.

Gondremark, the true ruler of this unfortunate country, is a more complex study. His position in Grünewald, to which he is a foreigner, is eminently false; and that he should maintain it as he does, a very miracle of impudence and dexterity. His speech, his face, his policy, are all double: heads and tails. Which of the two extremes may be his actual design he were a bold man who should offer to decide. Yet I will hazard the guess that he follows both experimentally, and awaits, at the hand of destiny, one of those directing hints of which she is so lavish to the wise.

On the one hand, as Maire de Palais to the incompetent Otto, and using the love-sick Princess for a tool and mouthpiece, he pursues a policy of arbitrary power and territorial aggrandisement. He has called out the whole capable male population of the state to military service; he has bought cannon; he has tempted away promising officers from foreign armies; and he now begins, in his international relations, to assume the swaggering port and the vague threatful language of a bully. The idea of extending Grünewald may appear absurd, but the little state is advantageously placed, its neighbours are all defenceless; and if at any moment the jealousies of the greater courts should neutralise each other, an active policy might double the principality both in population and extent. Certainly at least the scheme is entertained in the court of Mittwalden; nor do I myself regard it as entirely desperate. The margravate of Brandenburgh has grown from as small beginnings to a formidable power; and though it is late in the day to try adventurous policies, and the age of war seems ended, Fortune, we must not forget, still blindly turns her wheel for men and nations. Concurrently with, and tributary to, these warlike preparations, crushing taxes have been levied, journals have been suppressed, and the country, which three years ago was prosperous and happy, now stagnates in a forced inaction, gold has become a curiosity, and the mills stand idle on the mountain streams.

On the other hand, in his second capacity of popular tribune, Gondremark is the incarnation of the free lodges, and sits at the centre of an organised conspiracy against the state. To any such movement my sympathies were early acquired, and I would not willingly let fall a word that might embarrass or retard the revolution. But to show that I speak of knowledge, and not as the reporter of mere gossip, I may mention that I have myself been present at a meeting where

the details of a republican Constitution were minutely debated and arranged; and I may add that Gondremark was
throughout referred to by the speakers as their captain in
action and the arbiter of their disputes. He has taught his
dupes (for so I must regard them) that his power of resistance to the Princess is limited, and at each fresh stretch of
authority persuades them, with specious reasons, to postpone
the hour of insurrection. Thus (to give some instances of
his astute diplomacy) he salved over the decree enforcing
military service, under the plea that to be well drilled and
exercised in arms was even a necessary preparation for revolt.
And the other day, when it began to be rumoured abroad that
a war was being forced on a reluctant neighbour, the Grand
Duke of Gerolstein, and I made sure it would be the signal
for an instant rising, I was struck dumb with wonder to find
that even this had been prepared and was to be accepted. I
went from one to another in the Liberal camp, and all were
in the same story, all had been drilled and schooled and fitted
out with vacuous argument. " The lads had better see some
real fighting," they said; " and besides, it will be as well to
capture Gerolstein: we can then extend to our neighbours the
blessing of liberty on the same day that we snatch it for ourselves; and the republic will be all the stronger to resist, if
the kings of Europe should band themselves together to reduce it." I know not which of the two I should admire the
more: the simplicity of the multitude or the audacity of the
adventurer. But such are the subtleties, such the quibbling
reasons, with which he blinds and leads this people. How long
a course so tortuous can be pursued with safety I am incapable of guessing; not long, one would suppose; and yet
this singular man has been treading the mazes for five years,
and his favour at court and his popularity among the lodges
still endure unbroken.

I have the privilege of slightly knowing him. Heavily and
somewhat clumsily built, of a vast, disjointed, rambling
frame, he can still pull himself together, and figure, not without admiration, in the saloon or the ball-room. His hue and
temperament are plentifully bilious; he has a saturnine eye;

his cheek is of a dark blue where he has been shaven. Essentially he is to be numbered among the man-haters, a convinced contemner of his fellows. Yet he is himself of a commonplace ambition and greedy of applause. In talk, he is remarkable for a thirst of information, loving rather to hear than to communicate; for sound and studious views; and, judging by the extreme shortsightedness of common politicians, for a remarkable prevision of events. All this, however, without grace, pleasantry, or charm, heavily set forth, with a dull countenance. In our numerous conversations, although he has always heard me with deference, I have been conscious throughout of a sort of ponderous finessing hard to tolerate. He produces none of the effect of a gentleman; devoid not merely of pleasantry, but of all attention or communicative warmth of bearing. No gentleman, besides, would so parade his amours with the Princess; still less repay the Prince for his long-suffering with a studied insolence of demeanour and the fabrication of insulting nicknames, such as Prince Featherhead, which run from ear to ear and create a laugh throughout the country. Gondremark has thus some of the clumsier characters of the self-made man, combined with an inordinate, almost a besotted, pride of intellect and birth. Heavy, bilious, selfish, inornate, he sits upon this court and country like an incubus.

But it is probable that he preserves softer gifts for necessary purposes. Indeed, it is certain, although he vouchsafed none of it to me, that this cold and stolid politician possesses to a great degree the art of ingratiation, and can be all things to all men. Hence there has probably sprung up the idle legend that in private life he is a gross romping voluptuary. Nothing, at least, can well be more surprising than the terms of his connection with the Princess. Older than her husband, certainly uglier, and, according to the feeble ideas common among women, in every particular less pleasing, he has not only seized the complete command of all her thought and action, but has imposed on her in public a humiliating part. I do not here refer to the complete sacrifice of every rag of her reputation; for to many women these extremities are in

OF LOVE AND POLITICS

themselves attractive. But there is about the court a certain lady of a dishevelled reputation, a Countess von Rosen, wife or widow of a cloudy count, no longer in her second youth and already bereft of some of her attractions, who unequivocally occupies the station of the Baron's mistress. I had thought, at first, that she was but a hired accomplice, a mere blind or buffer for the more important sinner. A few hours' acquaintance with Madame von Rosen for ever dispelled the illusion. She is one rather to make than to prevent a scandal, and she values none of those bribes—money, honours, or employment —with which the situation might be gilded. Indeed, as a person frankly bad, she pleased me, in the court of Grünewald, like a piece of nature.

The power of this man over the Princess is, therefore, without bounds. She has sacrificed to the adoration with which he has inspired her not only her marriage vow and every shred of public decency, but that vice of jealousy which is so much dearer to the female sex than either intrinsic honour or outward consideration. Nay, more: a young, although not a very attractive woman, and a Princess both by birth and fact, she submits to the triumphant rivalry of one who might be her mother as to years, and who is so manifestly her inferior in station. This is one of the mysteries of the human heart. But the rage of illicit love, when it is once indulged, appears to grow by feeding; and to a person of the character and temperament of this unfortunate young lady, almost any depth of degradation is within the reach of possibility.

CHAPTER III

SO far Otto read, with waxing indignation; and here his fury overflowed. He tossed the roll upon the table and stood up. "This man," he said, "is a devil. A filthy imagination, an ear greedy of evil, a ponderous malignity of thought and language: I grow like him by the reading! Chancellor, where is this fellow lodged?"

"He was committed to the Flag Tower," replied Greisengesang, "in the Gamiani apartment."

"Lead me to him," said the Prince; and then a thought striking him, "Was it for that," he asked, "that I found so many sentries in the garden?"

"Your Highness, I am unaware," answered Greisengesang, true to his policy. "The disposition of the guards is a matter distinct from my functions."

Otto turned upon the old man fiercely, but ere he had time to speak, Gotthold touched him on the arm. He swallowed his wrath with a great effort. "It is well," he said, taking the roll. "Follow me to the Flag Tower."

The Chancellor gathered himself together, and the two set forward. It was a long and complicated voyage; for the library was in the wing of the new buildings, and the tower which carried the flag was in the old schloss upon the garden. By a great variety of stairs and corridors, they came out at last upon a patch of gravelled court; the garden peeped through a high grating with a flash of green; tall, old, gabled buildings mounted on every side; the Flag Tower climbed, stage after stage, into the blue; and high over all, among the building daws, the yellow flag wavered in the wind. A sentinel at the foot of the tower stairs presented arms; another paced the first landing; and a third was stationed before the door of the extemporised prison.

OF LOVE AND POLITICS

" We guard this mud-bag like a jewel," Otto sneered.

The Gamiani apartment was so called from an Italian doctor who had imposed on the credulity of a former prince. The rooms were large, airy, pleasant, and looked upon the garden; but the walls were of great thickness (for the tower was old), and the windows were heavily barred. The Prince, followed by the Chancellor, still trotting to keep up with him, brushed swiftly through the little library and the long saloon, and burst like a thunderbolt into the bedroom at the further end. Sir John was finishing his toilet; a man of fifty, hard, uncompromising, able, with the eye and teeth of physical courage. He was unmoved by the irruption, and bowed with a sort of sneering ease.

" To what am I to attribute the honour of this visit? " he asked.

" You have eaten my bread," replied Otto, " you have taken my hand, you have been received under my roof. When did I fail you in courtesy? What have you asked that was not granted as to an honoured guest? And here, sir," tapping fiercely on the manuscript, " here is your return."

" Your Highness has read my papers? " said the Baronet. " I am honoured indeed. But the sketch is most imperfect. I shall now have much to add. I can say that the Prince, whom I had accused of idleness, is zealous in the department of police, taking upon himself those duties that are most distasteful. I shall be able to relate the burlesque incident of my arrest, and the singular interview with which you honour me at present. For the rest, I have already communicated with my Ambassador at Vienna; and unless you propose to murder me, I shall be at liberty, whether you please or not, within the week. For I hardly fancy the future empire of Grünewald is yet ripe to go to war with England. I conceive I am a little more than quits. I owe you no explanation; yours has been the wrong. You, if you have studied my writing with intelligence, owe me a large debt of gratitude. And to conclude, as I have not yet finished my toilet, I imagine the courtesy of a turnkey to a prisoner would induce you to withdraw."

295

PRINCE OTTO

There was some paper on the table, and Otto, sitting down, wrote a passport in the name of Sir John Crabtree.

"Affix the seal, Herr Cancellarius," he said, in his most princely manner, as he rose.

Greisengesang produced a red portfolio, and affixed the seal in the unpoetic guise of an adhesive stamp; nor did his perturbed and clumsy movements at all lessen the comedy of the performance. Sir John looked on with a malign enjoyment; and Otto chafed, regretting, when too late, the unnecessary royalty of his command and gesture. But at length the Chancellor had finished his piece of prestidigitation, and, without waiting for an order, had countersigned the passport. Thus regularised he returned it to Otto with a bow.

"You will now," said the Prince, "order one of my own carriages to be prepared; see it, with your own eyes, charged with Sir John's effects, and have it waiting within the hour behind the Pheasant House. Sir John departs this morning for Vienna."

The Chancellor took his elaborate departure.

"Here, sir, is your passport," said Otto, turning to the Baronet. "I regret it from my heart that you have met inhospitable usage."

"Well, there will be no English war," returned Sir John.

"Nay, sir," said Otto, "you surely owe me your civility. Matters are now changed, and we stand again upon the footing of two gentlemen. It was not I who ordered your arrest; I returned late last night from hunting; and as you cannot blame me for your imprisonment, you may even thank me for your freedom."

"And yet you read my papers," said the traveller, shrewdly.

"There, sir, I was wrong," returned Otto; "and for that I ask your pardon. You can scarce refuse it, for your own dignity, to one who is a plexus of weaknesses. Nor was the fault entirely mine. Had the papers been innocent, it would have been at most an indiscretion. Your own guilt is the sting of my offence."

OF LOVE AND POLITICS

Sir John regarded Otto with an approving twinkle; then he bowed, but still in silence.

"Well, sir, as you are now at your entire disposal, I have a favour to beg of your indulgence," continued the Prince. "I have to request that you will walk with me alone into the garden so soon as your convenience permits."

"From the moment that I am a free man," Sir John replied, this time with perfect courtesy, "I am wholly at your Highness's command; and if you will excuse a rather summary toilet, I will even follow you as I am."

"I thank you, sir," said Otto.

So without more delay, the Prince leading, the pair proceeded down through the echoing stairway of the tower, and out through the grating, into the ample air and sunshine of the morning, and among the terraces and flower-beds of the garden. They crossed the fish-pond, where the carp were leaping as thick as bees; they mounted, one after another, the various flights of stairs, snowed upon, as they went, with April blossoms, and marching in time to the great orchestra of birds. Nor did Otto pause till they had reached the highest terrace of the garden. Here was a gate into the park, and hard by, under a tuft of laurel, a marble garden seat. Hence they looked down on the green tops of many elm-trees, where the rooks were busy; and, beyond that, upon the palace roof, and the yellow banner flying in the blue. "I pray you to be seated, sir," said Otto.

Sir John complied without a word; and for some seconds Otto walked to and fro before him, plunged in angry thought. The birds were all singing for a wager.

"Sir," said the Prince at length, turning towards the Englishman, "you are to me, except by the conventions of society, a perfect stranger. Of your character and wishes I am ignorant. I have never wittingly disobliged you. There is a difference in station, which I desire to waive. I would, if you still think me entitled to so much consideration—I would be regarded simply as a gentleman. Now, sir, I did wrong to glance at these papers, which I here return to you; but if curiosity be undignified, as I am free to own, falsehood is both cowardly and cruel. I opened your roll; and what did I find—what did I find about my wife? Lies!" he broke out. "They are lies! There are not, so help me God! four words of truth in your intolerable libel! You are a man; you are old, and might be the girl's father; you are a gentleman; you are a scholar, and have learned refinement; and you rake together all this vulgar scandal, and propose to print it in a public book! Such is your chivalry! But, thank God, sir, she has still a husband. You say, sir, in that paper in your hand, that I am a bad fencer; I have to request from you a lesson in the art. The park is close behind; yonder is the Pheasant House, where you will find your carriage; should I fall, you know, sir—you have written it in your paper—how little my movements are regarded; I am in the custom of disappearing; it will be one more disappearance; and long before it has awakened a remark, you may be safe across the border."

"You will observe," said Sir John, "that what you ask is impossible."

"And if I struck you?" cried the Prince, with a sudden menacing flash.

"It would be a cowardly blow," returned the Baronet, unmoved, "for it would make no change. I cannot draw upon a reigning sovereign."

"And it is this man, to whom you dare not offer satisfaction, that you choose to insult!" cried Otto.

"Pardon me," said the traveller, "you are unjust. It is because you are a reigning sovereign that I cannot fight with you; and it is for the same reason that I have a right to criticise your action and your wife. You are in everything a public creature; you belong to the public, body and bone. You have with you the law, the muskets of the army, and the eyes of spies. We, on our side, have but one weapon—truth."

"Truth!" echoed the Prince, with a gesture.

There was another silence.

"Your Highness," said Sir John at last, "you must not expect grapes from a thistle. I am old and a cynic. Nobody cares a rush for me; and on the whole, after the present interview, I scarce know anybody that I like better than your-self. You see, I have changed my mind, and have the uncommon virtue to avow the change. I tear up this stuff before you, here in your own garden; I ask your pardon, I ask the pardon of the Princess; and I give you my word of honour as a gentleman and an old man, that when my book of travels shall appear it shall not contain so much as the name of Grünewald. And yet it was a racy chapter! But had your Highness only read about the other courts! I am a carrion crow; but it is not my fault, after all, that the world is such a nauseous kennel."

" Sir," said Otto, " is the eye not jaundiced? "

" Nay," cried the traveller, " very likely. I am one who goes sniffing; I am no poet. I believe in a better future for the world; or, at all accounts, I do most potently disbelieve in the present. Rotten eggs is the burthen of my song. But indeed, your Highness, when I meet with any merit, I do not think that I am slow to recognise it. This is a day that I shall still recall with gratitude, for I have found a sovereign with some manly virtues; and for once—old courtier and old radical as I am—it is from the heart and quite sincerely that I can request the honour of kissing your Highness's hand? "

" Nay, sir," said Otto, " to my heart! "

And the Englishman, taken at unawares, was clasped for a moment in the Prince's arms.

"And now, sir," added Otto, " there is the Pheasant House; close behind it you will find my carriage, which I pray you to accept. God speed you to Vienna! "

" In the impetuosity of youth," replied Sir John, " your Highness has overlooked one circumstance. I am still fasting."

" Well, sir," said Otto, smiling, " you are your own master; you may go or stay. But I warn you, your friend may prove less powerful than your enemies. The Prince, indeed, is thoroughly on your side; he has all the will to help; but to whom do I speak?—you know better than I do, he is not alone in Grünewald."

" There is a deal in position," returned the traveller,

gravely nodding. "Gondremark loves to temporise; his policy is below ground, and he fears all open courses; and now that I have seen you act with so much spirit, I will cheerfully risk myself on your protection. Who knows? You may be yet the better man."

"Do you indeed believe so?" cried the Prince. "You put life into my heart!"

"I will give up sketching portraits," said the Baronet. "I am a blind owl; I had misread you strangely. And yet remember this; a sprint is one thing, and to run all day another. For I still mistrust your constitution; the short nose, the hair and eyes of several complexions; no, they are diagnostic; and I must end, I see, as I began."

"I am still a singing chambermaid?" said Otto.

"Nay, your Highness, I pray you to forget what I had written," said Sir John; "I am not like Pilate; and the chapter is no more. Bury it, if you love me."

CHAPTER IV

WHILE THE PRINCE IS IN THE ANTE-ROOM

GREATLY comforted by the exploits of the morning, the Prince turned towards the Princess's ante-room, bent on a more difficult enterprise. The curtains rose before him, the usher called his name, and he entered the room with an exaggeration of his usual mincing and airy dignity. There were about a score of persons waiting, principally ladies; it was one of the few societies in Grünewald where Otto knew himself to be popular; and while a maid of honour made her exit by a side door to announce his arrival to the Princess, he moved round the apartment, collecting homage and bestowing compliments, with friendly grace. Had this been the sum of his duties, he had been an admirable monarch. Lady after lady was impartially honoured by his attention.

"Madam," he said to one, "how does this happen? I find you daily more adorable."

"And your Highness daily browner," replied the lady. "We began equal; O, there I will be bold: we have both beautiful complexions. But while I study mine, your Highness tans himself."

"A perfect negro, madam; and what so fitly—being beauty's slave?" said Otto. "Madame Grafinski, when is our next play? I have just heard that I am a bad actor."

"O ciel!" cried Madame Grafinski. "Who could venture? What a bear!"

"An excellent man, I can assure you," returned Otto.

"O, never! O, is it possible!" fluted the lady. "Your Highness plays like an angel."

"You must be right, madam; who could speak falsely and yet look so charming?" said the Prince. "But this gentleman, it seems, would have preferred me playing like an actor."

301

PRINCE OTTO

A sort of hum, a falsetto, feminine cooing, greeted the tiny sally; and Otto expanded like a peacock. This warm atmosphere of women and flattery and idle chatter pleased him to the marrow.

"Madame von Eisenthal, your coiffure is delicious," he remarked.

"Every one was saying so," said one.

"If I have pleased Prince Charming?" And Madame von Eisenthal swept him a deep curtsey with a killing glance of adoration.

"It is new?" he asked. "Vienna fashion."

"Mint new," replied the lady, "for your Highness's return. I felt young this morning; it was a premonition. But why, Prince, do you ever leave us?"

"For the pleasure of the return," said Otto. "I am like a dog; I must bury my bone, and then come back to gloat upon it."

"O, a bone! Fie, what a comparison! You have brought back the manners of the wood," returned the lady.

"Madam, it is what the dog has dearest," said the Prince. "But I observe Madame von Rosen."

And Otto, leaving the group to which he had been piping, stepped towards the embrasure of a window where a lady stood.

The Countess von Rosen had hitherto been silent, and a thought depressed, but on the approach of Otto she began to brighten. She was tall, slim as a nymph, and of a very airy carriage; and her face, which was already beautiful in repose, lightened and changed, flashed into smiles, and glowed with lovely colour at the touch of animation. She was a good vocalist; and, even in speech, her voice commanded a great range of changes, the low notes rich with tenor quality, the upper ringing, on the brink of laughter, into music. A gem of many facets and variable hues of fire; a woman who withheld the better portion of her beauty, and then, in a caressing second, flashed it like a weapon full on the beholder; now merely a tall figure and a sallow handsome face, with the evidences of a reckless temper; anon opening like a flower to life and colour, mirth and tenderness :—Madame von Rosen had always a dagger in reserve for the despatch of ill-assured admirers. She met Otto with the dart of tender gaiety.

" You have come to me at last, Prince Cruel," she said. " Butterfly! Well, and am I not to kiss your hand? " she added.

" Madam, it is I who must kiss yours." And Otto bowed and kissed it.

" You deny me every indulgence," she said, smiling.

" And now what news in Court? " inquired the Prince. " I come to you for my gazette."

" Ditch-water! " she replied. " The world is all asleep, grown grey in slumber; I do not remember any waking movement since quite an eternity; and the last thing in the nature of a sensation was the last time my governess was allowed to box my ears. But yet I do myself and your unfortunate enchanted palace some injustice. Here is the last—O positively! " And she told him the story from behind her fan, with many glances, many cunning strokes of the narrator's art. The others had drawn away, for it was understood that Madame von Rosen was in favour with the Prince. None the less, however, did the Countess lower her voice at times to within a semitone of whispering; and the pair leaned together over the narrative.

" Do you know," said Otto, laughing, " you are the only entertaining woman on this earth! "

" O, you have found out so much," she cried.

" Yes, madam, I grow wiser with advancing years," he returned.

" Years! " she repeated. " Do you name the traitors? I do not believe in years; the calendar is a delusion."

" You must be right, madam," replied the Prince. " For six years that we have been good friends, I have observed you to grow younger."

" Flatterer! " cried she, and then with a change, " But why should I say so," she added, " when I protest I think the same? A week ago I had a council with my Father Director, the glass; and the glass replied, ' Not yet! ' I confess my face in this way once a month. O! a very solemn moment. Do you know what I shall do when the mirror answers, ' Now '? "

" I cannot guess," said he.

" No more can I," returned the Countess. " There is such a choice! Suicide, gambling, a nunnery, a volume of memoirs, or politics—the last, I am afraid."

" It is a dull trade," said Otto.

" Nay," she replied, " it is a trade I rather like. It is, after all, first cousin to gossip, which no one can deny to be amusing. For instance, if I were to tell you that the Princess and the Baron rode out together daily to inspect the cannon, it is either a piece of politics or scandal, as I turn my phrase. I am the alchemist that makes the transmutation. They have been everywhere together since you left," she continued, brightening as she saw Otto darken ; " that is a poor snippet of malicious gossip—and they were everywhere cheered—and with that addition all becomes political intelligence."

" Let us change the subject," said Otto.

" I was about to propose it," she replied, " or rather to pursue the politics. Do you know? this war is popular—popular to the length of cheering Princess Seraphina."

" All things, madam, are possible," said the Prince ; " and this among others, that we may be going into war, but I give you my word of honour I do not know with whom."

" And you put up with it? " she cried. " I have no pretensions to morality ; and I confess I have always abominated the lamb, and nourished a romantic feeling for the wolf. O, be done with lambiness! Let us see there is a prince, for I am weary of the distaff."

" Madam," said Otto, " I thought you were of that faction."

" I should be of yours, *mon Prince*, if you had one," she retorted. " Is it true that you have no ambition? There was a man once in England whom they called the kingmaker. Do you know," she added, " I fancy I could make a prince? "

" Some day, madam," said Otto, " I may ask you to help make a farmer."

OF LOVE AND POLITICS

"Is that a riddle?" asked the Countess.

"It is," replied the Prince, "and a very good one too."

"Tit for tat. I will ask you another," she returned. "Where is Gondremark?"

"The Prime Minister? In the prime-ministry, no doubt," said Otto.

"Precisely," said the Countess; and she pointed with her fan to the door of the Princess's apartments. "You and I, *mon Prince*, are in the ante-room. You think me unkind," she added. "Try me and you will see. Set me a task, put me a question; there is no enormity I am not capable of doing to oblige you, and no secret that I am not ready to betray."

"Nay, madam, but I respect my friend too much," he answered, kissing her hand. "I would rather remain ignorant of all. We fraternise like foemen soldiers at the outposts, but let each be true to his own army."

"Ah," she cried, "if all men were generous like you, it would be worth while to be a woman!" Yet, judging by her looks, his generosity, if anything, had disappointed her; she seemed to seek a remedy, and, having found it, brightened once more. "And now," she said, "may I dismiss my sovereign? This is rebellion and a *cas pendable*; but what am I to do? My bear is jealous!"

"Madam, enough!" cried Otto. "Ahasuerus reaches you the sceptre; more, he will obey you in all points. I should have been a dog to come to whistling."

And so the Prince departed, and fluttered round Grafinski and von Eisenthal. But the Countess knew the use of her offensive weapons, and had left a pleasant arrow in the Prince's heart. That Gondremark was jealous—here was an agreeable revenge! And Madame von Rosen, as the occasion of the jealousy, appeared to him in a new light.

CHAPTER V

THE Countess von Rosen spoke the truth. The great Prime Minister of Grünewald was already closeted with Seraphina. The toilet was over; and the Princess, tastefully arrayed, sat face to face with a tall mirror. Sir John's description was unkindly true, true in terms and yet a libel, a misogynistic masterpiece. Her forehead was perhaps too high, but it became her; her figure somewhat stooped, but every detail was formed and finished like a gem; her hand, her foot, her ear, the set of her comely head, were all dainty and accordant; if she was not beautiful, she was vivid, changeful, coloured, and pretty with a thousand various prettinesses; and her eyes, if they indeed rolled too consciously, yet rolled to purpose. They were her most attractive feature, yet they continually bore eloquent false witness to her thoughts; for while she herself, in the depths of her immature, unsoftened heart, was given altogether to manlike inviting, fiery, melting, and artful, like the eyes of a rapacious ambition and the desire of power, the eyes were by turns bold, syren. And artful, in a sense, she was. Chafing that she was not a man and could not shine by action, she had conceived a woman's part, of answerable domination; she sought to subjugate for by-ends, to rain influence and be fancy free; and while she loved not man, loved to see man obey her. It is a common girl's ambition. Such was perhaps that lady of the glove, who sent her lover to the lions. But the snare is laid alike for male and female, and the world most artfully contrived.

Near her, in a low chair, Gondremark had arranged his limbs into a cat-like attitude, high-shouldered, stooping, and submiss. The formidable blue jowl of the man, and the dull bilious eye, set perhaps a higher value on his evident desire to please. His face was marked by capacity, temper, and a kind of bold, piratical dishonesty which it would be calumnious to call deceit. His manners, as he smiled upon the Princess, were overfine, yet hardly elegant.

" Possibly," said the Baron, " I should now proceed to take my leave. I must not keep my sovereign in the ante-room. Let us come at once to a decision."

" It cannot, cannot be put off ? " she asked.

" It is impossible," answered Gondremark. " Your Highness sees it for herself. In the earlier stages, we might imitate the serpent; but for the ultimatum, there is no choice but to be bold like lions. Had the Prince chosen to remain away, it had been better; but we have gone too far forward to delay."

" What can have brought him ? " she cried. " To-day of all days ? "

" The marplot, madam, has the instinct of his nature," returned Gondremark. " But you exaggerate the peril. Think, madam, how far we have prospered, and against what odds ! Shall a Featherhead ?—but no ! " And he blew upon his fingers lightly with a laugh.

" Featherhead," she replied, " is still the Prince of Grünewald."

" On your sufferance only, and so long as you shall please to be indulgent," said the Baron. " There are rights of nature; power to the powerful is the law. If he shall think to cross your destiny—well, you have heard of the brazen and the earthen pot."

" Do you call me pot? You are ungallant, Baron," laughed the Princess.

" Before we are done with your glory, I shall have called you by many different titles," he replied.

The girl flushed with pleasure. " But Frédéric is still the Prince, *Monsieur le Flatteur*," she said. " You do not propose a revolution?—you of all men ? "

" Dear madam, when it is already made ! " he cried. " The

Prince reigns indeed in the almanack; but my Princess reigns and rules." And he looked at her with a fond admiration that made the heart of Seraphina swell. Looking on her huge slave, she drank the intoxicating joys of power. Meanwhile he continued, with that sort of massive archness that so ill became him, " She has but one fault; there is but one danger in the great career that I foresee for her. May I name it? may I be so irreverent? It is in herself—her heart is soft."

" Her courage is faint, Baron," said the Princess. " Suppose we have judged ill, suppose we were defeated? "

" Defeated, madam? " returned the Baron, with a touch of ill-humour. " Is the dog defeated by the hare? Our troops are all cantoned along the frontier; in five hours the vanguard of five thousand bayonets shall be hammering on the gates of Brandenau; and in all Gerolstein there are not fifteen hundred men who can manœuvre. It is as simple as a sum. There can be no resistance."

" It is no great exploit," she said. " Is that what you call glory? It is like beating a child."

" The courage, madam, is diplomatic," he replied. " We take a grave step; we fix the eyes of Europe, for the first time, on Grünewald; and in the negotiations of the next three months, mark me, we stand or fall. It is there, madam, that I shall have to depend upon your counsels," he added, almost gloomily. " If I had not seen you at work, if I did not know the fertility of your mind, I own I should tremble for the consequence. But it is in this field that men must recognise their inability. All the great negotiators, when they have not been women, have had women at their elbows. Madame de Pompadour was ill served; she had not found her Gondremark; but what a mighty politician! Catherine de Medici, too, what justice of sight, what readiness of means, what elasticity against defeat! But alas! madam, her Featherheads were her own children; and she had that one touch of vulgarity, that one trait of the good-wife, that she suffered family ties and affections to confine her liberty."

These singular views of history, strictly *ad usum Sera-*

phinæ, did not weave their usual soothing spell over the Princess. It was plain that she had taken a momentary distaste to her own resolutions; for she continued to oppose her counsellor, looking upon him out of half-closed eyes and with the shadow of a sneer upon her lips. " What boys men are! " she said; " what lovers of big words! Courage, indeed! If you had to scour pans, Herr von Gondremark, you would call it, I suppose, Domestic Courage? "

" I would, madam," said the Baron, stoutly, " if I scoured them well. I would put a good name upon a virtue; you will not overdo it; they are not so enchanting in themselves."

" Well, but let me see," she said. " I wish to understand your courage. Why we asked leave, like children! Our grannie in Berlin, our uncle in Vienna, the whole family, have patted us on the head and sent us forward. Courage? I wonder when I hear you! "

" My Princess is unlike herself," returned the Baron. " She has forgotten where the peril lies. True, we have received encouragement on every hand; but my Princess knows too well on what untenable conditions; and she knows besides how, in the publicity of the diet, these whispered conferences are forgotten and disowned. The danger is very real "—he raged inwardly at having to blow the very coal he had been quenching—" none the less real in that it is not precisely military, but for that reason the easier to be faced. Had we to count upon your troops, although I share your Highness's expectations of the conduct of Alvenau, we cannot forget that he has not been proved in chief command. But where negotiation is concerned, the conduct lies with us; and with your help, I laugh at danger."

" It may be so," said Seraphina, sighing. " It is elsewhere that I see danger. The people, these abominable people— suppose they should instantly rebel? What a figure we should make in the eyes of Europe to have undertaken an invasion while my own throne was tottering to its fall! "

" Nay, madam," said Gondremark, smiling, " here you are beneath yourself. What is it that feeds their discontent? What but the taxes? Once we have seized Gerolstein, the taxes are remitted, the sons return covered with renown, the houses are adorned with pillage, each tastes his little share of military glory, and behold us once again a happy family! ' Ay,' they will say, in each other's long ears, ' the Princess knew what she was about; she was in the right of it; she has a head upon her shoulders; and here we are, you see, better off than before.' But why should I say all this? It is what my Princess pointed out to me herself; it was by these reasons that she converted me to this adventure."

" I think, Herr von Gondremark," said Seraphina, somewhat tartly, " you often attribute your own sagacity to your Princess."

For a second Gondremark staggered under the shrewdness of the attack; the next, he had perfectly recovered. " Do I? " he said. " It is very possible. I have observed a similar tendency in your Highness."

It was so openly spoken, and appeared so just, that Seraphina breathed again. Her vanity had been alarmed, and the greatness of the relief improved her spirits. " Well," she said, " all this is little to the purpose. We are keeping Frédéric without, and I am still ignorant of our line of battle. Come, co-admiral, let us consult. . . . How am I to receive him now? And what are we to do if he should appear at the council? "

" Now," he answered, " I shall leave him to my Princess for just now! I have seen her at work. Send him off to his theatricals! But in all gentleness," he added. " Would it, for instance, would it displease my sovereign to affect a headache? "

" Never! " said she. " The woman who can manage, like the man who can fight, must never shrink from an encounter. The knight must not disgrace his weapons."

" Then let me pray my *belle dame sans merci*," he returned, " to affect the only virtue that she lacks. Be pitiful to the poor young man; affect an interest in his hunting; be weary of politics; find in his society, as it were, a grateful repose from dry considerations. Does my Princess authorise the line of battle? "

"Well, that is a trifle," answered Seraphina. "The council—there is the point."

"The council?" cried Gondremark. "Permit me, madam." And he rose and proceeded to flutter about the room, counterfeiting Otto both in voice and gesture not unhappily. "'What is there to-day, Herr von Gondremark? Ah, Herr Cancellarius, a new wig! You cannot deceive me; I know every wig in Grünewald; I have the sovereign's eye. What are these papers about? O, I see. O, certainly. Surely, surely. I wager none of you remarked that wig. By all means. I know nothing about that. Dear me, are there as many as all that? Well, you can sign them; you have the procuration. You see, Herr Cancellarius, I knew your wig.' And so," concluded Gondremark, resuming his own voice, "our sovereign, by the particular grace of God, enlightens and supports his privy councillors."

But when the Baron turned to Seraphina for approval, he found her frozen. "You are pleased to be witty, Herr von Gondremark," she said, "and have perhaps forgotten where you are. But these rehearsals are apt to be misleading. Your master, the Prince of Grünewald, is sometimes more exacting."

Gondremark cursed her in his soul. Of all injured vanities, that of the reproved buffoon is the most savage; and when grave issues are involved, these petty stabs become unbearable. But Gondremark was a man of iron; he showed nothing; he did not even, like the common trickster, retreat because he had presumed, but held to his point bravely. "Madam," he said, "if, as you say, he prove exacting, we must take the bull by the horns."

"We shall see," she said, and she arranged her skirt like one about to rise. Temper, scorn, disgust, all the more acrid feelings, became her like jewels; and she now looked her best.

"Pray God they quarrel," thought Gondremark. "The damned minx may fail me yet, unless they quarrel. It is time to let him in. Zz—fight dogs!" Consequent on these reflections, he bent a stiff knee and chivalrously kissed the Princess's hand. "My Princess," he said, "must now dismiss her servant. I have much to arrange against the hour of council."

"Go," she said, and rose.

And as Gondremark tripped out of a private door, she touched a bell, and gave the order to admit the Prince.

CHAPTER VI

THE PRINCE DELIVERS A LECTURE ON MARRIAGE, WITH
PRACTICAL ILLUSTRATIONS OF DIVORCE

WITH what a world of excellent intentions Otto entered his wife's cabinet! how fatherly, how tender! how morally affecting were the words he had prepared! Nor was Seraphina unamiably inclined. Her usual fear of Otto as a marplot in her great designs was now swallowed up in a passing distrust of the designs themselves. For Gondremark, besides, she had conceived an angry horror. In her heart she did not like the Baron. Behind his impudent servility, behind the devotion which, with indelicate delicacy, he still forced on her attention, she divined the grossness of his nature. So a man may be proud of having tamed a bear, and yet sicken at his captive's odour. And above all, she had certain jealous intimations that the man was false, and the deception double. True, she falsely trifled with his love; but he, perhaps, was only trifling with her vanity. The insolence of his late mimicry, and the odium of her own position as she sat and watched it, lay besides like a load upon her conscience. She met Otto almost with a sense of guilt, and yet she welcomed him as a deliverer from ugly things.

But the wheels of an interview are at the mercy of a thousand ruts; and even at Otto's entrance, the first jolt occurred. Gondremark, he saw, was gone; but there was the chair drawn close for consultation; and it pained him not only that this man had been received, but that he should depart with such an air of secrecy. Struggling with this twinge, it was somewhat sharply that he dismissed the attendant who had brought him in.

"You make yourself at home, *chez moi*," she said, a little ruffled both by his tone of command and by the glance he had thrown upon the chair.

PRINCE OTTO

"Madam," replied Otto, "I am here so seldom that I have almost the rights of a stranger."

"You choose your own associates, Frédéric," she said.

"I am here to speak of it," he returned. "It is now four years since we were married; and these four years, Seraphina, have not perhaps been happy either for you or for me. I am well aware I was unsuitable to be your husband. I was not young, I had no ambition, I was a trifler; and you despised me, I dare not say unjustly. But to do justice on both sides, you must bear in mind how I have acted. When I found it amused you to play the part of Princess on this little stage, did I not immediately resign to you my box of toys, this Grünewald? And when I found I was distasteful as a husband, could any husband have been less intrusive? You will tell me that I have no feelings, no preference, and thus no credit; that I go before the wind; that all this was in my character. And indeed, one thing is true, that it is easy, too easy, to leave things undone. But Seraphina, I begin to learn it is not always wise. If I were too old and too uncongenial for your husband, I should still have remembered that I was the Prince of that country to which you came, a visitor and a child. In that relation also there were duties, and these duties I have not performed."

To claim the advantage of superior age is to give sure offence. "Duty!" laughed Seraphina, "and on your lips, Frédéric! You make me laugh. What fancy is this? Go, flirt with the maids and be a prince in Dresden China, as you look. Enjoy yourself, *mon enfant*, and leave duty and the state to us."

The plural grated on the Prince. "I have enjoyed myself too much," he said, "since enjoyment is the word. And yet there were much to say upon the other side. You must suppose me desperately fond of hunting. But indeed there were days when I found a great deal of interest in what it was courtesy to call my government. And I have always had some claim to taste; I could tell live happiness from dull routine; and between hunting, and the throne of Austria, and your society, my choice had never wavered, had the choice been mine. You were a girl, a bud, when you were given me——"

"Heavens!" she cried, "is this to be a love scene?"

"I am never ridiculous," he said; "it is my only merit; and you may be certain this shall be a scene of marriage *à la mode*. But when I remember the beginning, it is bare courtesy to speak in sorrow. Be just, madam: you would think me strangely uncivil to recall these days without the decency of a regret. Be yet a little juster, and own, if only in complaisance, that you yourself regret that past."

"I have nothing to regret," said the Princess. "You surprise me. I thought you were so happy."

"Happy and happy, there are so many hundred ways," said Otto. "A man may be happy in revolt; he may be happy in sleep; wine, change, and travel make him happy; virtue, they say, will do the like—I have not tried; and they say also that in old, quiet, and habitual marriages there is yet another happiness. Happy, yes; I am happy if you like; but I will tell you frankly, I was happier when I brought you home."

"Well," said the Princess, not without constraint, "it seems you changed your mind."

"Not I," returned Otto, "I never changed. Do you remember, Seraphina, on our way home, when you saw the roses in the lane, and I got out and plucked them? It was a narrow lane between great trees; the sunset at the end was all gold, and the rooks were flying overhead. There were nine, nine red roses; you gave me a kiss for each, and I told myself that every rose and every kiss should stand for a year of love. Well, in eighteen months there was an end. But do you fancy, Seraphina, that my heart has altered?"

"I am sure I cannot tell," she said, like an automaton.

"It has not," the Prince continued. "There is nothing ridiculous, even from a husband, in a love that owns itself unhappy and that asks no more. I built on sand; pardon me, I do not breathe a reproach—I built, I suppose, upon my own infirmities; but I put my heart in the building, and it still lies among the ruins."

"How very poetical!" she said with a little choking laugh,

unknown relentings, unfamiliar softnesses, moving within her. "What would you be at?" she added, hardening her voice.

"I would be at this," he answered; "and hard it is to say. I would be at this:—Seraphina, I am your husband after all, and a poor fool that loves you. Understand," he cried almost fiercely, "I am no suppliant husband; what your love refuses I would scorn to receive from your pity. I do not ask, I would not take it. And for jealousy, what ground have I? A dog-in-the-manger jealousy is a thing the dogs may laugh at. But at least, in the world's eye, I am still your husband; and I ask you if you treat me fairly? I keep to myself, I leave you free, I have given you in everything your will. What do you in return? I find, Seraphina, that you have been too thoughtless. But between persons such as we, in our conspicuous station, particular care and a particular courtesy are owing. Scandal is perhaps not easy to avoid; but it is hard to bear."

"Scandal!" she cried, with a deep breath. "Scandal! It is for this you have been driving!"

"I have tried to tell you how I feel," he replied. "I have told you that I love you—love you in vain—a bitter thing for a husband; I have laid myself open that I might speak without offence. And now that I have begun, I will go on and finish."

"I demand it," she said. "What is this about?"

Otto flushed crimson. "I have to say what I would fain not," he answered. "I counsel you to see less of Gondremark."

"Of Gondremark? And why?" she asked.

"Your intimacy is the ground of scandal, madam," said Otto, firmly enough—"of a scandal that is agony to me, and would be crushing to your parents if they knew it."

"You are the first to bring me word of it," said she. "I thank you."

"You have perhaps cause," he replied. "Perhaps I am the only one among your friends——"

"O, leave my friends alone," she interrupted. "My

friends are of a different stamp. You have come to me here and made a parade of sentiment. When have I last seen you? I have governed your kingdom for you in the meanwhile, and there I got no help. At last, when I am weary with a man's work, and you are weary of your playthings, you return to make me a scene of conjugal reproaches—the grocer and his wife! The positions are too much reversed; and you should understand, at least, that I cannot at the same time do your work of government and behave myself like a little girl. Scandal is the atmosphere in which we live, we princes; it is what a prince should know. You play an odious part. Do you believe this rumour? "

" Madam, should I be here? " said Otto.

" It is what I want to know! " she cried, the tempest of her scorn increasing. " Suppose you did—I say, suppose you did believe it? "

" I should make it my business to suppose the contrary," he answered.

" I thought so. O, you are made of baseness! " said she.

" Madam," he cried, roused at last, " enough of this. You wilfully misunderstand my attitude; you outwear my patience. In the name of your parents, in my own name, I summon you to be more circumspect."

" Is this a request, *Monsieur mon mari?* " she demanded.

" Madam, if I chose, I might command," said Otto.

" You might, sir, as the law stands, make me a prisoner," returned Seraphina. " Short of that you will gain nothing."

" You will continue as before? " he asked.

" Precisely as before," said she. " As soon as this comedy is over, I shall request the Freiherr von Gondremark to visit me. Do you understand? " she added, rising. " For my part, I have done."

" I will then ask the favour of your hand, madam," said Otto, palpitating in every pulse with anger. " I have to request that you will visit in my society another part of my poor house. And reassure yourself—it will not take long—and it is the last obligation that you shall have the chance to lay me under."

317

" The last? " she cried. " Most joyfully ! "

She offered her hand and he took it; on each side with an elaborate affectation, each inwardly incandescent. He led her out by the private door, following where Gondremark had passed; they threaded a corridor or two, little frequented, looking on a court, until they came at last into the Prince's suite. The first room was an armoury, hung all about with the weapons of various countries, and looking forth on the front terrace.

" Have you brought me here to slay me? " she inquired.

" I have brought you, madam, only to pass on," replied Otto.

Next they came to a library, where an old chamberlain sat half asleep. He rose and bowed before the princely couple, asking for orders.

" You will attend us here," said Otto.

The next stage was a gallery of pictures, where Seraphina's portrait hung conspicuous, dressed for the chase, red roses in her hair, as Otto, in the first months of marriage, had directed. He pointed to it without a word; she raised her eyebrows in silence; and they passed still forward into a matted corridor where four doors opened. One led to Otto's bedroom; one was the private door to Seraphina's. And here, for the first time, Otto left her hand, and stepping forward, shot the bolt.

" It is long, madam," said he, " since it was bolted on the other side."

" One was effectual," returned the Princess. " Is this all? "

" Shall I reconduct you? " he asked, bowing.

" I should prefer," she said, in ringing tones, " the conduct of the Freiherr von Gondremark."

Otto summoned the chamberlain. " If the Freiherr von Gondremark is in the palace," he said, " bid him attend the Princess here." And when the official had departed, " Can I do more to serve you, madam? " the Prince asked.

" Thank you, no. I have been much amused," she answered.

OF LOVE AND POLITICS

" I have now," continued Otto, " given you your liberty complete. This has been for you a miserable marriage."

" Miserable! " said she.

" It has been made light to you; it shall be lighter still," continued the Prince. " But one thing, madam, you must still continue to bear—my father's name, which is now yours. I leave it in your hands. Let me see you, since you will have no advice of mine, apply the more attention of your own to bear it worthily."

" Herr von Gondremark is long in coming," she remarked.

" O Seraphina, Seraphina! " he cried. And that was the end of their interview.

She tripped to a window and looked out; and a little after, the chamberlain announced the Freiherr von Gondremark, who entered with something of a wild eye and changed complexion, confounded, as he was, at this unusual summons. The Princess faced round from the window with a pearly smile; nothing but her heightened colour spoke of discomposure. Otto was pale, but he was otherwise master of himself.

" Herr von Gondremark," said he, " oblige me so far: reconduct the Princess to her own apartment."

The Baron, still all at sea, offered his hand, which was smilingly accepted, and the pair sailed forth through the picture-gallery.

As soon as they were gone, and Otto knew the length and breadth of his miscarriage, and how he had done the contrary of all that he intended, he stood stupefied. A fiasco so complete and sweeping was laughable, even to himself; and he laughed aloud in his wrath. Upon this mood there followed the sharpest violence of remorse; and to that again, as he recalled his provocation, anger succeeded afresh. So he was tossed in spirit; now bewailing his inconsequence and lack of temper, now flaming up in white hot indignation and a noble pity for himself.

He paced his apartment like a leopard. There was danger in Otto, for a flash. Like a pistol, he could kill at one moment, and the next he might be kicked aside. But just

319

then, as he walked the long floors in his alternate humours, tearing his handkerchief between his hands, he was strung to his top note, every nerve attent. The pistol, you might say, was charged. And when jealousy from time to time fetched him a lash across the tenderest of his feeling, and sent a string of her fire-pictures glancing before his mind's eye, the contraction of his face was even dangerous. He disregarded jealousy's inventions, yet they stung. In this height of his anger, he still preserved his faith in Seraphina's innocence; but the thought of her possible misconduct was the bitterest ingredient in his pot of sorrow.

There came a knock at the door, and the chamberlain brought him a note. He took it and ground it in his hand, continuing his march, continuing his bewildered thoughts; and some minutes had gone by before the circumstance came clearly to his mind. Then he paused and opened it. It was a pencil scratch from Gotthold, thus conceived:

"The council is privately summoned at once.
"G. v. H."

If the council was thus called before the hour, and that privately, it was plain they feared his interference. Feared: here was a sweet thought. Gotthold, too—Gotthold, who had always used and regarded him as a mere pleasant lad, had now been at the pains to warn him; Gotthold looked for something at his hands. Well, none should be disappointed; the Prince, too long beshadowed by the uxorious lover, should now return and shine. He summoned his valet, repaired the disorder of his appearance with elaborate care; and then, curled and scented and adorned, Prince Charming in every line, but with a twitching nostril, he set forth unattended for the council.

CHAPTER VII

THE PRINCE DISSOLVES THE COUNCIL

IT was as Gotthold wrote. The liberation of Sir John, Greisengesang's uneasy narrative, last of all, the scene between Seraphina and the Prince, had decided the conspirators to take a step of bold timidity. There had been a period of bustle, liveried messengers speeding here and there with notes; and at half-past ten in the morning, about an hour before its usual hour, the council of Grünewald sat around the board.

It was not a large body. At the instance of Gondremark, it had undergone a strict purgation, and was now composed exclusively of tools. Three secretaries sat at a side table. Seraphina took the head; on her right was the Baron, on her left Greisengesang; below these Grafinski the treasurer, Count Eisenthal, a couple of non-combatants, and, to the surprise of all, Gotthold. He had been named a privy councillor by Otto, merely that he might profit by the salary; and as he was never known to attend a meeting, it had occurred to nobody to cancel his appointment. His present appearance was the more ominous, coming when it did. Gondremark scowled upon him; and the non-combatant on his right, intercepting this black look, edged away from one who was so clearly out of favour.

"The hour presses, your Highness," said the Baron; "may we proceed to business?"

"At once," replied Seraphina.

"Your Highness will pardon me," said Gotthold; "but you are still, perhaps, unacquainted with the fact that Prince Otto has returned."

"The Prince will not attend the council," replied Seraphina, with a momentary blush. "The despatches, Herr Cancellarius? There is one for Gerolstein?"

321

'A secretary brought a paper.

"Here, madam," said Greisengesang. "Shall I read it?"

"We are all familiar with its terms," replied Gondremark. "Your Highness approves?"

"Unhesitatingly," said Seraphina.

"It may then be held as read," concluded the Baron. "Will your Highness sign?"

The Princess did so; Gondremark, Eisenthal, and one of the non-combatants followed suit; and the paper was then passed across the table to the librarian. He proceeded leisurely to read.

"We have no time to spare, Herr Doctor," cried the Baron, brutally. "If you do not choose to sign on the authority of your sovereign, pass it on. Or you may leave the table," he added, his temper ripping out.

"I decline your invitation, Herr von Gondremark; and my sovereign, as I continue to observe with regret, is still absent from the board," replied the Doctor, calmly; and he resumed the perusal of the paper, the rest chafing and exchanging glances. "Madam and gentlemen," he said, at last, "what I hold in my hand is simply a declaration of war."

"Simply," said Seraphina, flashing defiance.

"The sovereign of this country is under the same roof with us," continued Gotthold, "and I insist he shall be summoned. It is needless to adduce my reasons; you are all ashamed at heart of this projected treachery."

The council waved like a sea. There were various outcries.

"You insult the Princess," thundered Gondremark.

"I maintain my protest," replied Gotthold.

At the height of this confusion the door was thrown open; an usher announced, "Gentlemen, the Prince!" and Otto, with his most excellent bearing, entered the apartment. It was like oil upon the troubled waters; every one settled instantly into his place, and Greisengesang, to give himself a countenance, became absorbed in the arrangement of his papers; but in their eagerness to dissemble, one and all neglected to rise.

OF LOVE AND POLITICS

"Gentlemen," said the Prince, pausing.

They all got to their feet in a moment; and this reproof still further demoralised the weaker brethren.

The Prince moved slowly towards the lower end of the table; then he paused again, and, fixing his eye on Greisengesang, "How comes it, Herr Cancellarius," he asked, "that I have received no notice of the change of hour?"

"Your Highness," replied the Chancellor, "her Highness the Princess . . ." and there paused.

"I understood," said Seraphina, taking him up, "that you did not purpose to be present."

Their eyes met for a second, and Seraphina's fell; but her anger only burned the brighter for that private shame.

"And now, gentlemen," said Otto, taking his chair, "I pray you be seated. I have been absent: there are doubtless some arrears; but ere we proceed to business, Herr Grafinski, you will direct four thousand crowns to be sent to me at once. Make a note, if you please," he added, as the treasurer still stared in wonder.

"Four thousand crowns?" asked Seraphina. "Pray, for what?"

"Madam," returned Otto, smiling, "for my own purposes."

Gondremark spurred up Grafinski underneath the table.

"If your Highness will indicate the destination . . ." began the puppet.

"You are not here, sir, to interrogate your Prince," said Otto.

Grafinski looked for help to his commander; and Gondremark came to his aid, in suave and measured tones.

"Your Highness may reasonably be surprised," he said; "and Herr Grafinski, although I am convinced he is clear of the intention of offending, would have perhaps done better to begin with an explanation. The resources of the State are at the present moment entirely swallowed up, or, as we hope to prove, wisely invested. In a month from now, I do not question we shall be able to meet any command your

323

Highness may lay upon us; but at this hour I fear that, even in so small a matter, he must prepare himself for disappointment. Our zeal is no less, although our power may be inadequate."

"How much, Herr Grafinski, have we in the treasury?" asked Otto.

"Your Highness," protested the treasurer, "we have immediate need of every crown."

"I think, sir, you evade me," flashed the Prince; and then turning to the side table, "Mr. Secretary," he added, "bring me, if you please, the treasury docket."

Herr Grafinski became deadly pale; the Chancellor, expecting his own turn, was probably engaged in prayer; Gondremark was watching like a ponderous cat. Gotthold, on his part, looked on with wonder at his cousin; he was certainly showing spirit, but what, in such a time of gravity, was all this talk of money? and why should he waste his strength upon a personal issue?

"I find," said Otto, with his finger on the docket, "that we have 20,000 crowns in case."

"That is exact, your Highness," replied the Baron. "But our liabilities, all of which are happily not liquid, amount to a far larger sum; and at the present point of time, it would be morally impossible to divert a single florin. Essentially, the case is empty. We have, already presented, a large note for material of war."

"Material of war?" exclaimed Otto, with an excellent assumption of surprise. "But if my memory serves me right, we settled these accounts in January."

"There have been further orders," the Baron explained. "A new park of artillery has been completed; five hundred stand of arms, seven hundred baggage mules—the details are in a special memorandum. Mr. Secretary Holtz, the memorandum, if you please."

"One would think, gentlemen, that we were going to war," said Otto.

"We are," said Seraphina.

"War!" cried the Prince. "And, gentlemen, with whom?

The peace of Grünewald has endured for centuries. What aggression, what insult, have we suffered? "

" Here, your Highness," said Gotthold, " is the ultimatum. It was in the very article of signature, when your Highness so opportunely entered."

Otto laid the paper before him; as he read, his fingers played tattoo upon the table. " Was it proposed," he inquired, " to send this paper forth without a knowledge of my pleasure? "

One of the non-combatants, eager to trim, volunteered an answer. " The Herr Doctor von Hohenstockwitz had just entered his dissent," he added.

" Give me the rest of this correspondence," said the Prince. It was handed to him, and he read it patiently from end to end, while the councillors sat foolishly enough looking before them on the table. The secretaries, in the background, were exchanging glances of delight; a row at the council was for them a rare and welcome feature.

" Gentlemen," said Otto, when he had finished, " I have read with pain. This claim upon Obermünsterol is palpably unjust; it has not a tincture, not a show, of justice. There is not in all this ground enough for after-dinner talk, and you propose to force it as a *casus belli*."

" Certainly, your Highness," returned Gondremark, too wise to defend the indefensible, " the claim on Obermünsterol is simply a pretext."

" It is well," said the Prince. " Herr Cancellarius, take your pen. ' The council,' " he began to dictate—" I withhold all notice of my intervention," he said, in parenthesis and addressing himself more directly to his wife; " and I say nothing of the strange suppression by which this business has been smuggled past my knowledge. I am content to be in time—" ' The council,' " he resumed, " ' on a further examination of the facts, and enlightened by the note in the last despatch from Gerolstein, have the pleasure to announce that they are entirely at one, both as to fact and sentiment, with the Grand Ducal Court of Gerolstein.' You have it? Upon these lines, sir, you will draw up the despatch."

" If your Highness will allow me," said the Baron, " your Highness is so imperfectly acquainted with the internal history of this correspondence, that any interference will be merely hurtful. Such a paper as your Highness proposes, would be to stultify the whole previous policy of Grünewald."

" The policy of Grünewald!" cried the Prince. " One would suppose you had no sense of humour! Would you fish in a coffee cup? "

" With deference, your Highness," returned the Baron, " even in a coffee cup there may be poison. The purpose of this war is not simply territorial enlargement; still less is it a war of glory; for, as your Highness indicates, the state of Grünewald is too small to be ambitious. But the body politic is seriously diseased; republicanism, socialism, many disintegrating ideas are abroad; circle within circle, a really formidable organisation has grown up about your Highness's throne."

" I have heard of it, Herr von Gondremark," put in the Prince; " but I have reason to be aware that yours is the more authoritative information."

" I am honoured by this expression of my Prince's confidence," returned Gondremark, unabashed. " It is, therefore with a single eye to these disorders, that our present external policy has been shaped. Something was required to divert public attention, to employ the idle, to popularise your Highness's rule, and, if it were possible, to enable him to reduce the taxes at a blow and to a notable amount. The proposed expedition—for it cannot without hyperbole be called a war—seemed to the council to combine the various characters required; a marked improvement in the public sentiment has followed even upon our preparations; and I cannot doubt that when success shall follow, the effect will surpass even our boldest hopes."

" You are very adroit, Herr von Gondremark," said Otto. " You fill me with admiration. I had not heretofore done justice to your qualities."

Seraphina looked up with joy, supposing Otto conquered;

but Gondremark still waited, armed at every point; he knew how very stubborn is the revolt of a weak character.

"And the territorial army scheme, to which I was persuaded to consent—was it secretly directed to the same end?" the Prince asked.

"I still believe the effect to have been good," replied the Baron; "discipline and mounting guard are excellent sedatives. But I will avow to your Highness, I was unaware, at the date of that decree, of the magnitude of the revolutionary movement; nor did any of us, I think, imagine that such a territorial army was a part of the republican proposals."

"It was?" asked Otto. "Strange! Upon what fancied grounds?"

"The grounds were indeed fanciful," returned the Baron. "It was conceived among the leaders that a territorial army, drawn from and returning to the people, would, in the event of any popular uprising, prove lukewarm or unfaithful to the throne."

"I see," said the Prince. "I begin to understand."

"His Highness begins to understand?" repeated Gondremark, with the sweetest politeness. "May I beg of him to complete the phrase?"

"The history of the revolution," replied Otto, drily. "And now," he added, "what do you conclude?"

"I conclude, your Highness, with a simple reflection," said the Baron, accepting the stab without a quiver, "the war is popular; were the humour contradicted to-morrow, a considerable disappointment would be felt in many classes; and in the present tension of spirits, the most lukewarm sentiment may be enough to precipitate events. There lies the danger. The revolution hangs imminent; we sit, at this council board, below the sword of Damocles."

"We must then lay our heads together," said the Prince, "and devise some honourable means of safety."

Up to this moment, since the first note of opposition fell from the librarian, Seraphina had uttered about twenty words. With a somewhat heightened colour, her eyes gen-

327

erally lowered, her foot sometimes nervously tapping on the floor, she had kept her own counsel and commanded her anger like a hero. But at this stage of the engagement she lost control of her impatience.

"Means!" she cried. "They have been found and prepared before you knew the need for them. Sign the despatch, and let us be done with this delay."

"Madam, I said 'honourable,'" returned Otto, bowing. "This war is, in my eyes, and by Herr von Gondremark's account, an inadmissible expedient. If we have misgoverned here in Grünewald, are the people of Gerolstein to bleed and pay for our misdoings? Never, madam; not while I live. But I attach so much importance to all that I have heard to-day for the first time—and why only to-day, I do not even stop to ask—that I am eager to find some plan that I can follow with credit to myself."

"And should you fail?" she asked.

"Should I fail, I will then meet the blow half way," replied the Prince. "On the first open discontent, I shall convoke the States, and, when it pleases them to bid me, abdicate."

Seraphina laughed angrily. "This is the man for whom we have been labouring!" she cried. "We tell him of change; he will devise the means, he says; and his device is abdication? Sir, have you no shame to come here at the eleventh hour among those who have borne the heat and burthen of the day? Do you not wonder at yourself? I, sir, was here in my place, striving to uphold your dignity alone. I took counsel with the wisest I could find, while you were eating and hunting. I have laid my plans with foresight; they were ripe for action; and then—" she choked—"then you return—for a forenoon—to ruin all! To-morrow, you will be once more about your pleasures; you will give us leave once more to think and work for you; and again you will come back, and again you will thwart what you had not the industry or knowledge to conceive. Oh! it is intolerable. Be modest, sir. Do not presume upon the rank you cannot worthily uphold. I would not issue my commands with so much gusto—it is from no merit in yourself they are obeyed. What are you? What have you to do in this grave council? Go," she cried, "go among your equals! The very people in the streets mock at you for a prince."

At this surprising outburst the whole council sat aghast.

"Madam," said the Baron, alarmed out of his caution, "command yourself."

"Address yourself to me, sir!" cried the Prince. "I will not bear these whisperings!"

Seraphina burst into tears.

"Sir," cried the Baron, rising, "this lady——"

"Herr von Gondremark," said the Prince, "one more observation, and I place you under arrest."

"Your Highness is the master," replied Gondremark, bowing.

"Bear it in mind more constantly," said Otto. "Herr Cancellarius, bring all the papers to my cabinet. Gentlemen, the council is dissolved."

And he bowed and left the apartment, followed by Greisengesang and the secretaries, just at the moment when the Princess's ladies, summoned in all haste, entered by another door to help her forth.

CHAPTER VIII

THE PARTY OF WAR TAKES ACTION

HALF an hour after, Gondremark was once more closeted with Seraphina.

" Where is he now? " she asked, on his arrival.

" Madam, he is with the Chancellor," replied the Baron. " Wonder of wonders, he is at work! "

" Ah," she said, " he was born to torture me! Oh, what a fall, what a humiliation! Such a scheme to wreck upon so small a trifle! But now all is lost."

" Madam," said Gondremark, " nothing is lost. Something, on the other hand, is found. You have found your senses; you see him as he is—see him as you see everything where your too-good heart is not in question—with the judicial, with the statesman's eye. So long as he had a right to interfere, the empire that may be was still distant. I have not entered on this course without the plain foresight of its dangers; and even for this I was prepared. But, madam, I knew two things: I knew that you were born to command, that I was born to serve; I knew that by a rare conjuncture, the hand had found the tool; and from the first I was confident, as I am confident to-day, that no hereditary trifler has the power to shatter that alliance."

" I, born to command! " she said. " Do you forget my tears? "

" Madam, they were the tears of Alexander," cried the Baron. " They touched, they thrilled me; I forgot myself a moment—even I! But do you suppose that I had not remarked, that I had not admired, your previous bearing? your great self-command? Ay, that was princely! " He paused. " It was a thing to see. I drank confidence! I tried to imitate your calm. And I was well inspired; in

330

my heart, I think that I was well inspired; that any man, within the reach of argument, had been convinced! But it was not to be; nor, madam, do I regret the failure. Let us be open; let me disclose my heart. I have loved two things, not unworthily: Grünewald and my sovereign!" Here he kissed her hand. " Either I must resign my ministry, leave the land of my adoption and the queen whom I had chosen to obey—or——" He paused again.

" Alas, Herr von Gondremark, there is no ' or,' " said Seraphina.

" Nay, madam, give me time," he replied. " When first I saw you, you were still young; not every man would have remarked your powers; but I had not been twice honoured by your conversation ere I had found my mistress. I have, madam, I believe, some genius; and I have much ambition. But the genius is of the serving kind; and to offer a career to my ambition, I had to find one born to rule. This is the base and essence of our union; each had need of the other; each recognised, master and servant, lever and fulcrum, the complement of his endowment. Marriages, they say, are made in heaven: how much more these pure, laborious, intellectual fellowships, born to found empires! Nor is this all. We found each other ripe, filled with great ideas that took shape and clarified with every word. We grew together —ay, madam, in mind we grew together like twin children. All of my life until we met was petty and groping; was it not—I will flatter myself openly—it *was* the same with you! Not till then had you those eagle surveys, that wide and hopeful sweep of intuition! Thus we had formed ourselves, and we were ready."

" It is true," she cried. " I feel it. Yours is the genius; your generosity confounds your insight; all I could offer you was the position, was this throne, to be a fulcrum. But I offered it without reserve; I entered at least warmly into all your thoughts; you were sure of me—sure of my support—certain of justice. Tell me, tell me again, that I have helped you."

" Nay, madam," he said, " you made me. In everything

331

you were my inspiration. And as we prepared our policy, weighing every step, how often have I had to admire your perspicacity, your man-like diligence and fortitude! You know that these are not the words of flattery; your conscience echoes them; have you spared a day? have you indulged yourself in any pleasure? Young and beautiful, you have lived a life of high intellectual effort, of irksome intellectual patience with details. Well, you have your reward: with the fall of Brandenau, the throne of your Empire is founded."

"What thought have you in your mind?" she asked. "Is not all ruined?"

"Nay, my Princess, the same thought is in both our minds," he said.

"Herr von Gondremark," she replied, "by all that I hold sacred, I have none; I do not think at all; I am crushed."

"You are looking at the passionate side of a rich nature, misunderstood and recently insulted," said the Baron. "Look into your intellect, and tell me."

"I find nothing, nothing but tumult," she replied.

"You find one word branded, madam," returned the Baron: "'Abdication!'"

"O!" she cried. "The coward! He leaves me to bear all, and in the hour of trial he stabs me from behind. There is nothing in him, not respect, not love, not courage—his wife, his dignity, his throne, the honour of his father, he forgets them all!"

"Yes," pursued the Baron, "the word Abdication. I perceive a glimmering there."

"I read your fancy," she returned. "It is mere madness, midsummer madness. Baron, I am more unpopular than he. You know it. They can excuse, they can love, his weakness; but me, they hate."

"Such is the gratitude of peoples," said the Baron. "But we trifle. Here, madam, are my plain thoughts. The man who in the hour of danger speaks of abdication is, for me, a venomous animal. I speak with the bluntness of gravity, madam; this is no hour for mincing. The coward, in a station of authority, is more dangerous than fire. We dwell on a volcano; if this man can have his way, Grünewald before a week will have been deluged with innocent blood. You know the truth of what I say; we have looked unblenching into this ever-possible catastrophe. To him it is nothing: he will abdicate! Abdicate, just God! and this unhappy country committed to his charge, and the lives of men and the honour of women . . ." His voice appeared to fail him; in an instant he had conquered his emotion and resumed: "But you, madam, conceive more worthily of your responsibilities. I am with you in the thought; and in the face of the horrors that I see impending, I say, and your heart repeats it—we have gone too far to pause. Honour, duty, ay, and the care of our own lives, demand we should proceed."

She was looking at him, her brow thoughtfully knitted. "I feel it," she said. "But how? He has the power."

"The power, madam? The power is in the army," he replied; and then hastily, ere she could intervene, "we have to save ourselves," he went on; "I have to save my Princess, she has to save her minister; we have both of us to save this infatuated youth from his own madness. He in the outbreak would be the earliest victim; I see him," he cried, "torn in pieces; and Grünewald, unhappy Grünewald! Nay, madam, you who have the power must use it; it lies hard upon your conscience."

"Show me how!" she cried. "Suppose I were to place him under some constraint, the revolution would break upon us instantly."

The Baron feigned defeat. "It is true," he said. "You see more clearly than I do. Yet there should, there must be, some way." And he waited for his chance.

"No," she said; "I told you from the first there is no remedy. Our hopes are lost: lost by one miserable trifler, ignorant, fretful, fitful—who will have disappeared to-morrow, who knows? to his boorish pleasures!"

Any peg would do for Gondremark. "The thing!" he cried, striking his brow. "Fool, not to have thought of it! Madam, without perhaps knowing it, you have solved our problem."

" What do you mean? Speak! she said.

He appeared to collect himself; and then, with a smile, " The Prince," he said, " must go once more a-hunting."

" Ay, if he would! " cried she, " and stay there! "

" And stay there," echoed the Baron. It was so significantly said, that her face changed; and the schemer, fearful of the sinister ambiguity of his expressions, hastened to explain. " This time he shall go hunting in a carriage, with a good escort of our foreign lancers. His destination shall be the Felsenburg; it is healthy, the rock is high, the windows are small and barred; it might have been built on purpose. We shall entrust the captaincy to the Scotchman Gordon; he at least will have no scruple. Who will miss the sovereign? He is gone hunting; he came home on Tuesday, on Thursday he returned; all is usual in that. Meanwhile the war proceeds; our Prince will soon weary of his solitude; and about the time of our triumph, or, if he prove very obstinate, a little later, he shall be released upon a proper understanding, and I see him once more directing his theatricals."

Seraphina sat gloomy, plunged in thought. " Yes," she said suddenly, " and the despatch? He is now writing it."

" It cannot pass the council before Friday," replied Gondremark; " and as for any private note, the messengers are all at my disposal. They are picked men, madam. I am a person of precaution."

" It would appear so," she said, with a flash of her occasional repugnance to the man; and then after a pause, " Herr von Gondremark," she added, " I recoil from this extremity."

" I share your Highness's repugnance," answered he. " But what would you have? We are defenceless, else."

" I see it, but this is sudden. It is a public crime," she said, nodding at him with a sort of horror.

" Look but a little deeper," he returned, " and whose is the crime? "

OF LOVE AND POLITICS

" His! " she cried. " His, before God! And I hold him liable. But still——"

" It is not as if he would be harmed," submitted Gondremark.

" I know it," she replied, but it was still unheartily.

And then, as brave men are entitled, by prescriptive right as old as the world's history, to the alliance and the active help of Fortune, the punctual goddess stepped down from the machine. One of the Princess's ladies begged to enter; a man, it appeared, had brought a line for the Freiherr von Gondremark. It proved to be a pencil billet, which the crafty Greisengesang had found the means to scribble and despatch under the very guns of Otto; and the daring of the act bore testimony to the terror of the actor. For Greisengesang had but one influential motive: fear. The note ran thus:

" At the first council, procuration to be withdrawn.

" CORN. GREIS."

So, after three years of exercise, the right of signature was to be stript from Seraphina. It was more than an insult; it was a public disgrace; and she did not pause to consider how she had earned it, but morally bounded under the attack as bounds the wounded tiger.

" Enough," she said; " I will sign the order. When shall he leave? "

" It will take me twelve hours to collect my men, and it had best be done at night. To-morrow midnight, if you please? " answered the Baron.

" Excellent," she said. " My door is always open to you, Baron. As soon as the order is prepared, bring it to me to sign."

" Madam," he said, " alone of all of us you do not risk your head in this adventure. For that reason, and to prevent all hesitation, I venture to propose the order should be in your hand throughout."

" You are right," she replied.

He laid a form before her, and she wrote the order in

335

a clear hand, and re-read it. Suddenly a cruel smile came on her face. " I had forgotten his puppet," said she. " They will keep each other company." And she interlined and initialed the condemnation of Doctor Gotthold.

" Your Highness has more memory than your servant," said the Baron; and then he, in his turn, carefully perused the fateful paper. " Good!" said he.

" You will appear in the drawing-room, Baron?" she asked.

" I thought it better," said he, " to avoid the possibility of a public affront. Anything that shook my credit might hamper us in the immediate future."

" You are right," she said; and she held out her hand as to an old friend and equal.

CHAPTER IX

THE pistol had been practically fired. Under ordinary
circumstances the scene at the council table would have
entirely exhausted Otto's store both of energy and anger;
he would have begun to examine and condemn his conduct,
have remembered all that was true, forgotten all that was
unjust in Seraphina's onslaught; and by half an hour after,
would have fallen into that state of mind in which a Catholic
flees to the confessional and a sot takes refuge with the
bottle. Two matters of detail preserved his spirits. For,
first, he had still an infinity of business to transact; and to
transact business, for a man of Otto's neglectful and pro-
crastinating habits, is the best anodyne for conscience. All
afternoon he was hard at it with the Chancellor, reading,
dictating, signing, and despatching papers; and this kept
him in a glow of self-approval. But, secondly, his vanity
was still alarmed; he had failed to get the money; to-
morrow before noon he would have to disappoint old Killian;
and in the eyes of that family which counted him so little,
and to which he had sought to play the part of the heroic
comforter, he must sink lower than at first. To a man of
Otto's temper, this was death. He could not accept the
situation. And even as he worked, and worked wisely and
well, over the hated details of his principality, he was secretly maturing a plan by which to turn the situation. It
was a scheme as pleasing to the man as it was dishonourable
in the prince; in which his frivolous nature found and took
vengeance for the gravity and burthen of the afternoon. He chuckled as he thought of it: and Greisengesang
heard him with wonder, and attributed his lively spirits to
the skirmish of the morning.

337

PRINCE OTTO

Led by this idea, the antique courtier ventured to compliment his sovereign on his bearing. It reminded him, he said, of Otto's father.

"What?" asked the Prince, whose thoughts were miles away.

"Your Highness's authority at the board," explained the flatterer.

"O, that! O yes," returned Otto; but for all his carelessness, his vanity was delicately tickled, and his mind returned and dwelt approvingly over the details of his victory. "I quelled them all," he thought.

When the more pressing matters had been dismissed, it was already late, and Otto kept the Chancellor to dinner, and was entertained with a leash of ancient histories and modern compliments. The Chancellor's career had been based, from the first off-put, on entire subserviency; he had crawled into honours and employments; and his mind was prostitute. The instinct of the creature served him well with Otto. First, he let fall a sneering word or two upon the female intellect; thence he proceeded to a closer engagement; and before the third course he was artfully dissecting Seraphina's character to her approving husband. Of course no names were used; and of course the identity of that abstract or ideal man, with whom she was currently contrasted, remained an open secret. But this stiff old gentleman had a wonderful instinct for evil, thus to wind his way into man's citadel; thus to harp by the hour on the virtues of his hearer and not once alarm his self-respect. Otto was all roseate, in and out, with flattery and Tokay and an approving conscience. He saw himself in the most attractive colours. If even Greisengesang, he thought, could thus espy the loose stitches in Seraphina's character, and thus disloyally impart them to the opposite camp, he, the discarded husband—the dispossessed Prince—could scarce have erred on the side of severity.

In this excellent frame he bade adieu to the old gentleman, whose voice had proved so musical, and set forth for the drawing-room. Already on the stair, he was seized with some compunction; but when he entered the great gallery and beheld his wife, the Chancellor's abstract flatteries fell from him like rain, and he re-awoke to the poetic facts of life. She stood a good way off below a shining lustre, her back turned. The bend of her waist overcame him with a physical weakness. This was the girl-wife who had lain in his arms and whom he had sworn to cherish; there was she, who was better than success.

It was Seraphina who restored him from the blow. She swam forward and smiled upon her husband with a sweetness that was insultingly artificial. " Frédéric," she lisped, " you are late." It was a scene of high comedy, such as is proper to unhappy marriages; and her aplomb disgusted him.

There was no etiquette at these small drawing-rooms. People came and went at pleasure. The window embrasures became the roost of happy couples; at the great chimney, the talkers mostly congregated, each full-charged with scandal; and down at the farther end the gamblers gambled. It was towards this point that Otto moved, not ostentatiously, but with a gentle insistence, and scattering attentions as he went. Once abreast of the card-table, he placed himself opposite to Madame von Rosen, and, as soon as he caught her eye, withdrew to the embrasure of a window. There she had speedily joined him.

" You did well to call me," she said, a little wildly. " These cards will be my ruin."

" Leave them," said Otto.

" I! " she cried, and laughed; " they are my destiny. My only chance was to die of a consumption; now I must die in a garret."

" You are bitter to-night," said Otto.

" I have been losing," she replied. " You do not know what greed is."

" I have come, then, in an evil hour," said he.

" Ah, you wish a favour! " she cried, brightening beautifully.

" Madam," said he, " I am about to found my party, and I come to you for a recruit."

"Done," said the Countess. "I am a man again."

"I may be wrong," continued Otto, "but I believe upon my heart you wish me no ill."

"I wish you so well," she said, "that I dare not tell it you."

"Then if I ask my favour?" quoth the Prince.

"Ask it, *mon Prince*," she answered. "Whatever it is, it is granted."

"I wish you," he returned, "this very night to make the farmer our talk."

"Heaven knows your meaning!" she exclaimed. "I know not, neither care; there are no bounds to my desire to please you. Call him made."

"I will put it in another way," returned Otto. "Did you ever steal?"

"Often!" cried the Countess. "I have broken all the ten commandments; and if there were more to-morrow I should not sleep till I had broken these."

"This is a case of burglary: to say truth, I thought it would amuse you," said the Prince.

"I have no practical experience," she replied, "but O! the good-will! I have broken a work-box in my time, and several hearts, my own included. Never a house! But it cannot be difficult; sins are so unromantically easy! What are we to break?"

"Madam, we are to break the treasury," said Otto; and he sketched to her briefly, wittily, with here and there a touch of pathos, the story of his visit to the farm, of his promise to buy it, and of the refusal with which his demand for money had been met that morning at the council; concluding with a few practical words as to the treasury windows, and the helps and hindrances of the proposed exploit.

"They refused you the money," she said, when he had done. "And you accepted the refusal? Well!"

"They gave their reasons," replied Otto, colouring. "They were not such as I could combat; and I am driven to dilapidate the funds of my own country by a theft. It is not dignified; but it is fun."

" Fun," she said; " yes." And then she remained silently plunged in thought for an appreciable time. " How much do you require? " she asked at length.

" Three thousand crowns will do," he answered, " for I have still some money of my own."

" Excellent," she said, regaining her levity. " I am your true accomplice. And where are we to meet? "

" You know the Flying Mercury," he answered, " in the Park? Three pathways intersect; there they have made a seat and raised the statue. The spot is handy, and the deity congenial."

" Child," she said, and tapped him with her fan. " But do you know, my Prince, you are an egoist—your handy trysting-place is miles from me. You must give me ample time; I cannot, I think, possibly be there before two. But as the bell beats two, your helper shall arrive: welcome, I trust. Stay—do you bring any one? " she added. " O, it is not for a chaperone—I am not a prude! "

" I shall bring a groom of mine," said Otto. " I caught him stealing corn."

" His name? " she asked.

" I profess I know not. I am not yet intimate with my corn-stealer," returned the Prince. " It was in a professional capacity——"

" Like me! Flatterer! " she cried. " But oblige me in one thing. Let me find you waiting at the seat—yes, you shall await me; for on this expedition it shall be no longer Prince and Countess, it shall be the lady and the squire—and your friend the thief shall be no nearer than the fountain. Do you promise? "

" Madame, in everything you are to command; you shall be captain, I am but supercargo," answered Otto.

" Well, Heaven bring all safe to port! " she said. " It is not Friday! "

Something in her manner had puzzled Otto, had possibly touched him with suspicion.

" Is it not strange," he remarked, " that I should choose my accomplice from the other camp? "

"Fool!" she said. "But it is your only wisdom that you know your friends." And suddenly, in the vantage of the deep window, she caught up his hand and kissed it with a sort of passion. "Now, go," she added, "go at once."

He went, somewhat staggered, doubting in his heart that he was overbold. For in that moment she had flashed upon him like a jewel; and even through the strong panoply of a previous love he had been conscious of a shock. Next moment he had dismissed the fear.

Both Otto and the Countess retired early from the drawing-room; and the Prince, after an elaborate feint, dismissed his valet and went forth by the private passage and the back postern in quest of the groom.

Once more the stable was in darkness, once more Otto employed the talismanic knock, and once more the groom appeared and sickened with terror.

"Good evening, friend," said Otto, pleasantly. "I want you to bring a corn sack—empty this time—and to accompany me. We shall be gone all night."

"Your Highness," groaned the man, "I have the charge of the small stables. I am here alone."

"Come," said the Prince, "you are no such martinet in duty." And then seeing that the man was shaking from head to foot, Otto laid a hand upon his shoulder. "If I meant you harm," he said, "should I be here?"

The fellow became instantly reassured. He got the sack; and Otto led him round by several paths and avenues, conversing pleasantly by the way, and left him at last planted by a certain fountain where a goggle-eyed Triton spouted intermittently into a rippling laver. Thence he proceeded alone to where, in a round clearing, a copy of Gian Bologna's Mercury stood tiptoe in the twilight of the stars. The night was warm and windless. A shaving of new moon had lately arisen; but it was still too small and too low down in heaven to contend with the immense host of lesser luminaries; and the rough face of the earth was drenched with starlight. Down one of the alleys, which widened as it receded, he could see a part of the lamplit terrace where a sentry silently paced, and beyond that a corner of the town with interlacing street-lights. But all around him the young trees stood mystically blurred in the dim shine; and in the stock-still quietness the upleaping god appeared alive.

In this dimness and silence of the night, Otto's conscience became suddenly and staringly luminous like the dial of a city clock. He averted the eyes of his mind, but the finger, rapidly travelling, pointed to a series of misdeeds that took his breath away. What was he doing in that place? The money had been wrongly squandered, but that was largely by his own neglect. And he now proposed to embarrass the finances of this country which he had been too idle to govern. And he now proposed to squander the money once again, and this time for a private, if a generous end. And the man whom he had reproved for stealing corn, he was now to set stealing treasure. And then there was Madame von Rosen, upon whom he looked down with some of that ill-favoured contempt of the chaste male for the imperfect woman. Because he thought of her as one degraded below scruples, he had picked her out to be still more degraded, and to risk her whole irregular establishment in life by complicity in this dishonourable act. It was uglier than a seduction.

Otto had to walk very briskly and whistle very busily; and when at last he heard steps in the narrowest and darkest of the alleys, it was with a gush of relief that he sprang to meet the Countess. To wrestle alone with one's good angel is so hard! and so precious, at the proper time, is a companion certain to be less virtuous than oneself!

It was a young man who came towards him—a young man of small stature and a peculiar gait, wearing a wide flapping hat, and carrying, with great weariness, a heavy bag. Otto recoiled; but the young man held up his hand by way of signal, and coming up with a panting run, as if with the last of his endurance, laid the bag upon the ground, threw himself upon the bench, and disclosed the features of Madame von Rosen.

343

" You, Countess!" cried the Prince.

" No, no," she panted, " the Count von Rosen—my young brother. A capital fellow. Let him get his breath."

" Ah, madam . . ." said he.

" Call me Count," she returned, " respect my incognito."

" Count be it, then," he replied. " And let me implore that gallant gentleman to set forth at once on our enterprise."

" Sit down beside me here," she returned, patting the further corner of the bench. " I will follow you in a moment. O, I am so tired—feel how my heart leaps! Where is your thief?"

" At his post," replied Otto. " Shall I introduce him? He seems an excellent companion."

" No," she said, " do not hurry me yet. I must speak to you. Not but I adore your theif; I adore any one who has the spirit to do wrong. I never cared for virtue till I fell in love with my Prince." She laughed musically. " And even so, it is not for your virtues," she added.

Otto was embarrassed. " And now," he asked, " if you are anyway rested?"

" Presently, presently. Let me breathe," she said, panting a little harder than before.

" And what has so wearied you?" he asked. " This bag? And why, in the name of eccentricity, a bag? For an empty one, you might have relied on my own foresight; and this one is very far from being empty. My dear Count, with what trash have you come laden? But the shortest method is to see for myself." And he put down his hand.

She stopped him at once. " Otto," she said, " no—not that way. I will tell, I will make a clean breast. It is done already. I have robbed the treasury single-handed. There are three thousand two hundred crowns. O, I trust it is enough!"

Her embarrassment was so obvious that the Prince was struck into a muse, gazing in her face, with his hand still outstretched, and she still holding him by the wrist. " You!"

he said, at last. "How?" And then drawing himself up, "O madam," he cried, "I understand. You must indeed think meanly of the Prince."

"Well then, it was a lie!" she cried. "The money is mine, honestly my own—now yours. This was an unworthy act that you proposed. But I love your honour, and I swore to myself that I should save it in your teeth. I beg of you to let me save it"—with a sudden lovely change of tone. "Otto, I beseech you let me save it. Take this dross from your poor friend who loves you!"

"Madam, madam," babbled Otto, in the extreme of misery, "I cannot—I must go."

And he half rose; but she was on the ground before him in an instant, clasping his knees. "No," she gasped, "you shall not go. Do you despise me so entirely? It is dross; I hate it; I should squander it at play and be no richer; it is an investment; it is to save me from ruin. Otto," she cried, as he again feebly tried to put her from him, "if you leave me alone in this disgrace, I will die here!" He groaned aloud. "Oh," she said, "think what I suffer! If you suffer from a piece of delicacy, think what I suffer in my shame! To have my trash refused! You would rather steal, you think of me so basely! You would rather tread my heart in pieces! O, unkind! O my Prince! O Otto! O pity me!" She was still clasping him; then she found his hand and covered it with kisses, and at this his head began to turn. "O," she cried again, "I see it! O what a horror! It is because I am old, because I am no longer beautiful." And she burst into a storm of sobs.

This was the *coup de grâce*. Otto had now to comfort and compose her as he could, and before many words, the money was accepted. Between the woman and the weak man such was the inevitable end. Madame von Rosen instantly composed her sobs. She thanked him with a fluttering voice, and resumed her place upon the bench at the far end from Otto. "Now you see," she said, "why I bade you keep the thief at distance, and why I came alone. How I trembled for my treasure!"

" Madame," said Otto, with a tearful whimper in his voice,
" spare me! You are too good, too noble! "

" I wonder to hear you," she returned. " You have
avoided a great folly. You will be able to meet your good
old peasant. You have found an excellent investment for a
friend's money. You have preferred essential kindness to
an empty scruple; and now you are ashamed of it. You
have made your friend happy; and now you mourn as
the dove! Come, cheer up. I know it is depressing to have
done exactly right; but you need not make a practice of it.
Forgive yourself this virtue; come now, look me in the
face and smile! "

He did look at her. When a man has been embraced by
a woman, he sees her in a glamour; and at such a time, in
the baffling glimmer of the stars, she will look wildly well.
The hair is touched with light; the eyes are constellations;
the face sketched in shadows—a sketch, you might say, by
passion. Otto became consoled for his defeat; he began
to take an interest. " No," he said, " I am no ingrate."

" You promised me fun," she returned, with a laugh.
" I have given you as good. We have had a stormy *scena*."

He laughed in his turn, and the sound of the laughter,
in either case, was hardly reassuring.

" Come, what are you going to give me in exchange,"
she continued, " for my excellent declamation? "

" What you will," he said.

" Whatever I will? Upon your honour? Suppose I asked
the crown? " She was flashing upon him, beautiful in
triumph.

" Upon my honour," he replied.

" Shall I ask the crown? " she continued. " Nay; what
should I do with it? Grünewald is but a petty state; my
ambition swells above it. I shall ask—I find I want nothing," she concluded. " I will give you something instead.
I will give you leave to kiss me—once."

Otto drew near and she put up her face; they were both
smiling, both on the brink of laughter, all was so innocent
and playful; and the Prince, when their lips encountered,

346

was dumfounded by the sudden convulsion of his being. Both drew instantly apart, and for an appreciable time sat tongue-tied. Otto was indistinctly conscious of a peril in the silence, but could find no words to utter. Suddenly the Countess seemed to awake. "As for your wife——" she began in a clear and steady voice.

The word recalled Otto, with a shudder, from his trance. "I will hear nothing against my wife," he cried wildly; and then, recovering himself and in a kindlier tone, "I will tell you my one secret," he added. "I love my wife."

"You should have let me finish," she returned, smiling. "Do you suppose I did not mention her on purpose? You know you had lost your head. Well, so had I. Come now, do not be abashed by words," she added, somewhat sharply. "It is the one thing I despise. If you are not a fool, you will see that I am building fortresses about your virtue. And at any rate, I choose that you shall understand that I am not dying of love for you. It is a very smiling business; no tragedy for me! And now here is what I have to say about your wife: She is not and she never has been Gondremark's mistress. Be sure he would have boasted if she had. Good-night!"

And in a moment she was gone down the alley, and Otto was alone with the bag of money and the flying god.

CHAPTER X

THE Countess left poor Otto with a caress and buffet simultaneously administered. The welcome word about his wife and the virtuous ending of his interview should doubtless have delighted him. But for all that, as he shouldered the bag of money and set forward to rejoin his groom, he was conscious of many aching sensibilities. To have gone wrong and to have been set right, makes but a double trial for man's vanity. The discovery of his own weakness and possible unfaith had staggered him to the heart; and to hear, in the same hour, of his wife's fidelity from one who loved her not, increased the bitterness of the surprise.

He was about halfway between the fountain and the Flying Mercury before his thoughts began to be clear; and he was surprised to find them resentful. He paused in a kind of temper, and struck with his hand a little shrub. Thence there arose instantly a cloud of awakened sparrows, which as instantly dispersed and disappeared into the thicket. He looked at them stupidly, and when they were gone continued staring at the stars. " I am angry. By what right? By none! " he thought; but he was still angry. He cursed Madame von Rosen and instantly repented. Heavy was the money on his shoulders.

When he reached the fountain, he did, out of ill-humour and parade, an unpardonable act. He gave the money bodily to the dishonest groom. " Keep this for me," he said, " until I call for it to-morrow. It is a great sum, and by that you will judge that I have not condemned you." And he strode away ruffling, as if he had done something generous. It was a desperate stroke to re-enter at the

348

point of the bayonet into his self-esteem; and, like all such, it was fruitless in the end. He got to bed with the devil, it appeared: kicked and tumbled till the grey of the morning; and then fell inopportunely into a leaden slumber, and awoke to find it ten. To miss the appointment with old Killian after all, had been too tragic a miscarriage: and he hurried with all his might, found the groom (for a wonder) faithful to his trust, and arrived only a few minutes before noon in the guest-chamber of the Morning Star. Killian was there in his Sunday's best and looking very gaunt and rigid; a lawyer from Brandenau stool sentinel over his outspread papers; and the groom and the landlord of the inn were called to serve as witnesses. The obvious deference of that great man, the innkeeper, plainly affected the old farmer with surprise; but it was not until Otto had taken the pen and signed that the truth flashed upon him fully. Then, indeed, he was beside himself.

"His Highness!" he cried, "His Highness!" and repeated the exclamation till his mind had grappled fairly with the facts. Then he turned to the witnesses. "Gentlemen," he said, "you dwell in a country highly favoured by God; for of all generous gentlemen, I will say it on my conscience, this one is the king. I am an old man, and I have seen good and bad, and the year of the great famine; but a more excellent gentleman, no, never."

"We know that," cried the landlord, "we know that well in Grünewald. If we saw more of his Highness we should be the better pleased."

"It is the kindest Prince," began the groom, and suddently closed his mouth upon a sob, so that every one turned to gaze upon his emotion. Otto not last; Otto struck with remorse, to see the man so grateful.

Then it was the lawyer's turn to pay a compliment. "I do not know what Providence may hold in store," he said, "but this day should be a bright one in the annals of your reign. The shouts of armies could not be more eloquent that the emotion of these honest faces." And the Brandenau lawyer bowed, skipped, stepped back and took snuff, with the air of a man who has found and seized an opportunity.

" Well, young gentleman," said Killian, " if you will pardon me the plainness of calling you a gentleman, many a good day's work you have done, I doubt not, but never a better, or one that will be better blessed; and whatever, sir, may be your happiness and triumph in that high sphere to which you have been called, it will be none the worse, sir, for an old man's blessing! "

The scene had almost assumed the proportions of an ovation; and when the Prince escaped he had but one thought: to go wherever he was most sure of praise. His conduct at the board of council occurred to him as a fair chapter; and this evoked the memory of Gotthold. To Gotthold he would go.

Gotthold was in the library as usual, and laid down his pen, a little angrily, on Otto's entrance. " Well," he said, " here you are."

" Well," returned Otto, " we made a revolution, I believe."

" It is what I fear," returned the Doctor.

" How? " said Otto. " Fear? Fear is the burnt child. I have learned my strength and the weakness of the others; and I now mean to govern."

Gotthold said nothing, but he looked down and smoothed his chin.

" You disapprove? " cried Otto. " You are a weathercock."

" On the contrary," replied the Doctor. " My observation has confirmed my fears. It will not do, Otto, not do."

" What will not do? " demanded the Prince, with a sickening stab of pain.

" None of it," answered Gotthold. " You are unfitted for a life of action; you lack the stamina, the habit, the restraint, the patience. Your wife is greatly better, vastly better; and though she is in bad hands, displays a very different aptitude. She is a woman of affairs; you are—dear boy, you are yourself. I bid you back to your amusements; like a smiling dominie, I give you holidays for life. Yes," he continued, " there is a day appointed for all when they shall turn again upon their own philosophy. I had grown to disbelieve impartially in all; and if in the atlas of the sciences there were two charts I disbelieved in more than all the rest, they were politics and morals. I had a sneaking kindness for your vices; as they were negative, they flattered my philosophy, and I called them almost virtues. Well, Otto, I was wrong; I have forsworn my sceptical philosophy; and I perceive your faults to be unpardonable. You are unfit to be a Prince, unfit to be a husband. And I give you my word, I would rather see a man capably doing evil than blundering about good."

Otto was still silent, in extreme dudgeon.

Presently the Doctor resumed: " I will take the smaller matter first: your conduct to your wife. You went, I hear, and had an explanation. That may have been right or wrong; I know not; at least, you had stirred her temper. At the council she insults you; well, you insult her back—a man to a woman, a husband to his wife, in public! Next upon the back of this, you propose—the story runs like wildfire—to recall the power of signature. Can she ever forgive that? a woman—a young woman—ambitious, conscious of talents beyond yours? Never, Otto. And to sum all, at such a crisis in your married life, you get into a window corner with that ogling dame von Rosen. I do not dream that there was any harm; but I do say it was an idle disrespect to your wife. Why, man, the woman is not decent."

" Gotthold," said Otto, " I will hear no evil of the Countess.

" You will certainly hear no good of her," returned Gotthold; " and if you wish your wife to be the pink of nicety, you should clear your court of demi-reputations."

" The commonplace injustice of a by-word," Otto cried. " The partiality of sex. She is a demi-rep; what then is Gondremark? Were she a man——"

" It would be all one," retorted Gotthold, roughly. " When I see a man, come to years of wisdom, who speaks in double meanings and is the braggart of his vices, I spit on the other side. 'You, my friend,' say I, 'are not even a gentleman.' Well, she's not even a lady."

"She is the best friend I have, and I choose that she shall be respected," Otto said.

"If she is your friend, so much the worse," replied the Doctor. "It will not stop there."

"Ah!" cried Otto, "there is the charity of virtue! All evil in the spotted fruit. But I can tell you, sir, that you do Madame von Rosen prodigal injustice."

"You can tell me!" said the Doctor, shrewdly. "Have you tried? have you been riding the marches?"

The blood came into Otto's face.

"Ah!" cried Gotthold, "look at your wife and blush! There's a wife for a man to marry and then lose! She's a carnation, Otto. The soul is in her eyes."

"You have changed your note for Seraphina, I perceive," said Otto.

"Changed it!" cried the Doctor, with a flush. "Why, when was it different? But I own I admired her at the council. When she sat there silent, tapping with her foot, I admired her as I might a hurricane. Were I one of those who venture upon matrimony, there had been the prize to tempt me! She invites, as Mexico invited Cortez; the enterprise is hard, the natives are unfriendly—I believe them cruel too—but the metropolis is paved with gold and the breeze blows out of paradise. Yes, I could desire to be that conqueror. But to philander with von Rosen; never! Senses? I discard them; what are they?—pruritus! Curiosity? Reach me my Anatomy!"

"To whom do you address yourself?" cried Otto. "Surely, you, of all men, know that I love my wife!"

"O, love!" cried Gotthold; "love is a great word; it is in all the dictionaries. If you had loved, she would have paid you back. What does she ask? A little ardour!"

"It is hard to love for two," replied the Prince.

"Hard? Why, there's the touchstone! O, I know my poets!" cried the Doctor. "We are but dust and fire, too arid to endure life's scorching; and love, like the shadow of a great rock, should lend shelter and refreshment, not to the lover only, but to his mistress and to the children that reward them; and their very friends should seek repose in the fringes of that peace. Love is not love that cannot build a home. And you call it love to grudge and quarrel and pick faults? You call it love to thwart her to her face, and bandy insults? Love!"

"Gotthold, you are unjust. I was then fighting for my country," said the Prince.

"Ay, and there's the worst of all," returned the Doctor. "You could not even see that you were wrong; that being where they were, retreat was ruin."

"Why, you supported me!" cried Otto.

"I did. I was a fool like you," replied Gotthold. "But now my eyes are open. If you go on as you have started, disgrace this fellow Gondremark, and publish the scandal of your divided house, there will befall a most abominable thing in Grünewald. A revolution, friend—a revolution."

"You speak strangely for a red," said Otto.

"A red republican, but not a revolutionary," returned the Doctor. "An ugly thing is a Grünewalder drunk! One man alone can save the country from this pass, and that is the double-dealer Gondremark, with whom I conjure you to make peace. It will not be you; it never can be you:— you, who can do nothing, as your wife said, but trade upon your station—you, who spent the hours in begging money! And in God's name, what for? Why money? What mystery of idiocy was this?"

"It was to no ill end. It was to buy a farm," quoth Otto, sulkily.

"To buy a farm!" cried Gotthold. "Buy a farm!"

"Well, what then?" returned Otto. "I have bought it, if you come to that."

Gotthold fairly bounded on his seat. "And how that?" he cried.

"How?" repeated Otto, startled.

353

"Ay, verily, how!" returned the Doctor. "How came you by the money?"

The Prince's countenance darkened. "That is my affair," said he.

"You see you are ashamed," retorted Gotthold. "And so you bought a farm in the hour of your country's need—doubtless to be ready for the abdication; and I put it that you stole the funds. There are not three ways of getting money: there are but two: to earn and steal. And now, when you have combined Charles the Fifth and Long-fingered Tom, you come to me to fortify your vanity! But I will clear my mind upon this matter: until I know the right and wrong of the transaction, I put my hand behind my back. A man may be the pitifullest prince, he must be a spotless gentleman."

The Prince had gotten to his feet, as pale as paper. "Gotthold," he said, "you drive me beyond bounds. Beware, sir, beware!"

"Do you threaten me, friend Otto?" asked the Doctor, grimly. "That would be a strange conclusion."

"When have you ever known me use my power in any private animosity?" cried Otto. "To any private man, your words were an unpardonable insult, but at me you shoot in full security, and I must turn aside to compliment you on your plainness. I must do more than pardon, I must admire, because you have faced this—this formidable monarch, like a Nathan before David. You have uprooted an old kindness, sir, with an unsparing hand. You leave me very bare. My last bond is broken; and though I take Heaven to witness that I sought to do the right, I have this reward: to find myself alone. You say I am no gentleman; yet the sneers have been upon your side; and though I can very well perceive where you have lodged your sympathies, I will forbear the taunt."

"Otto, are you insane?" cried Gotthold, leaping up. "Because I ask you how you came by certain moneys, and because you refuse——"

"Herr von Hohenstockwitz, I have ceased to invite your

aid in my affairs," said Otto. " I have heard all that I desire, and you have sufficiently trampled on my vanity. It may be that I cannot govern, it may be that I cannot love—you tell me so with every mark of honesty; but God has granted me one virtue, and I can still forgive. I forgive you; even in this hour of passion, I can perceive my faults and your excuses; and if I desire that in future I may be spared your conversation, it is not, sir, from resentment—not resentment —but, by Heaven, because no man on earth could endure to be so rated. You have the satisfaction to see your sovereign weep; and that person whom you have so often taunted with his happiness reduced to the last pitch of solitude and misery. No,—I will hear nothing; I claim the last word, sir, as your Prince; and that last word shall be—forgiveness."

And with that Otto was gone from the apartment, and Doctor Gotthold was left alone with the most conflicting sentiments of sorrow, remorse, and merriment; walking to and fro before his table, and asking himself, with hands uplifted, which of the pair of them was most to blame for this unhappy rupture. Presently, he took from a cupboard a bottle of Rhine wine and a goblet of the deep Bohemian ruby. The first glass a little warmed and comforted his bosom; with the second he began to look down upon these troubles from a sunny mountain; yet a while, and filled with this false comfort and contemplating life throughout a golden medium, he owned to himself, with a flush, a smile, and a half-pleasurable sigh, that he had been somewhat over plain in dealing with his cousin. " He said the truth, too," added the penitent librarian, " for in my monkish fashion I adore the Princess." And then, with a still deepening flush and a certain stealth, although he sat all alone in that great gallery, he toasted Seraphina to the dregs.

CHAPTER XI

AT a sufficiently late hour, or to be more exact, at three in the afternoon, Madame von Rosen issued on the world. She swept downstairs and out across the garden, a black mantilla thrown over her head, and the long train of her black velvet dress ruthlessly sweeping in the dirt.

At the other end of that long garden, and back to back with the villa of the Countess, stood the large mansion where the Prime Minister transacted his affairs and pleasures. This distance, which was enough for decency by the easy canons of Mittwalden, the Countess swiftly traversed, opened a little door with a key, mounted a flight of stairs, and entered unceremoniously into Gondremark's study. It was a large and very high apartment; books all about the walls, papers on the table, papers on the floor; here and there a picture, somewhat scant of drapery; a great fire glowing and flaming in the blue tiled hearth; and the daylight streaming through a cupola above. In the midst of this sat the great Baron Gondremark in his shirt-sleeves, his business for that day fairly at an end, and the hour arrived for relaxation. His expression, his very nature, seemed to have undergone a fundamental change. Gondremark at home appeared the very antipode of Gondremark on duty. He had an air of massive jollity that well became him; grossness and geniality sat upon his features; and along with his manners, he had laid aside his sly and sinister expression. He lolled there, sunning his bulk before the fire, a noble animal.

" Hey! " he cried. " At last! "

The Countess stepped into the room in silence, threw herself on a chair, and crossed her legs. In her lace and velvet, with a good display of smooth black stocking and of snowy petticoat, and with the refined profile of her face and slender plumpness of her body, she showed in singular contrast to the big, black intellectual satyr by the fire.

" How often do you send for me? " she cried. " It is compromising."

Gondremark laughed. " Speaking of that," said he, " what in the devil's name were you about? You were not home till morning."

" I was giving alms," she said.

The Baron again laughed loud and long, for in his shirt-sleeves he was a very mirthful creature. " It is fortunate I am not jealous," he remarked. " But you know my way: pleasure and liberty go hand in hand. I believe what I believe; it is not much, but I believe it. But now, to business. Have you not read my letter? "

" No," she said, " my head ached."

" Ah well! then I have news indeed! " cried Gondremark. " I was mad to see you all last night and all this morning: for yesterday afternoon I brought my long business to a head; the ship has come home; one more dead lift, and I shall cease to fetch and carry for the Princess Ratafia. Yes, 'tis done. I have the order all in Ratafia's hand; I carry it on my heart. At the hour of twelve to-night, Prince Featherhead is to be taken in his bed and, like the bambino, whipped into a chariot; and by next morning he will command a most romantic prospect from the donjon of the Felsenburg. Farewell, Featherhead! The war goes on, the girl is in my hand; I have long been indispensable, but now I shall be sole. I have long," he added exultingly, " long carried this intrigue upon my shoulders, like Samson with the gates of Gaza; now I discharge that burthen."

She had sprung to her feet a little paler. " Is this true? " she cried.

" I tell you a fact," he asseverated. " The trick is played."

" I will never believe it," she said. " An order? In her own hand? I will never believe it, Heinrich."

"I swear to you," said he.

"O, what do you care for oaths—or I either? What would you swear by? Wine, women, and song? It is not binding," she said. She had come quite close up to him and laid her hand upon his arm. "As for the order—no, Heinrich, never. I will never believe it. I will die ere I believe it. You have some secret purpose—what, I cannot guess—but not one word of it is true."

"Shall I show it you?" he asked.

"You cannot," she answered. "There is no such thing."

"Incorrigible Sadducee!" he cried. "Well, I will convert you; you shall see the order." He moved to a chair where he had thrown his coat, and then drawing forth and holding out a paper, "Read," said he.

She took it greedily, and her eye flashed as she perused it.

"Hey!" cried the Baron, "there falls a dynasty, and it was I that felled it; and I and you inherit!" He seemed to swell in stature; and next moment, with a laugh, he put his hand forward. "Give me the dagger," said he.

But she whisked the paper suddenly behind her back and faced him, lowering. "No, no," she said. "You and I have first a point to settle. Do you suppose me blind? She could never have given that paper but to one man, and that man her lover. Here you stand—her lover, her accomplice, her master—O, I well believe it, for I know your power. But what am I?" she cried; "I, whom you deceive!"

"Jealousy!" cried Gondremark. "Anna, I would never have believed it! But I declare to you by all that's credible, that I am not her lover. I might be, I suppose; but I never yet durst risk the declaration. The chit is so unreal; a mincing doll; she will and she will not; there is no counting on her, by God! And hitherto I have had my own way without, and keep the lover in reserve. And I say, Anna," he added with severity, "you must break yourself of this new fit, my girl; there must be no combustion. I keep the creature under the belief that I adore her; and if she caught a breath of you and me, she is such a fool, prude, and dog in the manger, that she is capable of spoiling all."

" All very fine," returned the lady. " With whom do you pass your days? and which am I to believe, your words or your actions? "

" Anna, the devil take you, are you blind? " cried Gondremark. " You know me. Am I likely to care for such a *preciosa?* 'Tis hard that we should have been together for so long, and you should still take me for a troubadour. But if there is one thing that I despise and deprecate, it is all such figures in Berlin wool. Give me a human woman—like myself. You are my mate; you were made for me; you amuse me like the play. And what have I to gain that I should pretend to you? If I do not love you, what use are you to me? Why, none. It is as clear as noonday."

" Do you love me, Heinrich? " she asked, languishing. " Do you truly? "

" I tell you," he cried, " I love you next after myself. I should be all abroad if I had lost you."

" Well, then," said she, folding up the paper and putting it calmly in her pocket, " I will believe you, and I join the plot. Count upon me. At midnight, did you say? It is Gordon, I see, that you have charged with it. Excellent; he will stick at nothing."

Gondremark watched her suspiciously. " Why do you take the paper? " he demanded. " Give it here."

" No," she returned; " I mean to keep it. It is I who must prepare the stroke; you cannot manage it without me; and to do my best I must possess the paper. Where shall I find Gordon? In his rooms? " She spoke with a rather feverish self-possession.

" Anna," he said sternly, the black, bilious countenance of his palace rôle taking the place of the more open favour of his hours at home, " I ask you for that paper. Once, twice, and thrice."

" Heinrich," she returned, looking him in the face, " take care. I will put up with no dictation."

Both looked dangerous; and the silence lasted for a measurable interval of time. Then she made haste to have the first word; and with a laugh that rang clear and honest, " Do not

be a child," she said. " I wonder at you. If your assurances
are true, you can have no reason to mistrust me, nor I to play
you false. The difficulty is to get the Prince out of the
palace without scandal. His valets are devoted; his chamberlain a slave; and yet one cry might ruin all."

"They must be overpowered," he said, following her to
the new ground, " and disappear along with him."

"And your whole scheme along with them!" she cried.
" He does not take his servants when he goes a-hunting: a
child could read the truth. No, no; the plan is idiotic; it
must be Ratafia's. But hear me. You know the Prince wor-
ships me? "

"I know," he said. "Poor Featherhead, I cross his
destiny!"

"Well now," she continued, "what if I bring him alone
out of the palace, to some quiet corner of the Park—the Flying Mercury, for instance? Gordon can be posted in the
thicket; the carriage wait behind the temple; not a cry, not
a scuffle, not a footfall; simply, the Prince vanishes!—What
do you say? Am I an able ally? Are my *beaux yeux* of
service? Ah, Heinrich, do not lose your Anna!—she has
power!"

He struck with his open hand upon the chimney.
"Witch!" he said, "there is not your match for devilry in
Europe. Service! the thing runs on wheels."

"Kiss me, then, and let me go. I must not miss my
Featherhead," she said.

"Stay, stay," said the Baron; "not so fast. I wish, upon
my soul, that I could trust you; but you are, out and in, so
whimsical a devil that I dare not. Hang it, Anna, no; it's
not possible!"

"You doubt me, Heinrich?" she cried.

"Doubt is not the word," said he. "I know you. Once
you were clear of me with that paper in your pocket, who
knows what you would do with it?—not you, at least—nor I.
You see," he added, shaking his head paternally upon the
Countess, " you are as vicious as a monkey."

"I swear to you," she cried, "by my salvation . . ."

OF LOVE AND POLITICS

"I have no curiosity to hear you swearing," said the Baron.

"You think that I have no religion? You suppose me destitute of honour. Well," she said, "see here: I will not argue, but I tell you once for all: leave me this order, and the Prince shall be arrested—take it from me, and, as certain as I speak, I will upset the coach. Trust me, or fear me: take your choice." And she offered him the paper.

The Baron, in a great contention of mind, stood irresolute, weighing the two dangers. Once his hand advanced, then dropped. "Well," he said, "since trust is what you call it . . ."

"No more," she interrupted. "Do not spoil your attitude. And now since you have behaved like a good sort of fellow in the dark, I will condescend to tell you why. I go to the palace to arrange with Gordon; but how is Gordon to obey me? And how can I foresee the hours? It may be midnight; ay, and it may be nightfall; all's a chance; and to act, I must be free and hold the strings of the adventure. And now," she cried, "your Vivien goes. Dub me your knight!" And she held out her arms and smiled upon him radiant.

"Well," he said, when he had kissed her, "every man must have his folly; I thank God mine is no worse. Off with you! I have given a child a squib."

CHAPTER XII

IT was the first impulse of Madame von Rosen to return
to her own villa and revise her toilette. Whatever else
should come of this adventure, it was her firm design to pay
a visit to the Princess. And before that woman, so little be-
loved, the Countess would appear at no disadvantage. It
was the work of minutes. Von Rosen had the captain's eye
in matters of the toilette; she was none of those who hang
in Fabian helplessness among their finery and, after hours,
come forth upon the world as dowdies. A glance, a loosened
curl, a studied and admired disorder in the hair, a bit of lace,
a touch of colour, a yellow rose in the bosom; and the instant
picture was complete.

"That will do," she said. "Bid my carriage follow me
to the palace. In half an hour it should be there in waiting."

The night was beginning to fall and the shops to shine
with lamps along the tree-beshadowed thoroughfares of
Otto's capital, when the Countess started on her high emprise.
She was jocund at heart; pleasure and interest had winged
her beauty, and she knew it. She paused before the glowing
jeweller's; she remarked and praised a costume in the
milliner's window; and when she reached the lime-tree walk,
with its high, umbrageous arches and stir of passers-by in
the dim alleys, she took her place upon a bench and began to
dally with the pleasures of the hour. It was cold, but she did
not feel it, being warm within; her thoughts, in that dark
corner, shone like the gold and rubies at the jeweller's; her
ears, which heard the brushing of so many footfalls, trans-
posed it into music.

What was she to do? She held the paper by which all
depended. Otto and Gondremark and Ratafia, and the state

itself, hung light in her balances, as light as dust; her little finger laid in either scale would set all flying: and she hugged herself upon her huge preponderance, and then laughed aloud to think how giddily it might be used. The vertigo of omnipotence, the disease of Cæsars, shook her reason. " O the mad world!" she thought, and laughed aloud in exultation.

A child, finger in mouth, had paused a little way from where she sat, and stared with cloudy interest upon this laughing lady. She called it nearer; but the child hung back. Instantly, with that curious passion which you may see any woman in the world display, on the most odd occasions, for a similar end, the Countess bent herself with singleness of mind to overcome this diffidence; and presently, sure enough, the child was seated on her knee, thumbing and glowering at her watch.

" If you had a clay bear and a china monkey," asked von Rosen, " which would you prefer to break? "

" But I have neither," said the child.

" Well," she said, " here is a bright florin, with which you may purchase both the one and the other; and I shall give it you at once, if you will answer my question. The clay bear or the china monkey—come? "

But the unbreeched soothsayer only stared upon the florin with big eyes; the oracle could not be persuaded to reply; and the Countess kissed him lightly, gave him the florin, set him down upon the path, and resumed her way with swinging and elastic gait.

" Which shall I break? " she wondered; and she passed her hand with delight among the careful disarrangement of her locks. " Which? " and she consulted heaven with her bright eyes. " Do I love both or neither? A little—passionately—not at all? Both or neither—both, I believe; but at least I will make hay of Ratafia."

By the time she had passed the iron gates, mounted the drive, and set her foot upon the broad flagged terrace, the night had come completely; the palace front was thick with lighted windows; and along the balustrade, the lamp on every twentieth baluster shone clear. A few withered tracks of sunset, amber and glow-worm green, still lingered in the western sky; and she paused once again to watch them fading.

"And to think," she said, "that here am I—destiny embodied, a norn, a fate, a providence—and have no guess upon which side I shall declare myself! What other woman in my place would not be prejudiced, and think herself committed? But, thank Heaven! I was born just!" Otto's windows were bright among the rest, and she looked on them with rising tenderness. "How does it feel to be deserted?" she thought. "Poor dear fool! The girl deserves that he should see this order."

Without more delay, she passed into the palace and asked for an audience of Prince Otto. The Prince, she was told, was in his own apartment, and desired to be private. She sent her name. A man presently returned with word that the Prince tendered his apologies, but could see no one. "Then I will write," she said, and scribbled a few lines alleging urgency of life and death. "Help me, my Prince," she added; "none but you can help me." This time the messenger returned more speedily and begged the Countess to follow him: the Prince was graciously pleased to receive the Frau Gräfin von Rosen.

Otto sat by the fire in his large armoury, weapons faintly glittering all about him in the changeful light. His face was disfigured by the marks of weeping; he looked sour and sad; nor did he rise to greet his visitor, but bowed, and bade the man begone. That kind of general tenderness which served the Countess for both heart and conscience, sharply smote her at this spectacle of grief and weakness; she began immediately to enter into the spirit of her part; and as soon as they were alone, taking one step forward and with a magnificent gesture—"Up!" she cried.

"Madame von Rosen," replied Otto, dully, "you have used strong words. You speak of life and death. Pray, madam, who is threatened? Who is there," he added bitterly, "so destitute that even Otto of Grünewald can assist him?"

"First learn," said she, "the names of the conspirators: the Princess and the Baron Gondremark. Can you not guess the rest?" And then as he maintained his silence—"You!" she cried, pointing at him with her finger. "'Tis you they threaten! Your rascal and mine have laid their heads together and condemned you. But they reckoned without you and me. We make a *partie carré*, Prince, in love and politics. They lead an ace, but we shall trump it. Come, partner, shall I draw my card?"

"Madam," he said, "explain yourself. Indeed I fail to comprehend."

"See, then," said she; and handed him the order.

He took it, looked upon it with a start; and then, still without speech, he put his hand before his face. She waited for a word in vain.

"What!" she cried, "do you take the thing downheartedly? As well seek wine in a milk-pail as love in that girl's heart! Be done with this, and be a man. After the league of the lions, let us have a conspiracy of mice, and pull this piece of machinery to ground. You were brisk enough last night when nothing was at stake and all was frolic. Well, here is better sport; here is life indeed."

He got to his feet with some alacrity, and his face, which was a little flushed, bore the marks of resolution.

"Madame von Rosen," said he, "I am neither unconscious nor ungrateful; this is the true continuation of your friendship; but I see that I must disappoint your expectations. You seem to expect from me some effort of resistance; but why should I resist? I have not much to gain; and now that I have read this paper, and the last of a fool's paradise is shattered, it would be hyperbolical to speak of loss in the same breath with Otto of Grünewald. I have no party; no policy; no pride, nor anything to be proud of. For what benefit or principle under Heaven do you expect me to contend? Or would you have me bite and scratch like a trapped weasel? No, madam; signify to those who sent you my readiness to go. I would at least avoid a scandal."

"You go?—of your own will, you go?" she cried.

"I cannot say so much, perhaps," he answered; "but I go with good alacrity. I have desired a change some time;

365

behold one offered me! Shall I refuse? Thank God, I am not so destitute of humour as to make a tragedy of such a farce." He flicked the order on the table. "You may signify my readiness," he added, grandly.

"Ah," she said, "you are more angry than you own."

"I, madam? angry?" he cried. "You rave. I have no cause for anger. In every way I have been taught my weakness, my instability, and my unfitness for the world. I am a plexus of weaknesses, an impotent Prince, a doubtful gentleman; and you yourself, indulgent as you are, have twice reproved my levity. And shall I be angry? I may feel the unkindness, but I have sufficient honesty of mind to see the reasons of this *coup d'état.*"

"From whom have you got this?" she cried in wonder. "You think you have not behaved well? My Prince, were you not young and handsome, I should detest you for your virtues. You push them to the verge of commonplace. And this ingratitude——"

"Understand me, Madame von Rosen," returned the Prince, flushing a little darker, "there can be here no talk of gratitude, none of pride. You are here, by what circumstance I know not, but doubtless led by your kindness, mixed up in what regards my family alone. You have no knowledge what my wife, your sovereign, may have suffered; it is not for you—no, nor for me—to judge. I own myself in fault; and were it otherwise, a man were a very empty boaster who should talk of love and start before a small humiliation. It is in all the copybooks that one should die to please his ladylove; and shall a man not go to prison?"

"Love? And what has love to do with being sent to gaol?" exclaimed the Countess, appealing to the walls and roof. "Heaven knows I think as much of love as any one; my life would prove it; but I admit no love, at least for a man, that is not equally returned. The rest is moonshine."

"I think of love more absolutely, madam, though I am certain no more tenderly, than a lady to whom I am indebted for such kindnesses," returned the Prince. "But this is unavailing. We are not here to hold a court of troubadours."

" Still," she replied, " there is one thing you forget. If
she conspires with Gondremark against your liberty, she may
conspire with him against your honour also."

" My honour? " he repeated. " For a woman, you surprise
me. If I have failed to gain her love or play my part of
husband, what right is left me? or what honour can remain
in such a scene of defeat? No honour that I recognise. I
am become a stranger. If my wife no longer loves me, I will
go to prison, since she wills it; if she love another, where
should I be more in place? or whose fault is it but mine? You
speak, Madame von Rosen, like too many women, with a man's
tongue. Had I myself fallen into temptation (as, Heaven
knows, I might) I should have trembled, but still hoped and
asked for her forgiveness; and yet mine had been a treason
in the teeth of love. But let me tell you, madam," he pursued,
with rising irritation, " where a husband by futility, facility,
and ill-timed humours has outwearied his wife's patience, I
will suffer neither man nor woman to misjudge her. She is
free; the man has been found wanting."

" Because she loves you not? " the Countess cried. " You
know she is incapable of such a feeling."

" Rather, it was I who was born incapable of inspiring it,"
said Otto.

Madame von Rosen broke into sudden laughter. " Fool,"
she cried, " I am in love with you myself."

" Ah, madam, you are most compassionate," the Prince
retorted, smiling. " But this is waste debate. I know my
purpose. Perhaps, to equal you in frankness, I know and
embrace my advantage. I am not without the spirit of adventure. I am in a false position—so recognised by public
acclamation: do you grudge me, then, my issue? "

" If your mind is made up, why should I dissuade you? "
said the Countess. " I own, with a bare face, I am the
gainer. Go, you take my heart with you, or more of it than
I desire; I shall not sleep at night for thinking of your
misery. But do not be afraid; I would not spoil you, you are
such a fool and hero."

" Alas! madam," cried the Prince, " and your unlucky

money! I did amiss to take it, but you are a wonderful persuader. And I thank God, I can still offer you the fair equivalent." He took some papers from the chimney. "Here, madam, are the title-deeds," he said; "where I am going, they can certainly be of no use to me, and I have now no other hope of making up to you your kindness. You made the loan without formality, obeying your kind heart. The parts are somewhat changed; the sun of this Prince of Grünewald is upon the point of setting; and I know you better than to doubt you will once more waive ceremony, and accept the best that he can give you. If I may look for any pleasure in the coming time, it will be to remember that the peasant is secure, and my most generous friend no loser."

"Do you not understand my odious position?" cried the Countess. "Dear Prince, it is upon your fall that I begin my fortune."

"It was the more like you to tempt me to resistance," returned Otto. "But this cannot alter our relations; and I must, for the last time, lay my commands upon you in the character of Prince." And with his loftiest dignity, he forced the deeds on her acceptance.

"I hate the very touch of them," she cried.

There followed upon this a little silence. "At what time," resumed Otto, "(if indeed you know) am I to be arrested?"

"Your Highness, when you please!" exclaimed the Countess. "Or if you choose to tear that paper, never!"

"I would rather it were done quickly," said the Prince. "I shall take but time to leave a letter for the Princess."

"Well," said the Countess, "I have advised you to resist; at the same time, if you intend to be dumb before your shearers, I must say that I ought to set about arranging your arrest. I offered"—she hesitated—"I offered to manage it, intending, my dear friend—intending, upon my soul, to be of use to you. Well, if you will not profit by my good will, then be of use to me; and as soon as ever you feel ready, go to the Flying Mercury where we met last night. It will be none the worse for you; and to make it quite plain, it will be better for the rest of us."

OF LOVE AND POLITICS

"Dear madam, certainly," said Otto. "If I am prepared for the chief evil, I shall not quarrel with details. Go, then, with my best gratitude; and when I have written a few lines of leave-taking, I shall immediately hasten to keep tryst. To-night, I shall not meet so dangerous a cavalier," he added, with a smiling gallantry.

As soon as Madame von Rosen was gone, he made a great call upon his self-command. He was face to face with a miserable passage where, if it were possible, he desired to carry himself with dignity. As to the main fact, he never swerved or faltered; he had come so heart-sick and so cruelly humiliated from his talk with Gotthold, that he embraced the notion of imprisonment with something bordering on relief. Here was, at least, a step which he thought blameless; here was a way out of his troubles. He sat down to write to Seraphina; and his anger blazed. The tale of his forbearances mounted, in his eyes, to something monstrous; still more monstrous, the coldness, egoism, and cruelty that had required and thus requited them. The pen which he had taken shook in his hand. He was amazed to find his resignation fled, but it was gone beyond his recall. In a few white-hot words, he bade adieu, dubbing desperation by the name of love, and calling his wrath forgiveness; then he cast but one look of leave-taking on the place that had been his for so long and was now to be his no longer; and hurried forth—love's prisoner—or pride's.

He took that private passage which he had trodden so often in less momentous hours. The porter let him out; and the bountiful, cold air of the night and the pure glory of the stars received him on the threshold. He looked round him, breathing deep of earth's plain fragrance; he looked up into the great array of heaven, and was quieted. His little turgid life dwindled to its true proportions; and he saw himself (that great flame-hearted martyr!) stand like a speck under the cool cupola of the night. Thus he felt his careless injuries already soothed; the live air of out-of-doors, the quiet of the world, as if by their silent music, sobering and dwarfing his emotions.

"Well, I forgive her," he said. "If it be of any use to her, I forgive."

And with brisk steps, he crossed the garden, issued upon the Park and came to the Flying Mercury. A dark figure moved forward from the shadow of the pedestal.

"I have to ask your pardon, sir," a voice observed, "but if I am right in taking you for the Prince, I was given to understand that you would be prepared to meet me."

"Herr Gordon, I believe?" said Otto.

"Herr Oberst Gordon," replied that officer. "This is rather a ticklish business for a man to be embarked in; and to find that all is to go pleasantly, is a great relief to me. The carriage is at hand; shall I have the honour of following your Highness?"

"Colonel," said the Prince, "I have now come to that happy moment of my life, when I have orders to receive but none to give."

"A most philosophical remark!" returned the Colonel. "Begad, a very pertinent remark! it might be Plutarch. I am not a drop's blood to your Highness, or indeed to any one in this principality; or else I should dislike my orders. But as it is, and since there is nothing unnatural or unbecoming on my side, and your Highness takes it in good part, I begin to believe we may have a capital time together, sir—a capital time. For a gaoler is only a fellow captive."

"May I inquire, Herr Gordon," asked Otto, "what led you to accept this dangerous and I would fain hope thankless office?"

"Very natural, I am sure," replied the officer of fortune. "My pay is, in the meanwhile, doubled."

"Well, sir, I will not presume to criticise," returned the Prince. "And I perceive the carriage."

Sure enough, at the intersection of two alleys of the Park, a coach and four, conspicuous by its lanterns, stood in waiting. And a little way off about a score of lancers were drawn up under the shadow of the trees.

CHAPTER XIII

WHEN Madame von Rosen left the Prince, she hurried
straight to Colonel Gordon; and not content with
directing the arrangements, she had herself accompanied the
soldier of fortune to the Flying Mercury. The Colonel gave
her his arm, and the talk between this pair of conspirators
ran high and lively. The Countess, indeed, was in a whirl of
pleasure and excitement; her tongue stumbled upon laughter,
her eyes shone, the colour that was usually wanting now per-
fected her face. It would have taken little more to bring
Gordon to her feet—or so, at least, she believed, disdaining
the idea.

Hidden among some lilac bushes, she enjoyed the great
decorum of the arrest, and heard the dialogue of the two men
die away along the path. Soon after, the rolling of a carriage and the beat of hoofs arose in the still air of the night,
and passed speedily farther and fainter into silence. The
Prince was gone.

Madame von Rosen consulted her watch. She had still,
she thought, time enough for the titbit of her evening; and
hurrying to the palace, winged by the fear of Gondremark's
arrival, she sent her name and a pressing request for a recep-
tion to the Princess Seraphina. As the Countess von Rosen
unqualified, she was sure to be refused; but as an emissary
of the Baron's, for so she chose to style herself, she gained
immediate entry.

The Princess sat alone at table, making a feint of dining.
Her cheeks were mottled, her eyes heavy; she had neither slept
nor eaten; even her dress had been neglected. In short, she
was out of health, out of looks, out of heart, and hag-ridden

371

by her conscience. The Countess drew a swift comparison, and shone brighter in beauty.

"You come, madam, *de la part de Monsieur le Baron*," drawled the Princess. "Be seated! What have you to say?"

"To say?" repeated Madame von Rosen. "O, much to say! Much to say, that I would rather not, and much to leave unsaid that I would rather say. For I am like St. Paul, your Highness, and always wish to do the things I should not. Well! to be categorical—that is the word?—I took the Prince your order. He could not credit his senses. 'Ah,' he cried, 'dear Madame von Rosen, it is not possible—it cannot be—I must hear it from your lips. My wife is a poor girl misled, she is only silly, she is not cruel.' '*Mon Prince*,' said I, 'a girl—and therefore cruel; youth kills flies.'—He had such pain to understand it!"

"Madame von Rosen," said the Princess, in most steadfast tones, but with a rose of anger in her face, "who sent you here, and for what purpose? Tell your errand."

"O, madam, I believe you understand me very well," returned von Rosen. "I have not your philosophy. I wear my heart upon my sleeve, excuse the indecency! It is a very little one," she laughed, "and I so often change the sleeve!"

"Am I to understand the Prince has been arrested?" asked the Princess, rising.

"While you sat there dining!" cried the Countess, still nonchalantly seated.

"You have discharged your errand," was the reply; "I will not detain you."

"O no, madam," said the Countess, "with your permission, I have not yet done. I have borne much this evening in your service. I have suffered. I was made to suffer in your service." She unfolded her fan as she spoke. Quick as her pulses beat, the fan waved languidly. She betrayed her emotion only by the brightness of her eyes and face, and by the almost insolent triumph with which she looked down upon the Princess. There were old scores of rivalry between them in more than one field; so at least von Rosen felt; and now she was to have her hour of victory in them all.

" You are no servant, Madame von Rosen, of mine," said Seraphina.

" No, madam, indeed," returned the Countess; " but we both serve the same person, as you know—or if you do not, then I have the pleasure of informing you. Your conduct is so light—so light," she repeated, the fan wavering higher like a butterfly, " that perhaps you do not truly understand." The Countess rolled her fan together, laid it in her lap, and rose to a less languorous position. " Indeed," she continued, " I should be sorry to see any young woman in your situation. You began with every advantage—birth, a suitable marriage —quite pretty too—and see what you have come to! My poor girl, to think of it! But there is nothing that does so much harm," observed the Countess finely, " as giddiness of mind." And she once more unfurled the fan, and approvingly fanned herself.

"I will no longer permit you to forget yourself," cried Seraphina. " I think you are mad."

" Not mad," returned von Rosen. " Sane enough to know you dare not break with me to-night, and to profit by the knowledge. I left my poor, pretty Prince Charming crying his eyes out for a wooden doll. My heart is soft; I love my pretty Prince; you will never understand it, but I long to give my Prince his doll, dry his poor eyes, and send him off happy. O, you immature fool! " the Countess cried, rising to her feet, and pointing at the Princess the closed fan that now began to tremble in her hand. " O wooden doll! " she cried, " have you a heart, or blood, or any nature? This is a man, child—a man who loves you. O, it will not happen twice! it is not common; beautiful and clever women look in vain for it. And you, you pitiful schoolgirl, tread this jewel under foot! you, stupid with your vanity! Before you try to govern kingdoms, you should first be able to behave yourself at home; home is the woman's kingdom." She paused and laughed a little, strangely to hear and look upon. " I will tell you one of the things," she said, " that were to stay unspoken. Von Rosen is a better woman than you, my Princess, though you will never have the pain of understanding it; and when I took the Prince your order, and looked upon his face, my soul was melted—O, I am frank—here, within my arms, I offered him repose!" She advanced a step superbly as she spoke, with outstretched arms; and Seraphina shrank. "Do not be alarmed!" the Countess cried; "I am not offering that hermitage to you; in all the world there is but one who wants to, and him you have dismissed! 'If it will give her pleasure I should wear the martyr's crown,' he cried, 'I will embrace the thorns.' I tell you—I am quite frank—I put the order in his power and begged him to resist. You, who have betrayed your husband, may betray me to Gondremark; my Prince would betray no one. Understand it plainly," she cried, " 'tis of his pure forbearance you sit there; he had the power—I gave it him—to change the parts; and he refused and went to prison in your place."

The Princess spoke with some distress. "Your violence shocks me and pains me," she began, "but I cannot be angry with what at least does honour to the mistaken kindness of your heart: it was right for me to know this. I will condescend to tell you. It was with deep regret that I was driven to this step. I admit in many ways the Prince—I admit his amiability. It was our great misfortune, it was perhaps somewhat of my fault, that we were so unsuited to each other; but I have a regard, a sincere regard, for all his qualities. As a private person I should think as you do. It is difficult, I know, to make allowances for state considerations. I have only with deep reluctance obeyed the call of a superior duty; and so soon as I dare do it for the safety of the state, I promise you the Prince shall be released. Many in my situation would have resented your freedoms. I am not—" and she looked for a moment rather piteously upon the Countess —"I am not altogether so inhuman as you think."

"And you can put these troubles of the state," the Countess cried, "to weigh with a man's love?"

"Madame von Rosen, these troubles are affairs of life and

death to many; to the Prince, and perhaps even to yourself, among the number," replied the Princess, with dignity. "I have learned, madam, although still so young, in a hard school, that my own feelings must everywhere come last."

"O callow innocence!" exclaimed the other. "Is it possible you do not know, or do not suspect, the intrigue in which you move? I find it in my heart to pity you! We are both women after all—poor girl, poor girl!—and who is born a woman is born a fool. And though I hate all women—come, for the common folly, I forgive you. Your Highness"—she dropped a deep stage courtesy and resumed her fan—"I am going to insult you, to betray one who is called my lover, and if it pleases you to use the power I now put unreservedly into your hands, to ruin my dear self. O, what a French comedy! You betray, I betray, they betray. It is now my cue. The letter, yes. Behold the letter, madam, its seal unbroken as I found it by my bed this morning; for I was out of humour, and I get many, too many, of these favours. For your own sake, for the sake of my Prince Charming, for the sake of this great principality that sits so heavy on your conscience, open it and read!"

"Am I to understand," inquired the Princess, "that this letter in any way regards me?"

"You see I have not opened it," replied von Rosen; "but 'tis mine, and I beg you to experiment."

"I cannot look at it till you have," returned Seraphina, very seriously. "There may be matter there not meant for me to see; it is a private letter."

The Countess tore it open, glanced it through, and tossed it back; and the Princess, taking up the sheet, recognised the hand of Gondremark, and read with a sickening shock the following lines:—

"Dearest Anna, come at once. Ratafia has done the deed, her husband to be packed to prison. This puts the minx entirely in my power; *le tour est joué;* she will now go steady in harness, or I will know the reason why. Come.

"HEINRICH."

"Command yourself, madam," said the Countess, watching with some alarm the white face of Seraphina. "It is in vain for you to fight with Gondremark: he has more strings than mere court favour, and could bring you down to-morrow with a word. I would not have betrayed him otherwise; but Heinrich is a man, and plays with all of you like marionettes. And now at least you see for what you sacrified my Prince. Madam, will you take some wine? I have been cruel."

"Not cruel, madam—salutary," said Seraphina, with a phantom smile. "No, I thank you, I require no attentions. The first surprise affected me: will you give me time a little? I must think."

She took her head between her hands, and contemplated for a while the hurricane confusion of her thoughts.

"This information reaches me," she said, "when I have need of it. I would not do as you have done, but yet I thank you. I have been much deceived in Baron Gondremark."

"O, madam, leave Gondremark, and think upon the Prince!" cried von Rosen.

"You speak once more as a private person," said the Princess; "nor do I blame you. But my own thoughts are more distracted. However, as I believe you are truly a friend to my—to the—as I believe," she said, "you are a friend to Otto, I shall put the order for his release into your hands this moment. Give me the inkdish. There!" And she wrote hastily, steadying her arm upon the table, for she trembled like a reed. "Remember, madam," she resumed, handing her the order, "this must not be used nor spoken of at present; till I have seen the Baron, any hurried step— I lose myself in thinking. The suddenness has shaken me."

"I promise you I will not use it," said the Countess, "till you give me leave, although I wish the Prince could be informed of it, to comfort his poor heart. And oh, I had forgotten, he has left a letter. Suffer me, madam; I will bring it you. This is the door, I think?" And she sought to open it.

"The bolt is pushed," said Seraphina, flushing.

"O! O!" cried the Countess.

A silence fell between them.

"I will get it for myself," said Seraphina; "and in the meanwhile I beg you to leave me. I thank you, I am sure, but I shall be obliged if you will leave me."

The Countess deeply courtesied, and withdrew.

CHAPTER XIV

BRAVE as she was, and brave by intellect, the Princess, when first she was alone, clung to the table for support. The four corners of her universe had fallen. She had never liked nor trusted Gondremark completely; she had still held it possible to find him false to friendship; but from that to finding him devoid of all those public virtues for which she had honoured him, a mere commonplace intriguer, using her for his own ends, the step was wide and the descent giddy. Light and darkness succeeded each other in her brain; now she believed, and now she could not. She turned, blindly groping for the note. But von Rosen, who had not forgotten to take the warrant from the Prince, had remembered to recover her note from the Princess: von Rosen was an old campaigner, whose most violent emotion aroused rather than clouded the vigour of her reason.

The thought recalled to Seraphina the remembrance of the other letter—Otto's. She rose and went speedily, her brain still wheeling, and burst into the Prince's armoury. The old chamberlain was there in waiting; and the sight of another face, prying (or so she felt) on her distress, struck Seraphina into childish anger.

" Go! " she cried; and then, when the old man was already half way to the door, " Stay! " she added. " As soon as Baron Gondremark arrives, let him attend me here."

" It shall be so directed," said the chamberlain.

" There was a letter . . . " she began, and paused.

" Her Highness," said the chamberlain, " will find a letter on the table. I had received no orders, or her Highness had been spared this trouble."

" No, no, no," she cried. " I thank you. I desire to be alone."

OF LOVE AND POLITICS

And then, when he was gone, she leaped upon the letter. Her mind was still obscured; like the moon upon a night of clouds and wind, her reason shone and was darkened; and she read the words by flashes.

"Seraphina," the Prince wrote, "I will write no syllable of reproach. I have seen your order, and I go. What else is left me? I have wasted my love, and have no more. To say that I forgive you is not needful; at least, we are now separate for ever; by your own act, you free me from my willing bondage; I go free to prison. This is the last that you will hear of me in love or anger. I have gone out of your life; you may breathe easy; you have now rid yourself of the husband who allowed you to desert him, of the Prince who gave you his rights, and of the married lover who made it his pride to defend you in your absence. How you have requited him, your own heart more loudly tells you than my words. There is a day coming when your vain dreams will roll away like clouds, and you will find yourself alone. Then you will remember

"OTTO."

She read with a great horror on her mind; that day, of which he wrote, was come. She was alone; she had been false, she had been cruel; remorse rolled in upon her; and then with a more piercing note, vanity bounded on the stage of consciousness. She a dupe! she helpless! she to have betrayed herself in seeking to betray her husband! she to have lived these years upon flattery, grossly swallowing the bolus, like a clown with sharpers! she—Seraphina! Her swift mind drank the consequences; she foresaw the coming fall, her public shame; she saw the odium, disgrace, and folly of her story flaunt through Europe. She recalled the scandal she had so royally braved; and alas! she had now no courage to confront it with. To be thought the mistress of that man: perhaps for that . . . She closed her eyes on agonising vistas. Swift as thought she had snatched a bright dagger from the weapons that shone along the wall. Ay, she would escape. From that world-wide theatre of nodding heads and buzzing whisperers, in which she now beheld herself unpitiably martyred, one door stood open. At any cost, through any stress of suffering, that greasy laughter should be stifled. She closed her eyes, breathed a wordless prayer, and pressed the weapon to her bosom.

379

PRINCE OTTO

At the astonishing sharpness of the prick, she gave a cry and awoke to a sense of undeserved escape. A little ruby spot of blood was the reward of that great act of desperation; but the pain had braced her like a tonic, and her whole design of suicide had passed away.

At the same instant regular feet drew near along the gallery, and she knew the tread of the big Baron, so often gladly welcome, and even now rallying her spirits like a call to battle. She concealed the dagger in the folds of her skirt; and drawing her stature up, she stood firm-footed, radiant with anger, waiting for the foe.

The Baron was announced, and entered. To him, Seraphina was a hated task: like a schoolboy with his Virgil, he had neither will nor leisure to remark her beauties; but when he now beheld her standing illuminated by her passion, new feelings flashed upon him, a frank admiration, a brief sparkle of desire. He noted both with joy; they were means. " If I have to play the lover," thought he, for that was his constant preoccupation, " I believe I can put soul into it." Meanwhile, with his usual ponderous grace, he bent before the lady.

" I propose," she said in a strange voice, not known to her till then, " that we release the Prince and do not prosecute the war."

" Ah, madam," he replied, " 'tis as I knew it would be! Your heart, I knew, would wound you when we came to this distasteful but most necessary step. Ah, madam, believe me, I am not unworthy to be your ally; I know you have qualities to which I am a stranger, and count them the best weapons in the armoury of our alliance:—the girl in the queen—pity, love, tenderness, laughter; the smile that can reward. I can only command; I am the frowner. But you! And you have the fortitude to command these comely weaknesses, to tread them down at the call of reason. How often have I not admired it even to yourself! Ay, even to yourself," he added tenderly, dwelling, it seemed, in memory on hours of more private admiration. " But now, madam——"

" But now, Herr von Gondremark, the time for these declarations has gone by," she cried. " Are you true to me? are

you false? Look in your heart and answer: it is your heart
I want to know."

"It has come," thought Gondremark. "You, madam!"
he cried, starting back—with fear, you would have said, and
yet a timid joy. "You! yourself, you bid me look into my
heart?"

"Do you suppose I fear?" she cried, and looked at him
with such a heightened colour, such bright eyes, and a smile
of so abstruse a meaning, that the Baron discarded his last
doubt.

"Ah, madam!" he cried, plumping on his knees. "Seraphina! Do you permit me? have you divined my secret? It
is true, I put my life with joy into your power—I love you,
love with ardour, as an equal, as a mistress, as a brother-in-
arms, as an adored, desired, sweet-hearted woman. O bride!"
he cried, waxing dithyrambic, "bride of my reason and my
senses, have pity, have pity on my love!"

She heard him with wonder, rage, and then contempt. His
words offended her to sickness; his appearance, as he grovelled
bulkily upon the floor, moved her to such laughter as we
laugh in nightmares.

"O shame!" she cried. "Absurd and odious! What
would the Countess say?"

That great Baron Gondremark, the excellent politician,
remained for some little time upon his knees in a frame of
mind which perhaps we are allowed to pity. His vanity,
within his iron bosom, bled and raved. If he could have
blotted all, if he could have withdrawn part, if he had not
called her bride—with a roaring in his ears, he thus regret-
fully reviewed his declaration. He got to his feet tottering;
and then, in that first moment when a dumb agony finds a
vent in words, and the tongue betrays the inmost and worst
of a man, he permitted himself a retort which, for six weeks
to follow, he was to repent at leisure.

"Ah," said he, "the Countess? Now I perceive the reason
of your Highness's disorder."

The lackey-like insolence of the words was driven home by
a more insolent manner. There fell upon Seraphina one of

those storm-clouds which had already blackened upon her reason; she heard herself cry out; and when the cloud dispersed, flung the blood-stained dagger on the floor, and saw Gondremark reeling back with open mouth and clapping his hand upon the wound. The next moment, with oaths that she had never heard, he leaped at her in savage passion; clutched her as she recoiled; and in the very act, stumbled and drooped. She had scarce time to fear his murderous onslaught ere he fell before her feet.

He rose upon one elbow; she still staring upon him, white with horror.

"Anna!" he cried, "Anna! Help!"

And then his utterance failed him, and he fell back, to all appearance dead.

Seraphina ran to and fro in the room; she wrung her hands and cried aloud; within she was all one uproar of terror, and conscious of no articulate wish but to awake.

There came a knocking at the door; and she sprang to it and held it, panting like a beast, and with the strength of madness in her arms, till she had pushed the bolt. At this success a certain calm fell upon her reason. She went back and looked upon her victim, the knocking growing louder. O yes, he was dead. She had killed him. He had called upon von Rosen with his latest breath; ah! who would call on Seraphina? She had killed him. She, whose irresolute hand could scarce prick blood from her own bosom, had found strength to cast down that great colossus at a blow.

All this while the knocking was growing more uproarious and more unlike the staid career of life in such a palace. Scandal was at the door, with what a fatal following she dreaded to conceive; and at the same time among the voices that now began to summon her by name she recognized the Chancellor's. He or another, somebody must be the first.

"Is Herr von Greisengesang without?" she called.

"Your Highness—yes!" the old gentleman answered. "We have heard cries, a fall. Is anything amiss?"

"Nothing," replied Seraphina. "I desire to speak with

you. Send off the rest." She panted between each phrase; but her mind was clear. She let the looped curtain down upon both sides before she drew the bolt; and, thus secure from any sudden eyeshot from without, admitted the obsequious Chancellor and again made fast the door.

Greisengesang clumsily revolved among the wings of the curtain; so that she was clear of it as soon as he.

"My God!" he cried. "The Baron!"

"I have killed him," she said. "O, killed him!"

"Dear me," said the old gentleman, "this is most unprecedented. Lovers' quarrels," he added ruefully, "*redintegratio*——" and then paused. "But, my dear madam," he broke out again, "in the name of all that is practical, what are we to do? This is exceedingly grave; morally, madam, it is appalling. I take the liberty, your Highness, for one moment, of addressing you as a daughter, a loved although respected daughter; and I must say that I cannot conceal from you that this is morally most questionable. And, O dear me, we have a dead body!"

She had watched him closely; hope fell to contempt; she drew away her skirts from his weakness, and, in the act, her own strength returned to her.

"See if he be dead," she said; not one word of explanation or defence; she had scorned to justify herself before so poor a creature: "See if he be dead" was all.

With the greatest compunction, the Chancellor drew near; and as he did so the wounded Baron rolled his eyes.

"He lives," cried the old courtier, turning effusively to Seraphina. "Madam, he still lives."

"Help him, then," returned the Princess, standing fixed. "Bind up his wound."

"Madam, I have no means," protested the Chancellor.

"Can you not take your handkerchief, your neckcloth, anything?" she cried; and at the same moment, from her light muslin gown she rent off a flounce and tossed it on the floor. "Take that," she said, and for the first time directly faced Greisengesang.

But the Chancellor held up his hands and turned away his

383

head in agony. The grasp of the falling Baron had torn down the dainty fabric of the bodice; and—" O Highness!" cried Greisengesang, appalled, " the terrible disorder of your toilette!"

" Take up that flounce," she said; " the man may die."

Greisengesang turned in a flutter to the Baron, and attempted some innocent and bungling measures. " He still breathes," he kept saying. " All is not yet over; he is not yet gone."

" And now," said she, " if that is all you can do, begone and get some porters; he must instantly go home."

" Madam," cried the Chancellor, " if this most melancholy sight were seen in town—O dear, the State would fall!" he piped.

" There is a litter in the Palace," she replied. " It is your part to see him safe. I lay commands upon you. On your life it stands."

" I see it, dear Highness," he jerked. " Clearly I see it. But how? what men? The Prince's servants—yes. They had a personal affection. They will be true, if any."

" O, not them!" she cried. " Take Sabra, my own man."

" Sabra! The grand-mason?" returned the Chancellor, aghast. " If he but saw this, he would sound the tocsin—we should all be butchered."

She measured the depth of her abasement steadily. " Take whom you must," she said, " and bring the litter here."

Once she was alone she ran to the Baron, and with a sickening heart sought to allay the flux of blood. The touch of the skin of that great charlatan revolted her to the toes; the wound, in her ignorant eyes, looked deathly; yet she contended with her shuddering, and, with more skill at least than the Chancellor's, staunched the welling injury. An eye unprejudiced with hate would have admired the Baron in his swoon; he looked so great and shapely; it was so powerful a machine that lay arrested; and his features, cleared for the moment both of temper and dissimulation, were seen to be so purely modelled. But it was not thus with Seraphina. Her victim, as he lay outspread, twitching a little, his big chest unbared, fixed her with his ugliness; and her mind flitted for a glimpse to Otto.

Rumours began to sound about the Palace of feet running and of voices raised; the echoes of the great arched staircase were voluble of some confusion; and then the gallery jarred with a quick and heavy tramp. It was the Chancellor, followed by four of Otto's valets and a litter. The servants, when they were admitted, stared at the dishevelled Princess and the wounded man; speech was denied them, but their thoughts were riddled with profanity. Gondremark was bundled in; the curtains of the litter were lowered; the bearers carried it forth, and the Chancellor followed behind with a white face.

Seraphina ran to the window. Pressing her face upon the pane, she could see the terrace, where the lights contended; thence, the avenue of lamps that joined the Palace and town; and overhead the hollow night and the larger stars. Presently the small procession issued from the Palace, crossed the parade, and began to thread the glittering alley: the swinging couch with its four porters, the much-pondering Chancellor behind. She watched them dwindle with strange thoughts: her eyes fixed upon the scene, her mind still glancing right and left on the overthrow of her life and hopes. There was no one left in whom she might confide; none whose hand was friendly, or on whom she dared to reckon for the barest loyalty. With the fall of Gondremark her party, her brief popularity, had fallen. So she sat crouched upon the window seat, her brow to the cool pane; her dress in tatters, barely shielding her; her mind revolving bitter thoughts.

Meanwhile, consequences were fast mounting; and in the deceptive quiet of the night, downfall and red revolt were brewing. The litter had passed forth between the iron gates and entered on the streets of the town. By what flying panic, by what thrill of air communicated, who shall say? but the passing bustle in the Palace had already reached and re-echoed in the region of the burghers. Rumour, with her loud whisper, hissed about the town; men

left their homes without knowing why; knots formed along
the boulevard; under the rare lamps and the great limes
the crowd grew blacker.

And now through the midst of that expectant company,
the unusual sight of a closed litter was observed approaching, and trotting hard behind it that great dignitary Cancellarius Greisengesang. Silence looked on as it went by;
and as soon as it was passed, the whispering seethed over
like a boiling pot. The knots were sundered; and gradually,
one following another, the whole mob began to form into
a procession and escort the curtained litter. Soon spokes-
men, a little bolder than their mates, began to ply the Chancellor with questions. Never had he more need of that great
art of falsehood, by whose exercise he had so richly lived.
And yet now he stumbled, the master passion, fear, betraying him. He was pressed; he became incoherent; and then
from the jolting litter came a groan. In the instant hubbub
and the gathering of the crowd as to a natural signal, the
clear-eyed quavering Chancellor heard the catch of the clock
before it strikes the hour of doom; and for ten seconds he
forgot himself. This shall atone for many sins. He plucked
a bearer by the sleeve. " Bid the Princess flee. All is lost,"
he whispered. And the next moment he was babbling for
his life among the multitude.

Five minutes later the wild-eyed servant burst into the
armoury. "All is lost!" he cried. "The chancellor bids
you flee." And at the same time, looking through the window, Seraphina saw the black rush of the populace begin
to invade the lamplit avenue.

"Thank you, Georg," she said. "I thank you. Go."
And as the man still lingered, "I bid you go," she added.
"Save yourself."

Down by the private passage, and just some two hours
later, Amalia Seraphina, the last Princess, followed Otto
Johann Friedrich, the last Prince of Grünewald.

BOOK III

FORTUNATE MISFORTUNE

FORTUNATE MISFORTUNE

CHAPTER I

PRINCESS CINDERELLA

THE porter, drawn by the growing turmoil, had vanished from the postern, and the door stood open on the darkness of the night. As Seraphina fled up the terraces, the cries and loud footing of the mob drew nearer the doomed palace; the rush was like the rush of cavalry; the sound of shattering lamps tingled above the rest; and overtowering all, she heard her own name bandied among the shouters. A bugle sounded at the door of the guard-room; one gun was fired; and then with the yell of hundreds, Mittwalden Palace was carried at a rush.

Sped by these dire sounds and voices, the Princess scaled the long garden, skimming like a bird the starlit stairways; crossed the Park, which was in that place narrow; and plunged upon the farther side into the rude shelter of the forest. So, at a bound, she left the discretion and the cheerful lamps of Palace evenings; ceased utterly to be a sovereign lady; and, falling from the whole height of civilisation, ran forth into the woods, a ragged Cinderella.

She went direct before her through an open tract of the forest, full of brush and birches, and where the starlight guided her; and beyond that again, must thread the columned blackness of a pine grove joining overhead the thatch of its long branches. At that hour, the place was breathless; a horror of night like a presence occupied that dungeon of the wood; and she went groping, knocking against the boles—her ear, betweenwhiles, strained to aching and yet unrewarded.

But the slope of the ground was upward, and encouraged

389

her; and presently she issued on a rocky hill that stood forth above the sea of forest. All around were other hilltops, big and little; sable vales of forest between; overhead the open heaven and the brilliancy of countless stars; and along the western sky the dim forms of mountains. The glory of the great night laid hold upon her; her eyes shone with stars; she dipped her sight into the coolness and brightness of the sky, as she might have dipped her wrist into a spring; and her heart, at that ethereal shock, began to move more soberly. The sun that sails overhead, ploughing into gold the fields of daylight azure and uttering the signal to man's myriads, has no word apart for man the individual; and the moon, like a violin, only praises and laments our private destiny. The stars alone, cheerful whisperers, confer quietly with each of us like friends; they give ear to our sorrows smilingly, like wise old men, rich in tolerance; and by their double scale, so small to the eye, so vast to the imagination, they keep before the mind the double character of man's nature and fate.

There sate the Princess, beautifully looking upon beauty, in council with these glad advisers. Bright like pictures, clear like a voice in the porches of her ear, memory re-enacted the tumult of the evening: The Countess and the dancing fan, the big Baron on his knees, the blood on the polished floor, the knocking, the swing of the litter down the avenue of lamps, the messenger, the cries of the charging mob; and yet all were far away and phantasmal, and she was still healingly conscious of the peace and glory of the night. She looked towards Mittwalden; and above the hilltop, which already hid it from her view, a throbbing redness hinted of fire. Better so: better so, that she should fall with tragic greatness, lit by a blazing palace! She felt not a trace of pity for Gondremark or of concern for Grünewald: that period of her life was closed for ever, a wrench of wounded vanity alone surviving. She had but one clear idea: to flee;—and another, obscure and half-rejected, although still obeyed: to flee in the direction of the Felsenburg. She had a duty to perform, she must free Otto—so her mind said, very coldly; but her heart embraced the notion of that duty even with ardour, and her hands began to yearn for the grasp of kindness.

She rose, with a start of recollection, and plunged down the slope into the covert. The woods received and closed upon her. Once more, she wandered and hasted in a blot, uncheered, unpiloted. Here and there, indeed, through rents in the wood-roof, a glimmer attracted her; here and there, a tree stood out among its neighbours by some force of outline; here and there, a brushing among the leaves, a notable blackness, a dim shine, relieved, only to exaggerate, the solid oppression of the night and silence. And betweenwhiles, the unfeatured darkness would redouble and the whole ear of night appear to be gloating on her steps. Now she would stand still, and the silence would grow and grow, till it weighed upon her breathing; and then she would address herself again to run, stumbling, falling, and still hurrying the more. And presently the whole wood rocked and began to run along with her. The noise of her own mad passage through the silence spread and echoed, and filled the night with terror. Panic hunted her: Panic from the trees reached forth with clutching branches; the darkness was lit up and peopled with strange forms and faces. She strangled and fled before her fears. And yet in the last fortress, reason, blown upon by these gusts of terror, still shone with a troubled light. She knew, yet could not act upon her knowledge; she knew that she must stop, and yet she still ran.

She was already near madness, when she broke suddenly into a narrow clearing. At the same time the din grew louder, and she became conscious of vague forms and fields of whiteness. And with that the earth gave way; she fell and found her feet again with an incredible shock to her senses, and her mind was swallowed up.

When she came again to herself, she was standing to the mid-leg in an icy eddy of a brook, and leaning with one hand on the rock from which it poured. The spray had wet her hair. She saw the white cascade, the stars wavering in the shaken pool, foam flitting, and high overhead the tall pines on either hand serenely drinking starshine; and in the sudden quiet of her spirit, she heard with joy the firm plunge of the cataract in the pool. She scrambled forth dripping. In the face of her proved weakness, to adventure again upon the horror of blackness in the groves were a suicide of life or reason. But here, in the alley of the brook, with the kind stars above her, and the moon presently swimming into sight, she could await the coming of day without alarm.

This lane of pine-trees ran very rapidly down hill and wound among the woods; but it was a wider thoroughfare than the brook needed, and here and there were little dimpling lawns and coves of the forest, where the starshine slumbered. Such a lawn she paced, taking patience bravely; and now she looked up the hill and saw the brook coming down to her in a series of cascades; and now approached the margin, where it welled among the rushes silently; and now gazed at the great company of heaven with an enduring wonder. The early evening had fallen chill, but the night was now temperate; out of the recesses of the wood there came mild airs as from a deep and peaceful breathing; and the dew was heavy on the grass and the tight-shut daisies. This was the girl's first night under the naked heaven; and now that her fears were overpast, she was touched to the soul by its serene amenity and peace. Kindly the host of heaven blinked down upon that wandering Princess; and the honest brook had no words but to encourage her.

At last she began to be aware of a wonderful revolution, compared to which the fire of Mittwalden Palace was but the crack and flash of a percussion cap. The countenance with which the pines regarded her began insensibly to change; the grass too, short as it was, and the whole winding staircase of the brook's course, began to wear a solemn freshness of appearance. And this slow transfiguration reached her heart, and played upon it, and transpierced it with a serious thrill. She looked all about; the whole face of nature looked back, brimful of meaning, finger on lip, leaking its glad secret. She looked up. Heaven was almost

emptied of stars. Such as still lingered shone with a changed
and waning brightness, and began to faint in their stations.
And the colour of the sky itself was the most wonderful;
for the rich blue of the night had now melted and softened
and brightened; and there had succeeded in its place a hue
that has no name, and that is never seen but as the herald
of morning. "O!" she cried, joy catching at her voice,
"O! it is the dawn!"

In a breath she passed over the brook, and looped up her
skirts and fairly ran in the dim alleys. As she ran, her
ears were aware of many pipings, more beautiful than
music; in the small dish-shaped houses in the fork of giant
arms, where they had lain all night, lover by lover, warmly
pressed, the bright-eyed, big-hearted singers began to
awaken for the day. Her heart melted and flowed forth to
them in kindness. And they, from their small and high
perches in the clerestories of the wood cathedral, peered
down sidelong at the ragged Princess as she flitted below them
on the carpet of the moss and tassel.

Soon she had struggled to a certain hilltop, and saw
far before her the silent inflooding of the day. Out of the
East it welled and whitened; the darkness trembled into
light; and the stars were extinguished like the street-lamps
of a human city. The whiteness brightened into silver, the
silver warmed into gold, the gold kindled into pure and living fire; and the face of the East was barred with elemental
scarlet. The day drew its first long breath, steady and
chill; and for leagues around the woods sighed and shivered.
And then, at one bound, the sun had floated up; and her
startled eyes received day's first arrow, and quailed under
the buffet. On every side, the shadows leaped from their
ambush and fell prone. The day was come, plain and garish;
and up the steep and solitary eastern heaven, the sun, victorious over his competitors, continued slowly and royally
to mount.

Seraphina drooped for a little, leaning on a pine, the shrill
joy of the woodlands mocking her. The shelter of the
night, the thrilling and joyous changes of the dawn, were

over; and now, in the hot eye of the day, she turned uneasily and looked sighingly about her. Some way off among the lower woods, a pillar of smoke was mounting and melting in the gold and blue. There, surely enough, were human folk, the hearth-surrounders. Man's fingers had laid the twigs; it was man's breath that had quickened and encouraged the baby flames; and now, as the fire caught, it would be playing ruddily on the face of its creator. At the thought, she felt a-cold and little and lost in that great out-of-doors. The electric shock of the young sunbeams and the unhuman beauty of the woods began to irk and daunt her. The covert of the house, the decent privacy of rooms, the swept and regulated fire, all that denotes or beautifies the home life of man, began to draw her as with cords. The pillar of smoke was now risen into some stream of moving air; it began to lean out sideways in a pennon; and thereupon, as though the change had been a summons, Seraphina plunged once more into the labyrinth of the wood.

She left day upon the high ground. In the lower groves there still lingered the blue early twilight and the seizing freshness of the dew. But here and there, above this field of shadow, the head of a great outspread pine was already glorious with day; and here and there, through the breaches of the hills, the sunbeams made a great and luminous entry. Here Seraphina hastened along forest paths. She had lost sight of the pilot smoke, which blew another way, and conducted herself in that great wilderness by the direction of the sun. But presently fresh signs bespoke the neighbourhood of man; felled trunks, white slivers from the axe, bundles of green boughs, and stacks of firewood. These guided her forward; until she çame forth at last upon the clearing whence the smoke arose. A hut stood in the clear shadow, hard by a brook which made a series of inconsiderable falls; and on the threshold, the Princess saw a sunburnt and hard-featured woodman, standing with his hands behind his back and gazing skyward.

She went to him directly: a beautiful, bright-eyed, and

haggard vision; splendidly arrayed and pitifully tattered; the diamond ear-drops still glittering in her ears; and with the movement of her coming, one small breast showing and hiding among the ragged covert of the laces. At that ambiguous hour, and coming as she did from the great silence of the forest, the man drew back from the Princess as from something elfin.

" I am cold," she said, " and weary. Let me rest beside your fire."

The woodman was visibly commoved, but answered nothing.

" I will pay," she said, and then repented of the words, catching perhaps a spark of terror from his frightened eyes. But, as usual, her courage rekindled brighter for the check. She put him from the door and entered; and he followed her in superstitious wonder.

Within, the hut was rough and dark; but on the stone that served as hearth, twigs and a few dry branches burned with the brisk sounds and all the variable beauty of fire. The very sight of it composed her; she crouched hard by on the earth floor and shivered in the glow, and looked upon the eating blaze with admiration. The woodman was still staring at his guest: at the wreck of the rich dress, the bare arms, the bedraggled laces and the gems. He found no word to utter.

" Give me food," said she,—" here, by the fire."

He set down a pitcher of coarse wine, bread, a piece of cheese, and a handful of raw onions. The bread was hard and sour, the cheese like leather; even the onion, which ranks with the truffle and the nectarine in the chief place of honour of earth's fruits, is not perhaps a dish for princesses when raw. But she ate, if not with appetite, with courage; and when she had eaten, did not disdain the pitcher. In all her life before, she had not tasted of gross food nor drunk after another; but a brave woman far more readily accepts a change of circumstances than the bravest man. All that while, the woodman continued to observe her furtively, many low thoughts of fear and greed contending in his eyes. She read them clearly, and she knew she must begone.

Presently she arose and offered him a florin.

" Will that repay you? " she asked.

But here the man found his tongue. " I must have more than that," said he.

" It is all I have to give you," she returned, and passed him by serenely.

Yet her heart trembled, for she saw his hand stretched forth as if to arrest her, and his unsteady eyes wandering to his axe. A beaten path led westward from the clearing, and she swiftly followed it. She did not glance behind her. But as soon as the least turning of the path had concealed her from the woodman's eyes, she slipped among the trees and ran till she deemed herself in safety.

By this time the strong sunshine pierced in a thousand places the pine-thatch of the forest, fired the red boles, irradiated the cool aisles of shadow, and burned in jewels on the grass. The gum of these trees was dearer to the senses than the gums of Araby; each pine, in the lusty morning sunlight, burned its own wood-incense; and now and then a breeze would rise and toss these rooted censers, and send shade and sun-gem flitting, swift as swallows, thick as bees; and wake a brushing bustle of sounds that murmured and went by.

On she passed and up and down, in sun and shadow; now aloft on the bare ridge among the rocks and birches, with the lizards and the snakes; and anon in the deep grove among sunless pillars. Now she followed wandering woodpaths, in the maze of valleys; and again, from a hilltop, beheld the distant mountains and the great birds circling under the sky. She would see afar off a nestling hamlet, and go round to avoid it. Below, she traced the course of the foam of mountain torrents. Nearer hand, she saw where the tender springs welled up in silence, or oozed in green moss; or in the more favoured hollows a whole family of infant rivers would combine, and tinkle in the stones, and lie in pools to be a bathing-place for sparrows, or fall from the sheer rock in rods of crystal. Upon all these things, as she still sped along in the bright air, she looked with a rapture of surprise and a joyful fainting of the heart; they seemed so novel, they touched so strangely home, they were so hued and scented, they were so beset and canopied by the dome of the blue air of heaven.

At length, when she was well weary, she came upon a wide and shallow pool. Stones stood in it, like islands; bullrushes fringed the coast; the floor was paved with the pine needles, and the pines themselves, whose roots made promontories, looked down silently on their green images. She crept to the margin and beheld herself with wonder, a hollow and bright-eyed phantom, in the ruins of her palace robe. The breeze now shook her image; now it would be marred with flies; and at that she smiled; and from the fading circles, her counterpart smiled back at her and looked kind. She sat long in the warm sun, and pitied her bare arms that were all bruised and marred with falling, and marvelled to see that she was dirty, and could not grow to believe that she had gone so long in such a strange disorder.

Then, with a sigh, she addressed herself to make a toilet by that forest mirror, washed herself pure from all the stains of her adventure, took off her jewels and wrapped them in her handkerchief, re-arranged the tatters of her dress, and took down the folds of her hair. She shook it round her face, and the pool repeated her thus veiled. Her hair had smelt like violets, she remembered Otto saying; and so now she tried to smell it, and then shook her head, and laughed a little, sadly, to herself.

The laugh was returned upon her in a childish echo. She looked up; and lo! two children looking on,—a small girl and a yet smaller boy, standing, like playthings, by the pool, below a spreading pine. Seraphina was not fond of children, and now she was startled to the heart.

" Who are you? " she cried, hoarsely.

The mites huddled together and drew back; and Seraphina's heart reproached her that she should have frightened things so quaint and little, and yet alive with senses. She thought upon the birds and looked again at her two visitors; so little larger and so far more innocent. On their clear faces, as in a pool, she saw the reflection of their fears. With gracious purpose she arose.

"Come," she said, "do not be afraid of me," and took a step towards them.

But alas! at the first movement, the two poor babes in the wood turned and ran helter-skelter from the Princess.

The most desolate pang was struck into the girl's heart. Here she was, twenty-two—soon twenty-three—and not a creature loved her; none but Otto; and would even he forgive? If she began weeping in these woods alone, it would mean death or madness. Hastily she trod the thoughts out like a burning paper; hastily rolled up her locks, and with terror dogging her, and her whole bosom sick with grief, resumed her journey.

Past ten in the forenoon, she struck a highroad, marching in that place uphill between two stately groves, a river of sunlight; and here, dead weary, careless of consequences, and taking some courage from the human and civilised neighbourhood of the road, she stretched herself on the green margin in the shadow of a tree. Sleep closed on her, at first with a horror of fainting, but when she ceased to struggle, kindly embracing her. So she was taken home for a little, from all her toils and sorrows, to her Father's arms. And there in the meanwhile her body lay exposed by the highwayside, in tattered finery; and on either hand from the woods the birds came flying by and calling upon others, and debated in their own tongue this strange appearance.

The sun pursued his journey; the shadow flitted from her feet, shrank higher and higher, and was upon the point of leaving her altogether, when the rumble of a coach was signalled to and fro by the birds. The road in that part was very steep; the rumble drew near with great deliberation; and ten minutes passed before a gentleman appeared, walking with a sober elderly gait upon the grassy margin of the highway, and looking pleasantly around him as he walked. From time to time he paused, took out his note-book and made an entry with a pencil; and any spy who had been near enough would have heard him mumbling words as though he were a poet testing verses. The voice of the wheels was still faint, and it was plain the traveller had far outstripped his carriage.

He had drawn very near to where the Princess lay asleep, before his eye alighted on her; but when it did he started, pocketed his note-book, and approached. There was a mile-stone close to where she lay; and he sat down on that and coolly studied her. She lay upon one side, all curled and sunken, her brow on one bare arm, the other stretched out, limp and dimpled. Her young body, like a thing thrown down, had scarce a mark of life. Her breathing stirred her not. The deadliest fatigue was thus confessed in every language of the sleeping flesh. The traveller smiled grimly. As though he had looked upon a statue, he made a grudging inventory of her charms: the figure in that touching freedom of forgetfulness surprised him; the flush of slumber became her like a flower.

"Upon my word," he thought, "I did not think the girl could be so pretty. And to think," he added, "that I am under obligation not to use one word of this!"

He put forth his stick and touched her; and at that she awoke, sat up with a cry, and looked upon him wildly.

"I trust your Highness has slept well," he said, nodding.

But she only uttered sounds.

"Compose yourself," said he, giving her certainly a brave example in his own demeanour. "My chaise is close at hand; and I shall have, I trust, the singular entertainment of ab-ducting a sovereign Princess."

"Sir John!" she said, at last.

"At your Highness's disposal," he replied.

She sprang to her feet. "O," she cried, "have you come from Mittwalden?"

"This morning," he returned, "I left it; and if there is any one less likely to return to it than yourself, behold him!"

"The Baron——" she began, and paused.

"Madam," he answered, "it was well meant, and you are quite a Judith; but after the hours that have elapsed, you will probably be relieved to hear that he is fairly well. I took his news this morning ere I left. Doing fairly well, they said, but suffering acutely. Hey?—acutely. They could hear his groans in the next room."

"And the Prince," she asked, "is anything known of him?"

"It is reported," replied Sir John, with the same pleasurable deliberation, "that upon that point your Highness is the best authority."

"Sir John," she said eagerly, "you were generous enough to speak about your carriage. Will you, I beseech you, will you take me to the Felsenburg? I have business there of an extreme importance."

"I can refuse you nothing," replied the old gentleman, gravely and seriously enough. "Whatever, madam, it is in my power to do for you, that shall be done with pleasure. As soon as my chaise shall overtake us, it is yours to carry you where you will. But," added he, reverting to his former manner, "I observe you ask me nothing of the Palace."

"I do not care," she said. "I thought I saw it burning."

"Prodigious!" said the Baronet. "You thought? And can the loss of forty toilettes leave you cold? Well, madam, I admire your fortitude. And the state, too? As I left, the government was sitting,—the new government, of which at least two members must be known to you by name: Sabra, who had, I believe, the benefit of being formed in your employment—a footman,—am I right?—and our old friend the Chancellor, in something of a subaltern position. But in these convulsions, the last shall be first and the first last."

"Sir John," she said, with an air of perfect honesty, "I am sure you mean most kindly, but these matters have no interest for me."

The Baronet was so utterly discountenanced, that he hailed the appearance of his chaise with welcome, and, by

400

way of saying something, proposed that they should walk back to meet it. So it was done; and he helped her in with courtesy, mounted to her side, and from various receptacles (for the chaise was most completely fitted out) produced fruits and truffled liver, beautiful white bread, and a bottle of delicate wine. With these he served her like a father, coaxing and praising her to fresh exertions; and during all that time, as though silenced by the laws of hospitality, he was not guilty of the shadow of a sneer. Indeed his kindness seemed so genuine that Seraphina was moved to gratitude.

"Sir John," she said, "you hate me in your heart; why are you so kind to me?"

"Ah, my good lady," said he, with no disclaimer of the accusation, "I have the honour to be much your husband's friend, and somewhat his admirer."

"You!" she cried. "They told me you wrote cruelly of both of us."

"Such was the strange path by which we grew acquainted," said Sir John. "I had written, madam, with particular cruelty (since that shall be the phrase) of your fair self. Your husband set me at liberty, gave me a passport, ordered a carriage, and then, with the most boyish spirit, challenged me to fight. Knowing the nature of his married life, I thought the dash and loyalty he showed delightful. 'Do not be afraid,' says he; 'if I am killed, there is nobody to miss me.' It appears you subsequently thought of that yourself. But I digress. I explained to him it was impossible that I could fight! 'Not if I strike you?' says he. Very droll; I wish I could have put it in my book. However, I was conquered, took the young gentleman to my high favour, and tore up my bits of scandal on the spot. That is one of the little favours, madam, that you owe your husband."

Seraphina sat for some while in silence. She could bear to be misjudged without a pang by those whom she contemned; she had none of Otto's eagerness to be approved, but went her own way straight and head in air. To Sir John, however, after what he had said, and as her husband's friend, she was prepared to stoop.

"What do you think of me?" she asked abruptly.

"I have told you already," said Sir John: "I think you want another glass of my good wine."

"Come," she said, "this is unlike you. You are not wont to be afraid. You say that you admire my husband: in his name, be honest."

"I admire your courage," said the Baronet. "Beyond that, as you have guessed, and indeed said, our natures are not sympathetic."

"You spoke of scandal," pursued Seraphina. "Was the scandal great?"

"It was considerable," said Sir John.

"And you believed it?" she demanded.

"O, madam," said Sir John, "the question!"

"Thank you for that answer!" cried Seraphina. "And now here, I will tell you, upon my honour, upon my soul, in spite of all the scandal in this world, I am as true a wife as ever stood."

"We should probably not agree upon a definition," observed Sir John.

"O!" she cried, "I have abominably used him—I know that; it is not that I mean. But if you admire my husband, I insist that you shall understand me: I can look him in the face without a blush."

"It may be, madam," said Sir John; "nor have I presumed to think the contrary."

"You will not believe me?" she cried. "You think I am a guilty wife? You think he was my lover?"

"Madam," returned the Baronet, "when I tore up my papers, I promised your good hubsand to concern myself no more with your affairs; and I assure you for the last time that I have no desire to judge you."

"But you will not acquit me! Ah!" she cried, "*he* will —he knows me better!"

Sir John smiled.

"You smile at my distress?" asked Seraphina.

FORTUNATE MISFORTUNE

"At your woman's coolness," said Sir John. "A man would scarce have had the courage of that cry, which was, for all that, very natural, and I make no doubt quite true. But remark, madam—since you do me the honour to consult me gravely—I have no pity for what you call your distresses. You have been completely selfish, and now reap the consequence. Had you once thought of your husband, instead of singly thinking of yourself, you would not now have been alone, a fugitive, with blood upon your hands, and hearing from a morose old Englishman truth more bitter than scandal."

"I thank you," she said, quivering. "This is very true. Will you stop the carriage?"

"No, child," said Sir John, "not until I see you mistress of yourself."

There was a long pause, during which the carriage rolled by rock and woodland.

"And now," she resumed, with perfect steadiness, "will you consider me composed? I request you, as a gentleman, to let me out."

"I think you do unwisely," he replied. "Continue, if you please, to use my carriage."

"Sir John," she said, "if death were sitting on that pile of stones, I would alight! I do not blame, I thank you; I now know how I appear to others; but sooner than draw breath beside a man who can so think of me, I would——O!" she cried, and was silent.

Sir John pulled the string, alighted, and offered her his hand; but she refused the help.

The road had now issued from the valleys in which it had been winding, and come to that part of its course where it runs, like a cornice, along the brow of the steep northward face of Grünewald. The place where they had alighted was at a salient angle; a bold rock and some wind-tortured pine-trees overhung it from above; far below the blue plains lay forth and melted into heaven; and before them the road, by a succession of bold zigzags, was seen mounting to where a tower upon a tall cliff closed the view.

"There," said the Baronet, pointing to the tower, "you see the Felsenburg, your goal. I wish you a good journey, and regret I cannot be of more assistance."

He mounted to his place and gave a signal, and the carriage rolled away.

Seraphina stood by the wayside, gazing before her with blind eyes. Sir John she had dismissed already from her mind: she hated him, that was enough; for whatever Seraphina hated or contemned fell instantly to Lilliputian smallness, and was thenceforward steadily ignored in thought. And now she had matter for concern indeed. Her interview with Otto, which she had never yet forgiven him, began to appear before her in a very different light. He had come to her, still thrilling under recent insult, and not yet breathed from fighting her own cause; and how that knowledge changed the value of his words! Yes, he must have loved her; this was a brave feeling—it was no mere weakness of the will. And she, was she incapable of love? It would appear so; and she swallowed her tears, and yearned to see Otto, to explain all, to ask pity upon her knees for her transgressions, and, if all else were now beyond the reach of reparation, to restore at least the liberty of which she had deprived him.

Swiftly she sped along the highway, and, as the road wound out and in about the bluffs and gullies of the mountain, saw and lost by glimpses the tall tower that stood before and above her, purpled by the mountain air.

CHAPTER II

TREATS OF A CHRISTIAN VIRTUE

WHEN Otto mounted to his rolling prison, he found another occupant in a corner of the front seat; but as this person hung his head and the brightness of the carriage lamps shone outward, the Prince could only see it was a man. The Colonel followed his prisoner and clapped to the door; and at that the four horses broke immediately into a swinging trot.

"Gentlemen," said the Colonel, after some little while had passed, "if we are to travel in silence, we might as well be at home. I appear, of course, in an invidious character; but I am a man of taste, fond of books and solidly informing talk, and unfortunately condemned for life to the guard-room. Gentlemen, this is my chance: don't spoil it for me. I have here the pick of the whole court, barring lovely woman; I have a great author in the person of the Doctor——"

"Gotthold!" cried Otto.

"It appears," said the Doctor, bitterly, "that we must go together. Your Highness had not calculated upon that."

"What do you infer?" cried Otto; "that I had you arrested?"

"The inference is simple," said the Doctor.

"Colonel Gordon," said the Prince, "oblige me so far, and set me right with Herr von Hohenstockwitz."

"Gentlemen," said the Colonel, "you are both arrested on the same warrant in the name of the Princess Seraphina, acting regent, countersigned by Prime Minister Freiherr von Gondremark, and dated the day before yesterday, the twelfth. I reveal to you the secrets of the prison house," he added.

405

"Otto," said Gotthold, "I ask you to pardon my suspicions."

"Gotthold," said the Prince, "I am not certain I can grant you that."

"Your Highness is, I am sure, far too magnanimous to hesitate," said the Colonel. "But allow me: we speak at home in my religion of the means of grace: and I now propose to offer them." So saying, the Colonel lighted a bright lamp which he attached to one side of the carriage, and from below the front seat produced a goodly basket adorned with the long necks of bottles. "*Tu spem reducis*—how does it go, Doctor?" he asked gaily. "I am, in a sense, your host; and I am sure you are both far too considerate of my embarrassing position to refuse to do me honour. Gentlemen, I drink to the Prince!"

"Colonel," said Otto, "we have a jovial entertainer. I drink to Colonel Gordon."

Thereupon all three took their wine very pleasantly; and even as they did so, the carriage with a lurch turned into the highroad and began to make better speed.

All was bright within; the wine had coloured Gotthold's cheek; dim forms of forest trees, dwindling and spiring, scarves of the starry sky, now wide and now narrow, raced past the windows; through one that was left open the air of the woods came in with a nocturnal raciness; and the roll of wheels and the tune of the trotting horses sounded merrily on the ear. Toast followed toast; glass after glass was bowed across and emptied by the trio; and presently there began to fall upon them a luxurious spell, under the influence of which little but the sound of quiet and confidential laughter interrupted the long intervals of meditative silence.

"Otto," said Gotthold, after one of these seasons of quiet, "I do not ask you to forgive me. Were the parts reversed, I could not forgive you."

"Well," said Otto, "it is a phrase we use. I do forgive you, but your words and your suspicions rankle; and not yours alone. It is idle, Colonel Gordon, in view of the order you are carrying out, to conceal from you the dissensions of my family; they have gone so far that they are now public property. Well, gentlemen, can I forgive my wife? I can, of course, and do; but in what sense? I would certainly not stoop to any revenge; as certainly I could not think of her but as one changed beyond my recognition."

"Allow me," returned the Colonel. "You will permit me to hope that I am addressing Christians? We are all conscious, I trust, that we are miserable sinners."

"I disown the consciousness," said Gotthold. "Warmed with this good fluid, I deny your thesis."

"How, sir? You never did anything wrong? and I heard you asking pardon this moment, not of your God, sir, but of a common fellow-worm!" the Colonel cried.

"I own you have me; you are expert in argument, Herr Oberst," said the Doctor.

"Begad, sir, I am proud to hear you say so," said the Colonel. "I was well grounded indeed at Aberdeen. And as for this matter of forgiveness, it comes, sir, of loose views and (what is if anything more dangerous) a regular life. A sound creed and a bad morality, that's the root of wisdom. You two gentlemen are too good to be forgiving."

"The paradox is somewhat forced," said Gotthold.

"Pardon me, Colonel," said the Prince; "I readily acquit you of any design of offence, but your words bite like satire. Is this a time, do you think, when I can wish to hear myself called good, now that I am paying the penalty (and am willing like yourself to think it just) of my prolonged misconduct?"

"O, pardon me!" cried the Colonel. "You have never been expelled from the divinity hall; you have never been broke. I was: broke for a neglect of military duty. To tell you the open truth, your Highness, I was the worse of drink; it's a thing I never do now," he added, taking out his glass. "But a man, you see, who has really tasted the defects of his own character, as I have, and has come to regard himself as a kind of blind teetotum knocking about

life, begins to learn a very different view about forgiveness.
I will talk of not forgiving others, sir, when I have made
out to forgive myself, and not before; and the date is like
to be a long one. My father, the Reverend Alexander Gordon, was a good man, and damned hard upon others. I
am what they call a bad one, and that is just the difference.
The man who cannot forgive any mortal thing is a green
hand in life."

" And yet I have heard of you, Colonel, as a duellist,"
said Gotthold.

" A different thing, sir," replied the soldier. " Professional etiquette. And I trust without unchristian feeling."

Presently after the Colonel fell into a deep sleep; and
his companions looked upon each other, smiling.

" An odd fish," said Gotthold.

" And a strange guardian," said the Prince. " Yet what
he said was true."

" Rightly looked upon," mused Gotthold, " it is ourselves
that we cannot forgive, when we refuse forgiveness to our
friend. Some strand of our own misdoing is involved in
every quarrel."

" Are there not offences that disgrace the pardoner? "
asked Otto. " Are there not bounds of self-respect? "

" Otto," said Gotthold, " does any man respect himself?
To this poor waif of a soldier of fortune we may seem respectable gentlemen; but to ourselves, what are we unless
a pasteboard portico and a deliquium of deadly weaknesses
within? "

" I? yes," said Otto; " but you, Gotthold—you, with
your interminable industry, your keen mind, your books—
serving mankind, scorning pleasures and temptations! You
do not know how I envy you."

" Otto," said the Doctor, " in one word, and a bitter one
to say: I am a secret tippler. Yes, I drink too much. The
habit has robbed these very books, to which you praise my
devotion, of the merits that they should have had. It has
spoiled my temper. When I spoke to you the other day
how much of my warmth was in the cause of virtue? how

much was the fever of last night's wine? Ay, as my poor fellow-sot there said, and as I vaingloriously denied, we are all miserable sinners, put here for a moment, knowing the good, choosing the evil, standing naked and ashamed in the eye of God."

"Is it so?" said Otto. "Why, then, what are we? Are the very best——"

"There is no best in man," said Gotthold. "I am not better, it is likely I am not worse, than you or that poor sleeper. I was a sham, and now you know me: that is all."

"And yet it has not changed my love," returned Otto, softly. "Our misdeeds do not change us. Gotthold, fill your glass. Let us drink to what is good in this bad business; let us drink to our old affection; and, when we have done so, forgive your too just grounds of offence, and drink with me to my wife, whom I have so misused, who has so misused me, and whom I have left, I fear, I greatly fear, in danger. What matters it how bad we are, if others can still love us, and we can still love others?"

"Ay!" replied the Doctor. "It is very well said. It is the true answer to the pessimist, and the standing miracle of mankind. So you still love me? and so you can forgive your wife? Why, then, we may bid conscience ' Down, dog,' like an ill-trained puppy yapping at shadows."

The pair fell into silence, the Doctor tapping on his empty glass.

The carriage swung forth out of the valleys on that open balcony of highroad that runs along the front of Grüne-wald, looking down on Gerolstein. Far below, a white waterfall was shining to the stars from the falling skirts of forest, and beyond that, the night stood naked above the plain. On the other hand, the lamplight skimmed the face of the precipices, and the dwarf pine-trees twinkled with all their needles, and were gone again into the wake. The granite roadway thundered under wheels and hoofs; and at times, by reason of its continual winding, Otto could see the escort on the other side of a ravine, riding well together in the night. Presently the Felsenburg came plainly in view,

409

some way above them, on a bold projection of the mountain, and planting its bulk against the starry sky.

" See, Gotthold," said the Prince, " our destination."

Gotthold awoke as from a trance.

" I was thinking," said he, " if there is danger, why did you not resist? I was told you came of your free will; but should you not be there to help her? "

The colour faded from the Prince's cheeks.

CHAPTER III

WHEN the busy Countess came forth from her interview with Seraphina, it is not too much to say that
she was beginning to be terribly afraid. She paused in the
corridor and reckoned up her doings with an eye to Gondremark. The fan was in requisition in an instant; but her
disquiet was beyond the reach of fanning. " The girl has
lost her head," she thought; and then dismally, " I have
gone too far." She instantly decided on secession. Now
the *Mons Sacer* of the Frau von Rosen was a certain rustic
villa in the forest, called by herself, in a smart attack of
poesy, Tannen-Zauber, and by everybody else plain Kleinbrunn.

Thither, upon the thought, she furiously drove, passing
Gondremark at the entrance to the Palace avenue, but
feigning not to observe him; and as Kleinbrunn was seven
good miles away and in the bottom of a narrow dell, she
passed the night without any rumour of the outbreak reaching her; and the glow of the conflagration was concealed
by intervening hills. Frau von Rosen did not sleep well;
she was seriously uneasy as to the results of her delightful
evening, and saw herself condemned to quite a lengthy so-
journ in her deserts and a long defensive correspondence,
ere she could venture to return to Gondremark. On the
other hand, she examined, by way of pastime, the deeds she
had received from Otto; and even here saw cause for disappointment. In these troublous days she had no taste for
landed property, and she was convinced, besides, that Otto
had paid dearer than the farm was worth. Lastly, the order
for the Prince's release fairly burned her meddling fingers.

411

PRINCE OTTO

All things considered, the next day beheld an elegant and beautiful lady, in a riding-habit and a flapping hat, draw bridle at the gate of the Felsenburg, not perhaps with any clear idea of her purpose, but with her usual experimental views on life. Governor Gordon, summoned to the gate, welcomed the omnipotent Countess with his most gallant bearing, though it was wonderful how old he looked in the morning.

"Ah, Governor," she said, "we have surprises for you, sir," and nodded at him meaningly.

"Eh, madam, leave me my prisoners," he said; "and if you will but join the band, begad, I'll be happy for life."

"You would spoil me, would you not?" she asked.

"I would try, I would try," returned the Governor, and he offered her his arm.

She took it, picked up her skirt, and drew him close to her. "I have come to see the Prince," she said. "Now, infidel! on business. A message from that stupid Gondremark, who keeps me running like a courier. Do I look like one, Herr Gordon?" And she planted her eyes in him.

"You look like an angel, ma'am," returned the Governor, with a great air of finished gallantry.

The Countess laughed. "An angel on horseback!" she said. "Quick work."

"You came, you saw, you conquered," flourished Gordon, in high good humour with his own wit and grace. "We toasted you, madam, in the carriage, in an excellent good glass of wine; toasted you fathom deep; the finest woman, with, begad, the finest eyes in Grünewald. I never saw the like of them but once, in my own country, when I was a young fool at College: Thomasina Haig, her name was. I give you my word of honour, she was as like you as two peas."

"And so you were merry in the carriage?" asked the Countess, gracefully dissembling a yawn.

"We were; we had a very pleasant conversation; but we took perhaps a glass more than that fine fellow of a Prince has been accustomed to," said the Governor; "and

FORTUNATE MISFORTUNE

I observe this morning that he seems a little off his mettle. We'll get him mellow again ere bedtime. This is his door."

"Well," she whispered, "let me get my breath. No, no; wait. Have the door ready to open." And the Countess, standing like one inspired, shook out her fine voice in "Lascia ch' io pianga"; and when she had reached the proper point, and lyrically uttered forth her sighings after liberty, the door, at a sign, was flung wide open, and she swam into the Prince's sight, bright-eyed, and with her colour somewhat freshened by the exercise of singing. It was a great dramatic entrance, and to the somewhat doleful prisoner within the sight was sunshine.

"Ah, madam," he cried, running to her—"you here!"

She looked meaningly at Gordon; and as soon as the door was closed she fell on Otto's neck. "To see you here!" she moaned and clung to him.

But the Prince stood somewhat stiffly in that enviable situation, and the Countess instantly recovered from her outburst.

"Poor child," she said, "poor child! Sit down beside me here, and tell me all about it. My heart really bleeds to see you. How does time go?"

"Madam," replied the Prince, sitting down beside her, his gallantry recovered, "the time will now go all too quickly till you leave. But I must ask you for the news. I have most bitterly condemned myself for my inertia of last night. You wisely counselled me; it was my duty to resist. You wisely and nobly counselled me; I have since thought of it with wonder. You have a noble heart."

"Otto," she said, "spare me. Was it even right, I wonder? I have duties, too, you poor child; and when I see you they all melt—all my good resolutions fly away."

"And mine still come too late," he replied, sighing. "Oh, what would I not give to have resisted? What would I not give for freedom?"

"Well, what would you give?" she asked; and the red fan was spread; only her eyes, as if from over battlements, brightly surveyed him.

413

"I? What do you mean? Madam, you have some news for me," he cried.

"O, O!" said madam, dubiously.

He was at her feet. "Do not trifle with my hopes," he pleaded. "Tell me, dearest Madame von Rosen, tell me! You cannot be cruel: it is not in your nature. Give? I can give nothing; I have nothing; I can only plead in mercy."

"Do not," she said; "it is not fair. Otto, you know my weakness. Spare me. Be generous."

"O, madam," he said, "it is for you to be generous, to have pity." He took her hand and pressed it; he plied her with caresses and appeals. The Countess had a most enjoyable sham siege, and then relented. She sprang to her feet, she tore her dress open, and, all warm from her bosom, threw the order on the floor.

"There!" she cried. "I forced it from her. Use it, and I am ruined!" And she turned away as if to veil the force of her emotions.

Otto sprang upon the paper, read it, and cried out aloud. "O, God bless her!" he said, "God bless her." And he kissed the writing.

Von Rosen was a singularly good-natured woman, but her part was now beyond her. "Ingrate!" she cried; "I wrung it from her, I betrayed my trust to get it, and 'tis she you thank!"

"Can you blame me?" said the Prince. "I love her."

"I see that," she said. "And I?"

"You, Madame von Rosen? You are my dearest, my kindest, and most generous of friends," he said, approaching her. "You would be a perfect friend, if you were not so lovely. You have a great sense of humour, you cannot be unconscious of your charm, and you amuse yourself at times by playing on my weakness; and at times I can take pleasure in the comedy. But not to-day: to-day you will be the true, the serious, the manly friend, and you will suffer me to forget that you are lovely and that I am weak. Come, dear Countess, let me to-day repose in you entirely."

FORTUNATE MISFORTUNE

He held out his hand, smiling, and she took it frankly. "I vow you have bewitched me," she said; and then with a laugh, "I break my staff!" she added; "and I must pay you my best compliment. You made a difficult speech. You are as adroit, dear Prince, as I am—charming." And as she said the word with a great courtesy, she justified it.

"You hardly keep the bargain, madam, when you make yourself so beautiful," said the Prince, bowing.

"It was my last arrow," she returned. "I am disarmed. Blank cartridge, *O mon Prince!* And now I tell you, if you choose to leave this prison, you can, and I am ruined. Choose!"

"Madame von Rosen," replied Otto, "I choose, and I will go. My duty points me, duty still neglected by this Featherhead. But do not fear to be a loser. I propose instead that you should take me with you, a bear in chains, to Baron Gondremark. I am become perfectly unscrupulous: to save my wife I will do all, all he can ask or fancy. He shall be filled; were he huge as leviathan and greedy as the grave, I will content him. And you, the fairy of our pantomime, shall have the credit."

"Done!" she cried. "Admirable! Prince Charming no longer—Prince Sorcerer, Prince Solon! Let us go this moment. Stay," she cried, pausing. "I beg, dear Prince, to give you back these deeds. 'Twas you who liked the farm— I have not seen it; and it was you who wished to benefit the peasants. And, besides," she added, with a comical change of tone, "I should prefer the ready money."

Both laughed. "Here I am, once more a farmer," said Otto, accepting the papers, "but overwhelmed in debt."

The Countess touched a bell, and the Governor appeared.

"Governor," she said, "I am going to elope with his Highness. The result of our talk has been a thorough understanding, and the *coup d'état* is over. Here is the order."

Colonel Gordon adjusted silver spectacles upon his nose. "Yes," he said, "the Princess: very right. But the warrant, madam, was countersigned."

"By Heinrich!" said von Rosen. "Well, and here am I to represent him."

"Well, your Highness," resumed the soldier of fortune, "I must congratulate you upon my loss. You have been cut out by beauty, and I am left lamenting. The Doctor still remains to me: *probus, doctus, lepidus, jucundus:* a man of books."

"Ay, there is nothing about poor Gotthold," said the Prince.

"The Governor's consolation? Would you leave him bare?" asked von Rosen.

"And, your Highness," resumed Gordon, "may I trust that in the course of this temporary obscuration, you have found me discharge my part with suitable respect and, I may add, tact? I adopted purposely a cheerfulness of manner; mirth, it appeared to me, and a good glass of wine, were the fit alleviations."

"Colonel," said Otto, holding out his hand, "your society was of itself enough. I do not merely thank you for your pleasant spirits; I have to thank you, besides, for some philosophy, of which I stood in need. I trust I do not see you for the last time; and in the meanwhile, as a memento of our strange acquaintance, let me offer you these verses on which I was but now engaged. I am so little of a poet, and was so ill inspired by prison bars, that they have some claim to be at least a curiosity."

The Colonel's countenance lighted as he took the paper; the silver spectacles were hurriedly replaced. "Ha!" he said, "Alexandrines, the tragic metre. I shall cherish this, your Highness, like a relic; no more suitable offering, although I say it, could be made. 'Dieux de l'immense plaine et des vastes forêts.' Very good," he said, "very good indeed! 'Et du geolier lui-même apprendre des leçons.' Most handsome, begad!"

"Come, Governor," cried the Countess, "you can read his poetry when we are gone. Open your grudging portals."

"I ask your pardon," said the Colonel. "To a man of my character and tastes, these verses, this handsome reference—most moving, I assure you. Can I offer you an escort?"

"No, no," replied the Countess. "We go incogniti, as we arrived. We ride together; the Prince will take my servant's horse. Hurry and privacy, Herr Oberst, that is all we seek." And she began impatiently to lead the way.

But Otto had still to bid farewell to Doctor Gotthold; and the Governor following, with his spectacles in one hand and the paper in the other, had still to communicate his treasured verses, piece by piece, as he succeeded in deciphering the manuscript, to all he came across; and still his enthusiasm mounted. "I declare," he cried at last, with the air of one who has at length divined a mystery, "they remind me of Robbie Burns!"

But there is an end to all things; and at length Otto was walking by the side of Madame von Rosen, along that mountain wall, her servant following with both the horses, and all about them sunlight, and breeze, and flying bird, and the vast regions of the air, and the capacious prospect: wildwood and climbing pinnacle, and the sound and voice of mountain torrents, at their hand: and far below them, green melting into sapphire on the plains.

They walked at first in silence; for Otto's mind was full of the delight of liberty and nature, and still, betweenwhiles, he was preparing his interview with Gondremark. But when the first rough promontory of the rock was turned, and the Felsenberg concealed behind its bulk, the lady paused.

"Here," she said, "I will dismount poor Karl, and you and I must ply our spurs. I love a wild ride with a good companion."

As she spoke, a carriage came into sight round the corner next below them in the order of the road. It came heavily creaking, and a little ahead of it a traveller was soberly walking, note-book in hand.

"It is Sir John," cried Otto, and he hailed him.

The Baronet pocketed his note-book, stared through an eye-glass, and then waved his stick; and he on his side, and the Countess and the Prince on theirs, advanced with somewhat quicker steps. They met at the reëntrant angle, where a thin stream sprayed across the boulder and was scattered in rain among the brush; and the Baronet saluted the Prince with much punctilio. To the Countess, on the other hand, he bowed with a kind of sneering wonder.

" Is it possible, madam, that you have not heard the news? " he asked.

" What news? " she cried.

" News of the first order," returned Sir John: " a revolution in the State, a Republic declared, the Palace burned to the ground, the Princess in flight, Gondremark wounded——"

" Heinrich wounded? " she screamed.

" Wounded and suffering acutely," said Sir John. " His groans——"

There fell from the lady's lips an oath so potent that, in smoother hours, it would have made her hearers jump. She ran to her horse, scrambled to the saddle, and, yet half seated, dashed down the road at full gallop. The groom, after a pause of wonder, followed her. The rush of her impetuous passage almost scared the carriage horses over the verge of the steep hill; and still she clattered further, and the crags echoed to her flight, and still the groom flogged vainly in pursuit of her. At the fourth corner, a woman trailing slowly up leaped back with a cry and escaped death by a hand's-breadth. But the Countess wasted neither glance nor thought upon the incident. Out and in, about the bluffs of the mountain wall, she fled, loose-reined, and still the groom toiled in her pursuit.

" A most impulsive lady! " said Sir John. " Who would have thought she cared for him? " And before the words were uttered, he was struggling in the Prince's grasp.

" My wife! the Princess? What of her? "

" She is down the road," he gasped. " I left her twenty minutes back."

And next moment, the choked author stood alone, and the Prince on foot was racing down the hill behind the Countess.

CHAPTER IV

BABES IN THE WOOD

WHILE the feet of the Prince continued to run swiftly, his heart, which had at first by far outstripped his running, soon began to linger and hang back. Not that he ceased to pity the misfortune or to yearn for the sight of Seraphina; but the memory of her obdurate coldness awoke within him, and woke in turn his own habitual diffidence of self. Had Sir John been given time to tell him all, had he even known that she was speeding to the Felsenburg, he would have gone to her with ardour. As it was, he began to see himself once more intruding, profiting, perhaps, by her misfortune, and now that she was fallen, proffering unloved caresses to the wife who had spurned him in prosperity. The sore spots upon his vanity began to burn; once more, his anger assumed the carriage of a hostile generosity; he would utterly forgive indeed; he would help, save, and comfort his unloving wife; but all with distant self-denial, imposing silence on his heart, respecting Seraphina's disaffection as he would the innocence of a child. So, when at length he turned a corner and beheld the Princess, it was his first thought to reassure her of the purity of his respect, and he at once ceased running and stood still. She, upon her part, began to run to him with a little cry; then, seeing him pause, she paused also, smitten with remorse; and at length, with the most guilty timidity, walked nearly up to where he stood.

" Otto," she said, " I have ruined all! "

" Seraphina! " he cried with a sob, but did not move, partly withheld by his resolutions, partly struck stupid at the sight of her weariness and disorder. Had she stood silent, they had soon been locked in an embrace. But she too had prepared herself against the interview, and must spoil the golden hour with protestations.

419

"All!" she went on, "I have ruined all! But, Otto, in kindness you must hear me—not justify, but own, my faults. I have been taught so cruelly; I have had such time for thought, and see the world so changed. I have been blind, stone-blind; I have let all true good go by me, and lived on shadows. But when this dream fell, and I had betrayed you, and thought I had killed——" She paused. "I thought I had killed Gondremark," she said with a deep flush, "and I found myself alone as you said."

The mention of the name of Gondremark pricked the Prince's generosity like a spur. "Well," he cried, "and whose fault was it but mine? It was my duty to be beside you, loved or not. But I was a skulker in the grain, and found it easier to desert than to oppose you. I could never learn that better part of love, to fight love's battles. But yet the love was there. And now when this toy kingdom of ours has fallen, first of all by my demerits, and next by your inexperience, and we are here alone together, as poor as Job and merely a man and a woman—let me conjure you to forgive the weakness and to repose in the love. Do not mistake me!" he cried, seeing her about to speak, and imposing silence with uplifted hand. "My love is changed; it is purged of any conjugal pretension; it does not ask, does not hope, does not wish, for a return in kind. You may forget forever that part in which you found me so distasteful, and accept without embarrassment the affection of a brother."

"You are too generous, Otto," she said. "I know that I have forfeited your love. I cannot take this sacrifice. You had far better leave me. O go away, and leave me to my fate!"

"O no!" said Otto; "we must first of all escape out of this hornet's nest, to which I led you. My honour is engaged. I said but now we were as poor as Job; and behold! not many miles from here I have a house of my own to which I will conduct you. Otto the Prince being down, we must try what luck remains to Otto the Hunter. Come, Seraphina; show that you forgive me, and let us set about this business of escape in the best spirits possible. You used to say, my dear, that, except as a husband and a prince, I was a pleasant fellow. I am neither now, and you may like my company without remorse. Come, then; it were idle to be captured. Can you still walk? Forth, then," said he, and he began to lead the way.

A little below where they stood, a good-sized brook passed below the road, which overleapt it in a single arch. On one bank of that loquacious water a footpath descended a green dell. Here it was rocky and stony, and lay on the steep scarps of the ravine; here it was choked with brambles; and there, in fairy haughs, it lay for a few paces evenly on the green turf. Like a sponge, the hillside oozed with well-water. The burn kept growing both in force and volume; at every leap it fell with heavier plunges and span more widely in the pool. Great had been the labours of that stream, and great and agreeable the changes it had wrought. It had cut through dykes of stubborn rock, and now, like a blowing dolphin, spouted through the orifice; along all its humble coasts, it had undermined and rafted-down the goodlier timber of the forests; and on these rough clearings it now set and tended primrose gardens, and planted woods of willow, and made a favourite of the silver birch. Through all these friendly features the path, its human acolyte, conducted our two wanderers downward,—Otto before, still pausing at the more difficult passages to lend assistance; the Princess following. From time to time, when he turned to help her, her face would lighten upon his—her eyes, half desperately, woo him. He saw, but dared not understand. " She does not love me," he told himself, with magnanimity. " This is remorse or gratitude; I were no gentleman, no, nor yet a man, if I presumed upon these pitiful concessions."

Some way down the glen, the stream, already grown to a good bulk of water, was rudely dammed across, and about a third of it abducted in a wooden trough. Gaily the pure water, air's first cousin, fleeted along the rude aqueduct, whose sides and floor it had made green with grasses. The path, bearing it close company, threaded a wilderness of briar and wild rose. And presently, a little in front, the brown top of a mill and the tall millwheel, spraying diamonds, arose in the narrows of the glen; at the same time the snoring music of the saws broke the silence.

The miller, hearing steps, came forth to his door, and both he and Otto started.

"Good-morning, miller," said the Prince. "You were right, it seems, and I was wrong. I give you the news, and bid you to Mittwalden. My throne has fallen—great was the fall of it!—and your good friends of the Phœnix bear the rule."

The red-faced miller looked supreme astonishment. "And your Highness?" he gasped.

"My Highness is running away," replied Otto, "straight for the frontier."

"Leaving Grünewald?" cried the man. "Your father's son? It's not to be permitted!"

"Do you arrest us, friend?" asked Otto, smiling.

"Arrest you? I?" exclaimed the man. "For what does your Highness take me? Why, sir, I make sure there is not a man in Grünewald would lay hands upon you."

"O, many, many," said the Prince; "but from you, who were bold with me in my greatness, I should even look for aid in my distress."

The miller became the colour of beetroot. "You may say so indeed," said he. "And meanwhile, will you and your lady step into my house?"

"We have not time for that," replied the Prince; "but if you would oblige us with a cup of wine without here, you will give a pleasure and a service, both in one."

The miller once more coloured to the nape. He hastened to bring forth wine in a pitcher and three bright crystal tumblers. "Your Highness must not suppose," he said, as he filled them, "that I am an habitual drinker. The time when I had the misfortune to encounter you, I was a trifle overtaken, I allow; but a more sober man than I am in my ordinary, I do not know where you are to look for; and even this glass that I drink to you (and to the lady) is quite an unusual recreation."

FORTUNATE MISFORTUNE

The wine was drunk with due rustic courtesies; and then, refusing further hospitality, Otto and Seraphina once more proceeded to descend the glen, which now began to open and to be invaded by the taller trees.

"I owed that man a reparation," said the Prince; "for when we met I was in the wrong and put a sore affront upon him. I judge by myself, perhaps; but I begin to think that no one is the better for a humiliation."

"But some have to be taught so," she replied.

"Well, well," he said, with a painful embarrassment. "Well, well. But let us think of safety. My miller is all very good, but I do not pin my faith to him. To follow down this stream will bring us, but after innumerable windings, to my house. Here, up this glade, there lies a cross-cut—the world's end for solitude—the very deer scarce visit it. Are you too tired, or could you pass that way?"

"Choose the path, Otto. I will follow you," she said.

"No," he replied, with a singular imbecility of manner and appearance, "but I meant the path was rough. It lies, all the way, by glade and dingle, and the dingles are both deep and thorny."

"Lead on," she said. "Are you not Otto the Hunter?"

They had now burst across a veil of underwood, and were come into a lawn among the forest, very green and innocent, and solemnly surrounded by trees. Otto paused on the margin, looking about him with delight; then his glance returned to Seraphina, as she stood framed in that sylvan pleasantness and looking at her husband with undecipherable eyes. A weakness both of the body and mind fell on him like the beginnings of sleep; the cords of his activity were relaxed, his eyes clung to her. "Let us rest," he said; and he made her sit down, and himself sat down beside her on the slope of an inconsiderable mound.

She sat with her eyes downcast, her slim hand dabbling in grass, like a maid waiting for love's summons. The sound of the wind in the forest swelled and sank, and drew near them with a running rush, and died away and away in the distance into fainting whispers. Nearer hand, a bird out of the deep covert uttered broken and anxious notes. All this seemed but a halting prelude to speech. To Otto it seemed as if the whole frame of nature were waiting for his words; and yet his pride kept him silent. The longer he watched that slender and pale hand plucking at the grasses, the harder and rougher grew the fight between pride and its kindly adversary.

"Seraphina," he said at last, " it is right you should know one thing: I never . . ." He was about to say " doubted you," but was that true? And, if true, was it generous to speak of it? Silence succeeded.

"I pray you, tell it me," she said; " tell it me, in pity."

" I mean only this," he resumed, " that I understand all, and do not blame you. I understand how the brave woman must look down on the weak man. I think you were wrong in some things; but I have tried to understand it, and I do. I do not need to forget or to forgive, Seraphina, for I have understood."

" I know what I have done," she said. " I am not so weak that I can be deceived with kind speeches. I know what I have been—I see myself. I am not worth your anger, how much less to be forgiven! In all this downfall and misery, I see only me and you: you, as you have been always; me, as I was—me, above all! O yes, I see myself: and what can I think? "

" Ah, then, let us reverse the parts! " said Otto. " It is ourselves we cannot forgive, when we deny forgiveness to another—so a friend told me last night. On these terms, Seraphina, you see how generously I have forgiven myself. But am not *I* to be forgiven? Come, then, forgive yourself —and me."

She did not answer in words, but reached out her hand to him quickly. He took it; and as the smooth fingers settled and nestled in his, love ran to and fro between them in tender and transforming currents.

" Seraphina," he cried, " O, forget the past! Let me serve and help you; let me be your servant; it is enough for me to serve you and to be near you; let me be near you, dear

—do not send me away." He hurried his pleading like the speech of a frightened child. " It is not love," he went on; " I do not ask for love; my love is enough . . ."

" Otto," she said, as if in pain.

He looked up into her face. It was wrung with the very ecstasy of tenderness and anguish; on her features, and most of all in her changed eyes, there shone the very light of love.

" Seraphina? " he cried aloud, and with a sudden, tuneless voice, " Seraphina? "

" Look round you at this glade," she cried, " and where the leaves are coming on young trees, and the flowers begin to blossom. This is where we meet, meet for the first time; it is so much better to forget and to be born again. O, what a pit there is for sins—God's mercy, man's oblivion! "

" Seraphina," he said, " let it be so, indeed; let all that was be merely the abuse of dreaming; let me begin again, a stranger. I have dreamed, in a long dream, that I adored a girl unkind and beautiful; in all things my superior, but still cold like ice. And again I dreamed, and thought she changed and melted, glowed and turned to me. And I—who had no merit but a love, slavish and unerect—lay close, and durst not move for fear of waking."

" Lie close," she said, with a deep thrill of speech.

So they spake in the spring woods; and meanwhile, in Mittwalden Rath-haus, the Republic was declared.

BIBLIOGRAPHICAL POSTSCRIPT

TO COMPLETE THÉ STORY

THE reader well informed in modern history will not require details as to the fate of the Republic. The best account is to be found in the memoirs of Herr Greisengesang (7 Bände: Leipzig), by our passing acquaintance the licentiate Roederer. Herr Roederer, with too much of an author's licence, makes a great figure of his hero—poses him, indeed, to be the centre-piece and cloud-compeller of the whole. But, with due allowance for this bias, the book is able and complete.

The reader is, of course, acquainted with the vigorous and bracing pages of Sir John (2 volumes: London: Longman, Hurst, Rees, Orme & Brown). Sir John, who plays but a toothcomb in the orchestra of this historical romance, blows in his own book the big bassoon. His character is there drawn at large; and the sympathy of Landor has countersigned the admiration of the public. One point, however, calls for explanation; the chapter on Grünewald was torn by the hand of the author in the palace gardens; how comes it, then, to figure at full length among my more modest pages, the Lion of the caravan? That eminent literatus was a man of method; "Juvenal by double entry," he was once profanely called; and when he tore the sheets in question, it was rather, as he has since explained, in the search for some dramatic evidence of his sincerity, than with the thought of practical deletion. At that time, indeed, he was possessed of two blotted scrolls and a fair copy in double. But the chapter, as the reader knows, was honestly omitted from the famous "Memoirs on the various Courts of Europe." It has been mine to give it to the public.

Bibliography still helps us with a farther glimpse of our

characters. I have here before me a small volume (printed
for private circulation: no printer's name; n.d.) "Poésies
par Frédéric et Amélie." Mine is a presentation copy, obtained for me by Mr. Bain in the Haymarket; and the name
of the first owner is written on the fly-leaf in the hand of
Prince Otto himself. The modest epigraph—"Le rime n'est
pas riche"—may be attributed, with a good show of likelihood, to the same collaborator. It is strikingly appropriate,
and I have found the volume very dreary. Those pieces in
which I seem to trace the hand of the Princess are particularly dull and conscientious. But the booklet had a fair success with that public for which it was designed; and I have
come across some evidences of a second venture of the same
sort, now unprocurable. Here, at least, we may take leave
of Otto and Seraphina—what do I say? of Frédéric and
Amélie—ageing together peaceably at the court of the wife's
father, jingling French rhymes and correcting joint proofs.

Still following the book-lists, I perceive that Mr. Swin-
burne has dedicated a rousing lyric and some vigorous son-
nets to the memory of Gondremark; that name appears twice
at least in Victor Hugo's trumpet blasts of patriot enumera-
tion; and I came latterly, when I supposed my task already
ended, on a trace of the fallen politician and his Countess. It
is in the "Diary of J. Hogg Cotterill, Esq." (that very interesting work). Mr. Cotterill, being at Naples, is intro-
duced (May 27th) to "a Baron and Baroness Gondremark—
he a man who once made a noise—she still beautiful—both
witty. She complimented me much upon my French—should
never have known me to be English—had known my uncle,
Sir John, in Germany—recognised in me, as a family trait,
some of his *grand air* and studious courtesy—asked me to
call." And again (May 30th) "visited the Baronne de
Gondremark—much gratified—a most *refined, intelligent*
woman, quite of the old school, now *hélas!* extinct—had read
my *Remarks on Sicily*—it reminds her of my uncle, but with
more of grace—I feared she thought there was less energy—
assured no—a softer style of presentation, more of the
literary grace, but the same firm grasp of circumstance and

force of thought—in short, just Buttonhole's opinion. Much encouraged. I have a real esteem for this patrician lady." The acquaintance lasted some time; and when Mr. Cotterill left in the suite of Lord Protocol, and, as he is careful to inform us, in Admiral Yardarm's flag-ship, one of his chief causes of regret is to leave " that most *spirituelle* and sympathetic lady, who already regards me as a younger brother."

THE END.